W.J. Burley lived near Newquay in Cornwall, and was a schoolmaster until he retired to concentrate on his writing. He died in 2002.

By W.J. Burley

A Taste of Power
Three Toed Pussy
Death in Willow Pattern
Wycliffe and How to Kill a Cat
Wycliffe and the Guilt Edged Alibi
Death in a Salubrious Place
Death in Stanley Street
Wycliffe and the Pea Green Boat
Wycliffe and the Schoolgirls
The Schoolmaster
Wycliffe and the Scapegoat
The Sixth Day
Charles and Elizabeth
Wycliffe in Paul's Court
The House of Care
Wycliffe's Wild Goose Chase
Wycliffe and the Beales
Wycliffe and the Four Jacks
Wycliffe and the Quiet Virgin
Wycliffe and the Winsor Blue
Wycliffe and the Tangled Web
Wycliffe and the Cycle of Death
Wycliffe and the Dead Flautist
Wycliffe and the Last Rites
Wycliffe and the Dunes Mystery
Wycliffe and the Redhead
Wycliffe and the House of Fear
Wycliffe and the Guild of Nine

Wycliffe and How to Kill a Cat

Wycliffe and the Four Jacks

W. J. BURLEY

Wycliffe and How to Kill a Cat
First published in Great Britain by Victor Gollancz Ltd in 1970
under the title *How to Kill a Cat*

Wycliffe and The Four Jacks
First published in Great Britain by Victor Gollancz in 1985

This omnibus edition published in 2008
by Orion Books Ltd
Orion House, 5 Upper St Martin's Lane
London WC2H 9EA

A CIP catalogue record for this book is available from the British Library.

ISBN 978-1-4072-1512-9

Printed and bound in Great Britain by
Clays Ltd, St Ives plc

The Orion Publishing Group's policy is to use papers that are natural,
renewable and recyclable products and made from wood grown in sustainable
forests. The logging and manufacturing processes are expected to conform to
the environmental regulations of the country of origin.

www.orionbooks.co.uk

Wycliffe and How to Kill a Cat

W.J.BURLEY

To Muriel – collaborator, critic and wife

CHAPTER ONE

Detective Chief Superintendent Wycliffe, Area CID, in a fawn linen jacket, checked shirt and grey slacks, looked even less like a policeman than usual. He had the right, he was on holiday though paying a courtesy call at the local police station.

'Don't be all day, Charles!' Instructions from Helen, his wife.

'Back to lunch, dear. Promise!'

'Is Inspector Warren in?'

'No, sir, afraid not. Can I help?'

Wycliffe introduced himself. 'A friendly call, sergeant. The inspector and I used to be in the same squad and I thought I would look him up. I'm in the town on holiday.'

Ferocious grin, the best the station sergeant could manage in the way of charm. 'Inspector Warren has been ill with stomach ulcers for more than a month, sir.'

'I'm sorry to hear that.' Conversation languished.

'As you're from Headquarters, sir, you might like a word with . . .'

'No, this is unofficial, sergeant, I expect you've got enough to do at this time of year.'

'Run off our feet, sir.'

And that might have been that, had not a constable appeared from one of the offices, handed the sergeant a slip of paper and murmured something in his ear.

'Right! Get hold of the police surgeon and send him there. Tell Wilkins to stay with it and I'll contact Division.'

'Trouble, sergeant?' Wycliffe, on the point of leaving, lingered.

'Woman found dead in a hotel bedroom, sir. They called in one of our chaps from a patrol car and he's just radioed in.'

'Is that all?'

'Our man thinks there's a good reason to suspect foul play.'

'You mean that the woman has probably been murdered?'

'Yes, sir.'

'Then why not say so?'

The sergeant said nothing.

Wycliffe hesitated, then plunged. 'I'll take a look, where is it?'

'Marina Hotel, Dock Crescent, sir. It's a bit of a dump, they cater for merchant seamen mainly. We had trouble there once before.'

'What sort of trouble?'

'Seaman stabbed a tart, sir. A year or two back that was. I believe the place has changed hands since then.'

'Right! You get on to Division, tell them I'm on the spot and ask them not to roll out the waggon until they hear from me.'

'You'll want a car, sir.'

'I've got one.'

Outside the sun was shining. They were queueing for the beach buses, mothers with bulging picnic bags, kids trailing plastic spades, girls in brief summer dresses and some playsuits conscientiously displaying their navels. The superintendent in holiday attire was not out of place, but he attracted curious glances as he crossed the square to the car park. Perhaps it was because he looked pleased with life. Few people do, or are. In fact he was humming a little tune;

he caught himself doing it and wondered. The reason for his complacency would scarcely bear examination. True, it was warm and sunny; true, he was on holiday, but it was not these things, it was the prospect of a case which made him sing. He felt in his bones that he was at the beginning of a case which he would remember, one which would go into the books. To be brutally frank then, he was happy because a woman lay dead in a sleazy hotel bedroom. Did he delight in crime? Surely a vicarious pleasure in vice must be at least as reprehensible as indulgence?

He got into his nice new shining black Zodiac and eased his way into the line of traffic. He was secretly proud of his car though Helen said that it was a trifle vulgar. He liked to cruise slowly, almost silently, aware of the power he had boxed up, waiting only for the gentle pressure of his foot. In fact, he had the Rolls mentality without the Rolls pay packet.

Now he had to crawl through the impossibly narrow main street where a carelessly parked wheelbarrow can snarl everything up. Then the shops thinned and he was running along by the harbour with a row of large, terraced Victorian houses on his right. Just before he came to the docks some of the houses were calling themselves hotels and one of these was the Marina. A couple of tired looking Dracaenas in a weedy patch of gravel and a rusted slatted iron seat. The stucco was peeling off the pillars of the porch and a snake of Elastoplast sealed over a crack in the plate-glass of the swing doors. Constable Wilkins was waiting for him in the vestibule.

'The sergeant telephoned to expect you, sir.'

'Doctor arrived yet?'

'Not yet, sir.'

'Where is she?'

'Second floor, sir, a little passage off the landing leads

9

to the extension. It's the door on your left at the end of the passage.'

Wycliffe grunted. 'Wait there, send the doctor up when he comes. What about the inmates?'

'I've told them to stay in their rooms, sir. Most of them are out anyway.'

The staircase had some elegance of design but the carpet was so threadbare that pattern and texture had long since disappeared. Paper peeled off the walls and a faint sickly odour suggested dry rot. But the place seemed reasonably clean. He braced himself for what he might find. After twenty years in the force he was still not shockproof. He could have asked the constable but that was not his way, he liked to form his own impressions from the very start.

As he turned on the first landing to tackle the next flight, he made up his mind that the woman would be fortyish, fleshy, blonde and strangled. She would be lying in a tangle of bedding staring up at the ceiling, fish eyed, her face and neck heavily cyanosed. He had seen it all before. This place was a likely hunting ground for whores and if one of the sisterhood got herself murdered it was ten to one on strangulation, frenzied and brutal.

But he was wrong in most of his surmises.

The figure on the double bed was that of a girl, twenty-one or two at most. Slim, petite, she lay on her back, sprawled across the bed. She was naked but, though her posture was suggestive enough, there was something innocent and virginal about her. Her auburn hair was splayed on the pillow, golden in the sunshine, and it was easier to believe her asleep than dead – until he saw her face. Her face, turned towards the wall and hidden by her hair, had been battered. Without disturbing the body it was difficult to determine the extent and nature of her injuries but Wycliffe noticed at once that the amount of swelling and bruising was disproportionately small for the bone damage which had been done. The upper lip and an area round the left eye were encrusted with dried blood but there was no sign of a free flow. Wycliffe was no doctor but he had seen enough of violent death to know the probable answer to that one. The odds were that the facial injuries had been inflicted after death. In which case, how had she died? Perhaps the initial blow had killed her but it seemed unlikely. Would she have lain there waiting to be clubbed? Not unless she was asleep. But she was lying naked on top of the bed clothes . . .

Wycliffe bent closer to examine the neck and found what he half expected, a tale-telling bluish tinge below the surface of the skin and a faint bruising on either side of the trachea above the larynx. She had been strangled, but by someone who had restrained the impulse to unnecessary violence – or never known it. And that was odd in view of what must have followed. What sort of nut would strangle a girl with such finesse, then smash her face in?

But he was running ahead of himself, time enough to speculate when he had the views of the experts.

He looked round the room – a back room. The window, which had its top sash wedged open an inch or two, looked on to a small yard and a railway cutting beyond with the back gardens of a row of houses on the other side. An iron fire escape crossed diagonally just below the window. There were net blinds but the Regency striped curtains would not draw. The carpet was worn through in places and of no discernible pattern. A built-in clothes cupboard with a full length mirror in the door, a dressing table, an upholstered chair with loose stuffing – these, with the bed, made up the furniture. The girl's underclothes were strewn over the chair and a sleeveless frock in gay op-art material hung from a hanger hooked over the picture rail. A nightdress and a quilted dressing-gown lay in a heap on the floor by the bed. A white pig-skin travelling case, elegant and incongruous, stood by the dressing table which was littered with expensive looking cosmetics. Among the bottles and jars he noticed a few items of jewelry, a pair of ear-rings, a garnet bracelet and a silver clip with another red stone inset. He looked at everything but touched nothing.

He went out on to the landing when he heard footsteps on the stairs. The police surgeon, tall, slim, immaculate in pepper and salt suiting, iron-grey hair faultlessly parted, and bifocals. A questioning glance at Wycliffe's informal dress.

'Chief Superintendent Wycliffe? Dr Rashleigh. Where is she?'

'As little disturbance as possible if you please, doctor.'

A faint lift of the eyebrows. 'We must assume that we know our respective jobs, superintendent.'

'Perhaps. But don't move her!' Wycliffe snapped. Pompous ass! He went downstairs; doctors always put him in a bad temper. 'Constable!'

'Sir?'

'Radio information room for the murder squad, pathologist, forensic – the lot. Then find the proprietor.'

While he waited, Wycliffe opened a door labelled *Lounge*. A large front room with a bay window which could have been pleasant. Several upholstered armchairs in varying styles and stages of decay, an octagonal table in veneered wood of revolting aspect, a nickel-plated flower stand and plastic flowers. A black iron grate stuffed with crinkly red paper and an overmantle with fairground ornaments. The room reeked of stale tobacco. They would need somewhere to interview witnesses and this would have to be it. He decided to ask for some kitchen chairs to spite possible fleas.

The proprietor was a little man, bald on top with a fringe

of grey hair. He was thin except for his paunch, which he carried low. He was smoking a home-made cigarette and his lips were stained yellow. A near down-and-out like his premises, but he had lively brown eyes which missed nothing.

'What's your name?'

'Ernest Piper.'

Wycliffe lowered himself on to the arm of one of the chairs. 'Who is she, Mr Piper?'

The little man raised a hand to his ear and stroked the lobe. 'According to the register she's Mrs Slatterly. Address given, W1.'

'When did she arrive?'

'Sunday evening, she's been here three nights.'

'Alone?'

He nodded. 'She said she was waiting for her husband to join her.'

'And did he?'

'Not to my knowledge, he didn't.'

'Had she booked in advance?'

'Telephone call the day before to reserve a double for three or four nights.'

'Not a common experience for you.'

Piper put in some more time fiddling with his ear. 'I don't know what you mean.'

The superintendent took out his pipe and began to fill it. He was entering into the spirit of the thing, beginning to get its flavour. 'I mean that you don't get many bookings, certainly not from husbands and their wives.'

A slow grin revealing blackened teeth. 'I don't have to draw pictures for you, do I?'

'What was your impression of her when she arrived?'

'Classy. Pretty too, a real eye catcher. Pity she got spoilt like that. To be frank, I couldn't make out what she was

13

doing in a place like this . . .' He hesitated then added in a burst of confidence, 'Look, superintendent, I got nothing to hide in this business and I hope you'll bear in mind that I'm being frank.'

Wycliffe struck a match and lit his pipe, puffing great clouds of smoke towards the ceiling. 'We'll see. Did she have any visitors?'

'Not to my knowledge.'

'Which doesn't take us very far.'

Piper shrugged. 'Well, you know how it is.'

'Did she go out much?'

'I passed her in the hall a few times. In any case she had to go out for food, we don't do meals other than breakfast.'

'Any mail?'

'One letter waiting for her when she arrived.'

'Postmark?'

'I didn't notice.'

'Who found her this morning?'

'Kathy, the girl who does the rooms.'

'When?'

Piper looked at his watch, a silver turnip which he took from a pocket in his unbuttoned waistcoat. 'About an hour ago. Say half nine. Kathy came to me in the kitchen and said, "I think something's happened to the girl in fifteen. I think she's dead." '

'Just like that.'

Piper nodded. 'Just like that, Kathy don't scare all that easy.'

'Then?'

'I went up to take a look.' He relit his cigarette which had gone out.

'Touch anything?'

He shook his head. 'Only her – just to see if she had really

14

croaked. I didn't see her face at first. Of course she'd been dead several hours, I should think.'

'You know about such things?'

'I seen a bit.'

'How long since you were last inside?'

A moment of reflection. 'Must be all of ten years.'

'Immoral earnings?'

He nodded. 'No violence though. I never been done for violence.'

Wycliffe noted and approved the precision of statement. The two men smoked placidly in complete accord.

'She was no trollop, super.'

Wycliffe sighed. 'They all have to start.'

The doctor interrupted them, shirt-sleeved and peevish, 'I suppose there is somewhere I can wash in this place?'

'Down the passage on the right, doctor, I'll show you.' Courtesy and service à la Marina! Wycliffe chuckled. He felt better and better. It wasn't crime which gave him pleasure, it was people. He made himself comfortable in the armchair. To hell with fleas!

Dr Rashleigh came back alone. 'I suppose you have notified the pathologist?'

'Of course! Perhaps you will be good enough to look in again when he is here?'

'Very well!' Rashleigh was still stuffy. 'But you may wish to hear my preliminary conclusions?'

Pretentious bastard! 'Certainly, doctor.'

Rashleigh smoothed his tie (Greyhounds 1934). 'I don't want to be too specific, but I think I may say that death was probably due to strangulation. The indications of asphyxia are slight and though there are marks on the neck they are faint.' He squinted up at the ceiling through his bifocals as though reading his lines there and mumbled

15

something about 'vagal inhibition'. Then he went on, 'The facial injuries were almost certainly inflicted after death. As to time of death, I would say that she has been dead from eight to twelve hours.'

'Between ten and two, then?'

'That would certainly agree with my preliminary findings, superintendent. If I were pressed I should incline towards the earlier time.'

'Very helpful, doctor. Anything else?'

Rashleigh hesitated. 'The girl was not a virgin, superintendent.'

Big deal! Surely he must know if anybody did that virginity beyond the age of twenty is a wasting asset?

'In fact, certain signs lead me to suppose that sexual intercourse probably took place shortly before death.'

'Not after?'

Rashleigh looked flustered. 'I'm not in a position to answer that question on the evidence I have seen.'

Surely the old goat must realize that it mattered! Never mind, the pathologist would see to all that.

When the divisional inspector arrived with his squad he found Wycliffe alone. He was standing beside the window, staring out at the docks. Born and reared and having lived most of his life in the Midlands, the sea and all that pertained to it fascinated him. Those tankers with their ugly grey hulls had probably rounded the Cape not so long ago on their way from some sun-scorched oil port in the Gulf . . .

Inspector Fehling coughed. He had not previously met the chief superintendent, who was a comparative newcomer to the area. His first impression was unfavourable and the inspector set great store by his first impressions. Wycliffe did not even look like a policeman, it was difficult to believe that he was tall enough and he seemed almost frail. A teacher, some kind of academic, perhaps a parson, but never a policeman.

'Inspector Fehling, sir.'

'How do you spell it?'

'F – E – H . . .'

'Ah, the solution, not a lack of success.'

'Sir?'

'Fehling's solution – Prussian blue stuff they used to use to test urine. Never mind, an unusual name, Inspector.'

'So they tell me. Now, do I have your permission to go ahead, sir?'

Wycliffe smiled as though at a secret joke. 'By all means. The pathologist should be here at any minute and the forensic people will be on their way. Let me know if you find anything – I shall be here.' When Fehling reached the door he called him back. 'Mr Fehling, I object to working in the middle of a circus – no cars outside this building. They must park on the car park down the street; and no uniformed men in evidence . . .'

Fehling was shocked. 'But there are several of our vehicles out there now . . .'

'Then please get them moved – damn quick!'

When Fehling was gone Wycliffe returned to the window. Delegation is a magic word. When you have the rank you can get out of almost any job you don't like doing. Not that chief superintendents are expected to search rooms, look for prints or photograph corpses. He had done his share in the past but never with much enthusiasm or faith. You may need such evidence to convict a man but crimes are about people and relationships. Wycliffe was of a contemplative disposition and he liked, on occasion, to talk. He was remarkable in that he had contrived to turn these dubious attributes into professional assets.

17

'He said you might like a cup of coffee.' A sleek, black-haired little West Indian girl carrying a tray with a cup of coffee on it, milk and sugar. She looked no more than sixteen but was probably twenty.

'Thanks, I would. Who are you?'

'I'm Kathy – Kathy Johnson – I work here.'

'It was you who found the dead girl?'

She nodded. Another surprise, he had expected some superannuated old pro with swollen legs and carpet slippers. 'I found her.'

'You sleep on the premises?'

'In one of the attics, yes.' She spoke with the attractive staccato precision of her people and she had a gravity of expression and demeanour which gave special weight to all she said.

'What do you know of the dead girl?'

'Not much. She was very pretty. I see her on the stairs once or twice and wish her good morning or good afternoon but that is all except one time . . .'

'What happened?'

She put her hand to her forehead in a quick gesture of recollection. 'I think it was on the first evening she is here, a man come and ask for her. No! it was the next evening – Monday.'

'Did this man ask for her by name?'

'Pardon?'

'Did this man say, "I want to speak to Mrs Slatterly" – that is the name she gave in the register isn't it?'

'Mrs Slatterly, that is right. No, I find him in the hall looking at the register and when I ask him what it is that he wants, at first he is unwilling to say then he say, "This Mrs Slatterly, is she young with auburn hair?" and I say, "Yes, but she is out".'

'What then?'

'He thinks for some time then he ask if there is a telephone in her room.' Kathy laughed at the very idea. 'When I say that there is not, he go off without another word.'

'Have you seen him since?'

'No, I do not see him again.'

'When you told Mrs Slatterly of his visit, did she seem worried?'

The little brown nose wrinkled. 'No, not worried.'

'Why don't you sit down?'

'Thank you.' She perched herself on the edge of one of the chairs, her tray in her lap. 'I do not think her name was Mrs Slatterly.'

'Why not?'

'When I have to tell her about the man who come to see her she is half way up the stairs, you understand?'

Wycliffe nodded.

'I say, "Mrs Slatterly!" and although she is sure to hear me she does not turn round. Twice I say it, then I have to go up after her.'

'You are a clever girl.'

'Thank you.'

'About this man, what was he like?'

'Not very tall, a bit fat, and he wore a dark suit with little stripes. It fitted very good, very smart and expensive looking. His hair is sandy coloured.'

'Oldish?'

'Pardon?'

'How old do you think he was?'

'Forty, maybe a little more. He is red in the face a little, perhaps he has had too much to drink, you understand?'

'Perfectly; anything else?'

She frowned. 'There was something about his face, something a little strange, like it was fixed.'

'You mean that his face lacked expression?'

She hesitated then gave up. 'I cannot say what it is that I mean, I am sorry.'

'But you would know him again if you saw him?'

'Of course!'

'Thank you, you are an excellent witness but you may have to say all this again so that it can be written down.'

'That is all right.' She got up, picked up his cup and was at the door when he said, 'You never saw her talking to anyone, I suppose?'

She turned, frowning. 'I almost forget. Yesterday morning when I am making the bed in one of the front rooms I happen to look out of the window. Mrs Slatterly was standing on the pavement by the gate talking to a man.'

'The same one?'

'No, I told you I do not see him again. This is a very tall thin man and, I think, younger, but I could not see him well. I know that he had on a cap and a mackintosh, but I cannot tell you any more.'

'Did they stay talking for long?'

She shook her head. 'I cannot say, I did not stop to watch.'

Progress, or so it seemed. It might not be too difficult to run down the chap in the natty pinstripe – if he was a local. Perhaps Fehling would find firm evidence of the girl's identity by the time he was through upstairs. It was more than likely. But if not . . . Wycliffe sighed and returned to the window, refilled his pipe and lit it. Never go to meet trouble. Two of the dockside cranes were performing complex evolutions, moving along their tracks and swinging their jibs in perfect harmony. Why did they do it? They never seemed to lift anything. Choreography by the shop steward.

Back to the sandy-haired chap in the pinstripes. If he had intended to kill the girl he wouldn't have made himself so conspicuous unless he was a kink. If he killed her it was probably unpremeditated, a sudden flare of anger or lust. Most murders by strangulation were like that but, a big but, the murderer invariably uses force far in excess of what is needed to kill. In this case there was remarkable restraint and restraint implies forethought. But what about the maniacal attack on the girl's face after death? It didn't add up. Wycliffe remembered a young thug in his old manor who made a study of the technique of strangulation, treating it as an art form. Four girls died before he was caught red-handed with the fifth, and none of them had showed any outward sign of the cause of death. Broadmoor. Detained at Her Majesty's Pleasure. He remembered the case with acute loathing, he had hated that youth and he hoped that Her Majesty would get a hell of a lot of pleasure. Violence of any sort appalled him and senseless self-indulgent violence left him biting his nails.

The pathologist and the forensic people arrived. Wycliffe had met the same team before and they exchanged amiable greetings, then the newcomers went about their business with that air of bored indifference which is their professional equivalent to the bedside manner. The little room was overcrowded and stuffy, but each man knew his job and scarcely a word was spoken. Wycliffe waited on the landing with the police photographers who had already taken pictures of the undisturbed room and were waiting to take more when the pathologist gave the word for the removal of the body.

It took them less than an hour. Dr Franks, the pathologist, a chubby little man, always in a hurry, bustled out. 'Ready now, superintendent. Perhaps you will get one of your chaps to bring up the shell.'

The girl's body would be put into a plastic shell, a temporary coffin, to be carted off to the mortuary.

Franks went into the bathroom and began to run lots of water. Wycliffe could hear him whistling to himself as he washed. It was all in the day's work for him too. 'Bit of a bug-house this, isn't it? What's a kid like that doing in this sort of dump? – Don't tell me, I'd rather keep my illusions. Where the hell is the soap? She was strangled all right. Bit of a fancy job or else a lucky hold by a tyro. Perhaps it was unlucky. Pressure on the jugulars. Even that mightn't have killed her by itself. I'll tell you more this afternoon, but not much. This bloody towel . . . For Christ's sake send somebody for a clean towel . . . Intercourse, as they say, had taken place – *was* taking place for all I know. Not the usual thing though, is it? Then he bashes her face in afterwards. Dear me! A nasty fellow he must be!'

A constable arrived with a fresh towel.

'Ah, that's better! I suppose Rashleigh told you how long she's been dead?'

'Between ten last night and two this morning.'

Franks nodded. 'I'd say after midnight.' He ran a pocket comb through his thinning hair. 'Are you going to join us this afternoon?'

'I shall be looking in.'

Wycliffe went downstairs to the lounge so as not to be in the way. A few minutes later he heard the men carrying her body down. The siren at the docks wailed. Half past twelve; lunchtime. A minute later a flood of bicycles burst through the gates and jammed the road outside. Fortunately they seemed too anxious to get home to bother about what was going on in the Marina.

Fehling came in looking important, a large briefcase under his arm. He whisked the flower stand with its plastic flowers on to the floor, removed the table runner and dusted the table top with a yellow duster from his briefcase. Then he displayed his finds. A photograph in a transparent polythene envelope with blue circles to indicate finger-prints, ten bundles of used pound notes, and a handbag.

'I'm not quite through yet, sir, but I doubt if there's much more of importance. Forensic have been over this lot.'

Inspector Fehling was a very large policeman, but he prided himself on the precision and economy of his move-ments. A gorilla, but a very refined gorilla. His simplest action was an exhibition – a performance, and one had the uncomfortable feeling that applause was expected. He reminded Wycliffe of those extraordinary athletes who contort themselves improbably while balanced on a narrow beam. He emptied the contents of the girl's handbag on to the table. Compact, lipstick, comb, unmarked handker-chief, five pound notes and some loose change, a tube of aspirin, and a little pocket knife with a mother-of-pearl handle. 'There was a cigarette case and lighter in the pocket of her outside coat.'

Wycliffe pointed to the bundles of notes. 'How much?'

'A thousand pounds, sir. It was in a drawer of the chest under some of her clothing.'

'Anything else?'

Fehling considered. 'Her clothes, of course, they seem to be of pretty good quality, a few pieces of jewelry and a sachet of oral contraceptives. She wore a ring but there is only a superficial mark on her finger so she probably put it on for the occasion.' He produced the ring in a plastic envelope; a gold wedding ring in an antique style, engraved inside with a monogram: $W \& J$, entwined. A moment of hesitation, then, 'That room had been searched before we got there, sir, I'd take my oath on it.'

'They couldn't have been looking for money.'

Fehling was ponderously judicial. 'That's what puzzles

23

me. You wouldn't think they would pass up a thousand quid in singles.'

'Is it possible that they wanted to remove anything that might identify her?'

'Could be! Could be, indeed, sir.' Fehling nodded his great head in approval. 'The West Indian girl says there was a framed photograph of the dead woman on the dressing table, but it's not there now.'

Wycliffe picked up the photograph in the plastic envelope. A half-length portrait of a young man with an electric guitar slung over his shoulder. A thin-faced youth with vacant eyes and the gloomy constipated look common to his kind. No signature, nothing written on the back. It was a studio portrait or the work of a good amateur but too glossy, like the publicity handouts from the big stars.

'Are you an authority on the Charts, Mr Fehling?'

'The charts, sir?'

'The Top Twenty.'

Fehling was disdainful. 'I'm afraid I'm too busy to bother with that nonsense.'

Wycliffe pushed the photograph towards him. 'Then you'd better consult an expert. If he's one of the idols he probably has nothing to do with our case, but if he's the boyfriend then we badly need his help.'

'What sort of expert would you suggest, sir?'

Wycliffe counted ten to himself then answered mildly, 'Try Kathy Johnson.'

'Kathy?'

'Kathy Johnson, the girl who seems to do all the work round here.'

'Oh, the West Indian girl!'

Wycliffe sighed. 'One more thing, the proprietor has got form but I don't want it rammed down his neck. Keep him sweet, he could be very useful.' Wycliffe began to fill his pipe. 'What do you make of it so far?'

The inspector picked up a bundle of notes and flicked them through as though he was about to perform a conjuring trick. 'This money suggests only one thing to me, sir – dope.'

'You think she was here to buy?'

Fehling hunched his immense shoulders. 'Stands to reason! I mean, this is a seaport, she's staying in a sleazy boarding house run for merchant seamen and she's got a thousand in used notes. She wouldn't be selling, would she? Not in this neck of the woods. I reckon we're on to something, sir.'

'In that case, the deal didn't go through – she was still in possession of the money. So she wasn't killed for it. So what was she killed for?'

This extraordinary verbal gymnastic did not baffle the inspector. 'Her boy friend probably knows something about that!'

'This laddie in the picture?' He shook his head. 'In that case we are dealing with two separate crimes both centred on the girl. It's not impossible but William wouldn't like it – neither do I.'

'William, sir?'

'Of Occam, a thirteenth-century gent who enunciated the axiom that in logic, entities must not be multiplied.'

'Ah!'

'Useful to remind oneself that the simplest possible explanation is probably the right one.'

'Quite so, sir.' (Christ! Where do they dig 'em up?) 'Well, sir, what next?'

Wycliffe opened the door and called, 'Kathy!' When she came he showed her the photograph of the boy with the guitar. 'Know him, Kathy?'

'I do not know that boy, superintendent.'

'Would you if he was famous?'

She grinned. 'Oh, yes! I have all their photographs in my room.' Wycliffe thanked her. 'And Kathy! I want you to write out a description of the man you found going through the register. Take your time over it and make it as complete as you can, then give it to Mr Fehling.'

Kathy went and he turned to Fehling. 'Have you found the blunt instrument?'

'Sir?'

'Whatever was used to hit her.'

'Ah. No, sir, we haven't found it, but there's a door stop missing. The door doesn't fasten properly from the inside and Piper put a seven pound brass weight there to keep it shut. Apparently it's one of those with a ring in the top to hold it by.'

'So, whoever it was didn't come prepared.'

Fehling chuckled. 'And it's not every bedroom in which you can count on finding a brass weight handy . . .'

Wycliffe looked at him blankly. 'You'd better set about finding that weight, hadn't you, Mr Fehling? And Mr Fehling, pass the word round, I don't want it known that the girl was disfigured. We'll keep that to ourselves for the moment.' He got up, searching in his pockets for sixpences for the telephone. Fehling stopped him at the door. 'There's one more thing, I forgot it – this, I found it under her bed.'

'What is it?'

He held out a shining ball the size of a marble. 'It's a steel ball-bearing, probably nothing to do with the girl. I expect it fell out of the pocket of the chap who had the room before her.'

Wycliffe took the little ball and slipped it into his pocket. 'I expect you're right.'

CHAPTER TWO

Wycliffe's hotel also overlooked the harbour, but higher up the estuary, away from the docks, next to the yacht club. The dining room was built out over the water and the racing dinghies often sailed brazenly close to the windows before going about. Wycliffe poured himself another glass of Chablis. 'Very pleasant wine, this, in fact they do us very well here altogether, very well.'

Helen laughed. 'Too well for your waist line, I think.'

He was feeling mellow after a good lunch. The water was like a mirror and if you looked with half closed eyes the whole scene dissolved into a living mosaic of colour, blue, yellow, red and white hulls with the green hill-side beyond. It would be pleasant to hire a boat and potter about the harbour for the afternoon. There was a little village of grey stone houses across the water and it would be fun to tie up at the jetty and stroll round the village, perhaps to have tea there. But he had a photo-graph in his pocket, a photograph of a young man who might, just possibly, be a murderer. He had put off telling Helen, not that she would fuss, she had been too long a policeman's wife, but it might have taken the edge off the enjoyment of their lunch.

'Something cropped up this morning.'

'I thought as much.'

'How could you?'

'You had that half smug, half guilty look I know so well, and you were late for lunch. Is it serious?'

'Murder. I should have been sent for anyway.'

Helen sighed. 'Oh, well, perhaps they will let you charge your hotel bill.'

Comforting woman.

As a concession to convention he changed his linen jacket and slacks for a lightweight suit of worsted and at two o'clock he was walking along the narrow twisting main street, smoking his pipe, one of the crowd returning to work. He would have liked to have been really a part of it, to have exchanged familiar greetings with the people he passed, to have known why the shutters were up at number forty-four, why the tobacconist at thirty-six was wearing a black arm band and the real story behind the newspaper placard which read: COUNCILLOR HILL WITHDRAWS.

This was a credible size for a community, you could identify yourself with it, live its life.

In the newspaper office a mini-skirted girl took time off to be polite. 'This is only a branch office but if you'd like to wait you could see Mr Brown, the local reporter. He's out to his lunch.'

In course of time Mr Brown arrived smelling of his liquid lunch, a red-headed young man, breezily efficient. 'Always ready to help the police, superintendent, what can we do for you?'

In a little office which had a desk, a chair, a type-writer, a telephone and nothing else, Wycliffe produced his photograph.

Brown studied it critically. 'Nasty business at the Marina, superintendent.'

'Very.'

'Is this the bloke?'

'Not as far as I know. Have you seen him before?'

As Brown spoke a cigarette danced up and down between his lips. 'They're all alike, aren't they? All the same

28

I should probably know him if he was a local lad. Can we print this? Say it was found on the scene of the crime?'

Wycliffe retrieved the photograph. 'We shall put it on the regional telly tonight. If that doesn't work I shall probably circulate it, you can print it then.'

'Who was she, super?'

Wycliffe shrugged. 'I wish I knew. Perhaps you could help, keep your eyes and ears open.'

Brown nodded. 'On a quid pro quo basis. I got precious little out of your chap at the Marina.'

'I'll see to it personally.'

'Thanks.'

'Any time!' The superintendent strolled out into the sunshine and this time he made for the car park.

He drove in a leisurely fashion the ten miles to the county town, infuriating other drivers who could only pass at those rare spots where the road had been straightened and widened. It took him twenty-three minutes. The white Jag chuntering behind would probably have done it in thirteen. Ten minutes lost! Save fivepence on the large packet! The kind of economics Wycliffe would never understand.

The afternoon sun beat down on the hospital campus so that the asphalt was soft underfoot and he was grateful for the cool tiled corridors of the pathology building. He made for the mortuary. It was overrun with people, some of whom had been at the Marina earlier. The police photographers were there with the tools of their trade, the people from forensic and a covey of policemen in and out of uniform. Wycliffe had arranged to meet some of his own Area squad there and he saw Chief Inspector James Gill pushing his way through the crowd towards him.

'Long time no see, sir! Must be all of a week!' Gill was young for his rank, craggy, tough and cynical enough to make Wycliffe feel, by contrast, comfortably warm-hearted. He liked working with Gill and had sent for him on this occasion.

'Who's with you?'

'Hartley, Wills and Manders, all we could spare. What's the Divisional set-up?'

Wycliffe shrugged. 'You'll meet Inspector Fehling directly. Impressive – that's the word, Jimmy, impressive.'

They were making their way through gossiping groups to the far end of the room where Franks and two of his assistants were working on the body of the dead girl. The acrid fishy smell of formalin was strong.

'Anything for me?'

Franks looked up. 'As far as the girl is concerned, nothing you'll want to hear. She was healthy, well nourished, between twenty and twenty-two, she had never given birth. No scars, no nice identifiable old fractures. She has a large mole on her left breast, her teeth have been well cared for, no extractions and only two fillings . . .'

Dr Bell of forensic joined them by the table. 'And there's no joy from the clothing either – there isn't much of it anyway.' He was bald headed, a little wisp of a man, with an oversized pipe which he sucked whether it was lit or not – 'Nipple fixation', he called it. 'Our job would be a pushover if women still wore calico drawers and shifts.'

'I can tell you one thing,' Franks said. He always saved the best till last. 'The man who made love to her is AB.' He looked absurdly pleased with himself, like a little boy who has just said his party piece. 'I ran the usual grouping tests on the seminal fluid and for once we hit the jack-pot.'

Wycliffe was unimpressed, or pretended to be. 'Big deal! If I remember rightly, about three per cent of the population are in the AB group, so, leaving women and

30

children aside, that gives us a round half million suspects in the UK to choose from.'

Franks's baby face wrinkled into a grin. 'You chaps want your job done for you! As it is we do most of it.'

Wycliffe looked down at the figure on the dissecting table. He was hardened by long usage, but it was in any case difficult to connect this gruesome cadaver with the eye-catching girl who had booked in at the Marina on Sunday night. It was that girl he wanted to know about, her living and her loving and the web of circumstance which had finally put an end to them both. He had to put the clock back to Sunday night at least, probably much further, and try to live with her that borrowed time.

He sent Chief Inspector Gill in search of the police photographer. 'I want you to work on your shots of the face and with Dr Franks's help, bring her alive. Let's have a photograph we can publish, one that her friends will recognize.'

Both men were doubtful but they agreed to try; and Kathy, Wycliffe said, would check the result.

Chief Inspector Gill rode back with Wycliffe in his nice new Zodiac to be put in the picture. Gill watched the countryside gliding sedately by and listened. It was one of Wycliffe's consolations that he didn't have to spell everything out for Gill; they had evolved a kind of conversational shorthand which, despite differences of temperament, they could use because their logical processes were similar.

'Three sets of prints on the photograph of the guitarist, one set belonging to the girl. Copies have gone to Area and to CRO.'

'So if he's got form, there's a chance, otherwise . . .'

'It's possible that none of the dabs are the killer's anyway.'

Gill let another mile or so slide by – they were trailing a

green double-decker bus at twenty with a queue of traffic behind waiting in vain for Wycliffe to make a move.

'Been this way before, Jim?'

'No sir, first visit. Seems pleasant enough, trees and all that.'

'You should bring your wife and kids down for a holiday.'

'Holiday? What's that? I thought it was something they gave to school kids. Going back to the case, this grouping test of Franks's, is it the same as a blood test?'

'Same thing.'

'Then it could help?'

Wycliffe drew to a halt behind the bus which had stopped to set down passengers. 'If we had a line-up of suspects it might, but we don't even know who the girl is. That's our first job and our best bet there is . . .'

'The laddie with the guitar.'

'Exactly. With any luck the photograph should be in all the papers tomorrow and it might be on television tonight.'

The cars behind had taken advantage of the bus stop and were streaming past. Finally the bus got going again and Wycliffe fell in behind.

'I suppose you couldn't pass that thing, sir? The diesel fumes . . .'

Wycliffe seemed surprised. 'Do they bother you? Anyway it's hardly worth it now, we're just coming into the town.'

They were cruising along a suburban road lined with Dracaenas and villas in a bewildering variety of architectural styles, each with its Bed and Breakfast sign. A canvas banner between two lamp-posts advertised a summer show at the Council's theatre.

Inspector Fehling had been busy establishing a murder

32

hunt HQ at the station. The recreation room had been cleared and equipped with tables and chairs, an epidiascope and a slide projector. A projection screen was fixed to one of the walls flanked by maps of the town and surrounding areas. Telephone engineers were busy installing additional instruments. Fehling looked at his achievement with pride.

'What are the magic lanterns for?' Wycliffe asked.

'A slide projector and epidiascope, sir, for projecting transparencies and prints.'

'Ah!'

'Visual aids, I think they call them, sir,' Gill said. 'All the rage in progressive forces.'

Opening off the main room were two little rooms which Fehling had set aside for the 'brass'. 'You take your choice, sir,' he offered generously, 'but this one is a bit bigger so I've taken the liberty of putting the reports there.' He pointed to a wire tray on the table containing an alarming bundle of typescript.

Wycliffe sat himself in one of the bentwood chairs on the wrong side of the desk and Gill chose the other. Fehling was left standing.

'For God's sake, sit down, Mr Fehling!'

So the inspector had to fit himself into the armchair behind the desk and he bulged over the arms. He started to sort the reports. Obviously he was good at paper work, which is the way to get on. If you make enough copies of bugger-all people think it and you must be important. Wycliffe filled his pipe, refused any papers and said, 'Tell us about it, Mr Fehling.'

Fehling passed a great hand over his brow and back over his thinning curls. 'There is only one new lead so far. You remember the house on the other side of the railway cutting?'

33

Wycliffe nodded. 'Their backs overlook the back of the hotel.'

'Exactly, they're good class houses, sir – respectable.'

'What's that got to do with it? Are you thinking of buying one?'

'Just that they're the sort of people who make reliable witnesses.'

Wycliffe questioned the assumption but said nothing. In his experience the more respectable people were, the more they had to hide. They didn't want to be mixed up in anything that wasn't quite nice.

'The lady at number twenty-six, a Mrs Foster, says that at a little after midnight she happened to be looking out of her landing window when she saw someone standing on the fire escape of the hotel.'

'Man or woman?'

'She thinks it was a man though she could only see a silhouette against the lighted window.'

'Which window?'

'Top floor of the extension, she says. It must have been the girl's room or the bathroom.'

'What was he doing?'

'Just standing there according to her. She says she watched him for nearly ten minutes.'

'The window of the girl's room won't open.'

'No, sir, it's screwed up.'

'And the curtains won't draw.' Wycliffe lit his pipe and blew clouds of smoke ceilingwards. 'What was she doing looking out of her window at that time of night?'

'I don't know, sir, but she says she's complained on several occasions to the police about goings on in that place.'

'I'll bet!' He caught Gill looking at him quizzically, wondering why he was knocking poor old Fehling who seemed to be doing a pretty good job. He hardly knew himself, not until he stopped to think, then he knew. It was the tacit assumption of Fehling and his like that the world is divided into two camps, the good and the bad, the respectable and the contemptible, the cops and the robbers. Never would Fehling look at one of his victims and say, 'There but for the grace of God . . .'

'Anything else?'

Fehling looked aggrieved, as well he might. 'The other two rooms on that floor of the extension, sir – one was occupied by an elderly tradesman sent down from Newcastle by his firm to do some special job on that cruise liner which is being refitted in the yard.'

'Could he tell you anything?'

'Nothing. He said he'd had a few drinks and slept like a log. The other room – the room next to the girl's – was let to a young man waiting to join his ship when she docks on Sunday. He was the worse for drink too and his recollections are hazy. But he had a girl with him . . .'

'What does she say?'

Fehling stroked his smooth chin which, in a few years, would extend in rolls down his neck. 'We haven't found her yet, sir. He picked her up in one of the pubs and he can't remember much about her except that she cleared off early this morning.'

'What about Piper?'

'Sir?'

'The proprietor of the place – what does he say about the girl?'

'Says he had no idea she was there, if he had he would have thrown her out. Respectable house, all that malarkey.'

'So what are you doing about it?'

'My chaps will be doing the rounds of the pubs tonight.'

'No.'

35

'Sir?'

'I said no, I expect they've got something better to do than a subsidized pub crawl.'

Fehling raised his eyes to the ceiling and pursed his lips. Chief Inspector Gill was enjoying himself.

'What about the other people staying in the place – anybody suspicious?'

Fehling fished some papers out of the wire tray. 'Here are the reports, sir.'

'Tell me about them, Mr Fehling.'

'Well, sir, there were nine other people staying in the hotel. All were men and all have been questioned by my chaps. They've given credible accounts of themselves, but we're checking, and they've been told not to leave the town without notifying us. Most of them – all but two, in fact – are waiting to join their ships. They've got seamen's books which seem to be in order.'

'What about the other two?'

'Lorry driver and his mate, sir, down here to pick up some turbine rotors which have to go back to the works for balancing.'

Wycliffe stood up. 'Well, I'm off! I'll leave you and Chief Inspector Gill together. No doubt you'll find that you have much in common.'

'Christ! Is he always like that?'

Gill looked at the door which had barely closed behind the Chief Superintendent. 'Mostly, but you'll get used to it.'

'I don't know that I want to,' Fehling grumbled. 'It's like tight boots, there don't seem to be much point in starting.'

Wycliffe left his car on the park and walked in the direction of the main street. It was just on six according to the clock over the post office, and visitors were streaming off the quay, returning from the afternoon boat trips,

36

making for their lodgings and dinner. The children trailed behind and were scolded while the toddlers had to be carried on daddys' shoulders. Wycliffe watched it all with interest and approval. He never tired of watching people, people about their business and their pleasure. Some men watched animals, building little hides to spy on badgers, birds or deer, but Wycliffe could not understand them. From a window on to a street, from a seat in a pub or a park, or strolling round a fairground, it was possible to observe a far more varied species, more complex, more intelligent, more perceptive and vastly richer in the pattern of their emotional response.

The narrow main street was almost deserted, the shops closed, the pubs and fried fish bars just opening their doors but with no customers as yet. Wycliffe ambled along window shopping. The bookshop he had noticed before, an especially good bookshop for a small town. Two large windows, one devoted to new and the other to secondhand books, well displayed and priced. A card invited inspection of *twenty thousand secondhand books inside – many of antiquarian interest and importance*. He promised himself that he would find time to spend an hour there. Good bookshops were getting all too rare. He noticed the name on the signboard:

W.P. COLLINS & SON.
NEW AND SECOND HAND BOOKSELLERS
Estab: 1847

Good for the Collinses!

He made his way through the street on towards the docks and the Marina. Apart from a few people on the pavement gawping, it looked serenely undisturbed. He pushed his way through the swing glass doors and found a constable in the hall. 'Is the room sealed?'

37

'Yes, sir.'

'Then report back, no need to waste your time here.' The constable went. 'Anybody home?' Silence. An appetizing smell led him by the nose to the kitchen. In better days it had been a conservatory and some of the smaller panes were red or blue or orange glass so that gay splashes of colour cropped up in unexpected places. Piper was seated at a large table covered with oilcloth, reading a racing paper and eating curried stew with a spoon. Opposite him, sitting bolt upright, prim as a maiden aunt at the Vicar's teaparty, Kathy, eating her stew very skilfully, with a fork.

Ernie Piper was too old a hand to be put off his food by a policeman. He looked up and grinned. 'Sit yourself down, superintendent, what can we do for you?'

'You like curry, superintendent? I make it myself and there is plenty.'

Wycliffe realized that he was hungry. 'It smells good!'

'She cooks like an angel,' Piper said. 'That's why I keep you, isn't it, Kathy?'

Kathy smiled but said nothing.

The curry was good – and hot. He had to suck in his breath after the first mouthful. Piper laughed. 'Try some bread, superintendent,' and he passed the board with the best part of a two pound loaf on it. 'She makes her own bread too. It makes going straight worth while.'

For a time they ate in silence. Piper opened a couple of bottles of beer and decanted them into glasses. Wycliffe wondered what Inspector Fehling would make of it if he could see them now.

'Who was the girl in sixteen last night?'

Piper shrugged, 'I told the inspector . . .'

'I know what you told the inspector, I also know your sort, my lad. Is your front door locked at night?'

'Well, no . . .'

38

'And is there, or is there not, a board in the hall which shows the rooms which are occupied?'

'I told you, I'm going straight, superintendent.' Piper took a great gulp of beer and wiped his lips with the back of his hand.

Wycliffe grinned. 'That's as may be but you're not going soft! Are you trying to tell me that any pick-up can have a free night's lodging and enjoy the other amenities of your establishment if she cares to bring her bloke here?'

Piper looked sheepish. 'Well no, but I can't stop the chaps who lodge here bringing back a bird if they feel that way, can I? I mean this isn't a Sunday school.'

Wycliffe had finished his curry and he was fiddling with the crusty top of the loaf. He broke off a generous chunk and began to nibble. It reminded him of when he used to be sent to buy bread when he was a kid – before they turned it into sponge rubber.

'Have some butter with it?'

'Not likely!' He chewed happily. 'I wouldn't like to be the girl who came back here with one of your boarders if she wasn't on your visiting list or if she didn't leave the proper cut. Where do they put it? Do they drop it in the potted palm as they go out?'

Piper chuckled. 'I'll say one thing for you, you know the score! It was Millie Ford, 46, Castle Hill. She's a good girl so don't you go upsetting her.'

'And don't you push your luck!' Wycliffe growled.

It was a mellow evening, a golden light over the harbour, softening the colours, blurring the outlines, the water still and gleaming.

Castle Hill was on his way back to the hotel, a minor hump in the low lying ground which fringes the harbour. You climb steeply from the main street between two rows of small and, for the most part, derelict shops, then the road falls away more slowly to the level of the harbour and the hotel. Millie lived over a shop which displayed a dusty collection of china and glass ornaments calling them, hopefully, antiques. The shop was shut so he knocked at the side door. An immensely fat woman across the street, standing in her doorway, shouted, 'You got to go up, dearie!' Despite all his years in the Force he was embarrassed.

The door opened on to a flight of wooden steps and at the top he was faced by three doors. He knocked on one marked *FORD*, and a voice called, 'Come in!' Of course the room overlooked the ubiquitous harbour, he couldn't escape from it, not that he wanted to. It was a bedsitter, a bit threadbare and over-used, but clean and tidy. 'What do you want, love?' Millie Ford in a housecoat and mules was standing by a tiny electric stove, waiting for a saucepan of milk to heat. 'I'm making some coffee, want some?'

Wycliffe refused. She was thirtyish, plump, a bit over-ripe, but attractive. 'I'm a police officer.'

She laughed in a bored way. 'I've heard that one before, dear, but I can spot a dick a mile off. Now, what do you want? Are you after something special?'

Wycliffe flapped his warrant card and she looked at it, incredulous. 'On the level? I wouldn't have said you was big enough, they must be making 'em in the handy pocket size. A chief super, too . . .!' She pointed to the only chair in the room. 'You better sit down.' She poured the milk into a half filled cup of coffee. 'Sure you won't? Well, what have I done now?'

Wycliffe looked round the room. He'd seen hundreds like it, most of them a great deal more squalid. She had been ironing a frock and the ironing board was wedged into the little space between the bed and the window. Over the bed there was a piece of poker-work: *Bless this house!*

She caught his eye and grinned. 'I expect you know why I'm here,' he began.

She shook her mop of black hair. 'I don't, love, honest.'

He looked at her suspiciously but she seemed to be telling the truth. 'A girl was strangled at the Marina last night.'

She stopped short in the act of sipping her coffee. 'But I was . . .'

'. . . there last night, I know.'

She was shocked and scared. She put her cup down on the stove, sat on the bed and faced him. 'Was it one . . . ?'

He shook his head. 'A stranger, we don't know who she was.'

She was relieved and he didn't blame her. She brought out a packet of cigarettes from the pocket of her housecoat and looked vaguely round for matches. He gave her a box and she lit a cigarette which set her coughing.

'She was in seventeen, next door to you.'

'Ah!'

'Now I want you to tell me all you can remember about last night from the time you picked up your man.'

She blew her nose after the coughing fit and seemed to be collecting her thoughts. 'I usually do The Ship, and I was there last evening. I got into conversation with a chap and we had a few drinks although he was three parts cut before we started. When they shut at half ten he asked me to come back with him. I asked him where and he said the Marina, so that was all right. He was only a youngster and when we got out in the air he made heavy weather of it so that it took me some time to get him there and then he just flaked out on the bed. Not that I was bothered, I got into bed and tried to get some sleep . . .'

'You didn't see anybody?'

41

'In the Marina? Only Ernie, he was poking about in the little office when we came in and he helped me to get his lordship upstairs.'

'Well?'

She drew on her cigarette thoughtfully. 'I could hear a couple next door and I thought it must be one of ours with a client. I couldn't get off to sleep so I lay there trying to guess who it was . . . you know how you do . . .'

'What could you hear?'

'Just voices, a man and a woman talking but I couldn't hear what they were saying. I only wished they would shut up. Oh yes! – the man coughed a lot – a smoker's cough.'

'Were they quarrelling?'

'No, just talking. A lot of men pick up a girl because they want a woman to talk to – funny really.'

Wycliffe sat there staring out of the window watching the purple dusk steal over the harbour like a mist and he was happy. He was feeling the texture of another life with sympathy and understanding – these encounters were the reward, not the penalty of his work. 'Then?'

'Well, it must have been around midnight when I heard somebody come out of the room and pass my door. I thought it must be the girl going home and wished I could go too but my fellow hadn't forked out and I would have to let Ernie have his cut anyway.'

'You're sure that this was around midnight?'

'No, I couldn't be sure of the time – not really.'

'And you heard nothing more all night?'

'Oh yes I did. Probably I dozed for a bit but some time later I heard them talking again and that seemed odd. She must have come back and I couldn't understand it. This time they did seem to be quarrelling but they kept their voices low . . .'

'The same voices?'

She looked puzzled. 'Well, they must have been, mustn't they?' Wycliffe said nothing and she went on, 'Then they stopped talking and started . . .'

'What?'

'To get down to it – I mean, there's no doubt about it with those beds in the Marina.'

'Anything more?'

'No, I didn't hear any more, I must have gone off to sleep properly after that. The next thing I knew it was getting light and my chap woke up. I told him I wanted my money and after a bit he pulled out his wallet and told me to take it. He had the father and mother of a hangover and I don't think he had a clue where he was or who I was . . . Anyway I took four quid and beat it . . . After all it wasn't my fault if . . .'

Wycliffe agreed.

'To think that next door that poor girl . . .' Millie found a handkerchief and dabbed her eyes. The most poignant grief of all when one can say, 'There but for the grace of God . . .'

Wycliffe walked back to the hotel and found Helen in the lounge reading. She looked up with a welcoming smile. 'Have you had a meal?'

'What? Oh, yes thanks.' He was still in a different world from this air-conditioned lounge with its soft lights, thick carpets and silent waiters. This world was less real to him, less comprehensible; it was not that he wanted to . . . He sighed. 'I had curried stew.'

Helen laughed. 'Was it good?'

What would she say if he told her that he had been entertained by a pimp and his Jamaican tart? 'Yes, very good.'

They had a drink together, then Helen said that she felt like bed.

'I'll be with you in ten minutes.'

43

He lit his pipe and went out on to the terrace. He stood, his arms resting on the balustrade. The waters of the harbour, dark and mysterious, dozens of riding lights sending their quivering ribbons of yellow across its surface. Well away to the right, the docks, a blaze of light, the only sounds a low pitched hum from some machinery and the hiss of escaping steam.

One man was with the dead girl until around midnight. They talked amicably. Had this man left before another appeared on the fire escape? Was the man on the fire escape spying on the couple? It seemed probable that he had come in through the bathroom window, the official way on to the escape in an emergency. In which case the girl had unfastened the window for him. This time the talk was less friendly: 'They seemed to be quarrelling but they kept their voices low'. But this visit had ended in copulation – and in murder.

Two men? It seemed so. So far he had heard of three in the case – four if he counted Ernie Piper. The boy with the guitar, the man in the pinstripes whom Kathy had found going through the register and the chap in cap and mackintosh she had seen talking to the dead girl. Was it one of these who had spent an hour with her? And another of them who had strangled her, then battered her face beyond recognition?

CHAPTER THREE

A morning conference in the superintendent's little office.

'As I see it, the bloke came the first time to make contact, to find out if she had the money and was able to do a deal. She satisfied him and he went off to get the stuff . . .' Fehling spoke in a ponderously judicial way which was one more source of irritation to Wycliffe.

'You still think that she was buying dope?'

The inspector blew out his cheeks. 'Oh, I don't think there can be any doubt on that score, it's another matter to decide what went wrong.' He studied his finger-tips then added, 'Quite another matter.'

Wycliffe was standing looking out of the window of the office. It was as though he had to keep in touch with the world outside, a room without windows would have been torture to him. The view was uninspiring, an exercise yard and beyond a great expanse of corrugated asbestos, the wall and roof of a garage. 'What do you think, Jim?'

Chief Inspector Gill's ugly expressive features creased in dissatisfaction. 'It sounds likely enough on the face of it but according to what you've just told us they must have spent the best part of an hour together just gossiping. That hardly sounds like a preliminary session to spy out the land – more as if they were old friends. But if they knew each other so well, why didn't he bring the goods with him? In any case, why was she killed?'

Fehling took up the challenge. 'There are at least two possible explanations. When he came back with the dope it's feasible that she wasn't satisfied, or that

45

she tried for a better deal – the girl says she heard them quarrelling.'

'So he makes love to her, strangles her, bashes her face in, then goes off without the money.'

Wycliffe's manner made Fehling flush. 'It sounds a bit thin, but you know as well as I do that you can't predict what a man will or won't do under stress.'

'You said that there were two possibilities – what was the other?'

'That they didn't quarrel about the deal but that her friend decided to round off the evening by giving her a tumble and she put up a fight.'

'So he strangled her?'

'It wouldn't be the first time!' Fehling was on the defensive.

'It couldn't have been much of a fight: Millie Ford heard nothing of it and she was next door.'

'But the girl was strangled and she did have her face battered.'

Wycliffe turned back to the window. 'Yes, and a thousand pounds was left untouched in a drawer. In any case, what about the chap on the fire escape? Where does he come into it?'

Fehling nodded. 'I've thought of that, I believe he was the same man. The front door of the hotel is fitted with a Yale-type lock which is kept clipped back but I found out from Piper that the catch is liable to slip and you find yourself locked out.'

'You think that's what happened to your friend?'

Fehling was pleased with himself. 'I do. Think of it, sir. After his first session with the girl he goes to get the stuff and when he comes back he finds the door locked. Naturally he doesn't want to rouse the house so he nips round and up the fire escape, taps on the girl's window and she lets him in through the bathroom.'

Chief Inspector Gill chuckled. 'That's very ingenious.'

Wycliffe grunted but said nothing. He hadn't a very high opinion of Fehling but he had to admit that there was some sort of case. If the girl wasn't buying dope, why would she hang around with a thousand pounds in used notes in a dockland hotel? Or had she *sold* something? He sighed. Speculation was useless until he knew who she was. 'What are you going to do next?'

Fehling felt that he had scored. 'I thought of looking into the docks angle. What ships are in? Itinerary of last trip? Who was sleeping ashore? – that sort of thing. I also planned to send out circulars – anybody in the vicinity of the Marina between, say, eleven and three.'

Wycliffe nodded. Fehling was right, whatever the reason for the crime it seemed to be linked with the docks or at least with the sea and seamen. 'I think you're on the right lines,' he said in a belated attempt to make amends.

Gill offered round a case containing thin black cheroots which were refused. He had changed to cheroots maintaining that they were less hazardous than cigarettes. He allowed himself only five a day, so that smoking one added something special to any occasion as the advertisement said that it would. Wycliffe lit his pipe in self defence. 'Yesterday evening,' Gill said, 'Inspector Fehling and I made a round of the cafés in the main street and as far as the docks. The Marina doesn't do meals other than breakfast and she must have eaten somewhere. It seems that she used a place almost by the dock gates and not above a hundred yards from the hotel. The chap who runs it had noticed an "auburn-haired dolly" whom he described "as the sort of bird to keep a man awake at night".'

'Poetic, really,' Wycliffe said. 'Was she always alone?'

'Always. The café owner was puzzled by her, she wasn't the sort he expected to get in a place like his.'

'What sort of place is it?'

Gill considered. 'It's really a lorry drivers' caf. Clean enough, friendly, but not much choice beyond the bangers and mash and a cuppa. I imagine it's used mainly by lorry drivers taking stuff in and out of the docks.'

'Not by the locals?'

Gill looked at him sharply. 'No, do you think that's why she went there?'

Wycliffe wished sometimes that Gill did not know him so well. He made an irritable movement to save a reply. He turned to Fehling. 'Why was her face battered in? That's what I want to know.'

'The chap went berserk, scared out of his wits,' Fehling said.

'Is that what you think?' Wycliffe's blank stare was turned on Gill.

The chief inspector shook his head. 'No, either her identification would lead direct to her killer or there are local associations which he doesn't want known.'

'Or both.'

'Could be.'

The telephone rang and Wycliffe answered it. 'Wycliffe.' It was the station sergeant. 'The guitarist, sir, whose photo went out on the telly last night – he's on the telephone, wants to know what it's all about.'

'Is he a local?'

'He's living in the town; he's got a flat in Marine Walk, chap by the name of Graham.'

'Tell him we'll send somebody along to talk to him – say during the next hour, then find out all you can about him from your chaps.'

'We could bring him in, sir.'

'No!' Wycliffe believed that when you brought a man into the police station you saw only half of him. He decided to interview Graham himself.

'He must be a cool one,' Gill said. 'The average man seeing his picture on the telly like that would be on to the nick before the news-reader got to the next item.'

'There aren't any average men left!' Wycliffe growled.

Before he left for Marine Walk he was briefed by the station sergeant. 'Kenneth Graham, sir, he runs a pop group and is known professionally as Kenny the Man. They seem to make a fairly plush living in the season, playing at several resorts up and down the West Country.'

Wycliffe set out.

A chief superintendent's place during a murder inquiry is usually established in the nearest police station but it can be in a village hall or even a caravan. As the officer in charge of the inquiry it is his job to remain at the centre coordinating all aspects of the investigation, receiving reports and deploying men and resources to the best advantage. The most Wycliffe had ever conceded to this official view of his duties was to telephone in at reasonable intervals or to keep in touch through his car radio. He had to get out and about, to get the smell of the chase. He had to meet witnesses in their normal surroundings. 'Field work,' he called it. He could, of course, have had his witnesses brought in. He could have carried out formal interrogations in the stultifying atmosphere of the police station where innocent people soon begin to behave like crooks. But Wycliffe believed that what he called *personal* crimes are more likely to be solved by getting to know the people involved, getting to know them so well that you begin to think as they do.

Two criticisms had been levelled at him at every stage of his career: 'He does not take well to discipline', and 'He often becomes too emotionally involved with his cases'. Damning criticisms of a policeman – Wycliffe never understood why they hadn't blocked his promotion, but he suspected that it was because the solemn Jacks who insisted on reams of paper rarely read what was on it. And he had a good reputation as a villain catcher.

Marine Walk circles the promontory which divides the harbour from the open sea. On the harbour side its low cliffs overhang the docks and on the sea side a fringe of sandy beaches, too small for exploitation, provide refuge for holidaymakers who enjoy peace and quiet. The houses are on the sea side and he drove round catching tantalizing glimpses of the sea through the trees which grow on the gentle slopes almost to the water's edge.

Graham lived in the upper flat of an Edwardian villa which had been modernized and converted into two flats with an outside staircase. The stairs ended on a glass roofed balcony with a magnificent panoramic view of the whole bay.

'Are you a copper?'

Kenny wore tight jeans and a floral shirt but he had changed his hair style since the photograph: instead of allowing it to hang lankly round his hatchet face he was now giving it the wave and set treatment.

'Chief Superintendent Wycliffe.'

'You'd better come in.'

To Wycliffe's surprise, the flat could hardly have been more conventional. Everything shone and though the taste was a bit *Coronation Street*, it had all been carefully chosen and cost money. In the lounge there was everything from a gleaming cocktail cabinet with chrome fittings to the most stupendous fake-log electric fire Wycliffe had ever seen, as well as china ducks clinging to the wall in frozen flight. Wycliffe was fascinated by the seeming incongruity of it

50

all. 'Do you live with your parents?' It seemed the most likely explanation.

But Kenny shook his head. 'You're looking at the gear? No, it's just that I like somewhere nice to come home to and I'm not short of a few bob. As a matter of fact I share with one of my mates.' He sat on the arm of a magenta-coloured cut moquette easy chair. 'Well, what's this all about then? It don't do a chap in my position any good to be put on the telly by the police. People will think I've done something.'

Wycliffe was perched on the edge of a settee trying to stop himself falling back into its monstrous clutches. 'About the photograph, Mr Graham, is it one you use for publicity purposes?'

'No, definitely not. We're a group and we sell as a group – private enterprise is out. That's one other reason why putting me on the telly won't do me any good.'

'The girl who had this photograph was murdered.'

'Yeh?' He sounded impressed and shocked. 'Who was she?'

'That's what we want to find out and it's why we need your help.'

Kenny took a cigarette from a dispenser on one of several little tables scattered about the room. He lit it and gave his attention once more to the superintendent. 'Got a photo?'

'No.'

'Well, I can't help, can I?'

'She was twenty-one or two, auburn haired, good looking, small, and she had a mole under her left breast. People who saw her when she was alive describe her as "eye-catching".'

Kenny had stopped smoking and was looking at the superintendent with close attention. 'Tell me some more.'

'There's not much else to tell, but these are some of the things she had with her . . .' He took a small parcel from his pocket, unwrapped it and spread out the few bits of jewelry they had found in her room. 'Recognize any of it?'

Kenny picked up the garnet bracelet. 'I gave her that. She had a thing about rubies but I couldn't run to that so we settled for the next best thing.'

'So you knew her.'

Kenny nodded, his eyes staring distantly, then he sighed, 'She was a doll!'

'What was her name and when did you know her?'

At that moment the door opened and a tousle-headed brunette in a baby-doll nightie came in. She was stretching her arms and yawning. 'What time is it?' She took a cigarette and looked vaguely round the room for a light. Wycliffe might not have been there for all the notice she took. 'God! I feel awful this morning!' She saw the jewelry. 'Are they for me?'

Kenny went over and took her by the shoulders. 'Go back to bed, Chick, or get yourself dressed.' He propelled her out of the room and rounded off his instructions with a resounding slap on her rump which made her squeal. He came back looking sheepish. 'Sorry about that.'

'All part of life's rich pattern,' Wycliffe said. 'Now, you were telling me . . .'

'Dawn Peters she was called, she did a summer season at the Voodoo last year.'

'The Voodoo is a club?'

'Yes, a plush place if you go by the prices. Anyway they hire two bands for the season, one pop and one trad. We was there last year and she was one of two strippers. *The Fabulous Dawn*, they billed her and for once they were right. She used to have the old men sitting

52

on the edges of their seats and begging. Every man in the place was convinced she was doing it for him and that included me – and I'm used to it.'

'You got to know her outside the club?'

He lit another cigarette. 'Yeh.' He was less anxious to talk now.

'Well?'

'Well enough.' He upset ash down the front of his shirt and took time off to brush it on to newspaper. 'I would have married her.'

'Did she live with you here?'

'I didn't have this place then; anyway she shared a flat with the other girl – Sadie. Sadie's still at the Voodoo, but she isn't in the same league.'

'You asked her to marry you?'

'Yeh, and she turned me down. I was lucky.'

'Lucky?'

He crushed out his cigarette in a huge plated ashtray with a press-down middle. 'That's what I said. For one thing she was married already and for another . . .' His voice trailed off. 'She was a case! She had the devil in her. It was any man any time but there was more to it than that.' He paused again, searching for words to describe something which had impressed him. 'She would always go to the limit and a bit further – you know what I mean? That sort of bird's fine to have fun with, but when it comes to the old steak and chips then you want something a bit more steady. Get me?

'It was the same in her act – I mean there are limits even for a stripper in a private club. When she turned it in at the Voodoo they lost a packet but old Quackers, the proprietor, told me himself that he was glad to see her go. With her antics on and off the stage she would have got the place shut down.'

'Where did she go when she left the Voodoo?'

Kenny shrugged. 'Up to the smoke but don't ask me where. She said she had a West End contract and she was probably telling the truth.'

'You said she was married. I take it she wasn't living with her husband?'

'I told you she was sharing with the other girl. I was new to the town then and I never knew the details but I heard gossip. Apparently she was married to some local square who took a pretty dim view of her goings on.' He grinned. 'I can't say as I blame him for that.'

Wycliffe stood up. From the window he could see the whole sweep of the bay from the lighthouse round a ten-mile stretch of coastline to the jagged teeth of the Meudon Rocks. He wondered if Kenny ever looked out of the window, or was it just another status symbol?

'Well, thank you for your help, Mr Graham. You haven't got a photograph of her, I suppose?'

Kenny shook his head. 'I never keep photos of dames, it makes for trouble, but there should be plenty at the club.'

Wycliffe moved towards the door. 'Is your group working at the moment?'

'Oh yeh, we're doing a season at the Scala.'

'Every night?'

'Except Tuesdays and Sundays. They have Bingo on Tuesdays.'

'Where were you on Tuesday night, then?'

Kenny looked shaken. 'Here! Come off it! You coppers are all alike.'

'Routine, Mr Graham, just routine. Where were you?'

He was aggrieved. 'I took the chick to that Indian place in Market Street for a nosh then we came back here early and went to bed.'

'Have you got a car?'

'Yeh. What of it?'

'Nothing. Did you know that Dawn Peters was back in the town?'

Kenny's aggressiveness increased with his nervousness. 'No, I didn't know, and if I had I wouldn't have been interested, copper!'

Wycliffe let himself out into the corridor and turned for a final word: 'Do you think Dawn Peters was her real name?'

'How the hell should I know?' Kenny the Man was disillusioned.

Wycliffe caught himself chuckling as he went down the steps, but if anybody had asked him why, he couldn't have told them. He would probably have grunted or he might have said, 'Just people.'

He drove back slowly to the centre of the town and parked on one of the quays, then he strolled in the main street. It was past one o'clock and the population of the town seemed to have its whole mind on food. It was too late to go back to the hotel for lunch but getting a meal otherwise was a competitive business and he was discouraged by the heat, by the crowded tables, by the queues and by the fact that every available potato seemed to have undergone a metamorphosis into chips. He took refuge in a pub and made a meal off ham sandwiches with mustard and a pint of beer. All round him the talk was of cricket, in which he had no interest. No-one so much as mentioned the murder. He stayed until two and followed his beer with a whisky.

'The Voodoo? They don't open till evening but you may find somebody there . . . Anyway, it's after you pass the church next to the off-licence.' Wycliffe walked once more in the sunshine while others were hurrying back to work.

The afternoon heat was oppressive, perspiration made his collar limp and his shirt stuck to his back. The Voodoo had no frontage, only a discreet entrance with a neon sign over the door, unlit. He pushed open the door and found himself at the top of a flight of carpeted stairs which led down below street level. At the bottom he was in a foyer with a cloakroom counter on his right and a couple of padded doors labelled by some retarded character *Adams* and *Eves*, respectively. Red, upholstered banquettes occupied every spare foot of wall space and above them there were framed photographs of show-business personalities, some of them well enough known to be vaguely familiar to the superintendent. Two showed an insipid looking blonde with nothing on but a head-dress and these were autographed *Sadie*. A pair of swing doors with figured glass panels opened into a very large dimly lit room with a curtained stage at one end, a central dance floor and tables and chairs disposed in two ranks on the carpeted fringe. The pervading colour was red, and the walls were hung with huge grinning masks and grotesque totems against a mural background depicting mythical monsters in vaguely erotic involvement. The stage and the bar on the far side were flanked by ten-foot-high figures which looked like refugees from Easter Island but were probably made of polystyrene. A faint smell of stale tobacco and alcohol blended with an indescribable synthetic scent out of an aerosol. But it was cool, like a cellar. There was nobody to be seen. 'Anybody about?'

After a second and a third try, a woman came down the steps from the stage. A bottle blonde, older than she tried to look; inclined to be fleshy, she looked naked rather than provocative in a psychedelic mini-dress which revealed too much white thigh. 'Who are you?'

'I want to see the owner.'

'He's not in.'

'I'm Chief Superintendent Wycliffe, Area CID.'

'What do you want?'

'I'll tell the owner when you've found him.'

She looked him over, then went back the way she had come. Wycliffe sat himself in one of the comfortable arm-chairs provided for the paying customers and lit his pipe. In about three minutes a man came down from the stage, forty plus, foppishly dressed in cavalry twill slacks, a modish shirt with green stripes and gold links, a green waistcoat with gilt buttons. His face was pink and rather podgy. His blue eyes looked out through rimless glasses and he spoke in an authoritative manner, intended to subdue. He was smooth, too smooth by half. 'Good afternoon, superintendent, nothing wrong, I trust?'

'I hope not, Mr . . .'

'Masson-Smythe – I'm the proprietor.' 'Quackers', Kenny the Man had called him, but not, Wycliffe was prepared to bet, to his face.

Wycliffe remained seated in his chair, smoking his pipe, Masson-Smythe stood over him, rocking on his heels. 'I am making enquiries about a Miss Dawn Peters, do you know her?'

The proprietor straightened the cuffs of his shirt, dis-playing the gold links. 'We had a cabaret artiste of that name who worked here last season.'

'A stripper?'

Masson-Smythe raised his eyebrows in disapproval. 'She was a speciality dancer and her act possessed great artistic merit.'

'I'm sure it did. She's been murdered.'

The eyes behind the spectacles widened.

'Was Dawn Peters her real name?'

'It was the name she used in her dealings with me.'

Wycliffe's manner hardened. 'But you employed her! What about insurance, income tax, S.E.T.?'

Masson-Smythe was curt. 'All our artistes have contracts, they are self-employed.'

'Was she good at her job?'

'She attracted patrons.'

There was something about Masson-Smythe's face which had been troubling the superintendent, now he realized what it was. Words came from his lips as from a ventriloquist's doll; there was scarcely any change of expression. 'You must have had photographs of her for display purposes?'

'Certainly.'

'I would like to see them.'

For some reason this seemed to touch a tender spot and the man lost something of his aggressive self-assurance. Wycliffe noticed little beads of perspiration on his upper lip. Something to hide. 'I'm sorry, we do not keep photographs of artistes who are no longer under contract with us, the rapid turnover in the entertainment business makes it . . .'

Wycliffe mentioned two or three names off the photographs in the foyer. 'Are these people under contract with you at present?'

'They are in quite a different category, superintendent, they are celebrities and the fact that they have performed here in the past is, itself, an advertisement.'

Wycliffe smoked placidly and Masson-Smythe continued to stand over him. 'I would like to know on what date Dawn Peters started to work here and under what circumstances she was offered a contract.'

For a moment it seemed that the man might refuse but after some hesitation he shrugged and said, 'Then we'd better move to my office.'

His office was on the street level but at the back of the building. It could have been the office of a prosperous accountant, and it occurred to Wycliffe that Masson-Smythe himself looked more like an accountant than a night club owner. He went to a filing cabinet, unlocked it, and drew out a file. He seated himself in an upholstered swivel chair behind his desk and waved Wycliffe to one of the client's chairs. 'Her contract is dated May tenth, and was to run for four months. I have a note here that I interviewed her first on the twenty-second of April.'

'Was she recommended to you?'

Masson-Smythe spread the papers on his desk and pretended to consult them. 'No, she turned up at a rehearsal and asked for a job. At first I didn't take her seriously; too many girls down on their luck think all they have to do is to take off their clothes in public to make their fortunes. It is not as simple as that.'

'Did she appear to be down on her luck?'

He considered. 'No, she was well dressed and well groomed, but she said that she needed money. I asked her if she had had any experience of cabaret work and she said that she had not. I was on the point of sending her away but there was something about her . . . She was an extremely attractive girl but in this business that isn't enough – a girl needs a certain personality and I thought that she might have it.'

'You gave her an audition?' (Do you audition a stripper?)

'There and then.' He took a cigarette from a box on his desk and lit it. 'She was a natural. It is not an easy thing, even for an experienced girl, to give a good performance under rehearsal conditions – no lights, no audience, no glamour, but despite all that she managed to make her performance intimate and provocative.'

'Yet you were not sorry when her contract ended?'

The blue eyes behind the glasses were cold. 'Indeed?'

Wycliffe fixed him with a bland stare. 'I have been told that you were glad to be rid of her, is that true or not?'

'Perfectly true!' It was the woman Wycliffe had seen downstairs. She came in and stood by Masson-Smythe's chair.

'My wife, Thelma, superintendent. I think that you have already met.'

After the civilities, he went on, 'The superintendent is making enquiries about Dawn Peters . . . Apparently she has been murdered.' No news to the little wife who had obviously been listening outside the door.

Wycliffe turned to her. 'You agree that you and your husband were glad to see her go – why?'

'She was a whore and this place is not a brothel. Does that answer your question?'

Masson-Smythe flushed but said nothing. His wife still stood by him, one hand on his chair as though asserting possession. A formidable woman, Wycliffe thought. Seen in a good light, the hard line of her jaw, a mean little mouth and slightly protuberant eyes disposed of what appeal she seemed to have in the dim light downstairs. Wycliffe knew the sort: hard with men, vicious with other women. Some of them had found their true vocations in the Nazi women's gaols.

'She persisted in dating the patrons which, of course, is strictly against the rules.'

And not only the patrons, Wycliffe thought. Hubby had probably taken a turn with the rest.

'When did she leave the Voodoo?'

Masson-Smythe glanced uneasily at his wife then referred to his papers. 'On August twenty-eighth.'

'Before her contract expired?'

'My husband was forced to terminate it.'

'Do you know where she went after she left?'

'I'm afraid her plans had no interest for us.'

Wycliffe took out his notebook and opened it. 'The other girl who worked with you last season is still with you, I should like her name and address.'

'Sadie Field, 4a, Mount Zion, but she can tell you nothing you don't know already.'

Thelma laughed. 'The original dumb blonde – that's Sadie.'

Wycliffe wrote down the address, put away his notebook and stood up. Thelma came out from behind the desk. 'One question, superintendent, was it Dawn Peters who was found strangled in a hotel bedroom?'

'It seems so.'

'I read about it in the papers.'

'Yes.'

Wycliffe had nothing against these people but he wished like hell he had. With most of the people he met, even the bent ones, it was all too easy to discover the common bond of their humanity, but not with this couple. Perhaps they had never been and never would be in trouble with the law but they repelled him. Mean. They lacked charity. St Paul said, 'Though I speak with the tongues of men and of angels and have not charity, I am become as a sounding brass or a tinkling cymbal.' Wycliffe thought so too.

The club owner came with him to the foyer and watched him as he walked up the stairs. As Wycliffe opened the street door he almost collided with a man coming in. A small dark chap with heavily lined features, shabbily dressed. Wycliffe had known plenty like him as bookie's runners before the new laws and he would probably never have given the incident another thought had it not been for the man's obvious nervousness. Before closing the door Wycliffe glanced down the stairs at Masson-Smythe who seemed anything but glad to see his visitor.

Outside the heat reflected from the pavements was like a blast from a baker's oven.

CHAPTER FOUR

Mount Zion, where Sadie lived, was a narrow, steep lane off the main street. It was so steep that there were steps at intervals and a rail running down the middle. Her flat comprised only two rooms and a share in the usual offices of an old tenement building which had been more or less modernized. It was on the second floor and over-looked a concrete yard festooned with washing. The living room, which had a curtained alcove for a kitchen, was furnished with a studio couch, a couple of easy chairs in faded chintz covers, a scratched dining table and two high-backed dining chairs, 1930 vintage. Evidently Sadie was dumb enough to be cheap.

'Miss Sadie Field?' Wycliffe introduced himself.

Sadie looked scared. She had a delicate prettiness, fair hair and freckles, and her figure was of the kind called 'trim', nothing exotic, certainly nothing erotic about her. When the patrons of the Voodoo watched Sadie take off her clothes they must have imagined themselves to be spying on the girl next door. She pulled her housecoat round her and retied the sash. 'Isn't it hot?'

'You were a friend of Dawn Peters?'

Nervous.'We used to share this flat. Is there something wrong?'

He encouraged her to sit and took a seat beside her on the couch. He had to shift a copy of the *Daily Mirror* and a paperback with a picture on the cover of a Dr Kildare character in gentlemanly embrace with a pretty nurse. A report on the finding of the body had a two-column spread at the foot of the front page of the *Mirror*. He pointed to it. 'Have you read this?'

'Yes.' Wide-eyed. She was gripping her hands together so tightly that the knuckles whitened. 'Was it her?'

'I'm afraid so.'

She looked as though she was going to cry but didn't.

'We know almost nothing about her and we need your help.'

She was staring out of the open window at the silhouettes of the buildings across the court. Between them you could glimpse the tops of the masts of craft in the harbour. 'I don't know much about her before she came to live with me and I haven't heard from her since she left . . .'

'When did she come here? Was it when she started to work at the club?'

She shook her head. 'Before. It was nearly two years ago – late August or early September.' She grinned. 'We met in the launderette, we got talking and she asked me if I knew of any cheap lodgings. The girl who shared with me had left so I brought her back. She liked it and stayed.'

'Did you know that she was married?'

'I didn't when she came here first, but people told me soon enough.'

'She didn't tell you herself?'

'Not till she'd been here a good while.'

'I understand that she was married to a local man?'

Sadie nodded. 'A man called Collins, he owns the bookshop. He's a lot older.'

'So that her real name wasn't Peters.'

'No, she wasn't called Dawn, either, her name was Julie.'

Julie Collins.

'I suppose you suggested that she should try for a job at the club?'

She looked surprised. 'No, I had no idea that she was even thinking of it until she turned up one afternoon at a rehearsal and Mr Masson-Smythe gave her an audition. She was like that – kept things to herself.'

'She lived here for eight or nine months before she started work at the club?'

'About that.'

'What did she live on?'

The translucent skin of her forehead wrinkled. 'She had money. It might not have been much but it was enough to live on. And she went with men though I don't know whether they paid her.'

A statement of fact with no overtones of comment but he felt suddenly irritated. Would nobody tell him what he wanted to know about this girl? She must have done most of the same things as other people, and some different, but all he could learn of her was that she went with men. 'Did she go out much?'

'Not much. For days at a time she wouldn't put a foot outside the door.'

'What did she do all day?'

Sadie picked at a loose thread in the chintz cover. 'She used to read a lot.'

'What did she read?' Probably a useless question.

She spread her hands in a little helpless gesture. 'Books from the library and she used to buy books sometimes.'

Wycliffe stood up and started to wander round the room. He was restless. Here he had his first chance to make some real contact with the dead girl. She had lived in these rooms for more than ten months. There must be something! He reached the door of the bedroom and pushed it open, Sadie close on his heels. 'It's not very tidy!' It wasn't, but neither was it dirty or squalid. Two single beds with nondescript coverlets, an old-fashioned dressing table with triple mirrors, a wardrobe with a front mirror and a grotesquely fretted top, a couple of wicker chairs littered with underwear. In an alcove there were shelves and on one of them books. 'Are these hers?' Hopeful.

'What? Oh yes, she left them behind.'

The random fall-out from almost any library: two or three book club selections, Durrell's *Justine*, a couple of Maigrets, a Nicolas Freeling, Dostoevsky's *Possessed* . . . the Collected Poems of Dylan Thomas, *Ulysses* . . . *Ulysses* had an inscription on the fly-leaf:

'To my love.

'Can men more injure women than to say
They love them for that, by which they are not they?
W.'

More ways than one of taking that. In any case it was an odd thing to quote to your girl friend. But literary. The other books were older and had passed through one or more secondhand shops, their decline recorded in pencilled prices on their fly-leaves. Several were books of poetry, Burns, Shelley, Keats . . . the rest were novels, *Wuthering Heights, Tess of the d'Urbervilles, Ann Veronica* . . .

A literary whore? Why not? Wycliffe was broadminded and had never believed in demarcation. And surely the tapestry of history must be the richer for its cultured courtesans?

He turned away from the books. 'You still share?'

'A staff supervisor from Wandell's.'

'Dawn . . . Julie, didn't tell you much about herself?'

She stood beside him, nervous, anxious to please. 'Not much, she didn't talk much about anything.'

'Have you got a photograph of her?'

'No, but there must be plenty at the club.'

66

'You got on with her? I mean, was she easy to live with?'

A small frown as she spotted and dived for a pair of tights lying on the floor. She picked them up and stuffed them under a cushion. 'Oh, yes.'

'No quarrels?'

A faint flush. 'Not quarrels . . .'

'Differences then – what about?'

'Several times she brought men home and I didn't like that so in the end I stopped it.'

'Apart from these men, did anybody ever come to see her?'

'Nobody.'

He caught the momentary hesitation in her manner. 'Sure?'

She sat on the edge of her bed and swept back her hair with the unselfconscious grace of a little girl. 'I don't know. One afternoon as I was coming up the stairs I saw a man coming out of our flat. It was just after I'd told her I wouldn't have men . . . Anyway, when I got in I asked her who the man was and she pretended there hadn't been anybody. I called her a liar and after a minute or two she said, "If you must know, that was my husband, he's been trying to persuade me to come back to him".'

'You believed her?'

'I don't know, I think so.'

'When was this?'

'Not long before she finished at the club and went off to London.'

'Surely you must know this man Collins?'

'Not really, I've seen him once or twice but the stairs are very dark – it could have been him.'

'Did she tell you anything about her husband?'

'Not really. I remember I said, "Why did you leave

67

him?" and she said, "He needed a mother not a wife; he didn't know what it was all about".'

'Perhaps he failed to love her for that by which she was not he.'

'What's that?' She looked at him sharply.

'Just thinking aloud.'

He wandered back into the living room and Sadie followed, watching his every move, puzzled by this strange man who was nothing like any policeman she had known. His questions, when they came, seemed almost incidental to some deeper preoccupation. And this was so: his mind was a turmoil of impressions, ideas, recollections, without pattern or purpose. At such times he seemed to lose his judgement, every fact seemed to carry the same weight, every possibility to be equally credible. Once, this state of mind had bothered him, he had supposed that his job demanded crisp, incisive logic; only when he found, to his surprise, that he was looked upon as successful, did he slowly acquire confidence to stifle his misgivings. Now, he rationalized his muddled thinking, saying that ideas crystallized from it.

The curtains of the kitchen alcove were drawn back and he found himself staring out through the little window above the sink. It gave a view of a cluster of mellow slate roofs which had changed little in a century and a half. They climbed steeply to a rising mound until, not far away, they cut the skyline in bold, jagged thrusts.

'Did she smoke?'

'Julie? A little, five or six a day, like me.'

There were so many possibilities. A slut sprawled on the couch all day, not bothering to dress until she put on her war paint to go to the club or to search for a man. Reading Dostoevsky.

'Drink?'

'Not more than you have to in our sort of job. I mean, we have to act as hostesses as well . . .'

Idly he opened the doors of one or two cupboards, a few utensils, a few groceries. A tiny refrigerator under the draining board, he stooped to open it. Half a small chicken, a bottle of milk and three or four bottles of Coca-Cola. He couldn't focus an image.

'The waiters know and whatever they bring is always watered down unless we ask for different.' She didn't seem to mind him poking about but she was puzzled by it.

'Was she sacked?'

'From the club? – No.'

'She left before her contract expired.'

'Because she wanted to.'

'That's not what they told me at the club.'

'You've been talking to Thelma, she hated her.'

'Because Julie went to bed with her husband?'

She frowned. 'That might have been part of it but they were at daggers drawn apart from that. Thelma is inclined to throw her weight about and Julie wasn't the sort to be put on.'

'They told me her contract was terminated because she dated patrons of the club.'

'Oh.'

For the first time she was holding out on him, her face resolutely closed.

Wycliffe sighed. 'She's been murdered. A man made love to her, then strangled her.'

She turned away quickly, her hand to her throat.

'We've got to find who did it – you agree?'

She still did not face him but she said, 'Yes.'

'All right! She broke one of the terms of her contract, Masson-Smythe says he sacked her for it, you say not . . .'

She faced him now, her face once more composed and frank. 'I think they wanted to get rid of her but they didn't dare.'

'Why not?'

'I think that she knew something about them – something which could have got them into serious trouble.'

'What?'

'I don't know. All I know is what happened one Monday afternoon – we have rehearsals then and this time it was the final one for a completely new show so everybody was on their toes. We had lights, costumes, everything, just like a real show. Dawn – Julie, had a new routine like the rest, this time she came on as a Firebird, dressed in dozens of chiffon scarves, all the colours of flame. She had to do a bit of ballet dancing in flickering red and orange lights as she got rid of the scarves and she did it very well. In the end of course she was naked and when she stood in the spot everybody gave her a hand – everybody except Thelma, that is.'

'She comes to rehearsals?'

'Thelma? She produces. She says she was once a Windmill girl and she seems to think that makes her an authority. Not but what she hasn't got some very good ideas.' Sadie was nothing if not fair. 'Anyway, when Julie finished her act, she said, "Well, dear, you aren't exactly a ballerina but I suppose it will have to do!" Julie didn't say anything, it wasn't easy to make her mad and Thelma went on, "After all, it isn't your dancing they come to see, is it?" Julie still said nothing and it would have passed off but when we were back in our dressing room – we shared – Thelma comes in. I could see she was up to something from the look on her face. She went straight up to Julie and said, "I didn't want to embarrass you in front of the others but I think you should have a bath before you do your act. Your legs, my dear – it shows under the lights".'

Sadie paused and moistened her lips like a little girl telling a story. 'Julie was sitting in front of the mirror brushing her hair and I could see her face in the glass. She went white then she turned round and looking up at Thelma she said, "You're doing your best to provoke me but it would be a big mistake. I know enough to put you and lover-boy out of harm's way for a very long time." You would have thought Julie had hit her. She never said another word, just stood there, then she walked out. But from then on there was never a criticism of anything Julie did, not so much as a sly dig.'

'You didn't discover what it was all about?'

'No. When she went out I asked Julie but she was quite rude. "Whatever it was about, Cheesy," she said, "it's nothing to do with you. It's better you don't know".'

'Cheesy?'

'That's what they call me, it's short for Cheesecake.' She seemed pleased to tell him.

'When did this happen? Was it shortly before she left?'

'Not long after she started to work at the club, perhaps four or five weeks.'

He made a move to go then hesitated. 'Did you like her?'

'Like her?' She echoed the words, stalling for time. 'She was easy to live with – I mean she wasn't catty like a lot of girls . . . in some ways she was quite kind.'

'But?'

Sadie searched painfully for words. 'She frightened me, I didn't understand her – she was *wild*.'

'Wild?'

'Reckless – always doing things just for kicks. You never knew what it would be next.'

'What sort of thing?'

She looked at him nervously then away again. 'She's dead now, so it can't hurt her. When she first came here we used to go shopping together and suddenly, in one of the shops, she would say, "We're going to have this on the house, Cheesy!" and she would nick something really valuable – not because she wanted it, either.'

Wycliffe nodded his understanding.

'It used to scare me rigid! But she was never happy unless she was taking risks . . .'

Food for thought, quite a lot of it; more might mean indigestion. 'You've been very helpful, Miss Field, I'm grateful and I may have to come back again.'

She had unwound during the time he had been there, now she was taut and nervous again. 'You won't say anything at the club? I can't afford to lose my job . . .'

'I'll be the soul of discretion.'

Four o'clock and the town shimmering in the heat. Over the sea, a canopy of purplish-black cloud slowly creeping up the sky like a giant shutter excluding the sunlight. He drove back to the station and as he got out of the car he felt a sudden chill with the sky darkening overhead. A moment later, a flicker of lightning and an explosive thunder clap heralding the rain. It came hissing and sweeping across the square like a wall of water as he hurried inside.

Fehling was in the HQ room typing his report, Gill was there too, his chair tilted back, his feet on the table, drinking tea. The lights were on because of the storm.

'The Deputy Chief has been asking for you.'

'Here?'

'On the blower. He wants you to ring him back at his home number.'

'What does he want?'

Gill lowered his feet to the floor. 'That's a moot point

at the moment, sir. Something with blood in it, I should think, preferably yours.'

Wycliffe poured himself a cup of cold tea. 'Well, what's new?'

'Not much. Fingerprints have matched one of the sets of dabs on your photograph of the guitar player and we've got the gen from Criminal Records.'

'Well?'

'A small-time crook who stepped out of line and tried for the big league. With four others he was concerned in a wages snatch – thirty thousand quid. They held up a security van in Battersea, the others got away but Allen was coshed by one of the security men and he got nicked.'

'Where is he now?'

Gill smiled. 'That's the point – he skipped while he was waiting to go up the steps – literally. He was below stairs in the Magistrates' Court waiting to be brought up and somehow he managed to get away. Nobody seems to know quite how but I gather there are some red faces.'

'It was all in the Crime Report a fortnight back,' Fehling volunteered.

'Was it.' Not a question, a mild snub. 'What do we know about this Allen?'

Gill picked up a typewritten sheet. 'Frederick Charles Allen, 27, five feet nine, one hundred and ninety pounds . . . blah blah . . . No fixed address . . . Approved School . . . Borstal at eighteen . . . six months housebreaking and assault in '61, two years for robbery in '64 . . . three months and six months for possession and trafficking in '66. There's a photograph.' Gill pushed over the information sheet with an attached photograph – a full-face and a profile. A square-faced young man with puffy unhealthy cheeks, deep-set eyes, a weak mouth and a low forehead, a mop of dark hair.

73

'He's still on the run?'

'Seems like it. Of course he could have got his mitts on that guitar player's photograph anywhere, there's nothing to say that he's in our manor.'

'There's nothing to say he isn't!' Wycliffe snapped. 'Is there any mention of a girl friend?'

'According to the notes he's a bit of a lad with the birds but no special one.'

They were interrupted by the most brilliant flash of lightning yet and a simultaneous clap of thunder which shook the building. The lights flickered but recovered. Wycliffe pointed to the photograph of Allen. 'Have you shown this to Piper at the Marina?'

'It's only just arrived. The chap I spoke to at the Yard was a bit toffee nosed but from what I could gather they're puzzled about Allen. This snatch was way out of his class.'

Wycliffe grunted. He was impatient, irritable, with the uncomfortable feeling that he was being side-tracked. 'Ask them to let us have all they can get on him.'

Then he told them about his own day. 'The Voodoo is being used as a cover for something and the girl found out about it. Admittedly that was months ago but it may still be the reason she was killed.' He turned to Fehling. 'I want you to put a round-the-clock watch on the club, but discretion above everything. If one of your flatfoots gives himself away . . .!' He made a dramatic gesture. 'And find out what you can about the Masson-Smythes, whether they've got any form, but I don't want the birds frightened off their nest. You'd better tell your fellows also to keep a special eye for Allen, if he puts in an appearance there it would mean something though I'm damned if I know what! The question is, what are they up to? What did the girl find out?'

'Trafficking. It's obvious!' from Fehling. 'Ties up with the money and with this chap Allen, he was done for possession and trafficking.'

Wycliffe took out his pouch and began to fill his pipe. 'I'll say one thing for you, you don't give up, but you may be right. It's possible that the girl bought herself into the racket as the price of her silence.'

'A dangerous thing to do, as we all know,' Gill said. He got out his cheroots and went through the ritual of lighting one. 'There are signs that cannabis is slipping through the south-western ports and that the traffic is getting organized with a distribution set-up in the area. Perhaps we've hit on it.'

Fehling drew the plastic cover over his typewriter and patted it like a pet dog. 'I'm sure of it.'

Wycliffe smoked in silence for a while. 'The resin would probably sell on the market for two-fifty a pound. What would they pay at the port?'

Gill shrugged. 'Say twenty-five to thirty.'

'So a thousand pounds should buy somewhere in the region of thirty-five or forty pounds – a tidy weight for a girl on her own.'

'We don't know that she would have been on her own, she said she was expecting her husband.' – Fehling, anxious to sustain his advantage.

'Why was she killed?'

'Probably because she was a thorn in the flesh of the Voodoo crowd.'

'Why was she battered after death?'

'I think you're making too much of that, sir.' Fehling, getting venturesome.

Wycliffe shook his head. 'If she was working for them would they kill her and leave her in possession of a thousand pounds of their money? In any case, does it *look* like

75

the sort of killing you get when rogues fall out?' He stood up and walked to one of the windows of the long room. He stood there, his hands on the sill, his pipe clenched in his teeth, looking down on the square. The rain had stopped, the clouds were thinning and people were on the move again. He got a kick from the fact that nature could still bring the ant-hill to a stop. 'It's possible that you are right, she may have been mixed up in a small time dope ring but that wasn't why she was killed. She was killed in a moment of passion, incidentally, perhaps almost accidentally . . .'

Sardonic grin from Gill. 'Incidental death by accident – that's a new one for the book.'

Wycliffe turned to face them. 'You're getting cheeky, my lad! Anything else?'

Fehling picked up the sheet he had been typing between finger and enormous spatulate thumb. It was a wonder he didn't hit three keys at once when he typed. 'She arrived in town on Sunday night by Royal Blue coach.'

'From London?'

'She took her ticket and boarded the bus at Victoria Coach Station. The driver remembers her because she was "so small and pretty". She got off the coach in the park here and while he was getting her luggage from the boot she said, "I have to get to the Marina, do you think I'll be able to pick up a taxi?" The driver got her a taxi and saw her into it.'

'There are times when I wish I was small and pretty,' Gill said. He watched a chance smoke ring rise from his cheroot, spread and vanish. 'Do you think we've got enough to start leaning on these Masson-Smythes?'

Wycliffe was definite. 'No! For the present we just watch.'

'What about the husband – the girl's husband – Collins, I think you said?'

'I don't know, I haven't seen him.'

Gill and Fehling looked at him in surprise. Gill said, 'You want one of us . . .?'

'No.' He glanced at the clock. 'The shop will be shut in a few minutes anyway.'

Fehling was on the point of asking what that had to do with it when a warning glance from Gill stopped him. Wycliffe added, as though in self justification, 'The girl's body was only found yesterday morning, it's not as though she'd been dead a month!'

He would have found it impossible to explain his thinking. He could hardly claim that it was logical. All he knew was that underneath his apparent acceptance of what Fehling and Gill had said, he didn't believe a word of it. He was certain that as yet they did not know what the case was about; they had been sidetracked. He knew of old that lift of the spirit which comes when you have one end of the thread in your hand. Suddenly there is a feeling of certainty. You *know*. He was a long way from that! But until then it was necessary to walk softly, to put out antennae, to get the feel and the smell of things. He would never do that if he gathered facts too quickly, there must be time to digest. He said, as though he still required to excuse himself, 'I'll see Collins in the morning. Meantime, Jim, I want you to do some snooping round the docks.'

'To find what, sir?' Gill thought it was best to get his brief clear.

'How the hell should I know? Just snoop.'

'I've been into that angle pretty thoroughly, sir.' Fehling was piqued.

'There's no reason why the chief inspector shouldn't go there himself, is there?' Fehling sighed, audibly, and Wycliffe went on, 'You know the score, Jim. One of the local lads must have a snout inside.'

'I think I get the message.'

'Good!' He envied Gill this job; loitering round the docks, hobnobbing with the men, snooping round the ships, having the odd drink with a hospitable skipper . . . You make a hell of a sacrifice for promotion. 'Have a chat with one or two of the blokes who tend on the ships; you see them lounging about the quay with their tongues hanging out so it shouldn't be too difficult or too expensive . . . And Jim! see if you come across a little dark chap with heavily lined features . . . fortyish – a little rat of a man. Reminds you of a bookie's runner. May have been a seaman, perhaps he still is.'

Gill's raised eyebrows forced him to go on, 'I saw a chap answering that description going into the Voodoo this afternoon, and I don't think Masson-Smythe was too pleased to see him.'

He was on the point of leaving when he remembered the Deputy Chief. He went into his temporary office, picked up the telephone and asked to be put through.

Deputy Chief Constable Bellings was an administrator, possibly a good one, Wycliffe was no judge, but he knew that Bellings could never have been a real policeman. No doubt he had once hammered a beat, no doubt he had done his share of CID work at the dirty end, house to house, drinking with snouts, hanging round warehouses, sleazy hotels and railway stations, questioning pimps, tarts, tearaways and, later, villains in the big time . . . But for Bellings this had been solely a means to an end, the distasteful and hazardous way to the top. Now he was nearly there, he had reached the stage where you could be objective about the disturbing variety of human weakness and wickedness which we call crime. He could smooth it all into a statistical curve and make it a matter of accounting. No wonder he disliked pegs which refused to stay in their proper holes.

'Mr Bellings? Wycliffe here, sir. I understand that you wish to speak to me.'

'To be accurate, I wished to locate you.'

'This is my HQ for the inquiry, sir.'

'I am delighted to hear it. I hope that it will be possible to contact you there. Good night, Charles!'

'Good night, sir!' And the same to you with embellishments!

He passed through the HQ room on his way out. 'I'm off!'

Fehling looked after him, mystified. 'He's cheered up! I thought he was in for a bollocking.'

'It takes him that way,' Gill said.

CHAPTER FIVE

Wycliffe and his wife stood side by side, arms resting on the balustrade, watching the harbour. The rain had gone leaving a fresh clean smell behind, everything looking sharp and incisive. The sun had set behind them but the sky was still a pale washed-out blue with smoky grey wisps of cloud tinged with gold. Out on the water a radio played a nostalgic waltz tune; further along the terrace a honeymoon couple stood close, arms round each other. Wycliffe rested his hand on his wife's. Twenty-four years ago, almost to the day, he had been a beat copper, standing on the pavement, watching people coming out of a cinema. A pretty fair girl hurried down the steps and dived past him in the direction of the bus stop. She wore an oatmeal summer coat and a saucy brown beret. And that might easily have been that, for the bus swept past and pulled in at the stop. But with only a few yards to go, she tripped and fell, badly ricking her ankle. He had rendered first aid. Helen Wills, typist; Charlie Wycliffe, copper. They had come a long way since then but for a long time the words, 'When I'm a sergeant', had seemed to be the Open Sesame to gracious living. 'We'll be able to afford a little car . . . ' Now he was a Detective Chief Superintendent and they stayed at four star hotels as a matter of course – or almost.

'A penny for them?'

'I was thinking what a smug bourgeois couple we've become.'

'Do you mind very much?'

'I don't know. I like to think I do.'

Somewhere a clock began to strike the hour. They counted though they knew the time. 'Nine o'clock.'

'Will Detective Chief Superintendent Wycliffe kindly come to reception?' A pause, then the message repeated by the young lady with a plum in her mouth, over the hotel loudspeaker system. 'Thank you!' Click! The voice had come faintly through the open windows of the lounge. Wycliffe went in obediently, stared at by the guests. Television should have convinced them that detectives don't have handcuffs hanging out of their pockets, or two heads. The girl in reception pointed to one of the telephone booths.

'Gill here, sir. I thought I'd better tell you that Ernie Piper at the Marina recognized Allen's photo. He's been staying there since Sunday in the name of Rawlings. Room twenty-one. He's one of those on Fehling's list supposed to be waiting for a ship and he's got a merchant seaman's book.'

'You've brought him in?'

Perceptible pause. ''Fraid not, he's skipped.'

Wycliffe's reply drew the attention of the girl in reception.

'He didn't sleep in his room last night. Piper had spotted him as an ex-con but he says he had no reason to think that he was a wanted man. Reasonable enough if you believe . . . '

Wycliffe did not try too hard to sound reasonable in return. 'If Piper could spot him what's wrong with the wall-eyed cretin who questioned him? What's Fehling playing at?'

'I don't think you can blame Fehling . . . '

'You must be joking! Anyway the thing is, what to do? It's too late to set up road checks, he's had twenty-four hours.' He hesitated. 'You'd better get on to the Met,

81

they'll want to amend their circular – and Jimmy, get on to our own boys and stir them up a bit – make the fur fly.'

He was nothing like as sore as he sounded; he rarely was. Early in his career he had realized that you have to put on a show. A reputation for bloody-mindedness which doesn't go too deep is an asset. Actually he was not displeased with the turn of events; something happening in a case is better than nothing, it gives you the chance to take a fresh hold.

'I have to go out, dear.'

'Will you be late?'

'I don't know but don't wait up for me.'

'The story of my life.'

He was going to take the car but, on an impulse, decided to walk. No point in rushing around. It was getting dark, the street lamps were on but the air was soft and balmy. Girls in their summer dresses without coats, young men in shirt sleeves. They paraded through the town and through the dusk in mixed groups, effervescent, noisy, predatory; looking for trouble. Most of them were restrained from making it by a flimsy barrier of convention. On that barrier, getting thinner every year, order and security depend. The educationalists ride their bandwagons, some of them doing the splits on two at once as an insurance. Some day, somebody will knock their heads together and tell them that education is about living. Meanwhile it's your job to seal the cracks, copper!

Beyond the main street he followed the road round the harbour to the Marina. A light high in one of the attics. Kathy's room? Or was she too parading the streets? He hoped so for her sake, anything is better than loneliness when you are young.

The vestibule of the Marina was dimly lit by a fly-blown bulb over the reception desk. Piper was there in his shirt sleeves, entering figures in a cash book. One of Gill's men was half asleep in a wicker chair by a dusty potted palm. He sprang up and tried to look efficient. 'Mr Gill left word that he will be at the station, sir.'

Wycliffe went straight for Piper. 'Where has he gone?'

Piper pulled the lobe of his ear. 'I haven't a clue, super, straight up I haven't! All I know is the bastard skipped without paying his bill.'

'Did he have any contact with the girl while he was here?'

'Not to my knowledge. I've never seen 'em together but you know how it is.'

'Did he go out much?'

A bit more ear pulling. 'Come to think of it I never saw him go out at all. I only ever saw him at breakfast and he was late for that.'

'What about his other meals?'

Piper shrugged. 'I suppose he must have gone out same as the rest.'

Wycliffe rested his arms on the desk and stared at the potbellied little man, compelling his reluctant gaze. Piper shook his head. 'It's no good leaning on me, Mr Wycliffe, I don't even know what all this is about. What's he done? He never murdered the kid, did he?'

Wycliffe straightened up. 'Where's Kathy?'

Piper brightened perceptibly. 'Probably in her room, I'll get her.'

'Don't bother! I'll find it.' He made for the stairs. What would Piper have thought, or Gill, if they knew that out of simple curiosity he wanted to see Kathy's room?

The attic passage was covered with lino instead of threadbare carpet and seemed cleaner because of it. There was only one room with a light under the door and he could hear the muffled sound of a transistor radio.

He knocked. The radio clicked off. 'Who is it?' Kathy opened the door and invited him in.

He was not disappointed. She had impressed herself on the little room. The sloping boarded ceiling was half covered with photographs of pop stars, there was a shelf with a few books, an ancient record player, a table, a chair and a bed with a bright orange coverlet. The sash window was wide open, the radio stood on the sill, and she had obviously been sitting by it sewing, for an embryonic garment lay, a little heap of green silky material, on the chair, needle and cotton stabbed into it. She cleared the chair and made him sit down, perching herself on the bed, knees together, dress pulled down. 'You have come about Mr Rawlings?'

'His real name is Allen and he is wanted by the police.'

'I am sorry, he seemed a harmless man.'

'You liked him?'

'I was sorry for him.'

Sitting by the open window he seemed to be almost on top of the docks; although it was night, clanking and hissing and a massive underlying throbbing filled the room. The superstructure of one ship, a pyramid of lights, seemed only a stone's throw away. 'Doesn't the noise keep you awake?'

'I'm used to it. It did at first.'

'Why were you sorry for him?'

'He was ill, always coughing. Although he was such a big man I do not think he is very strong, he must have something wrong with his lungs.'

'Did he go out much?'

She lowered her eyes. 'He did not go out, he spend most of his time in bed reading.'

'How did he manage for food?'

'He go down for breakfast but I bring him the rest. If not I think he would have gone without.'

84

'You brought him food; did Ernie know?'

She shrugged. 'Ernie!' Gentle, good-natured contempt.

Wycliffe regarded the solemn face, serene, composed. He wondered from what inner strength she derived her composure. The young need a sense of security! The answer to that seemed to be a raspberry. You were forced to blame it on the generation gap and give up trying to understand. 'Did he make a pass at you?'

'No, it wasn't like that.'

'Did he tell you anything about himself?'

'Only that he was waiting for his ship and he was afraid he would not be well enough to join her. He asked me not to talk about him for if the ship people hear he is ill they will not take him.'

'Did you ever see him with the girl who was killed?'

The question seemed to surprise her. 'But he never left his room except . . .'

'Let's take a look at his room.'

Room 21 was on the same floor as the dead girl's but in the main part of the house facing the front, a narrow room over a passage on the floor below. 'Is this how he left it?'

'Just as he leave it, I only pull back the curtains.'

Which meant that he had probably waited until after dark before leaving. It might help though he hadn't much hope. The room stank of eucalyptus, a smell which always revolted him. He looked round, pulling open the drawers of a rickety chest. Two or three sexy paperbacks, a dirty handkerchief. He turned to the tin which served as a wastepaper-basket. Three empty cigarette packets, dead matches and ash, an evening newspaper and part of a sheet of stiff paper, torn raggedly. On one side, the address of the hotel written in pencil, a feminine hand, on the other, at the torn edge, half – the lower half – of a scrawled signature, and below that, typewritten: *per pro Summit Theatrical Costumiers Ltd*.

A slender link but it might mean something. He fished out a plastic envelope and slipped it in. If Thelma Masson-Smythe had written that address – then . . . Then what? He could have pushed his reasoning powers a bit further but that had never been his way. Let it all mill around. He went to the window and looked out; the same view as from Kathy's room but a floor lower. He noticed a long low building on the other side of the road almost by the dock gates. A blue neon sign read: *SNACKS & CAFÉ*.

'Is that the place where she had her meals?'

'I think so, it is where most of our people go, but of course it is always men.'

'You wouldn't think it worth their while to stay open at this time of night.'

'Ah! In the day they serve men from the docks but at night a lot of young people from the town go there, almost like a club. It is cheap and they have a juke box and if he is in a good mood Joe will let you push the tables back and dance. Sometimes I go there, it is very good.'

A few minutes later Wycliffe was down in the street again. It was properly dark now; if you turned away from the glare of the docks you could see the stars against a velvet sky. He crossed the road to the café, looked up and saw Kathy at her window once more, waved and went inside.

A warm chippy smell. A counter with a coffee machine, a tea urn and a cash register, a few bar stools and behind the counter a fat man with a bald head reading the evening paper. But from the other side of a glass partition, plenty of noise, a juke box in full cry. Behind the counter an open door led into a kitchen.

'Evening.' The fat man stirred himself reluctantly.

Wycliffe produced his warrant card. The fat man, who must be Joe, looked at it indifferently. 'I suppose it's about that business across the way?' He nodded in the direction of the Marina. 'Your chaps have been in here already.'

'I know. You told them the girl came in here for her meals and that she came alone.'

'That's right. She did.' Joe looked at the superintendent through innocent china-blue eyes. 'Since they was here I been thinking and the more I think the more convinced I am – I seen that girl before.'

'Here?'

'Where else? I never go anywhere.'

A waitress came through from the other side of the partition, filled two cups at the coffee machine, rang up one and four and withdrew.

'You have a lot of young people in and out of here in the course of an evening, do you know them all?'

He shook his head. 'No, not all but I don't encourage strangers unless they got somebody I know with 'em. It's easier to keep the peace that way. You know where you stand.' He smoothed a massive hand over his bald head. 'How old would you say she was?'

'Twenty-one, give or take a few months.'

'That means she could have been coming in here anything up to say five or even six years ago.' He shook his head. 'I shall have to think about it.'

The street door opened and a girl put her head round, 'Joyce here tonight, Joe?'

'Ain't seen her.'

The head hesitated then made up its mind. 'OK. Thanks. See you!'

'Are you married?'

The fat man looked surprised. 'Me?' He laughed. 'I'm married all right with three kids and they're married too.'

87

He looked at Wycliffe speculatively. 'Like a coffee?'

Wycliffe nodded and waited while Joe drew two cups. When they were steaming on the counter he produced half a bottle of rum and added a tot to each. 'I've never known a copper yet who didn't prefer it this way.'

Two youths came through from the inner room. 'Night, Joe!'

'You're off early tonight, what's up?'

'We're going fishing with Freddie Bates, there's mackerel out in the bay – millions of 'em.'

Wycliffe and the fat man sipped their coffee. In the mellow mood of the moment he would have given a great deal to go fishing all night in the bay with Freddie Bates, or he would have swopped jobs with the fat man if that had been possible. Of course, what you see of another man's life is just the tip of the iceberg. He brought out his pouch and offered it across the counter but Joe refused. 'Don't smoke.'

'You must know a good many of the docks people?'

'I've been on their doorstep for thirty years.'

Wycliffe put a match to his pipe. 'If somebody wanted to get a man out of the country through this port – no questions asked – could it be done?'

The china-blue eyes studied him with disquieting serenity. 'I suppose it could; there'd be a risk of course.'

'How would you set about it?'

Joe smiled showing two rows of ostentatiously false teeth. 'I wouldn't, I like my peace of mind too much. But I suppose it could be done in one of two ways. A suitable man might get hold of false credentials and sign on as crew . . . '

'A suitable man, you say – that means he'd have to be a seaman?'

'He'd need to know his way round a ship.'

'And if he didn't?'

'Then he'd have to stow away and if he was going to do that and get ashore in a foreign port he'd need at least one friend in the crew, preferably somebody with a bit of authority.'

'You think it could be done?'

Joe smoothed his bald head. 'Of course it can be done. It would probably be more difficult with the bigger ships but one of the smallish foreigners . . . You might not have to search too long before you found even a skipper with a blind eye provided there was a big enough bait.'

'A thousand pounds?'

A shake of the head. 'I'm not up with the prices but in my opinion you'd get all you want for that.'

'Thanks.'

Joe grinned. 'Thinking of emigrating?'

'Something like that.'

Wycliffe moved away from the counter and pushed open the glass panelled door which led to the café. A long room with tables down both sides, green painted walls with advertisements for cigarettes and soft drinks, a couple of bagatelle machines and the juke box. Most of the tables were occupied by long haired youngsters of indeterminate sex. No dancing tonight, presumably because Joe's mood was inauspicious. He walked up the aisle between the tables glanced at indifferently. You would need to be a Siamese dwarf with three legs to really engage their attention. The waitress was at the end tables. Her skirt was so short that every time she bent over a table she showed her behind, but she seemed amiable. 'The girl that was killed? Yes, she used to come here. Are you a reporter?'

'Police.'

'Oh!' Her disappointment was obvious.

'Where did she sit?'

'This one by the window.'

'She arrived in the town on Sunday evening and she died on Tuesday night. How many meals did she have here? Lunch and evening meal on Monday, lunch and evening meal on Tuesday – four meals – is that it?'

'She came here Sunday night.'

'All right – five. Five meals but she sticks in your mind as though she'd been a regular customer for months . . . '

The girl swished crumbs from the plastic top of an empty table and wiped the surface with a damp cloth. 'Well, she would. I mean at lunch time she'd be the only woman in the place except me and Nelly and in the evening, well, she wasn't one of this lot, was she?'

'Too old?'

The little carmine lips screwed up. 'Not so much that but she was different.'

'How?'

'I dunno. The way she was dressed for one thing. She had style, and, for another, there was something about her, she was so small and yet she was . . . well, I know it sounds funny but she was perfect. I mean you could look at her as much as you like and you couldn't find anything wrong with her . . . '

'Did she spend long over her meals?'

'Quite a while. She brought a book and read, and after she had finished eating she would sit there with a cup of coffee, reading. She wasn't in any hurry to go.'

'She had lunch here twice when the place must have been full of men, did any of them get fresh with her?'

She shook her head. 'No, they watched her but they never spoke a word to her, not even a whistle.'

'So that each time she came in she sat at that table alone and spoke to no-one but you – is that right?'

'Well yes, except for one lunch time, it must have been Tuesday, a man came in and sat at her table.'

'A stranger?'

'No, a local, a man called Pellow – Dippy Pellow; he comes in for a meal now and then. He runs one of the launches that tend on the boats.'

'What sort of chap is he to look at?'

She screwed up her face. 'A dark little man, he must be forty-five to fifty. If you ask me a nasty bit of work.'

'In what way?'

She shrugged. 'For one thing he can't keep his hands to himself. I mean, at his age – it's disgusting!'

'Did you get the impression that he came here to meet her or was it by chance?'

She hesitated. 'I never thought, but now you mention it, perhaps he did. Don't you whistle at me, I aren't your dog! Some people!' The rebuke was for a youth, trying to attract her attention by whistling.

'Did the girl do more than pass the time of day with him?'

'Oh yes, they seemed quite matey. I was surprised.'

'You didn't hear anything of what they said to each other?'

She frowned. 'Believe me, mister, I got something better to do here at lunch time than listen to the customers. Which reminds me,' she added curtly, 'I got work to do now.'

'Wait!' His sudden peremptory manner brought her up short. 'Did she have anything to say to you?'

'Nothing more than just to give her order and say the usual things – nice weather an' all that.'

'You've lived in the town a long time?'

'All my life.'

'You didn't recognize or feel that she was familiar?'

The waitress looked puzzled. 'No, should I have?'

Wycliffe shook his head. 'I've no idea!'

He walked back to his hotel. A moist breeze had sprung up from the west and the air was chilly. Rain tomorrow. He pulled up the collar of his jacket and wished that he had worn his raincoat. The street was almost deserted and he felt depressed. An evening newspaper placard fluttered in the breeze: *Police Baffled by Hotel Murder*. For once they were dead right. Thirty-six hours after the discovery of the girl's body he ought to know a great deal more about her. Was she working for the Masson-Smythes? And if so, doing what? According to them they had kicked her out but according to Sadie she had left of her own free will knowing enough to put them both in gaol. Had she tried her hand at blackmail? That would account for the money and in certain circles blackmail is as good a way to get yourself murdered as any other. But surely not in the way this girl had been killed? Unless Masson-Smythe . . . But would he pay her hush money, make love to her, kill her and go away leaving the money? It didn't make sense. And why at a fifth-rate dump like the Marina? And where did the fugitive Allen come in?

At the back of his mind he had an idea which made sense of a good deal. He had scarcely realized that it was there until he had spoken to the café owner about stowaways. Now, to cheer himself up, he elaborated it in unaccustomed detail.

Assume that the girl had left the Voodoo as she said to go to a job in London. There she takes up with Allen, a small-time crook with ambitions beyond his class. He is nicked and charged, among other things, with attempted murder but he gets away. What if the Masson-Smythes were Travel Agents? Travel Agents for the underworld? Such organizations exist. From time to time the police uncover one and clean it up but where there is a demand . . . This might not be a bad base, especially with agents in some of the other ports of the south and west. If the girl had ferreted out their secret while she worked at the Voodoo the knowledge would seem heaven sent with her boy friend on the run. Allen is sent to lie low at the Marina until the girl arrives with the money. There she is contacted by Dippy Pellow who runs a launch . . . But why does it fall through? Why is she killed? Above all, why is she disfigured?

Wycliffe sighed audibly and drew curious glances from a couple in a shop doorway. He had to admit that there was only one aspect of the case which interested him – the fact that a girl of twenty-one had been strangled. Crimes of violence appalled him and murder most of all. There can be no restitution. Wycliffe numbered among the people he would call friends thieves, pick-pockets, pimps and forgers, but never once had he felt the least glimmer of sympathy or understanding for the man who used violence as one of the tools of his trade.

It was half past eleven when he reached the hotel and still there were two or three dedicated drinkers on the bar stools, the barman yawning behind his hand. Wycliffe ordered a brandy and drank it off.

'Good night to you.'

'Good night, superintendent.'

Now that they knew who he was there would be no chance of maintaining the illusion of being on holiday.

He went upstairs to bed and at last slipped in beside his wife. She spoke drowsily: 'Anything happened?'

'Enough.' He kissed her good night, turned over and fell asleep at once.

CHAPTER SIX

Drizzling rain from a slate grey sky. Friday morning. Wycliffe sat at a table in the HQ room looking at a photograph. Gill was having his first smoke of the day, perched on the edge of the same table, like a gargoyle. A detective constable hammered away at his report, his papers among the empty teacups. Wycliffe was absorbed: the photograph showed a girl with shoulder length hair gleaming in the light, fine open features, the forehead broad; thin, gently arched eyebrows, eyes wide, with long curving lashes, delicate nostrils and exquisite lips slightly parted and glistening with moisture as though she had just drawn her tongue across them. Yet this was the picture of a dead girl, the product of the pathologist's knowledge of anatomy and the police photographer's skill. Wycliffe had only to supply colour from memory and imagination, the hair was auburn, the eyes blue – almost violet, the skin . . .

'It's a work of bloody art!' Jim Gill said. 'It could have been on the front page of every newspaper tomorrow morning, now it's wasted.'

Wycliffe put the photograph down. 'She hasn't been officially identified yet so let them go ahead and publish. It will be interesting to see who admits to knowing her – and who doesn't.'

He stood up. 'I'm going to see Collins.'

The rain was hardly enough to keep people indoors but enough to make them wonder why they came out. The clock over the post office showed nine thirty-five and already visitors were trailing through the streets wondering whether to risk a boat trip or, if they didn't, what to do with the day. The narrow street was completely blocked by lorries unloading and several shopkeepers were still washing down their fronts.

At the bookshop a little man with brown eyes like buttons was cleaning the windows and had to move his ladder for Wycliffe to enter. Inside two girls were dusting down the shelves with feather dusters and one of them came over to him.

'I want to see Mr Collins.'

The girl obviously wanted to ask him his business but the blank impassive stare which he had cultivated as part of his stock-in-trade discouraged her and she went off down the shop, wiggling her bottom to show that she was not really impressed. He thought that she had gone to fetch Collins but he was mistaken. After a minute or two she came back with an older woman, a woman in her middle thirties, prickly with efficiency, the sort who has convinced herself that a business career is superior to a man in bed. 'Can I help you?'

'I want to see Mr Collins.'

Pursed lips. 'I'm Miss Rogers, I look after most of the firm's affairs.'

Defeated after all. 'This is personal. I am Detective Chief Superintendent Wycliffe.'

He saw her quick frown and, though her manner remained distant and slightly aggressive, he felt that she had become uneasy.

At the rear of the shop, hidden by bookcases, was a white painted iron spiral staircase, and a sign, pointing up it: *Secondhand Department*. He followed her up the steps and into the distilled mustiness of thousands of old books, a bitter sweet smell even to the booklover. The room was of indeterminate size, crammed with bookcases except for a clearing at the top of the stairs where there were two desks set near a window which overlooked the harbour. At the one nearest him an old lady sat knitting. She had an old fashioned box-till, an account book and a notice which read: *All purchases to be paid for here.* The other desk was littered with papers but there was no-one sitting at it.

'Where's Mr Willie?'

The old lady stopped knitting and looked at Wycliffe. She had cultivated her age; silver hair meticulously cared for; pouting, rather bad-tempered lips, lightly rouged; soft skinned fleshy cheeks with a dusting of powder to hide an unhealthy flush. 'Who is this?'

'A gentleman to see Mr Willie – where is he? Is he up in the flat?'

A measured silence through which the old lady asserted her refusal to be questioned. 'I'm Mrs Collins, you wish to see my son? What about?' She turned to the younger woman. 'No need for you to wait, Miss Rogers.'

It was an absurd situation though the tension was obvious. Miss Rogers stood irresolute for a moment, thought better of making a scene, and clattered off down the iron stairs making them vibrate. The old lady watched her go then turned to Wycliffe. 'You were saying?' But Wycliffe was saved the trouble of having to repeat himself.

'You wish to see me?' Willie Collins himself. Excessively tall, a scholarly stoop, pebble glasses distorting his eyes. He looked forty or more but a second look decided that he might be younger; his close-cropped sandy hair was almost boyish though his clothes drooped from his shoulders as though from the wasted frame of an old man.

'Detective Chief Superintendent Wycliffe, Mr Collins.'

Willie blinked down at him. 'Perhaps we should go somewhere where we can talk.' He darted bird-like glances from his mother to the superintendent and back again, the light glinting on his spectacles.

'Willie . . .'

'Yes, mother?'

The old lady hesitated. 'All right, take the superintendent up to the flat, I'll be there directly.'

'There's no need, mother.'

'Of course I shall come up!'

A small gesture of resignation. 'This way, superintendent.'

Through the bookcase maze to a green baize door and out on to a carpeted landing. Stairs down to a tiny hall and up to the flat.

'We have a side entrance, you see.'

Their sitting room overlooked the narrow chasm of the street and it was not a pleasant room. Wycliffe was vaguely aware of a sense of oppression, not entirely due to the poor light, the massive old-fashioned furniture, the sombre browns and fawns. But more to a feeling that this was a room in which people never lived. He would have sworn that the piano in its walnut case was never played, there was no wireless, no television, no books, newspapers, magazines – no knitting even. Yet within seconds the door opened and a woman bustled in. 'Oh! I didn't know there was anybody here.' Obvious that she was lying.

Willie was put out. 'This gentleman wants to talk to me, Aunt Jane.' But her fixed bland smile forced him to introductions. 'Miss Collins – my father's sister . . .'

She was at least twenty years younger than Willie's mother; leaner, harder, with a hint of fanaticism in her protuberant eyes and thin hard lips. Perhaps she had been born to be a nun and missed a turning somewhere, but she would certainly have looked at home in a convent of one of the stricter orders. She had mannish features accentuated

97

by an Eton-crop hairstyle, a bi-tonal voice like an adolescent boy's, and her frame was innocent of curves. 'My dear Willie! What have you been doing to bring a Chief Superintendent visiting us? I'm sure that it must be something quite dreadful!' Her boisterously arch manner irritated. She made no move to go and after an awkward silence she seated herself on a straight-backed chair and waited.

Wycliffe was by the window, peering out between the narrow gap in the curtains; he could look into a room across the street where two girls sat at a table piled high with flowers. They were putting them into bunches. Another world.

'When did you last hear from your wife, Mr Collins?'

Willie was still standing, fiddling with a china ornament on the mantelpiece.

'My nephew's wife left him two years ago and he hasn't heard from her since. It distresses him to speak of her, superintendent.' The melting glance she threw at Willie was not lost on the superintendent.

He produced the reconstructed photograph. 'Is this your wife, Mr Collins?'

Willie took the photograph and stared at it myopically. 'Where did you get this?'

'Is it your wife?'

'Yes.'

'Let me see it, dear.' Aunt Jane took the photograph from him, glanced at it and handed it to Wycliffe. What she had seen seemed to reassure her for she became more relaxed. 'It's her all right.'

'What is it, Willie?' His mother, flushed and out of breath. 'So you're here, Jane!' She looked from her sister-in-law to her son. 'Do you really want your aunt to hear all your business, Willie?'

Willie shrugged.

Wycliffe got down to business in self defence. 'I expect that you have heard of the death of a young woman at the Marina Hotel?'

Willie must have guessed what was coming but he gave no sign.

'I'm sorry to tell you that it was your wife who was killed – murdered.'

'Murdered.' Willie repeated the word in a curiously flat tone which seemed to signify complete acceptance.

'She was strangled.'

An incredibly smug look on the old lady's face. 'Well, it's nothing to do with us, superintendent! That girl walked out of here two years ago.'

Wycliffe said nothing. Willie might not have heard for all the impression the news seemed to have made on him. The old lady went on, her voice complacent like the cooing of a well-fed pigeon. 'Something was bound to happen to a girl like that – she was *wicked*! If she's been punished it's no more than she deserves.'

Aunt Jane remained unmoved but she frowned at her sister-in-law. 'That's foolish talk, Ada, it's natural that the superintendent will want to ask us questions.'

Wycliffe produced the ring which had been taken from the dead girl's finger. 'Was this her wedding ring?'

Willie reached out to take it but his mother forestalled him. She turned to Wycliffe, 'This ring belonged to my mother, she was called Jessica and she married William. You can see the two initials inside. Willie gets his name from both sides of the family . . . ' She fingered the ring for a moment and her face softened in recollection, but then the customary pout returned. 'That girl had no business to take it!'

'Don't be silly, Ada! You gave it her, it was her wedding ring!' Aunt Jane snapped. 'In any case you've changed your tune, when she first came here nothing was too good for her. I saw what she was from the start but you'd take no notice of me!'

Wycliffe never ceased to marvel at the scarcity value of human compassion and the meagre currency of charity. 'You are required to identify your wife's body, Mr Collins, and after that you will be asked to make a statement.' These people sickened him.

The old lady bristled. 'I really don't see why my son should be involved in the scandal surrounding this woman. He is respected in the town . . . '

'For God's sake shut up, mother!' Willie bleated and the outburst was so obviously unprecedented that it was followed by stunned silence.

His mother recovered first. 'How dare you speak to your mother like that!'

Wycliffe happened to be looking at Aunt Jane and saw the satisfaction on her face. He was physically as well as mentally ill at ease, the room was close, airless, and he could feel the perspiration round his neck soaking into his collar. Willie looked at him, a pleading look. 'Let's get out of here!' Willie got up and he followed him out of the room and across the passage. 'This is my room, I work and sleep here . . . '

The room looked out on the harbour, it was large, oblong, and more of a study than a bedroom. A narrow bunk tucked against one wall was the only apparent concession to sleeping. Apart from this the two long walls were occupied by benches with drawers below and shelves above. Several of the shelves were crowded with rank upon rank of brightly coloured toy soldiers, drawn up in parade ground order. The walls between the shelves were entirely hidden by coloured prints of eighteenth and nineteenth century uniforms. Under the benches, the smaller drawers were labelled: *Colours; Artillery; Small Arms* ... the large ones, with the names of battles: *Ramillies; Waterloo; Sedan* ... The wall by the door was a single nest of bookshelves reaching from floor to ceiling and all the books seemed to be concerned with warfare and the strategy of war, lives of famous generals and technical works on weapons.

Wycliffe looked round with appreciation. This was the sort of room of which he approved – professionally. It told him something of its owner, in this case, probably enough to prise off the lid of Willie's reserve. But he would have to go warily. He picked up a splendid hussar from the array of cavalry and examined it, expressing his admiration. 'I suppose these are accurate?'

'Of course! There would be no point in having them otherwise. I don't play with toy soldiers!' A practised answer to the soft impeachment.

'You are a student of warfare?'

The eyes behind the thick lenses were cautious. 'Of the eighteenth and nineteenth centuries. I know little of earlier times and less of modern war, the very thought of which appalls me.'

Wycliffe nodded, replacing the horseman carefully in his rank. Collins pointed to a comfortable looking wing-backed chair. 'Sit down, smoke if you want to.' He spoke in nervous jerks. 'I don't smoke myself.' He seated himself in a swivel chair by his desk and seemed to gain confidence in doing so. 'You wanted to ask me some questions about Julie?'

Wycliffe filled and lit his pipe. Collins seemed to be taking the news of his wife's death remarkably calmly – if it was news. But you could never tell with his sort; often, in self defence, they seemed able to contrive barriers of the mind, compartments in which unpleasant events could be more or less isolated, held for a time in cold storage. 'You don't strike me as a violent man, Mr Collins.'

Collins's quick glance darted round the room. 'Violent?' He made a broad gesture. 'You mean all this? No, I'm not in the least violent, quite the contrary. That's probably why my interest in war is historical. The present and the recent past are too immediate for me, but the battles of Marlborough and Napoleon are sufficiently remote for me to be objective about them. I can look at the strategy of a war or the tactics of a battle in much the same way as I might consider the problems presented by a game of chess.' He was undoubtedly shy, reticent, but he could not resist the chance to explain himself, probably because such opportunities came seldom. He fiddled with his blotter and scribbling pad, placing them geometrically on his desk, then he added, 'I *abhor* violence!'

'You think that it is never justified?'

A period of hesitation. 'I do think that but I also think that it is inevitable, human nature being what it is.'

Wycliffe dimly apprehended that as long as his questions remained general the scholar in Willie would see that he got honest answers. But he was less certain what would happen when the questions became personal. At heart, he believed, Willie was still the gangling gawky youth who had been the butt of his schoolfellows, the one who skulked in a corner of the playground, dreading to be noticed.

But Willie was still worrying away at the problem posed by Wycliffe's last question. 'I think that for any man, however mild, there is a point beyond which he may resort to violence.' He smiled vaguely. 'Call it the threshold of violence. We each have our different thresholds and those for whom it is low soon acquire a reputation for habitual violence while others have to be faced with extreme provocation before . . . ' His voice trailed off.

'But even the worm will turn at last – is that what you are saying?'

Collins looked at him, hesitated for a moment, then nodded. 'Yes.'

'How old are you, Mr Collins?'

'I am thirty-eight.'

'And your wife?'

'She is – was, twenty, almost twenty-one.' He crossed his spindly legs and started to beat a tattoo on his knee with his fingers. 'I married Julie two-and-a-half years ago when she was eighteen.' He spoke the name Julie in a special way; it occurred to Wycliffe that it was in a similar manner that priests spoke the name of Christ.

'Her parents?'

'She was an orphan, both her parents were killed in an air crash while she was still a child and she was in the care of the local authority – boarded out, I think that is the expression.'

'She was unhappy?'

'On the contrary, I think that she was quite at home with her foster parents. She had been with them for nine or ten years and they regarded her as their daughter. I think that they would have adopted her but for some legal quibble.'

'They raised no objection to her marrying a man seventeen years older?'

'No. Julie had to apply to the Court but her application was supported by her foster parents and by the local authority.'

'Was she pregnant?'

The restless fingers stopped tapping. 'She was not!'

Wycliffe hardly knew what to ask. He wanted some flesh to clothe the bare bones of this unlikely romance. A young, attractive girl immures herself with two shrewish women in order to marry a shy studious man twice her age. There must have been something.

'How did you first meet her?'

It was obvious that the question revived memories which had become painful. He spoke in a low voice and with long pauses. 'She was at school studying for her "A" levels. She was very serious about her work and her foster parents encouraged her. She read widely and she came to the shop first to buy cheap second-hand books – cheap copies of the poets. Then she found that I was interested in literature and she began to discuss her work with me. She would come in after school or on a Saturday and spend a lot of time in the bookroom. I would join her when I could and we would talk about what she had read, about her lessons, and we would plan her future work.'

'At that time you never met her outside?'

'I told you . . . '

'Always in the bookroom with your mother sitting at the cash desk?'

'Why yes. Mother is always there when the shop is open; she doesn't have to be there but it was her job when father was in the business and it would hurt her if she thought she was no longer needed.'

'Rather onerous conditions for courtship, surely?'

Willie flushed. 'There was no question of courtship!'

'But you married the girl!' He felt that he was moving in a realm outside the usual flesh and blood one that he knew, a world, perhaps, where an apt quotation took the place of hot hands in the back of the stalls. Not one that Julie would be at home in, of that he felt certain. 'Whose idea was it? Yours or hers?'

Willie took off his glasses and began to polish them for they had misted over. 'Actually it was my mother's.'

His mother's! Unexpected but it made sense. 'Your mother had a good opinion of Julie, then?'

'Yes, mother thought her a pleasant, well brought up girl.'

And mother thought too, 'A young girl can be guided – *moulded.*' With Willie well on the wrong side of thirty the alternative might be some mature woman with a mind of her own. Wycliffe thought that he could set the scene and write the script:

'*It's time you thought seriously about getting married, Willie.*'

'*I'm in no hurry. In any case, the chance would be a fine thing!*' Forced joke.

'*Don't be absurd, Willie! Scores of girls would jump at the chance.*'

'*All I can say is, I never come across them.*'

'*One in particular.*'

'*Oh?*'

'*Julie.*'

'*Julie! Don't be absurd, mother! She's only a child.*'

'*She's a woman, Willie. She knows it if you don't!*'

'*In any case it's ridiculous, Julie never thinks of me like that. To her I'm just an old buffer who helps her a bit with her work – just like another teacher.*'

'*In Julie's eyes you can do no wrong – I know.*'

'*Nonsense!*'

'*Ask her.*'

And in the end, of course, he did, as he did most things his mother wished. And because he was already in love with her youth and her mind, because he had a romantic vision of a relationship which was intellectual but deeply affectionate, because her foster parents saw it as a good match and because Julie wanted to get out of her council house home – they married.

That was it, or something like it.

The room was quiet, Wycliffe smoked peacefully, Willie stared at the carpet.

'Can men more injure women than to say
They love them for that, by which they are not they?'

The sentiment might well have appealed to Willie, but not, Wycliffe felt sure, to Julie, not to the girl he had seen lying dead at the Marina.

'What happened?'

Outside the pleasure boats were setting out across the harbour, some bound for the creeks and wooded reaches of the river, others for the more adventurous trip across the bay. A watery gleam of sunshine gave them encouragement. The siren of the ferry boat blasted, sharp, angry, as she changed course to avoid running down a dinghy drifting across her path with sails flapping. Wycliffe could see it all, just sitting there. In such a room he would never do any work.

'What went wrong?'

A stupid question about a situation which had never been right but Collins would not see it like that.

'I don't know. At first everything seemed to go well, then Julie started going out in the evenings, she would stay out late and offer no explanation. In the end she just went off.'

It seemed impossible to make any contact, to find common ground. 'Was she a virgin?'

Willie coloured. 'No.' His eyes darted round the room like an animal trying to escape. 'She told me that she had been . . . that she had been raped by a boy when she was fourteen.'

'Did you believe her?'

It was cruelty. 'I don't know.'

'The sexual side of your marriage – was it satisfactory?'

Willie could not have suffered more on the rack. 'I don't know. Why do you ask me these questions?'

'When she left you, where did she go?'

The relief was painful to see. 'She got a job in the town – in cabaret. Mother could never forgive her for that, she thought she did it on purpose to humiliate us.'

'And you – could you forgive her?'

The glasses glinted in the light. 'I had nothing to forgive, it was I who was wrong. I realize now that there was no life in this place for a young girl. I should have known, but if she had told me I would have given her anything . . . ' There was pathos in his simplicity.

But it wasn't difficult to imagine the situation. Julie treading on eggshells until she began to feel secure. Timid at first, overawed, watched by the two women. 'We don't do it that way dear! Never mind – you'll learn. We all have to be patient, don't we?' And a husband who believed that love could be equated with romance.

Was that how it had been? Or was there something more sinister behind it all?

'What did you do in the evenings before Julie started to go out?'

He looked surprised by the question. 'In the evenings? Julie used to play three-handed bridge with mother and my aunt.'

'And you?'

'I worked in here.'

'Did you expect her to leave you?'

'No, it came as a great shock.' He matched the tips of his fingers together and studied the result. 'She left a letter for mother which upset her very much.'

'Did you try to get her back?'

He nodded. It seemed for a moment that he could not trust himself to speak. 'Then she went away altogether.'

'And you didn't see her again until . . . until when, Mr Collins?'

'I never saw her again.'

'When she left, did she take any money with her?'

'She may have had a few pounds – not much.'

'She did not steal money from you or from the business?'

'Certainly not!' Collins looked startled. 'Why do you ask?'

Why did he ask? Wycliffe looked at the lean anxious face, at the tense body. Not a modicum of repose. What did he expect the poor devil to say in answer to all his questions? I killed my wife? Was that the object of the exercise? That, or to prove that he had done no such thing. Either way it was preposterous. If this man had murdered his wife it was because at thirty-eight he was still adolescent, because all his self control, all the restraints that were normal to him had been eroded by consuming jealousy; it was because he had a silly, selfish mother; because he had been a fool to marry a precocious child. Because of anything except wanting her dead. Now he had to live with his remorse – if he was guilty. What good would questions do him or Julie or anyone? And if there was no guilt then Wycliffe's very presence in the house was an impertinence.

The mood came and went. Julie was dead by violence and violence must be contained. When he had doubts about his calling, and he had them often, that was his answer.

'Who were her foster parents? I shall have to see them.'

'They are called Little. He is a welder at the docks and they live on the Three Fields Estate – 3, Trevellas Way.'

Wycliffe made a note. There was much more he wanted to know but he believed in short interviews with return visits. He stood up. 'Well, Mr Collins, if you are ready, we will get it over.'

'Now?' A scared look behind the thick lenses.

'These things won't wait.'

'All right. I'd better tell them. How long will it take?'

'You should be back in two hours.'

Wycliffe waited while Willie talked to his mother and aunt. Then they had to walk to the police station where Wycliffe had left his car. As they made their way through the busy streets a surprising number of people greeted Willie in a friendly fashion but he hardly seemed to see them.

'You are very popular in the town.'

'I've lived here all my life.'

They had to drive ten miles to the County Hospital and Willie sat staring at the road ahead. Wycliffe tried to start a conversation several times without result. It was only as they were pulling into the hospital car park that he started a topic of his own.

'Was there anything found in her room?'

'What sort of thing?'

He was quick to disclaim any preconceived idea. 'I don't know – anything.'

'A thousand pounds in used notes.'

Willie said nothing.

Dr Franks was in the pathology building and Wycliffe went to see him first. 'I've brought the husband.'

'Husband?' Franks's brows went up. 'I hadn't thought of her with a husband, is she local?'

'More or less. I wanted to ask you, did she dope?'

'Dope? No. There's no evidence of habitual drug taking – why?'

Wycliffe shrugged. 'Don't bother with it.'

As they went in, Franks whispered, 'You've warned him?'

'No.'

The white light shone down on Julie's shrouded form. 'Just one good look, Mr Collins, and I must warn you that what you will see will distress you.' He nodded to the attendant who lifted the sheet. 'Is that your wife, Mr Collins?'

Willie looked down at the body, he stared as though mesmerized; then he gave a queer pathetic little cry and collapsed on the tiles.

CHAPTER SEVEN

'Shall we eat out tonight?'

'If you like. Anywhere in mind?'

'A club, a place called the Voodoo, food, drinks, dancing and a floorshow.'

She looked at him suspiciously. 'It hardly sounds your sort of place.'

'It isn't but I think it might be interesting.'

Since the previous evening the club had been under observation. They had been lucky, an ex-policeman kept a tobacconist's shop across the road from the club and it was a simple matter to put a man in the stockroom over the shop. He had a personal radio and there was a telephone in the next room. His brief was vague, to note all the comings and goings when the club was closed and to try to spot any *known* persons entering or leaving when it was open. The watcher had Allen's photograph and instructions to look out for him in particular.

'He wouldn't be fool enough to try to hide out there,' Gill said but Wycliffe was less certain.

Keeping 'obo' sounds simple enough until you have tried spotting someone from a photograph, simple enough if you have the sort of memory which is an index of faces. Really simple only if you have a sixth sense for the job. Wycliffe had kept obo on countless occasions; having a room for it was luxury. For him, sitting in the soft darkness, looking out on the life of the street would have been a pleasure rather than a chore. A flask of coffee and a packet of sandwiches . . . But it is not a permissible recreation for chief superintendents. All the same he refused to be left out entirely. He decided that he wanted to put Masson-Smythe on edge without making any overt move against him. So he found himself an excuse for dining there.

Membership was by no means exclusive, a pound paid at the desk and a signature in the register, but the food and drink were expensive and there was a minimum charge.

Helen looked round the room with interest. It was dimly but cleverly lit by a red glow from hidden lamps so that the totem figures, the voodoo masks and the murals achieved their maximum effect. When they arrived several couples were dancing but most were at the tables eating. They were shown to a table not far from the stage and presented with monstrous menus which were difficult to read in the dim light.

'Why are these places always so dark?' Helen grumbled.

'I think it's supposed to make you feel naughty.'

'It makes me wonder if the cutlery is clean.'

They ordered roast lamb masquerading as *Filet d'agneau au four* and a bottle of Beaujolais.

During the meal Wycliffe saw Thelma from time to time. She moved among the tables saying the right things to the right people but she did not reach the tables near the stage. Her blue gown, high waisted in the classical style, made the best of her Junoesque figure. 'A striking woman,' Helen said.

'I prefer something more cuddly,' Wycliffe said. 'With her I should always be afraid of being eaten afterwards. Shall we have liqueurs?'

They were about to order when Wycliffe spotted Masson-Smythe himself, immaculate in evening dress, brooding over the floor. He saw them and came over, suave, ingratiating. Wycliffe introduced him to Helen.

'You are having liqueurs? Curaçao? Allow me. I insist!'

He instructed the waiter. 'I have a rather special Triple Sec which I keep for my friends . . . May I?' He seated himself at their table.

Wycliffe was astonished at the change in him but felt that this solicitous restaurateur act was a bit overdone.

Helen congratulated him on his club. 'Surprising to find such a place in a small town.'

'It doesn't make a fortune.' Masson-Smythe laughed. 'In fact, during the off-season we do no more than break even but we have to stay open to keep the nucleus of a competent staff.' He looked round with a certain pride at the well filled room. 'As you see at this time of year we do pretty well.'

'Have you always been in this business, Mr Masson-Smythe?'

He beckoned to the cigarette girl and selected two cigars from her tray. 'Mr Wycliffe?'

'That's very civil of you,' Wycliffe said, accepting a cigar.

When they were smoking he turned once more to Helen. 'No, I haven't always been in this business. I was chief steward on one of the Atlantic liners for a number of years. When I got tired of shuttling to and fro and had made enough money, I went to work for a London club to learn the business, then I started here.' Was there a challenge in the look he gave the superintendent? From time to time he dabbed with a white silk handkerchief at the beads of perspiration on his upper lip and once he removed and polished his glasses, squinting painfully while he did so.

Soon Helen was telling him about the twins. 'Have you a family, Mr Smythe?'

'Unfortunately, no. This business and a family don't mix I'm afraid.'

'You don't find it necessary to employ a bouncer?' Wycliffe showing a professional interest.

Masson-Smythe grinned. 'We get very little trouble and if the need arises I can give quite a good account of myself.' His candour was disarming.

They chatted amicably until the cabaret was due to start then he left them.

'What did you make of him?'

Helen was thoughtful. 'Smooth. Did you notice his face? He's had some sort of operation and plastic surgery to disguise the scar.'

Of course! That explained the facial immobility – his lack of expression.

'I also noticed that Thelma hardly took her eyes off us the whole time he was here.'

The bandleader announced the first act of the cabaret in a throaty contralto which made the audience laugh, putting them in the mood. A comedian told a seemingly endless stream of blue jokes and he was followed by a female impersonator whose sex might have been questioned anyway. A pretty girl with a guitar sang folk songs and the audience joined in the choruses. Picked out by a pink spotlight in the darkened room she looked young and appealing in her white mini-dress and everyone felt sentimental. Then it was Sadie's turn. It took her seven minutes of more or less graceful pirouettes and postures before she finally parted with her G-string and made her tour of the tables, her modesty protected by two Japanese fans. What her act lacked in skill was made up by her obvious desire to please and in this, to judge from the applause, she succeeded. When she saw the superintendent, she blushed.

Wycliffe looked at his watch. 'Eleven fifteen.'

'They don't close until three and there's another show with different acts in an hour . . . ' Helen was enjoying herself.

Wycliffe stood up. 'I'll be back.' He made his way across

the floor now crowded with dancers, out into the foyer. One or two couples were sitting out on the banquettes and a noisy crowd of Midlanders, just arrived, were being persuaded to sign the book. He pushed open the door marked *Adams* into the elegant washroom, all white tiles and gleaming chrome. He presented himself to the wall thinking vaguely about the case but he had had enough to drink to feel gratifyingly detached and benevolent. A cistern flushed in one of the cubicles behind him and he heard the sound of a door catch. A vague reflection of movement in the shining tiles and then a violent blow to the base of his skull drowned his senses in a great wave of pain.

When he recovered consciousness he was still lying on the tiled floor but now two men were bending over him, one was a stranger but the other was Masson-Smythe. His eyes were magnified by his glasses and Wycliffe was fascinated by them.

'What happened, superintendent? This gentleman found you lying here.'

The question irritated him and the base of his skull ached abominably. 'Somebody slugged me, what do you think happened?' He realized that he was very angry.

'There's a doctor in the club, I've sent for him.'

Wycliffe struggled to his feet. 'I don't need a doctor!' He looked at his watch and his eyes took a moment to focus; it was eleven twenty-five, only ten minutes since he had left Helen. 'Have you told my wife?'

'No . . . Shall I send . . . ?'

'No!'

A third man joined them, the doctor, a dapper little man with white hair but a springy step. Wycliffe was taken, protesting, to the staff rest room and made to sit while the doctor examined him.

'You've got a slight concussion, strictly speaking

you should spend the night in hospital but if you promise . . . '

'I'm going back to my hotel but first I want a telephone . . . ' And nothing they could say made any difference. The little doctor took himself off, grumbling, and Masson-Smythe hovered while he shut himself in the plush call-box. He dialled the station.

'Wycliffe here. I strongly suspect that Allen has just left the Voodoo, I want . . . '

'He's been picked up, sir. Wilson, who's on obo opposite the club, saw him come out and radioed in. He was picked up by a Panda . . . Excuse me, sir.' A momentary break. 'They're just bringing him in, sir. Do you want . . . ?'

'I want him locked up!' Wycliffe snapped and slammed down the receiver.

Outside Masson-Smythe had worked himself up into a state of indignation about the outrage committed on his premises but Wycliffe brushed past him growling, 'You need a good bouncer! But if you want to do something you can get me a taxi.'

Back at their table Helen looked at him startled. 'What's wrong?'

'Nothing much. Something's cropped up. Let's go.'

She knew him well enough to keep quiet until they were in the taxi and Masson-Smythe had made his final obsequious apology. 'Now!'

He told her, playing down the incident. 'It's bed for you, my boy!'

His head still ached and he wanted to take a couple of sleeping tablets but Helen was adamant. 'Not on top of all that alcohol!'

Actually he slept soundly until first light. When he woke, his head was still sore, though the pain was more localized. He had a raging thirst which the water from his bedside carafe, flat and warm, did little to cure, and he was tantalized by recollections of the heady chilled beer they serve on the terraces of continental cafés. He tried to occupy his mind with the case. There seemed little doubt that Allen had been hiding out at the Voodoo. If Masson-Smythe was fixing a passage for him it would be the logical place to go when he was forced out of the Marina. It might seem to him to be the last place the police would think of looking for him. Allen could reasonably assume that they would expect him to get as far away from the Marina as possible – not simply to move down the street. But, seeing Wycliffe, his logic deserted him and he panicked.

But what had all this to do with Julie? The only link seemed to be that they were both at the Marina . . . It was no good, he couldn't just lie there with his tongue seeming to swell in his mouth and a taste like sour vinegar. With the greatest care he slid slowly out of bed, but he might have saved himself the trouble.

'What's the matter?'

He mumbled something about the lavatory.

'Are you all right?'

'Fine!'

'You're sure?'

He put on his dressing gown and went out on to the verandah. The harbour lay under a pearly mist which merged into the sky. The land on the other side was a vague insubstantial shape. He could hear the steady chug-chug of a motor launch close by but could not see it, then it emerged abruptly from the mist, glided by and vanished again. An old man wearing a peaked cap and smoking a pipe stood with the tiller caught in his back, immobile as a statue. From somewhere below came the smell of coffee. He stole out of the room and downstairs where his status as a celebrity enabled him to get a cup from the kitchen staff who had just come on duty. He felt better. 'More hangover than concussion,' he told himself and hoped that he was right.

Instead of clearing, by breakfast time the mist had thickened to fog and at intervals they could hear the dismal blare of the fog-signal from the lighthouse in the bay. At nine o'clock, despite protests from Helen, he left for the station on foot. It was not actually raining but water condensed from the supersaturated air as from a steam-bath. He lit his pipe but the tobacco tasted like damp straw.

Saturday morning. The men of the new leisure wondering how to spend the time until *Grandstand*, their women bustling round the house, anxious to get out to do the weekend shopping before the best of everything was sold. Wycliffe felt dull, he had no clear idea what he intended to do. Presumably he would question Allen. The HQ room was empty save for a constable who had been typing and was now collecting his work into neat piles. He was young, probably ambitious.

'What's your name?'

'Rees, sir. Detective Constable.'

'What have you been typing?'

'Sir?'

'I asked you what you've been typing?'

'My report, sir.'

'On what?'

'Enquiries at the railway station, the bus station, taxi ranks and car-hire firms about Allen.'

'Allen is in custody.'

'I know that, sir, but I still have to make my report.'

'Do you think that all this paper work helps you to catch villains?'

The young man was too clever to fall head first into that

one. He considered. 'I think that catching villains is a team job, sir, and the team must know what all its members are doing. In the long run full communication saves work.'

'You've been brainwashed.'

'Sir?'

'You don't believe in the lone-wolf approach?'

'I think that it's out of date and dangerous, sir.'

Catch 'em young! He wondered if he was out of date and dangerous. To be more accurate, he knew that he was out of date and merely wondered whether he had reached the stage of being dangerous. He had no doubt that Deputy Chief Constable Bellings would say that he had. He went into his little room and stood by the window watching the condensed moisture run down the panes. His head still ached. Gill came in and found him there. 'How's the patient?' Wycliffe said nothing and he went on, 'We shall have to box a bit clever on this one. After all, he's already been charged with one major crime and the Yard'll want him back, pronto.'

'They can have him when we've finished with him. I want him as a witness in a murder case and for assaulting a police officer.'

Gill was about to say something but changed his mind. 'I'll be off.'

'Where?'

'To the docks, looking for a bent skipper.'

'Where's Fehling?'

'He's there already, waiting for me. I think he's avoiding you.'

'And well he might!'

When Gill had gone he picked up the telephone. 'Send Allen up . . . and send DC Rees with his notebook.' He hadn't prepared for the interrogation, never given it more than a fleeting thought. After all, he believed in playing things by ear. The great exponent of off-the-cuff detection. Old-fashioned! You get a feeling or you stop being a copper – that's what his first DI used to tell him.

His first reaction on seeing Allen at close quarters was one of incredulity. The man was built like a heavyweight wrestler; yet to hear Kathy talk you would have thought that he was a pitiably weak creature. And to imagine him with the fragile delicacy of the dead girl! The imagination boggled.

His eyes were brown, restless, they shifted focus like the eyes of a nervous animal. Probably his violence sprang from fright. Not that that was any excuse.

Wycliffe looked him up and down coolly. 'I've had you brought here to answer questions concerning the murder of Julie Collins at the Marina Hotel last Tuesday night. I am not concerned with the crime you have been charged with in the Metropolitan Police District – is that clear?'

'I don't know anything about any murder.'

'I said, "Is that clear?" '

'Yes.'

'Sit down.' He nodded to the uniformed constable who removed the cuffs.

Allen sat down and Wycliffe signed to the constable to leave. Rees came in and took his seat in a corner of the room.

'How old are you?'

'You've got it on the sheet.'

'How old are you?'

'Twenty-seven.'

Wycliffe relit his pipe, watching the man over the flickering flame of the match. 'Do you smoke?'

'Cigarettes.'

Wycliffe always carried a packet though he never smoked them; he tossed them over. 'Help yourself.'

Allen's fingers were clumsy and he bruised the cigarette as he drew it from the packet. He stood up, bending over the table for Wycliffe to light it, then he puffed greedily. A moment later he was shaken by a violent spasm of coughing.

'What's the matter with you?'

'I've got a weak chest. I was TB as a kid, perhaps I am again.'

A bid for sympathy? From time to time the bright little brown eyes lighted on Wycliffe only to flit away again as soon as they met his, but they kept coming back. 'He's wondering what to make of me.' Which was all to the good.

'You were staying at the Marina when that girl was killed, why were you there?'

A slow shrug of the massive shoulders. 'It's as good a place as the next to keep out of the way.'

'What was your connection with the girl?'

'None.'

'Your prints were found in the girl's room.'

Allen blew smoke through his nostrils. 'You can't con me, copper!'

'On a photograph in her handbag. How did you get to know her?'

An uneasy movement but no reply.

'She was strangled, then disfigured, her face beaten in with a brass weight which had been used as a door stop. You can imagine.'

The man's hands grasping the arms of his chair tightened and relaxed but he gave no other sign.

'Do I bore you?'

A quick frown.

'Where did you meet her?'

Silence.

Wycliffe reached for the telephone. 'You and I are going for a little trip.' He spoke into the mouthpiece. 'Have my car brought round and tell the constable who delivered Allen to come up.' He was play-acting and he hardly knew with what purpose. 'You too, Rees.'

The constable arrived and Allen was escorted down to Wycliffe's car. He was put into the back seat between his gaolers and Wycliffe drove to the county hospital. The fog was beginning to clear inland, the sun was struggling through and vapour rose from the wet roads and fields. He parked the car and led the way to the pathology building. Allen and his guards were left in a waiting room while he went in search of Dr Franks.

After half an hour Allen was escorted to the mortuary. The central lamp shone down on a covered trolley. Wycliffe and Franks stood on one side while Allen was brought to the other. 'Uncover the face.'

Allen's eyes darted round the room but were drawn at last to the mutilated face of the girl on the trolley. He had prepared himself but even so he could not suppress a movement of revulsion. 'This is your girl friend, Allen, somebody did this to her.'

Allen turned his head away. 'Let me get out of here!'

'Stay where you are!' Wycliffe's voice was like a whiplash. 'What's the matter with you? Don't you recognize her?' He drew the covering sheet further back. 'Perhaps you recognize the mole – look!' Brutal! But the only kind of language Allen and his like would understand.

Allen made a violent movement to shake off the two men who held him but failed. Wycliffe replaced the sheet. 'Have you ever had a blood test?'

It was obvious that the man was near the limit of endurance, but impossible to say which way further pressure would affect him. He might go berserk or simply fold up.

'I want you to have a blood test now; Dr Franks will prick the lobe of your ear and take a drop of blood.'

Allen looked at Wycliffe as a tormented dog looks at its tormentor, dumbly, uncomprehending. Franks came round the trolley, an assistant dabbed Allen's right ear lobe with surgical spirit and Franks produced a tiny lancet and phial. Allen winced as Franks squeezed a few drops of blood into the phial; then another dab of surgical spirit and it was done.

'What's it for?'

Wycliffe glanced at him indifferently. 'Just to check.'

'If you would care to wait in my office . . . ?' As they had planned, Franks led Wycliffe down the corridor to his office. Allen and the two policemen followed. Wycliffe seated himself in the swivel chair behind the metal desk and signed to Allen to take the other chair.

'Wait outside,' to the policemen.

It was a repetition of the scene in Wycliffe's office but now Allen was paler, even more nervous and less sure of himself. 'I didn't kill her.'

Wycliffe regarded him with a detached, impersonal stare. 'We shall see.' He looked round the white aseptic room; even the books and files looked as though they had been sterilized, but the window opened on to a little garden with fuchsias in flower and gladioli flaunting themselves. He had to shift his chair to avoid the direct path of the sunlight.

'Are your parents alive?'

'I don't know.'

'Why were you sent to an approved school in the first place?'

'What does it matter?'

'Was it a sex offence?'

'No!' The denial was prompt and vigorous.

'Women like you, I expect. I mean that you can have all the women you want?'

A glimmer of a smile which vanished at once. 'I've never had to twist their arms.'

'But you despise them?'

He raised his hands in a gesture. 'I take them as they come.'

'I gather that this girl who was murdered was pretty keen on it.'

No answer.

'Do you know what they were doing when he killed her? He was having her. Does that surprise you?'

Allen was sitting bolt upright in his chair, tense, scared.

'Have you ever felt like killing a woman at the very instant when . . . '

'I didn't kill her.'

Wycliffe went on as though he had not spoken. 'Of course, there is another possibility, her room is next to the fire escape, you could have been standing out there watching and then . . . '

The brown eyes were focused steadily on Wycliffe's now and Allen half rose from his chair. What would have happened if Dr Franks had not come bustling in is impossible to say. Ostentatiously Franks handed Wycliffe a slip of paper. 'This is what you are waiting for.' As he went out he gave Allen an inquisitive glance. Wycliffe looked at the paper: *Group A. Rh.+ve.* He folded it and put it carefully into his wallet, then he turned again to Allen. 'I think that you were on the point of telling me something.'

Allen hesitated, there was a moment while decision hung in the balance, then he suddenly went limp. 'All right, I'll tell you what I can.'

'You recognized the body in there as that of the girl who stayed at the Marina?'

'Yes.'

'She was your girl friend?'

'You could call her that.'

'What was her name?'

'She called herself Dawn Peters but I think that was for the business . . .'

'You are willing to make a statement?'

'I've said so, haven't I?'

Wycliffe relaxed. From now on it would all be plain sailing as far as Allen was concerned. A born bully, he hadn't the guts even to be a good crook. Wycliffe stood up and went briskly to the door. 'Right! We'll get back to the station.'

The two policemen escorted Allen out and Wycliffe, after a brief word with Franks to satisfy his curiosity, followed them. It was half past twelve when they arrived back and now Wycliffe was looking at Allen with a proprietary air, he was almost jovial. 'Hungry?'

'I haven't had anything since seven this morning.'

'Take him down, see that he gets a good meal, then he can have a sleep.'

Wycliffe had decided to go back to the hotel to lunch with his wife but when he went up to the HQ room he found Gill and Fehling there.

'I think Fehling has hit upon something, sir.'

Fehling, looking sullen, like a schoolboy with a grievance, said, 'I doubt if it's of any importance but this morning, when Mr Gill told me that you suspected the money might have been intended to get Allen out of the country, it set me thinking. My mind had been on drugs but if it's a question of an illicit passage, that narrows the field. There are very few ships where you could get away with that these days.'

'Well?'

'There's a freighter alongside the Eastern breakwater, the *Peruvia*, four thousand tons, Liberian registered. She was towed in several weeks back having had a fire which badly damaged her superstructure and accommodation. She's due to sail on Monday which would have suited Allen. The girl was there with the money. . . '

'I suppose it's a line of enquiry,' Wycliffe said without much enthusiasm, 'but we shall need more than that . . . '

'There is more,' Gill cut in with impatience. 'The skipper is a Spaniard but he speaks English of a sort, and he's been seen several times lately drinking ashore with Dippy Pellow, the chap who runs one of the tender launches. And finally, when she sails on Monday, she's bound for Barranquilla.'

'Never heard of it.'

'It's the Caribbean port of Colombia.'

'And that's supposed to mean something to me?'

'It will if you read this, it's the Yard's reply to your request for further information about Allen.' He handed Wycliffe a typewritten sheet. After details of the offences for which Allen had received his various sentences, the memo went on:

Allen comes from a respectable family. His father was a schoolteacher in Surbiton. Both parents are now dead but he has a sister who married an oil engineer and is believed to be residing in Venezuela. He seems to have had no contact with his parents after . . .

Wycliffe handed back the sheet. 'Geography is not my strong point but I assume that Venezuela is next door to Colombia – is that it?'

'That, sir, is it. I suggest we have a go at that skipper and that we pull in Pellow for questioning.'

'Have a go at the skipper by all means but Pellow will keep, he can't run away.'

Wycliffe could hardly admit it but he was bored with this side of the investigation, for he was convinced that it had no direct bearing on the girl's death and that was all that interested him. Why had she been strangled? And above all, why had she been disfigured? He was on the point of telling Gill to carry on when it occurred to him that here was a chance to potter round the docks in the line of duty and there must be some privilege for rank. 'I'll see this Spanish skipper.' He was cowardly enough to add, 'Then if there's any legation trouble it will be my problem.'

Fehling's face betrayed his thoughts. 'In that case, sir, I'll be off to lunch.'

'You're coming with me, Mr Gill can eat for both of us.'

For once Fehling's petulant expression changed to a smile.

They drove through the town to the dock gates. As they passed the Marina Wycliffe wondered what Fehling would say if he suggested dropping in on them for lunch. If he could have been sure of another curry he would have been sorely tempted. On the waste ground beside Joe's café four or five articulated lorries were drawn up. 'Do you fancy something?'

'In there?'

'Why not? He does a good line in coffee with a dash of rum.'

After a moment Fehling decided to treat this as a joke. Wycliffe pulled up at the police barrier which was immediately raised. Evidently they recognized Fehling. Inside the gates he drew into the car park.

'We can drive to the ship, sir.'

'Let's walk.'

Despite the interest of the place Wycliffe almost wished that he had taken the car. Against Fehling's immense bulk he felt insignificant and as Fehling had the length of leg to go with it he found himself hopping over railway tracks, dodging hawsers and almost running to keep up. Finally he had the courage to set his own pace, which forced the inspector into line. He grinned to himself. Easy really!

It was Saturday and the place was almost deserted. They skirted the four main graving docks but Wycliffe made a small diversion to look into the basin of the largest, which housed a monstrous tanker. From the twin propellers his eye swept up over the great bulbous curve of grey steel plates to the rail towering above him. *British Emblem. London.*

'Seventy thousand tons,' Fehling said.

It was high tide and along the wharf the steeply angled gangplanks to the high riding unladen ships worried Wycliffe who had no head for heights. But the *Peruvia*, when they reached her, seemed tiny by comparison. Her renovated superstructure gleamed with fresh white paint but her hull was mottled with great splashes of red oxide where rust had been chipped off. Near the head of the gangway, which Wycliffe climbed easily, a swarthy little man in blue dungarees lent on the rail smoking. He seemed not to see them until Wycliffe addressed him. 'We are police officers and we wish to see the captain.'

The man, without moving from the rail, looked them up and down and without a word returned to his contemplation of the wharf. Fehling's reaction was swift and effective. *'Policia! Captain Hortelano immediatamente!'*

Whether it was the basic Spanish or the drill sergeant's voice and manner, the little man was galvanized into action. 'You have hidden talents, Mr Fehling,' Wycliffe observed.

'His lot have a healthy respect for the police,' Fehling confided.

They were led up a companionway to the bridge and ushered into the presence of the captain with a single word, '*Policia!*'

The captain was small and dark and sallow, a wiry little man in a dusty creased uniform with tarnished buttons and braid. His breath smelt of whisky and his speech had that special precision of enunciation which comes when a hard drinker is at a particular stage of drunkenness. His manner was ingratiating and his English good. 'You will drink with me, gentlemen?'

'No thank you.'

'That is a pity, I look for an excuse as it is not good to drink alone. All the same . . .' He fetched a bottle from a wall cupboard and poured himself a generous double.

They were in his day cabin, which was fresh from the hands of the painters, and Wycliffe had the impression that the captain was not at home in it. Perhaps he was accustomed to a cosy squalor. 'Do you carry passengers on your ship, captain?'

'Passengers? She is not a passenger ship – no. But you understand it is sometimes done that we take one or two. To keep the law they must sign as crew but they do not work and they pay. Last year we have a famous English writer and he stay with us three trips.'

'You are proposing to take a passenger when you sail on Monday?'

The captain drank half his whisky in a single swig. 'No, it was spoken of but the gentleman had not the proper papers.'

Wycliffe was standing at the curtained porthole, staring

out over the harbour; the dinghies were racing in the Roads beyond the breakwater. Fehling, monumental and immovable, stood by the door. The skipper's nervous gaze flitted from one to the other.

'The gentleman in question is under arrest.'

'So? It shows, does it not, how careful one must be?'

'You did not know that this man was wanted by the British police for robbery with violence?'

The brown eyes widened. 'But certainly I do not know! Would I ever . . . ?'

'Then why do you suppose he was going to pay a thousand pounds for his passage?'

'*Dios mi!* A thousand pounds? That Pellow – he is . . . he is *sin vergüenza*! He has talk to you, señor, but you are not correctly informed. One hundred pounds is all I was to get for this man's passage to Barranquilla. One hundred English pounds!'

Wycliffe had turned away from the porthole and he was now facing the captain. 'Perhaps you will give me the address of your owners?'

'Owners? What is this? They must not hear of this man, it was not an official arrangement, you understand, and I am in much trouble already because of the fire. If I am in more trouble my career at sea will be finish!'

Wycliffe shrugged. 'If you want to sail on Monday and you don't want your owners to know about this spot of bother, all you have to do is to tell the truth.'

'But I have told you . . . '

Wycliffe took a step towards the door. 'We'll get the address from the docks office.'

'But señor, wait!'

'Well?'

'I was to have five hundred pounds to put this man ashore in Barranquilla.'

'Without passing through immigration?'

He nodded.

'That's better. Now listen to me! If you leave the docks premises or attempt to communicate with this man Pellow or anyone else before you sail on Monday, I'll have you arrested. You understand?'

'I understand, señor. Be assured . . . '

Wycliffe strolled out on to the bridge and stood for a moment by the wheel, looking for'ard over the holds to the bow and beyond. He could see her pitching into a great wall of water, shipping it green, the decks awash, then the shuddering recovery as she began to rear like a porpoise, only to be ready for the next plunge . . .

'Captain Mac Whirr, I presume!'

'Cheeky devil! So you read Conrad?'

'I like yarns about the sea.'

Wycliffe wondered if he might have to revise his opinion of Fehling.

The docks' clock on its steel tripod, rising above the sheds, showed a quarter to two. 'Is there anywhere we can get some lunch?'

'I know a good steakhouse . . . '

'With a glass of beer?'

'At two o'clock? You must be joking!'

'Well let's make for the nearest pub and have one before we eat.'

CHAPTER EIGHT

Allen looked more composed when they brought him to Wycliffe's room in the afternoon. He sat in the chair by the desk and waited. Wycliffe stood by the window which looked out on to the blank garage wall. Detective Constable Rees, the young man to whom Wycliffe had talked that morning, installed himself in a corner with his notebook. This day had a special significance for him: he had heard much of Wycliffe's reputation and had followed all his cases; now, in a manner of speaking, they were working together. With ball-point poised he waited for the great man to begin. Wycliffe turned from the window, seemed about to sit down then changed his mind. He felt in his pocket for his pipe, brought it out, lit it, then threw over a packet of cigarettes to Allen. 'You're going to need these.' He smoked for a while then said, 'Well, my friend, I'd better caution you – you are not obliged to say anything unless you wish to . . .'

The little alarm clock on the shelf showed a quarter past three. Allen was smoking and staring at the floor. Wycliffe was moving restlessly round in the tiny space between his desk and the window, like a caged animal.

'When did you first meet her?'

'Six months ago. She was working for a group of three Soho strip clubs. You know the sort of thing – they employ a dozen or so girls who shuttle between the clubs getting in twelve or more acts apiece between two and midnight, six days a week.'

'She must have been making good money.'

Allen lit another cigarette from the stub of the old. 'Seventy-five a week.'

'What were you doing?'

Allen looked blank.

'All right! Save it! You were looking round for a likely bird who would keep you until you did your next job.'

Allen was indignant. 'What if I was? It wasn't immoral earnings!'

Wycliffe chuckled. 'There could be two opinions about that! Anyway you turned on your charm and she fell for it.'

Allen made a gesture of dissent. 'I didn't have to turn on any charm with that one, she was like a bitch in heat and after the first time I couldn't be in a room with her for five minutes before she had her pants off.'

'Where was she living?'

'She shared lodgings with another girl in Bayswater.'

'Address?'

Allen hesitated. 'I can't remember, somewhere behind Paddington Station – Sussex Place, Sussex Gardens, Sussex something . . . I could take you there.'

'You moved in?'

He shook his head. 'It wasn't on, the landlady was an interfering old bag, in any case I didn't want that . . . '

'She came to your place?'

'No, I didn't want that either; if a chap is known by his bird it gives you coppers a bit of a lever.'

'So what did you do?'

'Hotel rooms – some nights and Sundays.'

'What was she like?'

'In bed? She'd been around and she knew all the tricks.'

'And yet you hooked her.' Wycliffe wondered what the young constable was making of all this. Was this the sort of interrogation he had expected?

Allen looked modest. 'She said she never got any satisfaction from other men.'

Wycliffe did not even smile. 'Did she tell you anything about her life before she met you?'

'Not much, she said that she had worked in a club down this way.'

'Nothing else?'

Allen grinned. 'She said she was married.'

'Did she give any details?'

'She said he was an old geezer.'

'Anything else?'

'She said he was creepy.'

'What does that mean?'

Allen shrugged. 'He played with toy soldiers like a kid.'

'Why did she marry him?'

'God knows! Why do women do things?' He paused, then added, 'She said she was an orphan and I think she lived in some sort of home. She wanted to get out and this guy had money.'

'And where did this idyll take place?'

'Search me!'

Poor Willie! He had been no more than an episode in her life. Amusing to look back on, to tell her friends about. A creep who played with toy soldiers. Why had she married him? To escape from a childhood hedged in by foster parents, children's officers and the featureless omnipotence of bureaucracy. By marrying Willie she transformed herself into a woman, a woman free to explore wider horizons from a secure base. And the base served its purpose. The truth? Even as the thoughts passed through his mind he knew that they were a ludicrous over-simplification. Julie must have had her fears and her frustrations, her disappointments and her moments

134

of bitter self reproach. Times when she felt sorry for her amiable husband and remorseful for what she was doing to him. But in the story she told, all this would be left out.

What was DC Rees thinking in his corner? Of the silences in particular? No doubt he had been told that when questioning a suspect the pressure must be kept up, never allow time for prevarication, change ground often . . . But now the suspect's eyes were closed, the room was warm and it was possible that he was dozing. The chief superintendent himself seemed near to it as he sat, elbows on the desk, his chin in his hands, staring into space.

'Was she still in these lodgings when she came down here?'

Allen opened his eyes. 'No, she'd moved to a flat.'

'Address?'

'Queensberry Mansions, Felton Terrace, Hampstead.'

'Up in the world.'

'You can say that again. She packed in with the strip joints about two months ago when she found she had a voice. Some agent took her up and she got a job in cabaret – real West End stuff . . . '

'Did you live in the flat?'

'No, she wanted me to but it suited me to carry on as before. You don't want to get in too deep with a bird.'

Wycliffe nodded as though he were in complete accord with this sentiment. 'And next thing she's staying at a crummy joint here in the far west with you on the same floor, pretending not to know her. And she gets herself murdered.' His manner changed suddenly from a lazy somnolence to vigorous aggression. 'Now, my lad, I want it straight. I know most of the story so don't try any tricks unless you want the murder rap slapped on you.'

Allen was wide enough awake now and resentful. 'I said I would talk and I will, there's no need for threats. You see, I got nicked for this wages job . . . '

'I don't want to hear about that, start from the time when you skipped.'

A moment for reorientation. 'Well, I was lucky and I got away clean. I dodged about for the rest of the day then when it was dark I made for her flat. She always said I could count on her if I was in trouble and now was her chance.'

'She knew you were bent?'

'She knew I'd done a few jobs.'

'She approved?'

He grinned. 'She seemed to get a kick out of it. She couldn't hear enough, wanted every detail. She used to egg me on, "Why don't you try something big? So far you've been taking risks for peanuts!" – that sort of talk.'

'So you went to her flat.'

'Yeh, and to give her her due, she made no bones about taking me in, she was tickled to death at the thought of the cops looking for me. I hadn't been there long when she asked me if I'd like to get out of the country. I said the chance would be a fine thing, then she said, "You told me you had a sister in Venezuela, would she take you if you could get there?" I said she would, partly because I believed it and partly because anything is better than going back inside. It may be some people's idea of a rest cure but not mine. I asked her what it was all about but she wouldn't tell me, she just said I'd be surprised at the contacts she had. Anyway, I didn't really believe her. We went on for a few days then one evening she came home and said it was all cut and dried. She told me to get a passport photo from a place down the road and some new clothes. When I was fitted out she gave me fifty quid and said I was to come down here and book in at the Marina.

I was to pretend that I was a seaman waiting for a ship and she would join me later. She told me to keep out of the way and not to let on I knew her when she arrived . . . '

'You didn't know the details of her arrangements?'

'No, she was queer like that, you had to let her make a mystery out of everything.'

'When did you arrive at the Marina?'

'I travelled down Saturday night and got there Sunday morning.'

'When did the girl arrive?'

'Sunday evening but I didn't see her until breakfast-time Monday. She didn't make any move then but she looked in my room afterwards and told me to come to her room that night round eleven. She said, "Later on I shall have company and it wouldn't do for you two to meet." '

'Well?'

Allen shifted his chair to avoid the sun which now streamed into the room from above the roof of the garage. 'Well, I went along at eleven and she told me everything was fixed. She was like a kid with a new toy – excited. She said I was to be put aboard a ship on Sunday night and that I should sail on Monday. Once outside British waters I would be treated like an ordinary passenger and on the other side they would put me ashore in Colombia with no questions asked. I should have five hundred dollars American and a passport good enough to get me across the border with Venezuela.' He lit another cigarette and inhaled deeply, starting off his cough again. When the cough had subsided he went on, 'I asked her where the money was coming from and she said that was the cream of it, her husband would pay.'

'Her husband?'

'That's what she said.'

'What happened then?'

'Happened? – nothing. I went back to my room.'

'You didn't give her a tumble to round off the evening?'

'No, she tried it on but I was in no mood for it. I'd been pretty low with bronchitis and – well, she just had to go without.'

'How did your prints come to be on the photograph in her handbag?'

'I've been thinking about that. I remember she asked me to get her handkerchief from her handbag. I saw the photo and asked her who it was.'

'Why did she carry it round?'

'Search me! She always had some man's photo in her bag, usually more than one.'

'Talking of photographs, did you notice one of her on her dressing table?'

Allen nodded. 'Yeh, in a frame, one she was fond of and carted everywhere with her.'

'When did you see her again?'

'I never did. Next day your blokes were swarming all over the place and as soon as I got the message I decided to beat it when I got the chance.'

'What were you doing in the Voodoo?'

'I had to keep off the streets and it was somewhere to go for the evening.'

'You're a liar!' Wycliffe spoke without heat. 'Do you think it was chance we picked you up as you came out?' He stood up and moved out of the sun, which was striking down exactly where he sat. 'You're not smart enough to be a crook, my lad! It would pay you to go straight. The girl arranged with the Masson-Smythes to have the thing set up for you and you thought you could go back to them and put the screw on a bit – "Look after me or else . . ."'

'That's not true!'

138

'Then why didn't you clear out altogether when you heard the girl had been murdered? Why hang about the town? You had twenty-four hours' start.'

'I was afraid of road checks.'

Wycliffe sighed. 'You make me tired! You're not even a good liar. What did you think when you heard that she'd been murdered?'

Allen looked at him, uncomprehending. 'I was scared – wouldn't you be? I mean, there was I on the spot, I'd been in her room and the police were already after me . . . '

Wycliffe was looking at him in detached appraisal, his stare was unnerving. In the end he made a little gesture. Impatience? Distaste? Helplessness? 'I'm going to send you back where you came from in the morning; you're no use to me. If it turns out that you did kill that girl . . . '

'I didn't kill her – why should I? I lost by it if anybody did!'

Wycliffe shook his head. 'For God's sake get him out of my sight!'

Allen sneered. 'That's the thanks you get – from cops!'

'Thanks for what?'

When they had taken him down Wycliffe stood for a long time looking out of the window and Gill found him there. 'Evening, Mr Wycliffe!'

Wycliffe did not turn round. 'I've just had a tête-à-tête with Allen. He seemed willing enough to talk about the girl but cagey on the subject of the Masson-Smythes. We want enough to put that pair inside so when Fehling comes in let him have another go at Allen – lean on him a bit.'

'I would enjoy leaning on that character myself . . . '

'No doubt, but you'll have to deprive yourself. I want you to ring the Yard, tell them we shall be returning Allen tomorrow. You can also tell them that you are coming up and that you'll need assistance.'

'To do what?'

'Contact the places she's worked at, get on to her former landlady and the neighbours in her new flat . . . Do the rounds, then ring me and tell me who did her in and why.'

Gill perched himself on the edge of Wycliffe's desk. 'When do I leave?'

'Tonight, there's a train around nine.'

'And how long have I got?'

Wycliffe turned to face him. 'Oh, don't hurry yourself, say twenty-four hours. Ring me tomorrow evening.'

Gill grinned. 'A cinch! Especially on a Sunday when London is like the Sahara desert.' He took out one of his cheroots and lit it. 'I haven't got Allen's story fitted in yet. If he's telling the truth, it was he who kept Millie awake in the next room. "Just voices", she said, "a man and a woman talking". Then she heard someone come out of the girl's room – that must have been Allen leaving. But Millie says next time she woke she heard a couple in there quarrelling and that the quarrel ended in lovemaking. We believe that the man who killed her was the man she made love with, so it couldn't have been Allen, he's the wrong blood group.' Gill broke off. 'Am I boring you, sir?'

'No, just confusing me, but carry on if you must.'

'Another visitor then. The man of the fire escape? If we believe Allen, that man could have been her husband come to deliver the money. If you ask me, it's a cock-up of a yarn. I mean, why kill your wife when you've just given her a thousand quid to help her get her lover out of the country?'

Wycliffe moved away from the window and sat at his desk. 'Get off my desk!'

Gill slid off the desk grinning. Wycliffe put his fingers together and stared at them thoughtfully. 'You have a way of making even the truth seem ridiculous, Jim. In any case, you haven't asked the most important question – how does one account for the restraint in killing and frenzied hatred suggested by the disfigurement?'

'I suppose it's possible that she was killed by one man and disfigured by another.'

'It's possible, certainly, but difficult to imagine a reason for it.'

A constable came in with a cup of tea on a tray. 'Sorry, sir, I'll fetch another cup, I didn't know the chief inspector was with you.'

'The chief inspector is leaving,' Wycliffe growled, and when the constable had gone, he went on, 'Run away, Jim. As a Dr Watson you're a dead loss and there isn't room for two Sherlocks.'

It was true, reasoned argument from Gill or from any-one else only confused him. Most of the time it hardly mattered but there came a stage in every case when it mattered a great deal. He seemed to have reached that stage now. He was like a man idly playing with a pack of cards, who finds that he has built or nearly built a clever little card house. Only two or three cards remain to be put in place and suddenly he values what he has contrived almost by accident and is afraid of spoiling it. In every difficult case in which he had eventually been successful, he had known such a time. Suddenly he would find himself in possession of a credible and convincing theory which seemed to need only a little more thought to work it out in compelling detail. It was then that he would pause, reluctant to discuss it, reluctant even to think about it.

Because his success seemed to be a matter of revelation rather than reason he had never developed any self confi-dence and set about every case with the feeling that this time he would be shown up at last. What an attitude of mind for a chief superintendent! He was humiliated by it and kept his self distrust a carefully guarded secret.

With Gill out of the way he felt better. He drank his tea and glanced through the reports in his tray. The Yard had sent someone to talk to the manager of Summit Theatrical Costumiers, the firm whose name appeared on the scrap of paper found in Allen's room with the address of the Marina scribbled on it. 'Yes, we have business dealings with Thelma Masson-Smythe at the Voodoo' . . . 'Yes, all the firm's letters are signed by me with the carbon in place.' Carbon copies of the correspondence with the Voodoo were produced and the fragment was found to match with the carbon copy of a letter dated 17th June regarding a disputed account. The carbon copy was being forwarded.

A bit of evidence linking the Masson-Smythes with Allen which might be useful if either or both persisted in denying the connection. It was obvious that the girl had sent him to the Voodoo and that he had been sent from there to the Marina.

Another of the reports also concerned the Masson-Smythes. They had been questioned about Allen's presence in the club and denied all knowledge of him. 'He is not a member, of course, but unfortunately it is all too easy for non-members to gate-crash . . . No, I've never seen him before.' Acting on instructions, the detective had seemed to accept this assurance without question. 'I hope he was convincing,' Wycliffe muttered. He wanted Allen's statement before he took any action against the Masson-Smythes and he thought that Fehling could be persuasive enough to make it good. He pushed the reports back into the tray and decided to spend the evening with his wife. He felt relaxed again.

He decided to walk, and not far from the station, by the Catholic Church, he almost collided with a woman coming out of the presbytery. She was vaguely familiar, tall and gaunt, wearing a severely tailored black costume and a black toque. Aunt Jane. He was sure that she had not recognized him, in fact, she had probably not even seen him and he could have sworn that her eyes were red with crying. He watched her stepping it out across the square. He wondered what secrets she had been whispering to her priest.

At the corner of Castle Hill a man selling newspapers, and a poster against the wall: *Moonlanding tonight?* He bought a paper and sharing the front page with the Apollo XI astronauts was a smudgy reproduction of Julie's photograph. The face looked back at him, the lips parted in a faint smile, the eyes wide and frank. Both Kathy and Piper had said that the photograph was 'like her' but that there was something not quite right about it. Could it be that the restoration gave her a look of innocence? It was his belief that satisfying sexual experience leaves its mark on the face of a girl. He could not define it but he thought that he knew it when he saw it and he had once called it the Mona Lisa smirk.

'Good evening, superintendent!' It was the little red-headed reporter. 'So you know who she was.'

Wycliffe wagged the paper. 'It doesn't say so here.'

'I write the stuff, I don't read it. What I can't understand is why you've been so coy about publishing the photograph. I could have told you who she was quick enough and so could a good many others in this town.'

'We had a good reason.'

'I suppose I could try the dailies with that.'

'With what?'

'Detective Chief Superintendent Wycliffe told our reporter that the police had good reason for withholding publication of the dead girl's photograph! A nasty-minded editor might smell a rat and come to the conclusion that somebody was getting the blanket treatment.'

Wycliffe laughed. 'What's the time?'

Brown looked at his watch. 'Just gone six.'

'Come and have a drink.'

The pub in Castle Hill backed on to the harbour; in fact, the main bar was built out on stilts so that at high tide it seemed to be afloat. They were the only customers. Wycliffe ordered two beers and carried them to the window seat at the far end of the room. They were close to the quay where the pleasure boats unloaded and at this time the boats were nuzzling each other for positions close to the steps. The passengers from less aggressive ones had to climb over two or even three other boats to reach the steps, but it was all part of the fun. And it was all as stale to the reporter as it was novel to Wycliffe. Brown sipped his beer.

'Now, young man!' Wycliffe ruffled through the papers in his briefcase and came out with one of the photographs taken by the police photographer of the injuries to the dead girl's face. 'Would you have identified her from that?'

Brown gave the photograph one glance and turned away. 'Christ!'

'Exactly. That was all we had to go on.'

Brown was white and for a moment Wycliffe thought he was going to be sick. 'Are you all right?'

'I suppose so. But nobody ever said that . . . '

'No, we deliberately kept quiet about that but it doesn't matter now. I intend to make a statement to the press on Monday. But if you jump the gun . . .!'

'You can rely on me.'

'I hope so. Now, I want something from you. Tell me about the Collinses.'

The reporter was recovering his poise. 'It makes a change being interviewed.'

'You're not being interviewed, my lad, you're being interrogated and don't you forget it.'

'OK. Have it your way. You've met them?'

'I've met them.'

'Well, you know what they're like. Everybody thought that Willie would end up by marrying the woman who does the books . . . ' He snapped his fingers in an effort to recall a name. 'Rogers – Iris Rogers. And she would have taken on where mother left off, if you see what I mean.'

Wycliffe nodded.

'People in the town used to say, "I wonder how much longer poor old Iris will have to wait" – of course they all knew that it would be until the old lady kicked the bucket.'

'The old lady is the boss?'

'You can say that again! Unless Willie was the product of a virgin birth, which wouldn't surprise me, there must have been a father round sometime but not in my day. Of course, the Collinses have got money – real money and it would be worth waiting for.'

'But he married Julie.'

Brown chuckled. 'It was a nine days' wonder – a kid of eighteen and a real doll at that! I mean, everybody wondered what he was going to do to her and what he was going to do it with . . . '

'You confine yourself to the facts, young man!'

'Sorry! I thought you wanted atmosphere, it must be the journalist in me. She was an orphan or something and as I remember it there was nobody at the wedding from her side except the foster mother.'

'Church?'

'You bet! With all the cake and trimmings, a real "do" for the town to gawp at and gossip about. Reception at the Royal.' He grinned. 'Even Aunt Jane was there.'

'Was that surprising?'

'I'll say! Aunt Jane is RC and she thinks the established church is the antichrist. They're a jolly family.'

'How long did Julie stay with them?'

'Six months, maybe. Even before that there was talk.'

'What sort of talk?'

Brown lit a cigarette and considered. 'After the excitement of the wedding had died down it all went quiet for a month or two, she was even helping in the shop and to everybody's surprise it looked as though it might work. Then she started living it up a bit; there's a country club on the Truro road and she was there most nights.'

'With her husband?'

'You must be joking! Anyway it wasn't long before she was involved in a car smash. She wasn't hurt but the driver was. It was Masson-Smythe, the chap at the Voodoo. I suppose he wanted to keep out of trouble with his wife so he said she'd thumbed a lift in the rain and he'd felt sorry for her. Could even have been true but it didn't make any difference to the gossip.'

'Anybody else?'

The reporter drained his glass. 'Have another?'

'No thanks. I asked you if there was anybody else?'

'There was plenty of talk but the only other name named, so to speak, was a chap called Byrne, a schoolteacher at the Greville Road Comprehensive.'

'Then she left him?'

Brown nodded. 'It was rumoured that she'd gone away with Byrne, I lost track of her, then at the beginning of last season she turned up doing her striptease at the

Voodoo. I reckon she did it deliberately and it was bloody cruel. I mean, in this town . . . '

Wycliffe stood up. 'You'll keep quiet about all this?'

Brown grinned. 'You're the boss, but you'll owe me something for Wednesday's issue.'

'It will be all over by then.'

'You're serious?'

Almost to his own surprise Wycliffe decided that he was. They left the pub together. Outside Brown had a final go. 'You'll be seeing Willie tonight?'

Wycliffe looked at him poker-faced. 'The shop's closed for the week-end.'

'Madame is in the Television Lounge, superintendent.'

Since his identity had become known he had received VIP treatment at the hotel and he hated it. He didn't know how to behave; in his anxiety not to appear patronizing he thought that he was probably churlish. All the same, the man called after him, 'A moment, if you please, sir!' The porter was holding a little book. 'Perhaps you will be kind enough to sign my boy's autograph, sir?'

Wycliffe took the book and scrawled his signature.

'And write Detective Chief Superintendent, if you will, sir.'

He found Helen in the television room watching a report on the astronauts. The room was fairly full and all heads turned to look as he came in. 'They put on a photograph of the girl who was murdered and they had one of you on too – one I haven't seen before. You looked as though . . . '

He sat watching the television until dinner time and after dinner they took their coffee out on to the terrace where the light was fading into warm, intimate summer darkness. It was a time for mellowness and ease but he was restless.

After he had lighted his pipe twice and put it out again, Helen asked, 'Why don't you ring the station?'

He pretended not to understand but after a while he said, 'I think I'll take a stroll before bed.'

'I'll expect you when I see you.'

CHAPTER NINE

He did not consciously direct his steps but without any clear idea in his mind about what he would do, he found himself outside the bookshop. Several of the shops in the street had their windows brilliantly lit, the florist's opposite, for example, had a window full of flowers cleverly lit from below and kept fresh by a fine spray which made rainbows in the light. But the bookshop was in total darkness, the old-fashioned blue canvas blinds were down. Looking up, he thought he could see a faint glimmer of light coming from the sitting room of the flat, one of the rooms which overlooked the street.

What were they doing? Was Willie in his room with his soldiers? Was he thinking of Julie? Wycliffe felt guilty; to confront him with the hideously mutilated features of his wife without warning was an act of cruelty. No wonder he had collapsed. In his own way he had deeply loved the schoolgirl to whom his mother had married him. At least he had loved the image he made of her.

What puzzled Wycliffe was his attitude afterwards. He had made no protest and seemed to bear no animosity against the superintendent, yet there had been a change in him not entirely explicable in terms of shock. At first Wycliffe could not make out what it was, then he decided that it was anger, cold anger, suppressed and dangerous. But against whom?

'I'm sorry that I had to submit you to that but it was necessary.'

No answer.

'You realize that your wife was dead before that was done to her?'

'Yes.'

'Have you any idea who could have done it?'

'No.'

'You are sure?'

'Quite sure!'

And that was all. Now he had to probe the wound.

He looked at his watch: a quarter to ten. Perhaps the two women were already in bed. When Julie was there they had played three-handed bridge. What did they do now?

He opened the door of the side passage which ran beside the shop. Almost at the far end there was a door in the left hand wall and a small light over a bell-push which shone on a printed card: *COLLINS. PRIVATE*. He rang the bell. Almost at once he was startled by a woman's voice from close at hand. A speak-box which he hadn't expected. He found the little metal grille and spoke into it.

'Come up, please.'

He opened the door and went up the carpeted stairs, past the green baize door to the bookroom and on up the next flight to the flat. The musty smell of the books pervaded everything. It was Miss Rogers who waited for him on the top landing – Iris, the reporter called her. She was tight lipped. 'You didn't waste much time getting here.'

'I beg your pardon?'

'It's barely ten minutes since Dr Rashleigh phoned you – or at least, he phoned the station.'

'What's the trouble?'

She looked surprised. 'Didn't he tell you?' She sniffed. 'As he was so anxious to drag in the police he'd better tell you himself. He's in the sitting room.'

In the dimly lit room where the brown velvet curtains met and overlapped across the window, Dr Rashleigh stood, elegant, yet restless and incongruous. He seemed relieved to see Wycliffe. 'So you've come yourself. I asked them to tell you but I didn't expect you to come. I don't want to make too much of this but I thought that in view of everything it would be better . . . '

'What exactly has happened?'

'She tried to poison herself it seems.'

'Who?'

Rashleigh looked impatient. 'Why, Aunt Jane, of course! Miss Collins.' Evidently the Collinses were such an established institution in the town that even this rather pompous doctor found it natural to speak of them with familiarity.

'What did she use?'

'Strychnine.'

'A pretty sure method.'

'As a rule, but not this time. She'll be up and about again tomorrow.'

'She's in hospital?'

'I thought it wiser for the night.'

Wycliffe sat down on one of the low armchairs and rested his head back against the embroidered runner. 'Tell me about it.' He got out his pipe and started to fill it. 'You said just now, "She tried to poison herself, it *seems*", – is there any doubt about it?'

Rashleigh looked distastefully at the other armchairs and chose instead a straight-backed dining chair. 'This *is* a depressing room, don't you think? Every time I come here . . . ' His voice trailed off, then he added in a burst of confidence, 'I've been coming to this house for twenty-five years and in all that time I don't think they've moved so much as an ornament!'

It was obvious that he was talking himself into more relevant disclosures. He fiddled with the perfect crease in the fine herringbone tweed of his trousers. It was difficult to credit that perhaps an hour earlier he was wrestling with a case of strychnine poisoning. 'I very much doubt if she intended to kill herself, superintendent. In fact, I strongly suspect that the effect of the strychnine she took was more than she'd bargained for, poor lady.'

'Then why did she take it at all?'

Rashleigh examined the long tapering fingers of a pale hand. 'Some people, especially women who are starved of . . . of affection, feel compelled to draw attention to themselves by some means, however drastic.'

Wycliffe felt like making a rude noise. 'You mean that she's tried it before?'

Rashleigh frowned. 'About three years ago; it was an overdose of a barbiturate which I had prescribed for her insomnia. On that occasion I persuaded her to enter a nursing home for a period.'

'A mental home?'

Rashleigh nodded unhappily. 'Yes.'

'Where did she get the strychnine?'

'Apparently it has been in the house for years, they had it for poisoning rats in the cellar. These old houses by the harbour . . . '

'Why did you send for me?'

Rashleigh bristled. 'I didn't *send* for you!'

'All right, why did you want me to be told?'

The doctor straightened his Greyhounds tie. 'One hears rumours. There must be few people in this town who have not heard that the girl murdered at the Marina was Collins's wife.'

Wycliffe had to acknowledge the truth of that. Kenny the Man, the Masson-Smythes, Sadie, the reporter, not to mention the Collinses themselves; somebody was bound to talk. But he was wilfully obtuse. 'You think that there may be a connection between the murder and this?'

'Certainly not!' Rashleigh was shocked. 'No direct connection that is. The emotional disturbance could well have been the trigger. With an unstable personality . . . '

'But do you discount entirely the possibility that Aunt Jane was poisoned by someone else?'

The doctor stood up to lend emphasis to his disclaimer. 'My dear superintendent! The very idea is unthinkable!'

'Who found her?'

Rashleigh smiled. 'You do not have to *find* someone suffering from strychnine poisoning. She was in her bedroom and her cries were heard by everyone in the flat – by Willie and his mother and by Iris Rogers.'

'What was *she* doing here?'

'You will be able to ask her that question yourself.'

It was odd, the more meticulous and precise the person he had to deal with the more abrupt and boorish his manner was apt to become. It was almost a reflex response. He invited snubs from such people and seemed oblivious of them. In fact, it was an aspect of his own sensitivity. In the presence of fastidiousness he felt that he and his job were being mutely criticized.

'I would like to see her bedroom.'

Rashleigh led the way. The room was next to the sitting room and, like it, overlooked the narrow street. It was large and sparsely furnished; an old-fashioned wooden single bed with slatted head and foot, a wardrobe, a chest of drawers and a table across the window which to judge from the few trinkets on it served as a dressing table. By the bed a small table held a reading lamp and several devotional books. Above the bed, a crucifix. The carpet was threadbare and the bedclothes lay on it in a twisted heap.

'She suffered convulsions, of course, but they were not excessively violent. I administered pentathol intravenously with success.'

Wycliffe looked round the room, bewildered at the perversity of human nature. Here was a woman, no more than middle aged, well-off, by no means stupid . . . He muttered to himself, 'It's masochistic!'

Rashleigh looked at him brightly. 'Isn't it?'

The tumbler was on the mantelpiece next to a plated alarm clock. Wycliffe picked it up; damp white crystals adhered to the sides and there was a similar sediment in the bottom. 'There must be enough here to kill an elephant!'

'There is, but it doesn't dissolve very easily in water, fortunately. She actually got very little down, I imagine.'

'But how do you know that she didn't intend . . . '

'I know my patient.'

'Where did you find the tumbler?'

'It had rolled under the bed.'

'How long after the call before you arrived here, doctor?'

'Not more than ten minutes. I was in my surgery as she well knew that I should be.'

Smug bastard! But he was probably right. 'She was conscious when you arrived?'

'Fully, but she said very little – just kept repeating the words, "God forgive me! God forgive me!" whenever the spasms allowed her to speak.'

'Where are the others?'

The doctor shrugged. 'Willie went to his room, I suppose that he is still there.'

'With his soldiers.'

A faint smile.

'And his mother?'

'Mrs Collins was somewhat excited. I gave her a sedative and she is sleeping.'

Wycliffe fiddled with the trinkets on the dressing table: a cameo brooch, a rosary, a locket . . . He sighed and became, abruptly, almost genial. He thanked the doctor for his cooperation and began to edge him out on to the landing.

'Good night, doctor! I expect that you can find your own way out.'

When Rashleigh had put on his hat and coat, collected his case and departed, Wycliffe stood in the passage outside Willie's door. He had his hand on the knob. In any other household . . . Then he changed his mind and went on down the passage to the kitchen. The door was open and the light was on.

'Here I am, superintendent.' Iris was standing just inside the kitchen door. Had she been eavesdropping? If so she was entirely composed.

The kitchen had been modern in the thirties; a mottled enamel gas cooker and washboiler, a refrigerator with a lot of polished wood in its structure. But everything shone, and, as a bonus, the kitchen overlooked the harbour. The curtains were undrawn and he could see, vaguely, the outline of boats in the darkness.

'I thought you might want to talk to me.'

'Yes.'

'We could go to the sitting room.'

'I like kitchens,' Wycliffe said, which was true.

They sat on cane chairs placed on opposite sides of a large, square, scrubbed table, just like the one that had taken up most of the room in his mother's kitchen. Iris looked out of place in her severely cut two-piece and her no-nonsense blouse. She belonged to an office as surely as a typewriter or a filing cabinet. Wycliffe had known scores like her, hardworking, dependable, their one satisfaction in life being indispensable. She was not bad looking, big boned with a tendency to fleshiness, but her features were good. A slightly pinched look round the nostrils might mean a shrewish temper and when the light caught her at a certain angle it was possible to see golden hairs on her upper lip. Her hair was straw coloured and her skin freckled.

'I want you to know where I stand . . . ' He could have forecast the opening. 'I've worked in this business for sixteen years.'

'A long time.'

She nodded. 'But there's more to it than that; if it hadn't been for that girl – Julie – I should have been married to him by now. I thought that it was better for you to hear it from me rather than from gossip.'

'Are you trying to tell me that you had a motive for the murder?' He couldn't resist provoking her.

She was contemptuous. 'Don't be absurd, I merely wanted you to have your facts right.'

'Thank you. Now, what do you know about this evening's business?'

She reached into her handbag, which lay open on the table, and drew out a silver cigarette case and a lighter to match. 'Smoke?' Wycliffe refused and she lit a cigarette but the hand holding the lighter trembled. Evidently she had less self possession than she liked to admit. 'If you think this affair tonight has anything to do with Julie's death then you're barking up the wrong tree. Aunt Jane is queer in the head – she's done this sort of thing before but she's no intention of killing herself.'

'Then why pretend? It's a hazardous business.'

Iris blew out a thin spiral of smoke and watched it rise. 'She did it to bring Willie to heel.'

'I don't understand.'

She looked at him doubtfully. 'Have you ever seen them together – Willie and his aunt?'

'I have.'

'Then you must have noticed. She dotes on him, it's

pathological. To her, he's the son she's never had and the man she's never married.'

Wycliffe smiled faintly. He took out his half smoked pipe and asked permission to light it. 'What about tonight?'

She reached a saucer from the dresser to do duty as an ashtray. 'There was a row, I don't know what about. On Saturday nights I stay on late to square up the books for the week. I'd finished downstairs and when I came up to the flat as usual to tell Willie I was going, she was outside his door begging him to let her in. She was crying.'

'What happened?'

'When she saw me she went to her own room. I called to Willie to let me in and he did. He was obviously very upset but I couldn't get out of him what it was about. It was while I was with him that she started to scream.'

Wycliffe was watching her with a mild fixity of expression, almost as though his thoughts were elsewhere and when he spoke it was to say something not directly relevant. 'You would have married Mr Collins if . . .?'

'If I'd had the chance – yes.' She stubbed out her cigarette in the saucer with a vigorous jab.

'The match he made seems to have been unfortunate.'

'Unfortunate! It was absurd and disastrous!'

'One would have thought that his mother and his aunt would have persuaded him . . .'

'They encouraged him! At least his mother did.'

'Indeed?'

'Yes. That seems odd to you, doesn't it? But she had a good reason – to stop him marrying me.'

'Mrs Collins disapproved of you?'

Her nostrils looked more pinched now and there were spots of colour in her cheeks. 'As a daughter-in-law, yes. She knew that once I was Willie's wife things would be different. I'm no teen-aged girl to dance to her tune. In her eyes, Willie's interest in Julie was an answer to a prayer, a young girl, an orphan, who could be brought up in the way she should go. With her, "Yes, Mrs Collins, No, Mrs Collins, It's very kind of you, Mrs Collins", the old lady thought that butter wouldn't melt in her mouth. For once, she was wrong!' Iris lit a second cigarette and smoked rapidly, making the tobacco glow and crackle and expelling the smoke in bursts. As Wycliffe watched her he was mildly perturbed at the antagonism he felt towards her. Surely she had the right to be resentful?

'How did he first meet the girl?'

'She used to come to the shop – into the secondhand department. At first she came with other girls and I think they did it for a lark, there used to be a lot of giggling, but the rest soon got tired of it and she came alone. She was at the grammar school doing "A" levels in history and English and, to give her her due, I think she had a genuine feeling for books. She soon got talking to Willie, who is more of a scholar than a business man, and he used to help her with her essays and advise her on her reading. Of course she was flattered by the attention of an older man and it was a novel experience for Willie to have a pretty young girl with auburn hair and violet eyes hanging on his every word. Of course, she saw her chance . . . '

'Are you saying that she set out to . . . '

'To seduce him – certainly she did!'

'A man double her age?'

She made a little contemptuous noise with her lips. 'You men are all the same, even policemen who should know better! You'll never believe that young girls can be truly wicked – certainly not the ones with a pretty face and nice legs. You should have seen this one go to work! "You make me feel so stupid! It's all crystal clear when you explain it. If you were a teacher . . . I feel so guilty, wasting your time like this . . . " And on another tack: "I suppose I've had a sad life, really . . . I often wonder . . . if my parents hadn't been killed. Daddy was a painter . . . " Actually daddy was a carpenter and they were taking their first holiday abroad – Majorca, I think it was, but she made it sound as though they took planes as we take buses.'

'She seems to have fooled Mrs Collins successfully, a difficult feat if I'm any judge.' Wycliffe was cool.

'She was taken in because she wanted to be!' Iris was more at her ease now. 'Of course you are writing off most of what I say on the grounds that I'm a frustrated old maid, a bit warped and more than a bit spiteful. Up to a point you may be right but there's more to it than that. As I said, I've worked in this business for sixteen years and without any false modesty I've saved it from the fate of most bookshops in towns of this size. I felt I had a stake in the place and I didn't see why I should be cheated of it by a scheming chit of a girl!'

Wycliffe looked at the chin, the set of the jaw and the pursed lips. 'The marriage lasted only a few months and it is two years since she left him – a year since she left the town altogether. During that time have you resumed your old relationship?'

She stubbed out her cigarette butt. 'Obviously we couldn't get married.'

'He had grounds for divorce.'

For some reason she flushed and shook her head. 'He wouldn't – at least . . . '

'What were you going to say?'

She hesitated. 'I was going to say that his attitude seemed to be changing in recent months. Given time I think he might have agreed, then she came back . . . '

Whether she realized it or not she was gilding the lily as far as motive went. She had reason enough to kill but surely not in the particular way that Julie died?

'And now that she is dead?'

She looked up angrily and seemed on the point of protesting but changed her mind. 'I don't know. I don't know anything any more.'

Wycliffe smoked in silence for a while. 'Before he met his wife, were you engaged?'

'No, there was an understanding, I told you.'

'What does that mean?'

'I don't know what you're asking me.'

'Did you go to bed with him?'

Again the colour flooded her cheeks. 'Yes.'

'And now?'

Her reply was barely audible. 'Yes.' She made an angry movement. 'What does that make me?'

'I don't know. Compassionate or determined, it depends on your motive.'

She looked at him sharply but said nothing. Wycliffe sat with his elbows on the table and for at least two minutes the silence was unbroken except for the ticking of the kitchen clock. 'What has been the effect on Willie of his wife's death?'

She leaned back in her chair, more relaxed. 'I wish I knew. I can't understand him. I mean, he knew that she was dead on Wednesday and of course he was upset – desperately upset, but he was normal, if you know what I mean. He was just as you might expect him to be . . . '

'But now?'

'Since you were here yesterday he's changed. I can't explain it but it frightens me. I mean, he's doing all the usual things and when you speak to him he answers you quite sensibly, but you get the impression he isn't really there at all. He's like a man walking in his sleep but I can't find out what it is.'

'He won't discuss it with you?'

'No.'

'You know that I took him to identify his wife's body?'

'Yes, but seeing her shouldn't have affected him like that, surely?'

Wycliffe reached for his briefcase and took out the photograph of the dead girl's face. He placed it on the table within her reach. 'That may explain it.'

She took the photograph and glanced at it. 'My God! You let him see that!'

'The girl was murdered, that's all that matters to me – murdered and mutilated after death.'

'Whoever did that must be mad!' She shuddered involuntarily then went quiet, 'You don't think that he . . . '

'How do I know what to think?'

'But Willie couldn't! I mean violence of any sort appalls him. He's gentle . . . ' She stopped, looking at Wycliffe. 'Nothing I can say will make any difference, will it?'

He shrugged.

After a while she got up. 'I'd better go.'

'No.'

She looked at him in surprise but sat down again.

'Does the old lady suffer from heart trouble?'

'Why, yes . . . '

'Serious?'

'I suppose so, the doctor says any sudden shock might kill her. Actually I think she's shock proof except where Willie is concerned.'

'What about Aunt Jane?'

His manner was different, more relaxed. The way he said 'Aunt Jane' almost made her laugh. 'She's as strong as a horse.'

'Any insanity in the family?'

She became guarded once more. 'Well, you know about

161

Aunt Jane – whether you call that insanity I don't know.'

'And?'

She fiddled with the clasp of her bag. 'Willie's father died in the asylum but that was before I started to work here.' She looked across at Wycliffe meeting his placid gaze. 'I know what you're thinking, but Willie is as sane as you or me.'

'When did you first hear that Julie had been murdered?'

She became obviously agitated. 'I heard about the murder Wednesday lunchtime but I didn't know that it was her.'

'Who told you that it was?'

She hesitated. 'I heard it from somebody yesterday – after you'd been.'

'You're a bad liar!'

She stood up, flushed and angry. 'I'm leaving!'

'No!' His manner startled her. 'I'm conducting a murder inquiry, Miss Rogers, and I will not listen to fairy tales. Please sit down and answer my questions truthfully. When did you first hear that Julie was back in town?'

'I don't know what you're talking about.'

He leaned forward in his chair and spoke confidentially. 'If you are frank now you may save yourself a great deal of embarrassment later. You have already told me – perhaps unwittingly – that Mr Collins and, by implication, you also, knew on Wednesday that it was Julie who had been murdered. Now I want to know when it was you heard that she had come back?'

She gave in and sat down. 'I saw her just as she got off the coach on Sunday evening when I was on my way home from church.'

'Where do you live?'

She gestured vaguely. 'Up on the terraces, I have a flat.'

'Alone?'

'Yes.'

'Did Julie see you?'

'I'm sure she didn't; she was getting her luggage from the boot of the coach and talking to the driver.'

'But you had no doubt that it was she?'

'I'd know her anywhere.'

'How did you find out that she was staying at the Marina?'

'I followed her.'

'She took a taxi.'

'So did I – from the same rank.'

'Why?'

'Because I wanted to know where she was going. I've never made the mistake of underestimating her ability to cause trouble.'

'Didn't it strike you as odd that she should stay at a place like the Marina?'

'I couldn't understand it.'

'You told Willie you'd seen her?' It was inevitable that he would drop into the habit of calling them all by their intimate family names.

'I rang him as soon as I got home, it seemed the natural thing to do.'

'Of course, what was his reaction?'

She hesitated. 'It's difficult to say.'

'You mean that he seemed to know already?'

She looked steadily at the table top and said nothing. He could see that she was close to tears and tears did not come easily to her. He stood up and went to the window to give her a moment to recover. Not much to be seen, just the shadowy outlines of the moored craft and the shimmering paths of their riding lights. 'Did you expect Julie to leave him?'

He heard her stifle a sob. 'I didn't know at first, I wasn't sure what she was prepared to give up. Then she started going out in the evenings and there were rumours about one or two men . . . '

'Masson-Smythe?'

'Smythe first, he runs the club where she went to work in the end, then there was a schoolteacher called Byrne.' She shook herself as though to rid her body of some cloying contact. 'Can you understand a girl like that? It was Byrne she went off with but it only lasted a week or two.' She laughed. 'Not even a long hot summer. Then she was back again.'

'You saw her go into the Marina on Sunday evening, was that the last you saw of her?'

'Yes.'

'Did you or Willie mention her again?'

'No.'

'Not even when you heard about the murder?'

'Well, yes. I heard about the murder from a customer. Willie had been at the printing works all the morning and when he came back, I said, "Was it her?" He was as white as death and he just said, "Yes".'

'Nothing more?'

She shook her head. 'He burst out crying.'

Wycliffe stood for a while, apparently lost in thought. Actually, though ideas chased each other through his mind they could hardly be said to have any pattern of rational consecutive thought. A mother's boy at thirty-six finds himself in love, probably for the first time in his life. The man on the fire escape – who was he? What did he see? Group AB? A question easily answered – too easily; he wasn't ready for that yet. He had once shocked a subordinate by saying, 'I like to have a theory before I get lumbered with too many facts!' Now the story was often told against him, but it was true. In this case he wanted to get the psychology right before he blundered into accusations of guilt. Could Willie have battered his dead wife's features into an unrecognizable tangle of skin and flesh and bone? Wycliffe felt sure that if he had killed his wife it was an unpremeditated crime – 'almost accidental' he had said to Gill. The restraint in the killing, the violence of the disfigurement – he kept coming back to it. Fear? Who else would need or want to disfigure the girl?

He was half surprised to find himself still in the kitchen with Iris sitting at the table watching him. The clock showed five minutes to eleven. It was beginning to rain, he could see the water beginning to run down the window panes, playing tricks with the harbour lights. 'Is there much cash kept in the flat or in the shop?'

The question surprised her. 'Some nights there may be as much as three or four hundred pounds in the safe in my office.'

'That money is in your charge?'

'Of course.' She added, 'Willie has a key.'

'Are cheques drawn on the business account signed by Willie alone?'

'They are not signed by Willie at all, the business belongs to his mother for her lifetime and she signs the cheques.'

'What about Aunt Jane?'

Iris bridled. 'It has nothing whatever to do with her!'

'But surely she must have shared in her father's will?'

'She was left certain investments which, by all accounts, have done very well for her.'

'Well, thank you Miss Rogers, you've been very helpful.'

'You're going?'

'Yes.'

'You're not seeing Willie?'

'Not tonight.'

165

She seemed reluctant to let him go. 'I hope that I haven't given you the impression . . . ' She saw the look on his face and stopped. 'All right, I'm on the telephone at home as well as here. If you want me . . . '

'Yes.' He hesitated. 'Will the old lady be all right in the house with only Willie?'

Iris smiled. 'I've been thinking about that, perhaps I'd better stay here tonight.'

He decided to look in at the station on his way back to the hotel. To his surprise he found Fehling in the HQ room, his bulk squeezed into one of the bentwood armchairs, busy writing. 'Still here? Any progress with Allen?'

Fehling's satisfaction was unmistakable. 'He's made a fresh statement, sir.'

'Involving the Masson-Smythes?'

'Up to the neck! The girl sent him to the Masson-Smythes and they made the arrangements. This fellow Pellow is their go-between with the ships and he's done similar jobs before. Allen isn't very bright and when the girl was killed he panicked and went there.'

'Good!'

Wycliffe stood by the window watching the rain. A constable came in and began to collect dirty teacups from among the litter on the tables. Outside the rain was falling vertically, thin threads that gleamed in the light of the street lamps. The square was almost deserted, a single taxi on the rank, a man and a girl under one umbrella hurrying home. He turned to Fehling. 'It's time you got some sleep, Mr Fehling, but there are a couple of things I'd like you to lay on tomorrow. Pick up Dippy Pellow, quietly, without making a fuss. With Allen's statement and what you get from him, you should have enough to book him. Make sure the Voodoo is kept under observation but don't bring the Masson-Smythes in unless they try to make a bolt for it. One more thing, fix it so that Kathy Johnson can see Masson-Smythe without him knowing. I want to see if she recognizes him.'

'Anything else, Mr Wycliffe?'

Wycliffe was wandering aimlessly round the room as though loath to leave. 'What? Oh, no! Have a good night.'

He went down the stairs and out of the front door into the rain, his shoulders hunched, and by the time he reached his hotel he was soaked to the skin.

CHAPTER TEN

Wycliffe hoped that Sunday would prove uneventful and
that he would have time to think. After breakfast – nine
o'clock on Sundays – he went out on to the terrace to
smoke his first pipe of the day. He was on his own –
Helen had made friends with some local people who had
a motor launch and she was going with them across the
bay to explore a bit of Daphne du Maurier country. He
could have gone with them but though he intended to
have a lazy day his conscience would not allow him to
break contact for eight or nine hours. In any case it was
pleasant on the terrace. The sky was deep blue with fleecy
white clouds and at dozens of moorings peppered all over
the harbour boat owners were bailing out, scrubbing down,
checking motors or rigging – whatever they were doing it
seemed to be delectable employment to Wycliffe. Nearby
a boy and a girl were cooking breakfast on a bottle-gas
stove on the deck of a little sailing craft. They must
have been hard put even to sleep in the tiny cabin. The
boy wore shorts and the girl a bikini. Wycliffe secretly
wished that he could have his youth over again in this
permissive society on which so much is blamed. It looked
good enough to him that morning.

He sat in one of the wicker chairs and read the two
glossy Sundays, mostly about Apollo XI, until the church
bells started ringing. One, close by, a cracked bell, tolled
so rapidly that it imparted a sense of urgency to its message
while across the water a more melodious cadence nicely
countered its monotony. Sunday: there was something in

the air at the same time relaxing and inhibiting. Because of his Methodist upbringing he associated it with the smell of pitch pine pews and hymn books. When the bar opened he had a drink brought to him on the terrace.

'Excuse me . . . Superintendent Wycliffe? . . . My name is Byrne . . . '

A stockily built young man, fair haired with a good-natured, not very intelligent face, and rugby player written all over him. 'It's about the photograph in the newspaper – I knew the girl . . . ' He loomed over Wycliffe, standing first on one leg then on the other.

'Pull up a chair. Drink?'

'What? – No thank you . . . yes, I think I will, a beer if I may . . . '

Wycliffe signalled the waiter. The terrace was getting busy with people who wanted to get in some drinking time before lunch. They sat watching the harbour while they waited for the drinks. The young couple from the sailing boat were swimming now, chasing each other in the water and laughing. Byrne looked miserable, *la dolce vita* had landed him where he was now. The waiter came back with his beer and a whisky for Wycliffe.

'Cheers!'

'Cheers!'

Wycliffe put down his glass, his grey eyes on the young man. 'You went off with her, stayed with her about three weeks, then came back without her. Now let's have the details.'

Byrne looked relieved by this approach, he relaxed. 'I met her at a Rugby Club dance.'

'Are you married?'

'I am now but I wasn't then.' He hesitated. 'I want to keep my wife out of this if it can be managed. She's Welsh and just a bit . . . '

'Go on.'

'Well, I know it sounds odd but she made a bee line for me. You'd have thought I was the only man in the room.'

'She must like 'em stocky,' Wycliffe muttered, remembering Allen.

'Pardon?'

'Never mind!'

'Afterwards I wanted to take her home but she said that wasn't on.'

'Did you know who she was?'

'No, not then. Anyway, she asked me if I lived with my parents and I said I didn't, I had a flat. I must admit I was a bit taken aback when she said, "That's all right then, I'll take *you* home".' He looked out over the water. 'I suppose I was still a bit wet behind the ears but I couldn't make her out; I wondered if I'd picked up a pro without knowing it.'

'What happened?'

He turned his frank blue eyes on Wycliffe. 'I never knew a girl could be like that! And yet she was so small and so . . . ' He fumbled for a word.

'Exquisite.'

He agreed at once. 'Yes, that's the word for her – exquisite and yet she was like . . . like . . . Well, I suppose every man has sort of sex fantasies. I mean he never expects them to come true, he never expects to find a woman who . . . But she *insisted* . . . ' He broke off, at a loss for words to describe his relationship with the girl. The language of eroticism is limited and follows a tricky path between mere clinical description and obscenity.

'So you owe her something?'

He looked at the superintendent suspecting a joke but the grey eyes were serious. 'Owe her something?'

'For helping to make a man of you. You are probably a better husband because of her.'

He looked surprised. 'Yes, I suppose so, I'd never thought of it like that.'

Wycliffe emptied his glass. 'You continued to see her and finally took her away with you although, by then, you must have known that she was a married woman. Did you intend to go for good?'

Byrne felt that in some way the question was loaded against him and he bungled his answer. 'For good? I don't know, I suppose so, but I had my work to think of, hadn't I?' He paused, his brows creased in an effort to recall the past and to present it in a not too damaging light. 'During the few months from the time we met until we parted in Torquay it was as though I was permanently drunk. I mean, here was I, an ordinary chap to whom this tremendous thing had happened! That's how it seemed to me at the time – you understand?' He was pathetically anxious to be understood, like most people with a guilty conscience. '*Nothing* else mattered. If she'd been married to my own brother it wouldn't have made any difference.'

'And yet you walked out on her.'

The young couple were back on their boat. She was lying face downwards on the cabin roof, she had removed her bra and he was rubbing her back with sun lotion. Byrne was watching them, his mind in a whirl. He had rationalized and tidied up the whole episode with Julie months ago, before he got married, seeing himself, relatively, in a favourable light. At least he had had the sense to get away from a dangerous woman! Now here was this grave-faced policeman turning the whole thing topsy turvy, making it seem that he had been the prime mover, that he was in the girl's debt, that he had 'walked out on her'!

'Why did you leave her?'

He clasped his hands round one knee and rocked gently to and fro in his chair. 'I suppose I realized that there was no future in it.' It was not the answer he would have given ten minutes earlier.

'You came back together?'

'No, I left her in Torquay, I didn't even know that she had come back until I heard that she was appearing at the club.'

'Did you see her again?'

'No. About a year ago I heard that she had left the town. I got married shortly afterwards and I neither saw nor heard anything of her until last week.'

'Then?'

'I had a letter from her saying that she was coming back and that she might look me up for old times' sake.'

'You still have the letter?'

'No, I destroyed it in case Gwyn should come across it.'

'Did she tell you where to find her?'

'No.'

'Did you try to find her?'

He shook his head. 'No, I was terrified that she would come looking for me.'

'You didn't go to the Marina?'

'I swear I didn't. I might have done if I'd known, just to persuade her to let bygones be bygones.'

Wycliffe sat back in his chair. 'All right, Mr Byrne, thank you for coming, I'll get in touch if I need you again.'

'You'll remember about Gwyn – not knowing?' The eyes were pleading.

'I'll remember.' He almost added, 'Why don't you tell her before her friends do?' But his job was crime not marriage guidance. All the same he chuckled as he went in to his lonely lunch. 'I wonder if he's managed to teach Gwyn any of Julie's little tricks.'

He had just finished his lunch and was considering smoking a pipe on the terrace when he was paged by the loudspeakers. Fehling was on the telephone, obviously pleased with himself.

'Any luck?'

'Kathy Johnson identified Masson-Smythe as the man she found going through the register at the Marina. I found out that he patronizes the bar at the Royal on Sunday mornings so I sent DC Hartley along with Kathy to have a drink. She's positive he's the man.'

'Good!'

'And we've picked up Pellow. He was a bit truculent at first but once he realized we had it on him he was ready to cough fast enough. Actually he's not too sorry to get one in on the Masson-Smythes for getting mixed up with Allen. "A small time runt who'd grass on his own mother!" – Pellow's description.'

Wycliffe could almost sympathize. No professional would have loused up an organization like the Voodoo, if only because he might need it one day.

'He's admitted to three other cases in the past eighteen months, including Frank Ellison.'

'The Hatton Garden chap?'

'That's the man. Eighty thousand pounds' worth of uncut stones, never traced.'

'It will be a feather in your cap if you can get a line on that lot, Mr Fehling!' But to tell the truth, Wycliffe was not interested. 'Where is Pellow now?'

'In the cells.'

'And Allen?'

'We packed him off on the train this morning.'

'No news of Jim Gill yet?'

'He only arrived in London at six this morning, sir.'

'All right. You've done very well, Mr Fehling. Did you get any sleep last night?'

'A few hours, sir.'

'What about lunch?'

'I've had a canteen lunch, sir, but don't worry about me, if there's anything I can do . . .'

Fehling had the enthusiasm of a very young schoolboy. Wycliffe hesitated. 'I'll ring you back in a few minutes.' He dropped the receiver, looked up the number of the Voodoo and dialled.

'Masson-Smythe speaking.'

'Chief Superintendent Wycliffe.'

'Yes?' A blend of caution and habitual self confidence.

'I would like to see you as soon as possible.'

Thelma's voice in the background: 'Who is it?' And her husband too concerned to remember to cover the mouthpiece: 'Wycliffe.'

'Shall we say this afternoon at the police station?'

A momentary hesitation. 'I'm afraid that this afternoon will not be convenient, perhaps tomorrow at my office.'

Wycliffe recognized the professional, feeling out the ground. He was decisive. 'I think that it had better be this afternoon, here.'

'Very well, if you insist, though what more I can tell you . . .'

'Let us say at two thirty, then.'

A moment later Wycliffe was speaking to Fehling again. 'I've made an appointment with Masson-Smythe at the station for two thirty and I want you to keep it. Question him about his travel agency – lean on him, but keep off the girl and her death. I'll give you an hour, then I'll take over.'

Fehling was pleased.

The superintendent spent half an hour on the terrace. He then strolled through the deserted streets to the police station. It seemed that most of the population must be on the beach or out in boats and the square had been taken over by the pigeons, strutting up and down between the rows of parked cars. Outside the station, an E-type Jag, parked against the kerb. The wages of sin. From the desk he phoned Fehling, who came down a few minutes later.

'We've got him, sir. He's a slippery customer but he knows that he can't talk his way out of this one. We can slap half a dozen charges on him over the Allen business but it's going to be the devil of a job to get him on the others. It's Pellow's word against his.'

Wycliffe looked sympathetic but at heart he was only interested in Masson-Smythe in so far as he might shed light on Julie's murder. 'All right, I'll take over now and you can have another go later.'

Masson-Smythe was in Wycliffe's office, sitting in the chair by the desk. He looked changed; despite his natty summer suiting in fashionable cinnamon, he looked bedraggled. He was holding his glasses in his hand, leaving white circles round his eyes in contrast with his flushed features.

'Well, Mr Smythe, this man Allen seems to have caused both of us quite a lot of trouble.'

Masson-Smythe looked at him dully. Wycliffe beamed. 'Amateurs! Fortunately you and I are professionals and we know the score.'

Masson-Smythe said nothing but wiped his glasses and put them back on.

Wycliffe turned over the papers on his desk. 'You told me that you employed Julie Collins in your cabaret on the strength of a visit she made to your club on a rehearsal afternoon. You auditioned her and offered her a four month contract.'

'That is correct.'

'You did not tell me that for some time before you had, as the phrase goes, been on terms of intimacy with her.'

Masson-Smythe drew out a silver cigarette case. 'May I smoke?' He lit a Turkish cigarette and blew a cloud of pungent, silver grey smoke into the air. He was recovering confidence. 'I answered the questions you asked, superintendent.'

'I see. Would it be true to say, then, that you engaged her because she threatened to tell your wife of your relationship?'

'That would not be true. I offered her a contract because I thought she had the makings of a first-class cabaret artiste and events have proved me right.'

Wycliffe smiled. 'A club like yours, although it makes its money out of visitors, depends for its continued existence on the good will or at least the tolerance of influential locals. Knowing this, you employ the wife of one of the town's most respected business men simply because she's pretty good at taking her clothes off in public. Frankly, I don't believe it!' He brought out his half-smoked pipe and relit it, watching Masson-Smythe over the undulant flame of the match. 'But that is unimportant . . . ' He broke off abruptly, looking across at DC Rees who sat in the corner taking notes. 'I suppose Mr Masson-Smythe has been formally cautioned? . . . Good! We must keep the record straight.'

The superintendent seemed to be in no hurry, he shuffled through the litter of papers on his desk and then, without looking up, 'What were you doing in the Marina on Monday evening?' Make your man comfortable, then kick the chair away.

Masson-Smythe stopped with his cigarette halfway to his lips. 'I don't know what you're talking about.'

Wycliffe was as bland as mother's milk. 'Oh, come, Mr Smythe! I have a statement here from a witness; not a shadow of doubt. In any case I can't see why you need be so coy. After all, we know that it was at Julie's instigation that you were arranging Allen's passage. Surely, that's what you've been talking to Mr Fehling about?'

Masson-Smythe leaned forward in his chair. 'All right, I went to the Marina to see her but she wasn't in.'

'So when did you see her?'

Now he was like a chess player, trying to foresee his opponent's next move. His hand went to his waistcoat pocket and his fingers searched for something they did not find. 'She telephoned me.'

'Saying what?' Wycliffe was intrigued by the movement of his right hand, he was passing his thumb over his fingers continuously in a rolling movement. A nervous idiosyncrasy, but an odd one.

'She telephoned to fix up details about Allen.'

'She must have had a considerable hold over you for you to take on that job. After all, Allen hadn't a penny and you must have known that he was no more than a petty thief. She was blackmailing you, wasn't she, Mr Smythe?'

Again the fruitless investigation of his waistcoat pocket and a resumption of the rolling movement of fingers and thumb.

'Think about your answer by all means. I have a colleague in London at this moment, searching her flat. I also have a witness who will state that Julie had a hold over both you and your wife while she was still under contract at the club. You were in a cleft stick over this man Allen. Far from turning him down or even making a little on the deal, you had to subsidize him. Julie had a thousand pounds in notes in her room when she died – when did you hand them over, Mr Smythe?'

'I gave her no money, I swear it!' Fingers and thumb were working overtime now, and suddenly their message was clear to Wycliffe. He put his hand into the pocket of his jacket and his fingers closed over a little steel ball-bearing, the one Fehling had found under the girl's bed.

'Do you think we could have the window open?' Masson-Smythe was sweating profusely, the perspiration running down his temples and filming his spectacles.

Wycliffe got up and opened the window himself, letting in the raucous screaming of gulls who were quarrelling over scraps thrown out from the canteen.

'I don't deny that I have given her money in the past. If your people have searched her flat they must have evidence that she was blackmailing me anyway.'

'How much and how often?'

'Perhaps five or six hundred over the past year.'

'Not bleeding you, then?'

'No, I had the impression that she thought I might be useful in other ways and, of course, I was right.'

'Her threat was exposure to the police?'

'She didn't threaten.' He lit another cigarette and inhaled deeply. He was silent for some time and Wycliffe let him be. The little clock on the mantelpiece dominated the room with its loud metallic tick. When he next spoke his whole manner seemed to have changed. 'I've knocked about the world since I was a boy of sixteen and there isn't much that can surprise me now. But that girl . . . ! I knew I was a damn fool to get mixed up with her. She was a shrewd, calculating bitch, but she had what it takes to hold a man. She was like a drug, you kept coming back though you knew she would finish you in the end. I was like a kid with his first girl.'

'How did she find out?'

He laughed. 'Pillow talk! Me! I wanted to impress her and she would lie there with her ears pinned back cooing away and then – Wham!' The suave tight-lipped mask had slipped to reveal a coarser, more violent personality

178

underneath. His speech was different, even his postural reflexes seemed to have changed for he lounged in his chair where previously he had sat almost primly, conscious of his dignity. Now he looked out of place in his smart dandified clothes.

But he had stopped the rolling movement of his fingers and thumb, the tension had gone.

Wycliffe looked at the almost expressionless, almost immobile features and suddenly he understood. 'It was something more than your little racket which Julie held over you, wasn't it? It was not so much what you were doing as *who you were*.'

'There's no point in denying it now, is there, copper? I've known for eight years that I had only to get myself nicked once and it would be all up.' He stroked his cheek. 'They can alter your face but they can't change your dabs.'

'Where did you break from?'

'The Moor.'

It had become a parlour guessing game with Smythe furnishing the clues and Wycliffe doing the guessing.

'Eight years ago . . . McClaren, the bank robber.' Wycliffe racked his memory. 'A bank in Holborn, you and three others, a bystander was shot and killed – shot when he tried to interfere. You got over the wall with . . . '

'Nick Crane but he was picked up.' Masson-Smythe seemed delighted to be remembered as though they were old friends meeting after a lapse of years.

Wycliffe remembered the case, not because he was involved, but because of the cold-blooded killing of a courageous young man who had tried to stop them getting away. 'You got fifteen years and you served two . . . '

'Three.'

'And they never recovered the money.'

'No.'

Young Rees had become so absorbed in the drama being played out before him that he had forgotten to take notes. Not that it mattered, Masson-Smythe, or McClaren, had gone beyond the point of no return. Wycliffe picked up the telephone. 'Ask Dr Rashleigh if he will kindly come to the station to do a blood test – a grouping test . . . Yes, as soon as possible, please.'

'What's that in aid of?'

'You'll see.'

'I didn't kill her.'

'No? You had ample motive and you've killed before.'

'That's not true. I didn't know there was a shooter in the outfit. Even the judge said there was no evidence to show which of us fired the shot.'

He was right, the gun had been left at the scene and it hadn't been possible to establish which of the three men had used it.

'Why did you go to the Marina on Tuesday night?'

'You mean Monday, surely?'

'Don't stall! It will do you no good as well you know! Why did you go to the girl on Tuesday night, the night she was killed?'

Smythe still hesitated and Wycliffe took the little steel ball from his pocket and lobbed it over. 'You left your calling card and you left the money – a thousand pounds in used notes.'

Smythe caught the steel ball, glanced at it and laid it on the desk in the ashtray. 'All right, I went there, but I didn't leave her any money.'

'Why did you go?'

'She insisted. As far as the money goes you can check my bank account . . . '

'A fat lot of good that would be. It would surprise me if you don't keep that amount of cash on hand. Anyway, if she didn't want money why did she tell you to come?'

He shook his head. 'I don't know but it was just like her. She could never resist cracking the whip. The point is, when I got there she was already dead.'

Wycliffe looked at him through narrowed eyes. 'You expect me to believe that?'

'It's straight up.'

'What time did you get there?'

'One o'clock was the time she gave me but I was early, say twenty or a quarter to.' He stopped to light a cigarette. 'The front door was unlocked as she told me it would be and I followed her directions. The bedroom door was a bit open and there was a light on. I think I called her name, but there was no answer and then I pushed the door wide open and went in . . .'

'Go on.'

'She was lying on the bed, naked. At first I thought that she was up to her games, then I thought she might be asleep and I touched her. She was warm but completely limp. I wondered if she was drugged but when I tried her heart and pulse there was nothing – not a dicky bird.'

'So?'

'I scarpered. I got out of that place like a bat out of hell! I mean, what else could I do?'

'When you saw her on the bed how did she look?'

'Look? I've just told you, like she was sleeping though it seemed a bit odd to be sleeping naked with no bedclothes over her.'

'Did you see a door-stop in the room? A brass weight?'

'Was that what it was? I nearly tripped over the bloody thing in the middle of the floor.'

'Did you have intercourse with her?'

'Christ, no! What sort of bloody pervert do you take me for?'

'Did you search her room?'

Masson-Smythe leaned forward in his chair. 'Look, skip, do me a favour and get this straight: I went to the room, I found her lying there, I made sure she was dead and I scarpered. With my problems what else could I do?' He looked at Wycliffe intently, his eyes anxious. 'You do believe me?'

'There's no reason why I should.' Wycliffe picked up the telephone once more. 'I'm having you taken down. Later you'll be asked to make a formal statement.'

DC Rees went out with Masson-Smythe and Wycliffe remained in his chair, staring into space. Was Smythe telling the truth? Convicted of robbery with violence, an escaped convict with the strongest motive for killing the girl, was it likely that someone else had murdered her and that he had arrived, innocently, to find her dead? Yet it was too easy to pin the thing on him. And what about the disfigurement? If Masson-Smythe had found her dead, did he then set about destroying her features? And if so, why? A sudden flooding tide of anger? Most professionals were not like that, they seldom let their hearts rule their heads. But had he a motive for disfiguring her? Perhaps. An unidentified corpse found in a hotel bedroom doesn't worry anybody much but the police *as long as it remains unidentified*. But Julie Collins's corpse would soon bring the cops to his doorstep.

Wycliffe sighed and turned his thoughts to Julie herself. He knew quite a lot about her now, but the facts, put together, made a strange pattern – or no pattern at all. Although he knew well enough that human motives are always complex, that every man is a battleground of conflicting desires and emotions, he had still found it useful to try to pin-point a single dominant drive in accounting for any course of action. Greed, jealousy, love, ambition, lust . . . Single words, powerful words, and convenient shorthand with which to label the motives of a man – or of a woman. But Julie refused to be pigeon-holed. His mental vision of her remained as enigmatic as his first actual sight of her, lying across her hotel bed, naked, in the posture of love.

Plenty of amateur psychologists would have little difficulty in explaining Julie. A neglected child, orphaned at an age when she needed a sense of security most – they would see in her ruthlessness, in the exercise of her power over men, a desire to hit back. And into her frenzied promiscuity they might read a continuing and unsatisfied yearning to identify herself with other human beings, to be accepted. Perhaps they would be right, but Wycliffe felt that such explanations were too facile, they were little better than his word labels. For one thing, neither Julie nor anyone else is simply a product of an environment. Nature, in his book, was at least as important as nurture. Look at Kathy Johnson. He got up from his chair, profoundly dissatisfied, and went into the HQ room.

It was empty but he could hear voices in the little office used by Fehling and Gill. He pushed open the door. Fehling heaved himself out of the chair behind the desk. 'Mr and Mrs Little, sir. Julie's foster parents.'

The Littles were in their late fifties. He was tall, his best suit hung loose on his bony frame and his face was creased with deep lines from nostrils to mouth. His domed head was bald and shining. A Geordie, he turned out to be, who had come south in the Depression and never gone back. His wife was local, plump, comfortable, with a mind of her own though ready enough to play second fiddle in deference to her belief in proper male dominance. They sat close, posed as though waiting for a picture to be taken.

'I only saw her photo in the paper after dinner when I settled down to have a read. It knocked us sideways and we thought we'd better come straight away . . . '

Mrs Little dabbed her eyes with a screwed-up handkerchief. 'I was telling this gentleman, nine years we had her, she was like our own flesh and blood.'

Under some pressure they admitted that Julie had not been an easy child. 'But we loved her none the less for that!' Mrs Little's features threatened to dissolve at any moment into uncontrollable weeping. 'Once we thought they might make us take her away from school.' She lowered her voice and murmured the dreaded word – 'Stealing! And no need for it, we'd always given her everything she wanted, hadn't we, Bert?'

Mr Little nodded and blinked. He had a habit of blinking nervously whenever he was addressed. 'And we had a bit of trouble with boys – not that I'm narrow, we didn't mind her having boy friends, but this was different. She got herself mixed up with a lot of young thugs. The things we found in her room! I mean it was obvious that she was going all the way and her not fifteen!' He broke off and sighed. 'But she was reasonable, she listened, which is more than some of them will.' He blinked furiously.

'And she was such a clever girl!' Mrs Little redressed the balance. 'You should see her school reports – everything "Excellent" – all her subjects, only at the bottom her headmaster would write something about her attitude and conduct being unsatisfactory.'

'What about her marriage?'

They looked at each other and tacitly agreed that it was mother's turn. 'We didn't know anything about it until young Collins came along and asked our permission. We was taken aback, I can tell you! At first we was all against it; for one thing she was too young to marry and he was a man of thirty-six . . . '

Mr Little, revolving his trilby hat in his lap, took up the tale: 'Of course it wasn't for us to decide really, it was up to the Children's Officer, but we talked it over and in the end we agreed it might be the best thing for her. She was set on it anyway.'

'It was a good chance,' Mrs Little said. 'The Collinses are a respected family in the town, she wouldn't want for anything. But it didn't work.'

'Have you heard from her since she went away?'

Mrs Little shook her head and her husband answered, 'Not so much as a Christmas card.'

'Did you know her parents?'

Mrs Little looked at her husband, her tiny mouth pursed in disapproval. He blinked and said, 'Yes, we knew them.'

'We used to feel sorry for the little girl, they neglected her, always gallivanting off and leaving her to fend for herself, poor little mite!'

'Her mother was on the stage before she married him – or said she was. She made up enough.'

'He was a carpenter, wasn't he?' Wycliffe asked.

Mr Little smiled. 'You could call him that, I suppose. He used to make old-fashioned chairs and tables in a shed behind the house. I suppose he must have sold them because they never seemed to be short of money.'

'He was all right in his way,' Mrs Little argued. 'It was her!'

'They lived near you?'

'Next door when we lived down on the Plain, before we moved to the estate. Julie used to spend most of her time in our place even then.'

CHAPTER ELEVEN

It was after eight when Gill finally telephoned and Wycliffe had been sitting at his desk since six. From time to time he pretended to work on the reports but most of the time he dozed. His head would sag on his chest and he was asleep. It was a warm evening and he envied the people still messing about in boats in the harbour, the sea like glass on the evening flood. He even envied the people in church with the west doors open and the sun streaming down the nave. When the phone rang he woke with a start and it took him a moment to remember where he was. 'Any luck?'

'Not so's you'd notice. It's no rest cure trying to find anybody in London on a fine Sunday. Anyway I had a word with the owner of the strip joints where she used to work and with her landlady of those days. Nothing much we don't know already. Then I ran down the manager of the night club where she's under contract – or was. I found him at a sort of pansies' *soirée* in Camden Town. He was a mite peeved at first . . . '

'Never mind the local colour, let's have the facts,' Wycliffe growled.

'Yes, sir! He's definitely cheesed off. Says he'll lose a mint through this. Apparently her act was a sensation. She used to come on all in white silk, down to her ankles, hair to her shoulders, innocent and virginal. Then she'd sing obscene little ditties in a husky contralto. All the time she'd never fetch a smile and look vaguely shocked when the audience laughed their heads off. The manager told me she's already made two records and was all set to be a money spinner.'

'There are easier ways of making a living than being a policeman.'

Gill cackled. 'You can say that again. You ought to see this chick's bankbook! Lovely figures all down one side – in black.'

'I gather you've been to her flat?'

'Eager Beaver – that's me! Nice place, nice neighbourhood. People don't care what you do as long as you don't disturb them doing it. Her place, all white and oatmeal . . . '

'What? I thought you said oatmeal?'

'I did, it's a sort of beige . . . '

'Never mind. Any books?'

'Books? Hundreds! Place is like a public library. Some of them are quite interesting.'

'In what way?'

'Let's call them text books of sexual technology. She must have made a study of it.'

'I expect she did, it was her living one way or another.'

'She seems to have done a spot of blackmail as a side-line – nothing spectacular – chicken feed compared with what she got more or less legit. A little book with several addresses and against one or two of them sums of money at intervals. Amounts between fifty and three or four hundred. One of the providers is on our patch – our friend Masson-Smythe.'

'I've been talking to him this afternoon. Any evidence?'

'Evidence?'

'Don't be difficult, Jim! If she's blackmailing she must have something.'

'Not a thing!'

That was the irony of it. So many victims of blackmail

are paying up on evidence long since destroyed.

'Anything else?'

'No, sir. Sufficient unto the day . . . '

'You'd better come home, my lad.'

Wycliffe put the telephone back on its rest, stretched and yawned. Sufficient unto the day . . . It was too late for dinner but he would be able to get cold meat and salad.

He had his cold meat and salad with half a bottle of Beaujolais, but only just. He was sitting back and thinking about lighting his pipe when the loudspeaker paged him. Helen, her hair bleached, her skin pink after a day on the water, looked at him with concern. 'You're dog tired.'

'Don't be silly, I've been sleeping most of the evening!'

It was Fehling, who had been given the job of getting a warrant and organizing the search of the Voodoo premises. 'I was beginning to think that every magistrate had emigrated! Anyway, I made it in the end. I'm speaking from the club now.'

'Any luck?'

Fehling was hesitant. 'Of course we're not through yet, sir, but I've got a feeling this place is clean. There's nothing here which could incriminate a monk. They were ready for us!'

Wycliffe was not very interested but he tried to sound consoling. 'I shouldn't worry, we've got more than enough to cook Masson-Smythe's goose.'

'That's not the point, sir! I was counting on getting a lead on some of his pals – past and present.'

'Very frustrating!' Wycliffe couldn't get worked up over Fehling's yearning for promotion. 'Anything else?'

'Yes, the Masson-Smythe woman made a break for it just before I arrived. Not very clever! Apparently she phoned for a taxi and when it arrived just turned up on the step all ready for the off. Of course, DC Hartley, who was keeping obo, put paid to that! He's with me now, by the way, not much point in him going back on obo when . . . '

'None,' Wycliffe agreed. He saw no reason so far for stirring out of the hotel again. He wished that Fehling would dry up and he struggled to light his pipe with the receiver wedged between his cheek and his shoulder.

'There was one other thing, sir. In a drawer of Smythe's desk I found a silver framed photograph of the dead girl. I wondered . . . '

'The one from her dressing table?' Wycliffe was on the ball now. All that kerfuffle before coming to the point! Of course it might not *be* the point for Fehling.

'It could be, sir. We shall have to show it to the girl at the Marina.'

'Prints?'

'Only one or two smears, nothing identifiable.'

'I'll be down. Give me ten minutes.'

Thelma Masson-Smythe was composed and inclined to offence rather than defence. 'I don't know by what right . . . '

Wycliffe ignored her. She was lounging among the cushions of an overblown settee like some Hollywood *femme fatale* of the twenties. Her baggage, two suitcases, was still on the floor beside her.

'Open them up,' to Hartley who hovered in the background.

'They've been searched, sir, there's nothing . . . '

'Never mind, open them.'

Hartley lifted one of the cases on to a chair, snapped the catches and lifted the lid. Thelma Masson-Smythe sat up to get a better view. Her manner was indifferent, almost sardonic. The case was half empty, a few underclothes thrown in on two or three summer dresses neatly folded in polythene bags. Wycliffe lifted out a couple of slips, a brassiere and two pairs of briefs.

'You get a kick out of that?' As with her husband, the thin veneer was peeling off and the real woman beginning to show through, a hard-faced tart.

The second case held a coat and skirt, a nightdress and a few more items of underwear. Wycliffe closed the lid and turned to the woman. He was puzzled; sure that she had hoaxed them, but he could not see what she had achieved by doing it. 'You intended to travel light?' The first words he had spoken to her since his arrival.

She puffed cigarette smoke ceilingwards and watched it rise. 'I was in a hurry.' The plain orange dress she wore was sleeveless, tight, and so brief that it made Wycliffe slightly uneasy to look at her, embarrassed by the sheer bulk of naked pink flesh.

'No woman is in too much of a hurry to put in her toilet things.'

'I forgot.'

Wycliffe lit his pipe. 'You were told this afternoon that your husband had been arrested and that you would be able to talk to him if you came to the station.'

'I'm not responsible for his troubles!'

Wycliffe left her, still puzzled and disgruntled, and wandered about the premises, watching Fehling's men at work, searching every drawer, every cupboard. No stone unturned. But he agreed with the inspector, it was a waste of time. He looked at the silver framed photograph of the dead girl, a head and shoulders, a colour print like the stills outside cinemas.

'You think Masson-Smythe took it when he went to the Marina?' Fehling asked.

'It's possible.'

Fehling shook his massive head. 'I don't see why he should have unless he also battered her face in. I mean, if he wanted to destroy clues to her identity, there wouldn't be much point in taking the photo and leaving the girl . . . '

They were in Smythe's office and Wycliffe perched himself on the edge of the desk. 'Have you thought that it might have been a woman who did the battering?'

It was obvious that the idea had not occurred to Fehling, equally obvious that he was taken by it. 'Thelma?'

'I don't know.'

'She could have followed her husband . . . ' He was getting enthusiastic. 'By all accounts she had reason enough to hate the girl.'

Wycliffe was still holding the photograph and he began to remove it from its frame. 'There, on the back in pencil: *Voodoo* and a serial number. That would be reason enough for Smythe to take it away with him, it was one of his publicity shots of the girl and he wouldn't want that found beside her body . . . '

'The same would apply to Thelma.'

'Of course!' He was chasing an elusive idea which had nothing to do with the photograph. 'Why did she call a taxi?'

Fehling looked surprised. 'To make a bolt for it, I suppose.'

'Nonsense! She's too wily a bird not to know that we had the place covered.'

'Then I don't follow . . . '

'She *wanted* to be stopped. She had no intention of taking that taxi.' He broke off. 'Send for Hartley.'

DC Hartley was a Wiltshireman and his voice would have been God's gift to a radio gardening programme. 'Sir?'

'Did anybody enter the premises during the evening before Mrs Masson-Smythe tried to leave?'

Hartley's expression was sufficient answer.

'All right, you forgot, what happened afterwards put it out of your mind . . . '

'I noted it, sir.' He brought out his notebook and flipped over the pages. 'Four thirty, sir. A girl, blonde, smallish, light blue summer dress and white handbag. . . '

'When did she come out?'

Hartley flushed. 'She didn't, sir.'

'Then she must be here now. Have you found her?' Nasty. Wycliffe didn't wait for a reply but turned to Fehling. 'That's where your evidence is gone. Now, Hartley, what did you do when you saw Mrs Masson-Smythe about to clear out in a taxi?'

'I went over and stopped her, sir.'

'Was she abusive?'

'Resigned, I would have said, sir. She didn't seem very surprised.'

'What did you do then?'

'Why, I went in with her to the lounge, I was about to phone through to the station and report when Inspector Fehling turned up . . . '

'And while you were escorting her indoors, the other young woman skipped out with a suitcase containing what Inspector Fehling is looking for.'

'And now,' said Fehling, ominously, 'we're looking for a smallish blonde who wears a light blue dress and carries a white handbag. Hartley!'

Wycliffe had found that the chance to play the great detective came rarely and when it did you had to avoid sounding smug. 'I should try 4a, Mount Zion, Hartley. Ask for Sadie Field.'

'The stripper?' Fehling was incredulous. 'I thought you said she was a decent sort of girl?'

'She is but she's also a bit dumb and scared of losing her job, just the sort Thelma would choose to do her dirty work. In any case, Sadie won't have heard yet that her employer has been nicked.'

'Well! What are you waiting for, Hartley?' Fehling was smarting a bit.

'Go easy on her!' Wycliffe ordered. 'She's more sinned against than sinning.'

He wandered out of the office and down the steps to the club. The lights were on, and two solemn dicks were shaking one of the giant polystyrene statues between them, to see if it rattled. It was too much for Wycliffe and he made his way back to the lounge.

Thelma seemed not to have moved but she was sipping a drink and there was a tray of drinks on a small table by the settee. 'Found what you're looking for, superintendent? If you would tell me what it is, perhaps I could help you?'

Wycliffe perched on the arm of a voluptuous black leather monster which seemed ready to engulf and perhaps digest anyone with the temerity to sit in it properly.

'Whisky, superintendent?' Her assurance was brittle and when he merely sat and stared at her without speaking he was gratified to see her shift her position slightly and make an ineffective effort to pull down the hem of her dress.

'I found an interesting photograph, a photograph of Julie Collins in a silver frame. It was last seen on the dressing table in her bedroom at the Marina.'

She stopped with her glass midway to her lips. 'That's not possible.'

'Oh, it's possible all right, your husband admits that he went to see the girl on the night she was murdered. He says, of course, that she was dead when he got there.'

She was off the settee in a flash, upsetting her drink down the front of her dress. 'You filthy, lying, stinking cop! You can't pin that on him!'

193

Wycliffe was unmoved. 'That remains to be seen, but what interests me at the moment is your share in the business.'

'Me?' Her surprise could have been genuine. Standing there with the gin soaking into the bodice of her dress, without shoes, her hair and eyes wild, it was hard to connect her with the woman in the blue gown whom Helen had described as 'striking', who moved about the club, suave and graceful, the experienced professional hostess.

'You haven't been told that Julie's face was destroyed by an attacker who battered her with a heavy brass weight.'

This stopped her. She went to the settee and sat on the edge, her legs apart, her hands drooping between them. 'Serves her bloody well right, she was a dirty whore!'

'You had reason to be jealous of her. Is it possible that you followed your husband that night . . . ?'

'Me? You think that I . . . ?'

'You hated the girl and you are obviously vicious.'

'You can't set me up, copper!' But there was no longer any punch behind the words. She was shaken, and she continued to sit in the same posture as before, for once unselfconscious, like a little girl, a little girl with a problem.

He drove back to his hotel. The town was deserted and as he passed through the square the town clock was doling out the strokes of midnight. The hotel garage was full so he left his car in the forecourt. The night porter admitted him. 'Developments, sir?' Wycliffe grunted. He had his foot on the carpeted stair, then he noticed that there was still light in the television lounge.

'They're down, sir.'

'Down?'

'The astronauts, they've touched down on the moon.'

He had forgotten and the fact unsettled him. But he did not go into the television lounge, instead he went through to the terrace. He lit his pipe and rested his arms on the balustrade, staring out over the harbour. It was very quiet, a noise of purring machinery from the docks, and that was all. He could make out the shape of the little sailing boat belonging to the young couple. There was a riding light at the masthead and he thought that he could distinguish a dim glow from the porthole of the tiny cabin.

Tonight men would walk on the moon. He tried to take it in, to grasp and hold the thought that this moment of time was shared with two men in their fragile capsule on the surface of the moon a quarter of a million miles away. He tried and failed. It was when he made an effort to think in a disciplined way about anything that he was most conscious of his shortcomings. And this reflection brought him back to the case. Not only did he find sustained logical thought difficult but he was always short of written data. He had the official reports but these were so full as to be almost useless. Any other detective would have a sheaf of private notes, but he rarely wrote anything down and if he did he either lost it or threw it away. Notes were repugnant to him. Even now he ought to be sitting at a desk with a notepad in front of him, jotting down his ideas, transposing and relating facts like a jig-saw.

Like hell!

But the price he paid was heavy, his thoughts went in circles.

Julie Collins had been strangled, then viciously assaulted. If Masson-Smythe spoke the truth, one did not immediately follow the other. Had the murderer been interrupted in his work? Had he retreated somewhere when he heard Smythe coming? The figure on the fire-escape? It seemed improbable. He could only have left the girl's room through the door, in which case Smythe would almost certainly have seen him. *Had* Smythe seen him? Unlikely but not impossible. But if the murderer had already gone when Masson-Smythe arrived, that presupposed that someone else had come after him and disfigured the girl.

Had the man on the fire-escape watched the murder, seen Smythe enter and leave, and *then* come in through the bathroom window to carry out his task? But why?

There was movement on the little yacht, a lithe figure climbing on to the cabin roof, standing by the mast; the glimmer of a cigarette.

And if Smythe was lying? It was possible though unlikely that the man who had intercourse with the girl was not her murderer. That let Smythe out, for according to Rashleigh he was Group O. But he could have been responsible for the disfigurement to make identification difficult and reduce the risk of being linked with the crime. Far fetched? But there had to be some explanation and if he had rejected every far fetched hypothesis in his cases a good many would have remained unsolved.

The girl had joined her lover, they were standing side by side now, he could see the glow of both cigarettes; from time to time one or the other would describe a small trajectory in the darkness.

As to suspects, he had plenty. Allen, Smythe, Collins, Byrne – though he could hardly take Byrne seriously. And if hate was the motive for the mutilation, who had better reason to hate her than the women?

He went inside.

'Not staying up for the walk, sir?'

'No.'

As he slid in beside his wife he could feel the glowing warmth from her sun-tanned skin. 'You'll be sore tomorrow,' he whispered.

CHAPTER TWELVE

He woke with his course of action clear in his mind and with the confidence that it would bring results. By the time he went to bed again the case would be over. A sanguine view considering his vague speculations of the previous night but it was a familiar pattern. Somehow the alchemy of sleep had once more cleared and ordered his thoughts. He could not explain it, he just knew, and because he knew he hummed a little tune in the bathroom. Helen, still in bed, called to him, 'You sound happy this morning!'

'I am! How are the shoulders?'

'Sore.'

'That'll teach you to go to sea decently clad.'

'The twins rang up last night.' The Wycliffes had twin children, a boy and a girl of nineteen and they had been camping in France.

'Oh, they're back are they?'

'They came back on somebody's yacht of all things – somebody they met in Cherbourg while they were waiting for the ferry.'

He couldn't help remembering his own youth when a day trip to Barmouth was something to look forward to and back on for weeks.

He was in the bedroom now, in his dressing gown. Out of the window he could see the little boat belonging to the young couple. They were swimming again, although it was raining. For some reason he felt a sudden pang of sadness and sighed.

'What's the matter?'

'Old age – what else?'

Before breakfast they watched a telerecording of the moon walk. 'That's one small step for man, one giant leap for mankind.' Neil Armstrong's words, they impressed him. He wondered why he felt that men who walked on the moon should have come from a better world.

When he arrived at the station there were half-a-dozen pressmen lounging round the enquiry desk, including Brown from the local paper.

'Good morning, lads!'

'Has Masson-Smythe been arrested?'

'What's he charged with?'

'Off the record . . . '

'Is the case over?'

Wycliffe lit his pipe. 'If you got all the answers you know very well you couldn't print 'em. Mr Masson-Smythe was with me yesterday afternoon . . . '

' . . . helping with enquiries!' they finished for him.

'Exactly! However, certain charges have been made but they have no direct connection with the murder.'

'What are the charges?'

'He will be coming up before the magistrates this morning.'

'What about Allen?'

'He is back in custody and, presumably, the law will proceed against him where it left off.'

'But he slugged you on Friday night at the club.'

'Did he? I shouldn't print that if I were you, he might have you for libel.'

One shrivelled little fellow who looked in need of a good meal but was, in fact, the most experienced of them, spoke for the first time. 'The super promised a statement and that's all we're going to get. Let's have it.'

'Good! Here it is: "For reasons connected with the

inquiry, the police have not previously disclosed that the dead girl's features had been so mutilated after death as to make them unrecognizable." '

This silenced them and by the time they found fresh questions Wycliffe was half-way up the stairs to his office. Fehling was waiting for him. 'What about the Spaniard? He's due to sail at six this evening.'

'Let him!' Wycliffe growled. 'We've got enough crooks of our own.'

It was half past nine when he arrived at the book-shop. The little rat-faced man was scrubbing the steps but Wycliffe went to the side door. He did not ring, it was unlocked, so he climbed the carpeted stairs without invitation. At the top he called, 'Is anyone at home?' Aunt Jane came out of the kitchen at the end of the dimly lit corridor.

'I'm extremely sorry! I hope you don't mind me coming up but I think your bell must be out of order.'

'Superintendent!' She was all of a flutter but welcoming. 'Let me get out of this overall. Just step into the lounge, superintendent, I'll be with you in a moment.'

He found himself once more in the depressing room overlooking the street; nothing had changed. He stood by the window watching the traffic until she joined him. She was nervous, alternately patting her cropped hair and smoothing the creases from her blue linen dress. Except for a difference in length, it seemed to be a replica of a dress Wycliffe's grandmother had worn when he first remembered her. She made him sit down in one of the easy chairs and perched herself on one of the straightbacks.

'I'm glad to see you recovered, Miss Collins.'

'Oh, yes, I'm quite recovered, thank you, superintendent. They wanted me to spend a few days in a nursing home but I told them I have a few things to clear up here first. After that we shall see.'

Wycliffe scarcely knew where to begin.

'By all means smoke, superintendent! My father and my brother smoked a pipe and I like the smell of tobacco.'

It was something. He lit up.

'It was clever of you to come, superintendent.'

'Clever?'

'Of course! To realize that it was I who could tell you about Willie. Ada is his mother but she's never been *close* to him. Even when he was a little boy it was to me that he came with all his troubles and we would sit down together and work something out. He was such a sensitive child, superintendent, and Ada never really understood him. Willie is a Collins.'

'You've lived here for a long time, Miss Collins?'

'All my life, it's my home.' She looked down at her large bony hands, clasped in her lap. 'Ada always frustrated Willie; she still does. She seems to think it's a sin for people to do what they want, a sin not to be always *busy*. Yet we know our Lord's answer to Martha, don't we?' She spoke as though they shared a cosy but rather guilty secret. 'I can remember so well, when Willie was a little boy, she used to say, "You can play with your soldiers, Willie, but only until tea-time", "You can read *one* chapter of your book", or "You can go out for half-an-hour". Of course, she was just the same with his father. I've always said he wouldn't have gone like he did if it hadn't been for her.'

'And Willie still comes to you with his troubles?'

She flashed him a quick, anxious look from her slightly protuberant eyes, and for some reason her lower lip trembled. He was afraid that she would cry but she recovered herself. 'He always confides in me.'

'Did he tell you that Julie had written to him to say that she was coming back?'

Her face hardened. 'Iris has been talking to you, I know. She's no right, she's only an employee!'

Wycliffe stood up. 'I could call him up and ask him now . . . '

'No!' Her reaction was so sharp that it startled him. 'No, I don't want him here.' She smoothed the material of her dress. 'He told me.'

'Did he think that she was coming back to him?'

'He hoped that she would.'

'And you?'

'I wanted what he wanted.'

He could see her mental conflict reflected in her face. 'She was a slut!' And she added, 'He would never have married her if it hadn't been for Ada's scheming.'

'When did you give him the money, Miss Collins?'

Her jaw set in a firm line. 'I don't know what you're talking about!'

He was gentle. 'I can get a court order in a case of this sort. Your bank would have to tell the truth.'

She gave in at once. 'Ada always kept him short! My brother never intended it to be like that. He left the business to Ada for her lifetime, just to protect her, but she's used the will to keep her son tied to her apron strings. The poor boy's never had any money of his own, just the pittance he draws as salary . . . It makes my blood boil!'

'So you gave him a thousand pounds in cash. What did he say it was for?'

'For Julie. He told me exactly what it was for, we don't have any secrets from each other. The money was for her.'

'Why, exactly, did she need a thousand pounds?'

'She said in her letter that she was in trouble with the

202

police and that she needed the money to avoid going to prison. She hinted that if he helped her she would come back to him.'

'You believed all this?'

She gave him an odd look. 'Certainly not! But he did. It was very thinly disguised blackmail!'

'Yet you let him go through with it – gave him the money to go through with it.'

She laughed without humour. 'You don't keep people's love by telling them the truth, superintendent. You have to let them find that out for themselves – then be there waiting for them.'

Love should never repel but Wycliffe was repelled. The Marina seemed to him at that moment a haven of sanity and decency compared with this little bourgeois household. But what was the point in making such comparisons? Such judgements? People lived their lives and who was he to moralize? He had never had the Collinses for a family or Julie for a wife. If he had, who could say?

She sat watching him, a tentative smile on her lips. 'Anyhow, it will come right now.'

'Come right?'

'She's dead, isn't she?'

'Murdered.'

She shook her head.

'Julie was strangled, Miss Collins, there can be no doubt of that.'

But she continued to shake her head.

'Are you afraid that it was Willie who killed her? Perhaps you know that it was he – did he confide in you?'

The look she gave him sprang from a sudden flare of hatred. 'Don't be absurd! Willie wouldn't hurt a fly, you have only to look at him . . . Nobody but a fool would . . . '

'Then what are you afraid of?'

'That you will get things wrong.' She made an effort to control herself. 'After all, you don't know him as I do.'

Wycliffe looked at her for some time, his eyes steady and grave. At last she raised hers and their gaze met. They sat for a little longer in silence, then Wycliffe stood up. 'Well, Miss Collins, thank you for talking to me. I will go through the bookroom, if I may, to the shop.'

'You are going to see him?'

'There are one or two points.'

She would have liked to stop him but she realized that she was helpless. 'Very well! You know the way. But remember, superintendent, he's not himself.'

He went down to the next landing while she stood at the top of the stairs watching. The only light in the corridor and down the stairs came from fanlights over the doors of the rooms. The atmosphere was oppressive, claustrophobic. He paused at the green baize door. 'To spend one's whole life in such a place!'

One old gentleman burrowed among the books but otherwise the secondhand department was deserted. Willie's mother's chair was empty though her knitting lay beside the till. He went down the spiral staircase. At the bottom, a door which he had noticed before was standing slightly ajar; he pushed it open without knocking and came upon a tableau which interested him. Iris, Willie and his mother in attitudes which they held as though petrified. The old lady had an unhealthy flush, Iris was pale, Willie looked sullen. The room was a little office and in contrast with the gloom of the flat which he had just left, it was gay with reflected sunlight, the ceiling and walls brilliant with dancing patterns of light from the waters of the harbour outside. He must have blinked foolishly in the doorway. The old lady was first to recover. 'You wished to speak to me, superintendent?' Precisely the right blend of courtesy and rebuke. He had to admit to a grudging admiration, and yet she had made a substantial contribution to the wrecking of two lives and, perhaps, to the premature ending of a third. But was it fair to blame her? No doubt she had told herself that she had to provide the drive which Willie lacked. No doubt she had said the same of his father. Perhaps she was right.

'I want to talk to your son, Mrs Collins.'

Willie seemed to awake from a trance. 'To me? Then we'd better go upstairs.' The old lady made a move but he added, 'No, mother!' He followed Wycliffe out, leaving the two women together.

Willie's room was as gay as the office. Wycliffe sat himself in a chair facing the window while Willie took the swivel chair by his work table. He had been busy, the table was covered by a large sheet of cardboard on which a large-scale map had been drawn and in one corner a legend: *Austerlitz: December 2nd. 1805*. Fragments of card in various shapes and sizes with evocative labels were pinned to the map. Willie had sought refuge from reality in the reconstruction of one of Napoleon's most famous victories.

'So the money came from your aunt.' Frontal attack.

'She told you!'

'She had no option. Now, Mr Collins, last time I was here you told me that you hadn't seen your wife since she left the town. Now you will have to tell a different story so make sure this one is the truth.'

Willie looked older and vaguer, it was impossible to know whether his attention had been gained, whether he understood the seriousness of his position. Wycliffe suspected that he was too withdrawn, too self absorbed.

'When did you give her the money?'

He looked as though he did not understand the question and made no attempt to answer.

'I have a witness who will say that your wife was expecting a visitor at midnight on the night of her death. He will also say that she was expecting to receive certain money from her husband – from you, Mr Collins.'

The words seemed to be lost on him. He passed his hand over his forehead and murmured, 'I want to know who did that to her; if only I could be sure!'

Wycliffe remembered times in his own life when he had seemed to lose contact with the world outside, to become aware of it only when it obtruded in some unwelcome fashion. At such times he might have voiced his thoughts aloud and been ashamed and irritated if someone overheard and tried to answer. But it was not for him to be sympathetic. 'It is my belief that on Tuesday night, just before midnight, you went to the Marina to give your wife the thousand pounds you had obtained from your aunt. You did this by arrangement with your wife, an arrangement made over the telephone or, perhaps, you discussed it when you met her outside the hotel on Tuesday morning. You were seen talking to her,' he added and Willie did not deny it.

Willie stood up and began moving restlessly about the room. Wycliffe was still not sure how far he had penetrated the depths of his introspection. 'Why did you kill her?'

The thick lenses flashed in the light but Willie said nothing.

'You made love to her, then you strangled her – why? Did she ridicule you? Did she tell you that she had fooled you again? That she had no intention of coming back to the life you could offer her?' There was no doubt now that he had riveted Willie's attention. 'Or did she make you intolerably jealous by taunting you with the affairs she had had with other men? Worse still, were you standing on the fire escape, watching, while she tried to persuade Allen to make love to her?'

He paused and though Willie said nothing his eyes never left Wycliffe's.

'You said yourself that there is a point beyond which the worm will turn. For everyone, according to you, there is a threshold of violence. Did Julie push you over that threshold?'

He was gambling on the assumption that in the five days since Julie's death Willie's guilt had become an insupportable burden, that he would find immeasurable relief in confession. For Wycliffe was satisfied that Willie had killed his wife and equally convinced that he had not mutilated her afterwards. The sight of her in the mortuary had overwhelmed him and Wycliffe believed that eventually the blend of guilt, bewilderment, horror and fear would be too much for him. All his life he had taken his troubles to someone, usually to Aunt Jane; the two of them would 'sit down and work something out together'. Had he gone to her and blurted out, 'I've killed Julie'? From Aunt Jane's manner Wycliffe was inclined to think not. Willie was carrying this, his greatest burden, alone – so far.

He was standing by the shelves where his soldiers were deployed, fiddling with them, shifting one here and another there, then putting them back to their original positions. His hand hovered over a troop of cavalry and he lifted one of the red-coated horsemen and held it, seeming to study the modelling intently. Wycliffe let him be and looked out of the window, watching three tugs fussing round a giant tanker like Lilliputians round a Gulliver.

'She said in her letter that I mustn't come to the hotel until she sent for me but I couldn't keep away. I walked past the place six or seven times on the Monday without catching sight of her, but on Tuesday morning I was lucky, I met her just as she was coming out of the gate . . . ' His voice faltered and he stopped speaking. No doubt he was reliving the moment when he had first set eyes on her after months of separation. 'She seemed no different, it was just as though we had run into one another in the street as we sometimes did when she was . . . when we were living together. She said, "Oh, Willie! this will save me phoning", and she told me what she wanted me to do – to bring the money that night.'

'She had told you in her letter how much?'

He resented the interruption and dismissed it with a nod. 'She told me to come by the fire escape which goes up to the bathroom window at the back of the hotel. There's a footpath which runs along by the railway cutting round the backs of the houses . . . ' His voice trailed off into silence. He put down his horseman and picked up another.

'Did you tell anyone of your appointment?'

He looked at Wycliffe for some time before answering, as though debating in his mind what to say, then, 'I told my aunt.' As he spoke, his hand closed on the little horseman and the delicate metal legs snapped. He opened his hand and looked blankly at the fragments then he allowed them to slide off his hand on to the carpet.

'Why did you kill her?'

No answer.

Wycliffe was conscious of the delicacy of his task, to exert enough pressure to make him talk without reducing him to hysterical incoherence. 'You loved her?'

'She was the only . . . ' He broke off and after a moment said, simply, 'Yes.'

'Have you ever had a blood test, Mr Collins?'

'A blood test?' Surprise, but not apprehension.

'To determine your blood group.'

'Yes, I'm AB.'

'A rather rare group.'

'Yes.'

'The man who had intercourse with your wife immediately before her death was of that group.'

The sensitive mouth twitched but he said nothing.

'It is possible to tell from the semen.'

No response.

Wycliffe was beginning to be oppressed by a curious lethargy. The warm room, the dazzling light, Willie's answer drawn from him laboriously, flat and colourless. He lit his pipe. When he spoke again his manner was friendly. 'You are not the stuff of which criminals are made, Mr Collins. Sooner or later you will find it imperative to talk. Already you are torn apart by a conflict between your instinct for self preservation and an almost irresistible longing to discharge some measure of your guilt by confession and by explanation. To explain – to be able to say, "This is *why* I did it; this is how it happened!"

'Believe me, the conflict is spurious. You cannot, whatever you do, preserve yourself, you have already destroyed the person you were.'

Willie was still standing by the shelves but he was watching Wycliffe and listening. 'Confession, atonement, absolution – is that the formula?' Except for a tremor in his voice the question might have been part of a cosy academic discussion.

'No. Because in my view there is no atonement for murder.'

'A priest would do better.'

'But I am a policeman.' He knew that Willie was on the brink of decision, he knew too that silence would be his best advocate, but at that moment the door opened and Aunt Jane came in.

Wycliffe stood up. 'I think, Miss . . . '

But she turned on him, silencing him with a look. 'I wish to make a statement, superintendent.'

'About what, Miss Collins?'

'I killed Julie.' She spoke triumphantly, the slight smile which so often seemed to hover round her lips was more pronounced, and, as always, it was a smile of satisfaction. 'I killed her, there is no need to torture this poor boy any longer.'

Wycliffe was surprised less by the confession than by Willie's reaction. He gazed at his aunt and in his gaze there was nothing of incredulity or relief or bewilderment, only hatred, and hatred so intense that Wycliffe wondered if he might attack her.

'Well? Are you going to arrest me?'

'I shall need more than a simple assertion of guilt before I do that, Miss Collins.'

'All right! I'll tell you about it. Am I allowed to sit down?'

'Of course!' He gave her his own chair and perched himself on one corner of a built-in cabinet. She sat on the edge of the chair, bolt upright, bony hands clasped in her lap. Her grey eyes seemed more protuberant, her wispy hair more wild. 'I must caution you . . . '

She brushed aside his words. 'When Willie showed me her letter I knew that it would be useless to refuse to help or to argue with him but I was determined that he shouldn't be trapped by that creature a second time.'

Wycliffe glanced across at Willie but he had resumed his seat by the table and his head was bent over his reconstruction of the battle.

'When he told me that he was to see her on Tuesday night I decided to follow him.' She pursed her lips.

Wycliffe looked at the hard embittered features, the

mean mouth, and wondered how the love of this woman differed from that of another. Why should it repel instead of attract? Why should it isolate rather than unite? Because it was selfish? Possessive, certainly, but hardly selfish . . .

'You followed your nephew to the hotel?'

She chose to think that he was doubting her and turned to Willie for confirmation. 'You know that I'm speaking the truth, don't you, Willie?'

But Willie continued to stare at the desk as though he had not heard.

'He came into my room next morning just as it was getting light and saw my wet things. It started to rain just before one o'clock when I was coming back and I got nearly wet through. When Willie opened my door I was awake and he was about to speak when he caught sight of my wet coat spread over the dressing table to dry. I could see by the look on his face that he understood.'

'Understood what, Miss Collins?'

She looked at him craftily. 'That I had followed him.'

Wycliffe waited, but no more came. 'Is this true, Mr Collins?'

Silence for a moment, then the single word, 'Yes.'

This confirmation seemed to be what she had waited for and she continued her story. 'As I said, I followed him when I heard him leave the house just before twelve on Tuesday night. There was nobody about and I had to stay well back for fear of being seen but I knew where he was going so it hardly mattered. I was surprised when he walked right past the Marina but he continued round the corner towards the railway and I understood. He took the narrow path that leads behind the houses on the edge of the cutting and at one of the back doors he stopped and let himself in. After a minute or two I followed. Luckily I waited by the door for a while for it was some time before

I saw him on the fire escape; he seemed to be waiting but after a little while I heard a window opening and he disappeared inside. There was only one light on in the place and that was in the room next to the top of the escape.'

'What did you intend to do? What was the point of following your nephew?'

She gave the question thought, frowning as though in an effort to recall her exact state of mind. 'I'm not sure what I intended to do. I think I meant to wait until Willie had gone and then go in and talk to her . . . I don't know for certain because everything turned out differently. At any rate I climbed the escape and when I got level with the lighted window I could see that it had no blind and the curtains were not drawn so I could look right into the room.' She hesitated and for the first time seemed to have difficulty in going on.

'What did you see?'

She sighed. 'They were both there, Willie and the girl. Willie must have given her the money before I got there and they were talking. She was sitting on the bed in her dressing gown and Willie was standing over her. He seemed to be reasoning with her or arguing, then she started to laugh. She stood up and took off her dressing gown so that she was naked, then she . . . she began to . . . ' She broke off and there were spots of colour in her cheeks. 'I never imagined that any woman could be so degraded!' She made a curious little noise, between a sob and a snort. 'We all know that men . . . She undressed him – literally and I had to watch while . . . And she was laughing all the time, that made it worse. She seemed to be taunting him and even while he . . . while he was under the spell of her lust, she continued to laugh at him and provoke him. I could see that he was angry because there were tears in his eyes and from a child he has always cried when he was angry and not when he was hurt. She was a devil and she deserved to die!' The telling of her story had excited her so that she was breathing rapidly and her hands twisted incessantly in her lap.

He looked at Willie, still slumped in his chair without a movement. Her gaze followed Wycliffe's and for a moment her features softened. Wycliffe looked from one to the other and felt sick. 'What happened?'

'Afterwards he got up and dressed himself . . . '

'Leaving Julie on the bed?'

A moment of hesitation, then, 'Yes, leaving her lying there, watching him.'

'Did she lie still?'

Her eyes narrowed. 'She wasn't dead if that's what you mean. She continued talking to him and laughing.'

'And what did he do?'

'He just dressed and left.'

'And she was alive when he left?'

'Certainly she was alive.'

'What did you do?'

'I was afraid for a moment that he would come out on to the fire escape and find me there but he didn't, he must have left by the front door. The window of the bathroom was still open and I climbed in. When I got to her she was still lying on the bed.'

'She must have been surprised to see you.'

'I suppose she was, I didn't give her much chance to think about it. I stood over her and told her what I thought of her.'

'What did she say?'

'She . . . she called me obscene names.'

'Then you strangled her?'

She looked at him curiously. 'I am a strong woman,

superintendent, she had much less strength than I and it was surprisingly easy.'

'There must have been a struggle.'

'Hardly any.' She stopped for a moment, apparently to order her thoughts. 'I don't think I really meant to kill her. I didn't . . . '

'You were going to say?'

'Nothing.'

Wycliffe studied her gravely, his eyes steady and un-blinking. 'Having strangled her, you then battered her face to make it unrecognizable.'

'No.' Again the crafty look. 'I did not. I heard the front door open and shut and footsteps on the stairs. I was frightened because I felt sure that whoever it was would come to her room. I don't know why I thought so but I was right.'

'So what did you do?'

Incredibly, in view of what had gone before, she looked embarrassed. 'I hid in the clothes cupboard.' She gave a self conscious little laugh. 'I hadn't more than got inside when a man came into the room. He called out, "Julie", in a loud whisper. Then he made some joking remark and walked over to where she was lying on the bed. I couldn't see what he was doing there but I heard him let out an oath.'

'Then?'

'Then he went. He went so quickly and quietly it took me a moment to realize that he had gone.' She sighed deeply. 'I came out of the cupboard . . . '

'Did you see the man?'

'Only his back and that not very clearly, I was afraid to open the door more than a crack.'

'Did the man search the room or take anything from it?'

'I told you, as soon as he found that she was dead he

couldn't get away fast enough, but there was one thing, I'd forgotten it until now – he took away her photograph.'

'Her photograph?'

'Yes, one in a silver frame, I noticed it when I was looking in the window and when I came to look for it afterwards, it was gone. He must have taken it.'

'All right go on.'

'I knew what I had to do; if I could prevent that vile woman from causing any more wickedness, I would do it. First I searched the room for anything that would identify her or link her with Willie and . . . '

'But the man had already seen her, lying there – dead.'

She smiled unpleasantly. 'It was obvious that he wouldn't talk. Why didn't he rouse the house? In any case it was a risk I had to take.'

'When you searched the room did you find anything?'

She nodded with satisfaction. 'I found a book of poetry Willie had given her. Apart from the shop label there was an inscription on the fly-leaf in Willie's writing.' She looked across at her nephew, 'I have the book still.'

Willie gave no sign that he had heard.

'It was then that I missed the photograph and realized the man must have taken it.'

'You did not recover your money.'

Her look was enough to tell him that the money had no importance for her. 'I had other things to think about. I had to make her unrecognizable and I was afraid that I should make too much noise and wake the house.'

'What did you use? What weapon?'

'There was a heavy brass weight in the middle of the floor. I suppose they used it as a door stop. It was the weight which gave me the idea in the first place.' She glanced across at Willie and lowered her voice to a whisper, 'I *wanted* to destroy her, she had no right . . . '

'To do what?'

She looked at Willie and back to Wycliffe. 'To live.'

'And having done all this, you walked out. Did you use the fire escape?'

She nodded. 'I went the way I had come.'

'What time was this?'

'It was striking one when I passed the church, just when it started to rain. When I got back here I got out of my wet things and before going to bed I looked in Willie's room. His bed had not been slept in and he was not there. I heard him come in about an hour later.' She looked at Wycliffe challengingly. 'I have told you what happened, superintendent, now you can do what you have to do.'

Wycliffe sat staring at her for a long time but his eyes had lost focus. There was silence in the room except for the noises from the docks and the muffled sounds of traffic in the street. He could hardly believe in the reality of his experience, it was like one of those pointless but infinitely depressing dreams from which one knows there will be an awakening. He stirred himself. 'Mr Collins!'

No response.

His temper was wearing thin. 'Mr Collins! Kindly turn round and give me your attention!'

Willie obeyed and faced him with a blank stare.

'I want to know if you have been listening to what your aunt has told me?'

'I have been listening.'

Aunt Jane watched her nephew with a solicitude which was at once pathetic and nauseating. He avoided her eyes. Wycliffe concentrated all the force of his personality on getting Willie to look at him and to answer his question. 'To the best of your knowledge, is your aunt's account of what happened true?'

Willie stared at the superintendent and the silence

lengthened. Aunt Jane made a small movement as though she would have stretched out her hand to touch him but a frown from Wycliffe stopped her.

'What my aunt has told you is true.'

'You say this, realizing the full implication of her story?'

Another interval. 'Yes.'

'Now, I suppose, you will arrest me,' from Aunt Jane.

'I shall ask you to come with me to the police station and to make a statement. After that we shall see.' He reached for the telephone on Willie's desk and dialled a number. Aunt Jane sat bolt upright on the edge of her chair, serene and content. Willie sat with his head in his hands staring at the carpet.

CHAPTER THIRTEEN

Wycliffe was back in his little office; the clock on the mantelpiece showed a quarter past three and outside the sun still shone. On his desk, two statements, neat little wads of typescript, one from William Reginald Collins, the other from his aunt, Jane Alicia Collins. The two statements corroborated each other in every detail for which corroboration was possible and on the strength of them Jane Alicia Collins had been charged with murder. Jim Gill, who had travelled down overnight, sat on the other side of the desk.

'So it's in the bag?'

Wycliffe was morose. 'You've read the statements?'

Gill nodded. 'I have and it seems watertight to me. What's the matter? Are you afraid they won't stand up in court?'

'I feel sure that they will.'

'Well then!'

Wycliffe stood up. 'She didn't do it, Jim.'

'Didn't do it? But she's made a perfectly reasoned and credible statement full of circumstantial details and Fehling found the weight, locked away in a drawer in her bedroom, with blood and hair still adhering to it . . . '

'And covered with her prints – I know all that, Jim. She battered the girl's face in, there's no doubt of that, but she didn't kill her. I've known from the start that the strangling and the mutilation were irreconcilable, the one came of too much loving, the other from passionate hatred and jealousy.'

Gill took out his cheroots and lit one. 'With all due respect, sir, that's just your reading of the case . . . '

Wycliffe was impatient. 'Read her statement again! It would have been better if you could have listened to her as I did. Circumstantial, as you say, until you come to the bit where she is lying, the bit where she claims to have strangled the girl. Apart from anything else, can you imagine a young and healthy girl being overwhelmed and strangled without one hell of a struggle?'

'You think Collins did it while he was making love to her?'

'I'm sure of it. I very much doubt if he meant to but she was provoking him beyond endurance and unwittingly she reached his threshold of violence.'

'Come again?'

'According to Collins, the point at which the worm turns. Of course, Aunt Jane saw it all through the window and when Willie had cleared out she went in and tidied things up in her own inimitable way.'

Gill studied the ash as it grew on his cheroot. 'If you thought like that, why did you have her charged?'

'What else could I do?'

Gill made a sudden movement which scattered the grey ash over his blue pinstripe. 'Give me ten minutes with Master Willie and I'll give you a confession to beat that one! Little runt, hiding behind a woman's bloody apron!'

Wycliffe smiled. 'He's done that all his life and he's too old to change now. But assuming you got him to talk, what good would it do? Julie's death would blight four other lives – Willie's, his mother's, his aunt's and probably Iris Rogers's too.'

Gill shook his head. 'You mustn't try to play God in this game, Mr Wycliffe.'

Wycliffe looked at him with great gravity. 'I'm not

playing God, Jim, you've got the roles mixed, I'm cast as Pontius Pilate.'

That evening at a little after six, Wycliffe and his wife were sitting near the edge of the low cliff which juts out into the sea to form the main bastion of the harbour, a natural breakwater. The tide had turned but the ebb had not yet acquired strength and the flat calm of the evening flood imparted a stillness to everything encouraging a mood of nostalgic sadness.

'What shall we do tomorrow?'

She turned to him in surprise. 'What about the case?'

'It's all over, Gill and Fehling will deal with the paper work.'

She smiled. 'In that case . . . ' She broke off. 'Look! There's a ship coming out.'

Creeping out of the harbour, a small vessel with gleaming white paint on her superstructure but the black hull gashed with ugly red splashes. The name on her bows was clearly visible: *SS Peruvia.*

'She's bound for Barranquilla, a port in Colombia, and her skipper is a Spaniard called Hortelano.'

'How on earth do you know that?'

'It's a long story!' He leaned towards her suddenly and kissed her.

'What was that for?'

'For being more or less normal.'

THE END

Wycliffe and
the Four Jacks

W.J.BURLEY

People who know Roseland will recognize the places described, and they may be irritated by inaccuracies in the topography. These are deliberate in order to reduce any risk, through and accidental resemblance, that a real person might be identified with one of the characters in this book – all of whom are imaginary.

W. J. B.

CHAPTER ONE

Thursday June 16th

As usual Cleeve was in his library study by nine-thirty. He stood by the window gazing out over his own garden and the clustered rooftops of the village below, across the creek to the headland where a line of pine trees descended with the profile of the promontory in a perfect curve, almost to the fringe of white water and the sea. Grey slate roofs, the glittering surface of the creek, rising green fields, and the arc of the pines against a misty-blue windy sky. Rain in the offing.

Seven or eight years ago, when he first came to live at Roscrowgy, there had been twenty pines, now there were thirteen; gales and old age had taken an erratic toll. It was absurd, but each morning he counted them in a ritual act, not that he needed to, for any fresh gap would have been immediately obvious.

June 16th; on June 16th, 28 years ago . . .

He heard his secretary moving about in the next room; in a few minutes she would bring in his mail and then he would know.

He watched a fly, a large grey fly with a chequered pattern on its abdomen, crawling up the window pane; it reached the top without finding a way out and went back to the bottom again. He watched while the performance was repeated twice more, then he opened the window and let the creature out, to be whisked away on the wind. As a small boy he had often sought to appease a hostile fate by such little acts of grace.

There was a tap at the door and Milli came in with the mail. She had opened and vetted most of it – everything from his publishers and his agent, everything addressed to him as Peter Stride; she was not permitted to open his Cleeve mail.

He did not turn round, determined to be casual, ordinary.

'Good morning, Mr Cleeve.' Milli bright and brittle.

He said, 'Good morning!' with just the right degree of preoccupation.

Milli was small, with black hair and dusky skin; lithe and agile as a monkey; he sometimes thought she might be capable of all 30 classical positions, but not with him; athletic sex was diversion for the young.

'Anything in the post?'

'Nothing I can't deal with.'

'Then take it away. I want to get on with the *Setebos* revision, so Milli – no telephone.' She was already moving to the door having left the Cleeve mail on his desk. Normally he would have added something facetious. 'Tell 'em I'm suffering from premenstrual tension.'

It seemed all right but at the door she looked back and he fancied she had sensed his unease; not that it mattered.

Childlike, he counted to a hundred before he would allow himself to look at the few items of mail on his desk: four buff-coloured envelopes, probably bills; two white ones with typewritten superscriptions and a third, addressed in bold, well-formed capitals. That was it! He held the envelope for a time without opening it. When he did, he drew out a single playing card – the Jack of Diamonds. Along the top margin of the card someone had written: Thursday June 16th and the number four.

He sat at his desk and with a key from his pocket unlocked the bottom left-hand drawer. It was here that he kept his automatic pistol, the current volume

8

of his journal, and certain lists which might be of use to his executors. There was also a cardboard box which had once held a hundred cigarettes. From the box he removed three envelopes similar to the one he had just received. From each of the envelopes he extracted a playing card, three Jacks of Diamonds identical with the fourth he now had, but each carrying a different date and number. He arranged them on his desk, from left to right: Saturday September 4th – 1, Tuesday March 8th – 2, Friday May 13th – 3, and Thursday June 16th – 4.

He stared at the cards for some time, then with a grimace gathered them up. He put them back in their envelopes and returned the envelopes to the box and the drawer.

Still seated at his desk he reached for the fat wad of typescript which was *Setebos*, picked up a ball-point and set to work. He had thought the opening chapter good, now it had the impact of a wet sponge, but he persevered, making deletions and insertions, knowing they would come out again in a later revision.

Writers come in all shapes and sizes but Cleeve was a surprise to the few people who penetrated his privacy. They found it hard to accept that David Cleeve, who looked and sometimes spoke like a prosperous farmer, must be reconciled with Peter Stride, the sophisticated creator of the terrifying Manipulators in *Xanadu* and the sadistic Preceptors in *Medicus*. A generous build, an open countenance, a fresh school-boy complexion and guileless blue eyes – these, with an exuberant moustache, sandy hair and freckles, must surely mean innocence and simplicity of soul.

The room darkened as clouds crept up the sky and the first flurry of raindrops spattered against the window. At eleven o' clock Milli came in with a cup of black coffee and when she had gone he laced it with whisky.

He existed in two worlds; in this comfortable room

9

with his books and the paraphernalia of his work about him; defined, secure and purposeful; and in that other world of more than a quarter of a century ago through which he had prowled like some feral young animal. That world was no longer real, even his memories of it were vague, like the recollections of a dream, yet it acquired fresh substance through those four cards.

He drank his coffee and when it was gone he went to the drinks cupboard again and poured himself a whisky. He took it to the window and stood there, looking out. A vestige of sunlight silvered the edge of the blue-black clouds and miniature white horses reared on the dark water of the creek, sending the sailing dinghies scurrying for shelter like a flock of frightened geese. During the next hour or so he made other visits to the drinks cupboard and between times sat at his desk brooding over the typescript.

Patricia would diagnose one of his Occasionals – her word for episodes which occurred without warning and at longish intervals, but always with the same scenario. He would start drinking in the morning, contrive some sort of scene over lunch, then continue drinking through the afternoon. In the evening he would go to sleep in a small bedroom near his study and stay there until morning.

The buzzer sounded for lunch and he got to his feet; he was not yet drunk, for his step was firm. In the corridor outside his study he paused by the open door of his secretary's office where she was working, oblivious.

'Milli!' A bellow.

She looked up, startled and annoyed.

'Lunch!'

Roscrowgy sprawled across the flank of a hill, two storeys at each end, single-storeyed between, built on split levels and accommodating to vagaries of contour like a Tibetan monastery. Cleeve had his working suite of rooms on the upper floor at one end, while the dining and reception rooms were at the other. He went down an oak staircase and along the length of a broad passage which had occasional steps both up and down; the floors were of polished wood with Afghan rugs, and the white walls were relieved by a series of large uniform pictures of a Graham Sutherland genre. Patricia's taste; it reminded him of a well-endowed nunnery and he was accustomed to refer to the pictures as Stations of the Cross.

'Bloody hell!' An inarticulate protest.

The dining-room continued the monastic theme; oak floor with rugs, white walls, furniture in natural beech. The table was laid for five but the room was empty. He went to the sideboard and poured himself a whisky.

His wife came in silently and he did not see her at once. Cleeve might have been mistaken for a farmer but there was no mistaking Patricia Cleeve for a farmer's wife. She was a Tull of the Oxfordshire Tulls and God had thoughtfully endowed her with features admirably suited to half-tone reproduction in *The Tatler*. Patricia was forty-three, nine years younger than her husband; an English rose, not yet faded; a blonde, with a pink and white complexion, but with large limpid eyes whose steady gaze could unsettle the most hardened conscience.

Cleeve saw his wife and turned away, but not before she had recognized the symptoms.

Carrie Byrne wheeled in a trolley of food; bowls of salad and other vegetables and a platter of sliced chicken-breast. Carrie, a Tull cousin of thirty-eight, occupied an ambivalent position in the household; somewhere between a member of the family and a housekeeper. In colouring, personality and opinions Carrie was neutral, a congenital 'don't know'. In Cleeve's words, 'Clay which had waited too long for the potter.'

11

They took their places at table; Milli joined them with a muttered apology. Patricia said, 'There's chilled fruit juice if anybody wants it.'

Cleeve mumbled unintelligibly. It was a relief to take refuge in the established routine of an Occasional. No one would question it. 'Are we not to have the twins' company at lunch?' Ponderously aggressive.

'I told you. Andrew is at the School of Mines today. Some vacation work he has to do for his course at the university. Christine is changing; she came back wet from the dig.'

Cleeve looked out of the window at the rain sweeping in from the sea. 'What does she want to spend her time up there for? Surely at her age she's got better things to do.'

Nobody spoke. Plates and bowls passed from hand to hand. With an imperious gesture Cleeve refused the salad but speared several large slices of chicken breast with his fork. Seated at the head of the table he munched the chicken with pieces of bread roll, scattering crumbs and eyeing the three women with sullen aggression. The syndrome was complete.

Christine came in; a slim girl of nineteen with her mother's looks and her father's colouring. She wore skin-tight jeans and a denim shirt; the bloom was intact. She sat in her place, glanced at her father, then at her mother – questioning; her mother answered with the faintest shrug.

At the age of three Christine had dubbed her father 'daddy bear', and it had never been improved upon. It spanned the whole repertoire of his moods, from playful, affectionate whimsicality to the aggressive unpredictability of his Occasionals.

They ate in silence; when it seemed that someone might speak the tension rose, only to subside again when nothing happened. It was Patricia who finally took the plunge: 'How is the dig going, Christie?'

Christie responded with self-conscious enthusiasm.

'Oh, very well. Of course, we spent most of this morning in the shed sorting out pottery sherds; there was nothing we could do outside, but Gervaise says that with any luck we should finish excavating the third hut by Tuesday or Wednesday. Of course, it all depends on the weather. . .'

Christine was a lively, kindly girl with boundless enthusiasm, searching for a cause; the present candidate was archaeology and she had given up her vacation to an Iron-Age dig in Henry's Field, a site adjoining Roscrowgy. The enemy was philistinism in the shape of developers, farmers, tourist boards and planners of every ilk.

Cleeve made a sound which could only be described as a deep growl and turned to Carrie Byrne. 'Did you hear that, Carrie? I don't suppose you've been up to the dig this morning?'

Carrie, realizing that she was to be the focus of today's scene, seemed to shrink into her thin frame like a snail into its shell. She said, 'No, David, I've been doing the shopping.'

'Pity!' He mimicked his daughter's enthusiasm with grotesque cruelty: ' "Gervaise says that with any luck we shall finish excavating the third hut by Tuesday or Wednesday." Think of that now, Carrie! Of course it all depends on the weather.' After a pause he said, 'Gervaise . . .! Bloody pouf!'

Christie flushed but she said nothing. Cleeve glared round the table as though challenging a response and when none came he went on: 'Who cares about the sodding huts anyway? Or the squalid little savages who lived in 'em? If it hadn't been for their screwing we wouldn't be here now and the world would be a better place.'

Patricia turned her steady, disquieting gaze on her husband. 'You are being quite disgusting, David.'

'Me?' He feigned surprise. 'Oh, I forgot! We don't screw in the Shires, we "make love" or we "have sex".'

13

Patricia said nothing but she persisted in her gaze until he lowered his eyes. The meal continued in silence; only Milli seemed quite unaffected by the exchanges; she behaved as though the others did not exist.

When there was no more chicken on the platter Cleeve got to his feet, pushing back his chair so that the legs scraped over the floor.

'Aren't you staying for dessert?'

He glared at his wife and turned away without a word. For an instant he seemed to stagger, but recovered his balance and walked to the door which he left open behind him. They listened to his footsteps down the corridor.

Carrie got up and closed the door. 'David isn't himself today.' Carrie had an unchallenged mastery of the banal. Before sitting down again she went to the kitchen and returned with a bowl of fruit.

They helped themselves except for Christie; she got up from her chair: 'If you will excuse me . . .'

'Aren't you having any, Christie? You mustn't let father upset you like that.'

The girl was near to tears. 'It's so unfair. I mean, it's his land; he gave permission for the dig and he's even paying for it. It doesn't make sense!'

Patricia looked uneasily at Milli, but she was busy dissecting an orange. 'You must know your father's moods by now, darling; he'll be up there as usual tomorrow, telling you all what a good job you're doing.'

'Will he!' Christie went out and her mother watched her go.

'Don't get up again, Carrie; I'll make the coffee.'

While Patricia was in the kitchen the telephone rang; there was a phone in the short passage between kitchen and dining-room and she answered it there.

'Roscrowgy, Mrs Cleeve speaking.'

A man's voice: 'It's me. . . . Is it all right to talk?'

14

'I suppose so; what is it?' She had lowered her voice, so that she would not be overheard in the dining-room.

'I must talk to you, can you come down?'

'If I must.' She was in no mood for her brother's problems.

'It really is important, Tricia.'

'It usually is; I'll be there in about an hour.'

'Can't you make it sooner? I'm really worried.'

'All right, I'll come as soon as I can.'

'Thanks, darling! I know you think—'

'I'll be there as soon as I can, Geoffrey.' And she replaced the receiver. She finished preparing the coffee tray and carried it into the dining-room. 'Where's Milli?'

Carrie said, 'She's gone back to work; she didn't want any coffee. Was that Geoffrey?'

Patricia nodded. 'He's really upset. Of course, it's money. I'm going down there. If anybody asks, I'm taking Biddy for a run.'

A few minutes later Patricia, followed by her English setter, walked down the drive and through the white gates. The rain had eased to a fine mist blown landward by the wind. The estuary and the bay beyond were a waste of grey waters under a grey sky; only the tower of the little lighthouse, like a stumpy candle, stood out white in the gloom. June in Cornwall; but tomorrow, or the next day, or the next, could be gloriously fine.

Down the steep hill, past expensive villas, hidden in their own grounds, to the fringes of the old village. Mount Zion Chapel, then Mount Zion Steps, leading down to the waterfront and the harbour – really a steep, narrow, cobbled street with steps at intervals to ease the slope. Several of the little granite cottages had been tarted up and three or four had been turned into shops.

Patricia made her way down the Steps among tourists,

15

disconsolate in the rain. They turned to look at her and her dog, an unselfconsciously elegant pair. Near the bottom of the Steps a shop with a bow window exhibited a neat sign, gold-on-green: 'Geoffrey Tull, Herbalist and Naturopath.'

There was a 'closed' sign on the door, but Patricia tapped on the glass and a man in his middle thirties came to open it. Geoffrey was fair and good-looking, a blond moustache glistened in the light. But his features were too soft and he was slightly overweight. He wore a green silk shirt and fawn trousers.

Patricia angrily evaded a kiss. 'Don't be so foolish, Geoffrey!'

He was immediately contrite. 'Sorry, darling! But bless you for coming. I would have phoned before but I wanted to make sure that secretary of David's wasn't listening-in at the other end.'

Patricia snapped. 'You know perfectly well that the house phone is a separate line.'

Inside, the shop was laid out like a small Edwardian pharmacy with gilded glass jars on the shelves and a battery of little polished wooden drawers behind the counter, each labelled with its white-enamelled plaque: *Arctium lappa, Laurus nobilis, Spiraea ulmaria* . . .

'Come through to the back where we can talk.'

Biddy settled complacently on the doormat.

The back room was a laboratory-cum-kitchen where the herbal decoctions, extracts and tinctures were prepared.

They sat on stools. 'Now, what is this about?'

He put on an absurdly guilty look, like a small boy confessing to naughtiness. 'It's about money, Tricia, dear.'

'So I imagined.'

'But this is worse than anything . . . Connors from the bank rang this morning and asked me to come and see him.'

'Well?'

16

'He's stopping my cheques unless I can find a guarantor or pay off my overdraft.'

'You must have seen this coming.'

Geoffrey squirmed. 'Actually, Tricia, I didn't. The money has been coming in pretty well lately; business is brisk, and I just didn't do my sums.'

Patricia sighed. 'Will you never learn?' She shifted impatiently on her stool. 'What exactly are you asking me to do? I'm not made of money, Geoffrey: I only have what David gives me and he likes to have some idea where it goes.'

Saturday July 16th

In a rented cottage on the waterfront Wycliffe stood at the window and looked across to that same headland and those same pine trees which Cleeve contemplated ritually each morning. Only the narrow road to the castle and the low sea wall separated the cottage from the water. In the creek, sailing dinghies formed a fixed pattern on the surface of an unrippled sea. A boy in a rowing-boat, oars shipped, trailed a fishing line; children idled in the shallows. There was a raft moored off-shore for swimmers and on it a girl in a bikini stood motionless. It seemed to Wycliffe that the scene had been frozen in an instant of time, as though a ciné-film had suddenly cut to a single frame. Then, into this static world, came a bustling ferry boat, pushing a moustache of white water ahead of blue bows; another cargo of trippers from Falmouth, and more to come. They would spill out on to the quay and spread through the village spending their money in the shops and cafés, helping to sustain the inhabitants through the long close season.

The Wycliffes had arrived that morning for a fortnight's holiday walking in the Roseland peninsula. It was no more than 50 miles from home, and part of his police territory, yet they had never explored the area, never visited the places with those evocative names

17

which sprinkled the map: St Just, St Mawes, St Anthony, St Gerrans, Percuil. . .

They had lunched at a wine bar a few doors away; crab salad with a carafe of white wine. Since then Helen had made up their bed in the little upstairs room which had a timbered ceiling and a latticed window. It was beginning to feel like a holiday.

Helen was taking off her apron. 'I thought we could look round the village this afternoon – perhaps go over the castle, then tomorrow we could start our real walking. . .'

They joined the drifting movement of visitors and trippers along the waterfront in the direction of the quay. There were shops and pubs, toytown banks with original opening hours, and some elegant little houses that had metamorphosed from fishermen's cottages. Most of them had their pots of geraniums, begonias or mesembryanthemums outside.

The beach was a strip of grey shingle. White and pink flesh was exposed there within the limits of decency; there were no deckchairs, no life-guards (only a leaden soldier could drown there) no radios – in fact, no anything but the rather grubby-looking shingle and the well-mannered sea.

The shops seemed unexciting, at least resistible, but Helen dawdled and Wycliffe said, 'I'll wait for you by the harbour.'

He rejoined the meandering groups; all ages and both sexes clad in shorts, T-shirts and bikinis, sometimes with startling effect. Alone among them an elderly man made his dignified way, immaculate in a pale-grey suit and a white straw hat; he carried two library books; a relic. To Wycliffe he seemed like a gentle dinosaur loose among baboons.

Arrived at the harbour, Wycliffe lit his pipe and rested his arms on the sea wall to watch three youngsters – two girls and a boy, putting off in a tiny drop-keel sailing boat. Orange lifejackets and blue shorts.

He had been brought up on Arthur Ransome long before he had even seen the sea. Did these children lead story-book lives? After 30 years in the police he was still looking for the kinds of people he had read about as a child. The man in the white straw hat, these children . . .

Helen joined him and they continued their walk but almost at once she was diverted again.

'Look!'

A narrow cobbled street, little more than an alley, rose steeply away from the waterfront, the knobbly spine of the old village. A blue-and-white-enamelled sign read: Mount Zion Steps – and there were steps at intervals to ease the slope and a tubular iron handrail to assist the weary. The granite-fronted houses were stacked against each other like steps themselves; one had a 'Police' sign over the front door. There were a few shops, rather twee: a herbalist's with a bow-fronted window, a vegetarian restaurant all varnished pine ('We must eat there sometime'). Further up a shop sold silver brooches and buckles of Celtic design, and next to that was a photographer's which looked as though it had been left behind by the 'twenties.

Helen was attracted by the brooches displayed on simple velvet cushions in the little window of the jewellery shop; they were oddly interspersed with books bearing esoteric titles: Earth Magic, Leys and Power Centres, The Psi Connection . . . There was also a hand-written poster headed, 'The Celtic Society of Roseland' and announcing, 'There is still time to halt the desecration of Henry's Field! Details inside.'

The shop was so small that they had just room to stand between the counter and the door. Jewellery was displayed in the glass-topped counter-case, and on shelves behind the counter were more books of pseudo-science for the lunatic fringe.

A woman came from somewhere at the back: middle forties, big-boned, strong features, with blonde, shoulder-

19

length hair, a striking woman. She wore an emerald-green frock that was almost a gown, a silver torque round her neck and silver bangles on her arms which were bare to the elbows. Theatrical but effective.

Her manner was crisp. 'As you see, the showcase is divided into three: hallmarked silver pieces to authentic Celtic designs on your right; modern enamel-on-copper pieces in the middle; and a selection of similar enamel-on-silver designs to your left.'

She stood, monumentally immobile, an operatic princess awaiting her cue. Helen asked to see a particular tray of the Celtic designs and it was lifted out on to the counter without a word.

Helen pointed to a brooch of intricate pattern, 'I think this one is very beautiful, don't you, Charles?'

The princess volunteered, 'That is late-Irish – the triskele design is based on an eighth-century medallion in the National Museum, Dublin.'

A Siamese cat came from somewhere and leapt on to the counter, examining the customers with green-eyed suspicion. Wycliffe reached out to stroke it.

'I shouldn't touch her! She can be quite aggressive with strangers.'

Helen, concentrating on the brooches, said, 'Do you make these lovely things yourself?'

'I do.'

They bought the brooch and while it was being packed in its box with a certificate of provenance Wycliffe said, 'What's this about Henry's Field?'

The blue eyes sized him up. 'Henry's Field is on the hill above the village. With the Stone Field next to it, it is one of the sacred places of the Celtic people and the ground should never be broken or ploughed. It is situated at the convergence of ley-lines from early Celtic settlement sites over the whole Roseland peninsula and is a centre of power.'

'So, what are they doing with it, building council houses?'

She suspected him of levity and became more severe. 'If you are genuinely interested you should read the Society's leaflet.' She handed over a couple of pages of duplicated typescript, clipped together. 'You will see that after remaining undisturbed for close on two thousand years the site is now being excavated by archaeologists who should know better.'

They escaped. Outside, with her brooch, Helen said, 'It cost a lot of money, Charles.'

'Never mind, call it an unbirthday present.'

At the top of the Steps they were brought face to face with the non-conformist Gothic of Mount Zion Chapel; they had reached the boundary of the old village. Further up the hill, nineteen-twentyish villas peeped out from behind their thickets of laurel and bamboo, escallonia and hebe, and there was a larger building which looked like an hotel. A black-on-yellow AA sign pointed still further up the hill: *To the Excavations*.

Wycliffe said, 'This must be what Boadicea was talking about; shall we take a look?'

The hill was steep and the sun was hot but the climb was short and, looking back, they could see the creek, the Fal estuary, and the bay spread out like a sixteenth-century map, with Henry VIII's two castles facing each other across the narrows, and the lighthouse at the bottom of its grassy promontory, its feet almost in the water. A container ship in ballast, putting out from the harbour, churned up a foamy wake.

They passed an estate with Roscrowgy on the white drive-gate, and immediately beyond there was open land covered with gorse and heather. At a considerable distance from the road they could see, well spread out, a large wooden shed, two bell-tents which looked like army surplus from the Boer war, and a caravan. Another AA sign directed them down a narrow, stony lane and brought them to the shed. Over a large area, where gorse and heather had been cleared, the ground was

21

marked out with surveying poles and ribbons and a number of young people, minimally clad, were working in trenches.

A notice on the shed read: 'Henry's Field Iron-Age Site. Visitors welcome. Please report here.' Field archaeologists are usually polite, probably because they are territorial intruders.

The wooden hut was part office, part museum and part laboratory, all in a space less than 20 feet square. A pretty, auburn-haired girl was scrubbing something in a sink and a minute or two went by before she became aware of the Wycliffes and came over, wiping her reddened hands on a towel.

'My name is Christine. If you know anything about archaeology please say so; there's no point in me nattering on about things you know already.'

They were shown aerial photographs of the site before excavation began.

'These were taken in winter when the vegetation had died down. You see the outlines of the hut-circles? They seem to be cut off abruptly at the Roscrowgy boundary, that's because the settlement extended into what is now part of the garden of the house . . . We'll look at the actual dig first, then we'll come back here and you can see some of our finds. . .'

They followed her out of the hut to where the work was going on and she dutifully kept up the flow of information. 'Henry's Field is most likely a corruption of an old Cornish name for the place, *Henros* – hen means old and *rōs* means heath . . . the field bit has been added. This is the hut numbered "one" in the photograph—'

'Mr Wycliffe! A surprise to see you here!' Gervaise Prout, whom Wycliffe had met in connection with security arrangements for a touring exhibition of archaeological goodies from the Far East. A man in his early fifties, with a mass of white curly hair, a long thin face with a healthy outdoor tan and slightly

22

protruding teeth. His voice was high-pitched and there were occasional disconcerting ascents into actual falsetto.

The girl looked disappointed at losing her audience and Prout apologized handsomely: 'I really am sorry, Christie, but Mr Wycliffe and I are already acquainted.'

This disposed of, he turned to Helen and greeted her with nervous cordiality. 'A pleasure, Mrs Wycliffe! I hope you and your husband will allow me to show you round.'

So they were shown round the site by Prout instead of the girl. 'Actually it's a very promising dig. Plenty of "B" pottery as we expected, but I'm fairly sure some of the fragments are from the "A" period which would put us in the same league with Bodrifty . . .'

They had reached the highest point of the field where they were able to overlook the house and part of the garden next door.

Helen said, 'How extraordinary! It's like a ranch house – who lives there?'

'Don't you know?' Prout seemed surprised. 'That's Roscrowgy – David Cleeve's place. He owns this field and the Stone Field next to it. As a matter of fact he's our patron. He put up most of the money for this dig.'

Wycliffe asked, 'Should we know him?'

Prout laughed. 'Perhaps not as Cleeve but you will have heard of Peter Stride. You must have seen his books in the shops even if you haven't read them. I must confess, I'm no addict.'

But Helen was, with a row of Stride's fat masterpieces on her shelves. She was impressed. 'You mean he lives there? Is he there now?'

Prout seemed pleased to display his intimacy with a celebrity. He glanced at his watch. 'Half-past three. You may see him while you are here. He often takes a stroll round the site about this time. Incidentally, Christine, the auburn-haired girl who brought you over, is his daughter. Charming girl!'

23

Wycliffe had read Stride's books and seen three or four of them serialized on TV, though with less enthusiasm than Helen. The man had a remarkable ability to create an atmosphere of brooding dread, a chilling awareness of violence.

Wycliffe said, 'I gather you've had some opposition to your dig.'

A short laugh. 'Madam Laura and her ley-lines! There's an old superstition about this having been an ancient Celtic burial ground for the whole Roseland peninsula, so anyone who disturbs the dead et cetera et cetera . . . It seems that the tale got a fresh lease of life some years back when the previous owner of Roscrowgy took part of Henry's Field into his garden and was dead within the year. Nobody mentions that the poor man was a cardiac case.' Prout made a dismissive gesture. 'In any case this has never been a burial place nor was it a sacred enclosure. It is an ordinary settlement site which seems to have enjoyed an unusually long period of occupation, making it more interesting than most.'

They completed their tour and Prout led them back to the wooden hut. He pushed open the door and they were confronted by two men in earnest conversation; one was large and pleasant-looking with a luxuriant reddish moustache. There was something expansively Edwardian about him and he carried a polished cherry-wood stick with a silver mount that was almost a staff. The other was very tall, of a skeletal leanness, with a completely bald head; he was terribly disfigured down the left side of his head, face and neck, as if by burns.

Prout, for no obvious reason, was clearly displeased by the encounter, but with contrived affability he performed the introductions – 'Mr and Mrs Wycliffe, Mr David Cleeve, of whom you have heard, and Mr Kitson, a neighbour who takes a great interest in our work here.'

A mild surprise for Wycliffe to discover that the amiable-looking one with the reddish moustache was Cleeve.

A shaking of hands and murmured exchanges without meaning. Kitson immediately excused himself and left. Wycliffe noticed that the disablement extended down the whole left side of his body, for he limped badly and held the arm on that side at a curious angle.

Cleeve had been formally polite, then his manner changed to sudden interest: 'Wycliffe? Not Superintendent Wycliffe?'

'I'm afraid so.'

Cleeve laughed. 'This is my lucky day! I've always wanted to meet a real live detective. I cut my literary teeth on what French call *le roman policier* and criminal investigation fascinates me still.'

Hard to believe that this pleasant man, apparently anxious to be agreeable, was the author of a dozen books which were not only money spinners but considered worthy of detailed study and analysis by literary critics and psychologists, so that there was already a considerable literature on the Stride phenomenon.

They chatted easily for a few minutes then Helen said, 'You live in a beautiful place, Mr Cleeve, and you seem to have a delightful garden.'

'Are you interested in gardening – either of you?'

Wycliffe said dryly, 'Helen is, and I'm learning.'

Cleeve chuckled. 'I sympathize; it's the same with us. Patricia – my wife – is the gardener but I have to sort of caddy for her and make the right noises.' He broke off abruptly. 'Why don't you come over while you are here and let Patricia take you round? She never misses a chance to show off her garden.'

They displayed a proper reluctance, but allowed themselves to be persuaded. They were shepherded across the field, through a wicket gate into the garden of the house, and along a mossy path through a rhododendron tunnel which brought them to a door at one end of the long, rambling building.

Cleeve pushed open the door and they were in a garden room with a blue-and-white-tiled floor, ornamental white tables and chairs with striped cushions. Almost the whole of one wall was open to a courtyard garden where there was an ornamental pool and a fountain with Berniniesque figures.

'I'll find Patricia – do make yourselves at home. What can I get you to drink?'

They refused drinks.

'Later perhaps,' Cleeve said.

Helen whispered, 'What a charming man! But not a bit like I expected; he's so *ordinary*.'

Cleeve came back with his wife, a slimly elegant blonde. She wore a cornflower-blue frock which fitted without a crease and made Helen feel uncomfortable in her M & S slacks and blouse. But Patricia Cleeve was cordial in her welcome.

'David is quite right; I love showing off my garden but I get little opportunity. Most of our visitors are only interested in publication schedules, copyrights and royalties. But really a garden is not much fun unless friends come to look at it – don't you agree, Mrs Wycliffe?'

It seemed obvious that the two women would hit it off.

'Shall we start here in the courtyard?'

Cleeve said, 'I'm going to be selfish and cut the garden routine, if I may. I want to show Charles my workshop.'

A fairly smooth operation, but Wycliffe was in no doubt that it was one, and had been from the first moment of their meeting.

Cleeve took him along a corridor, elegant but severe, with disquieting pictures and institutional undertones, up a flight of stairs to a landing with doors opening off. Wycliffe could see into one room, a business-like office where a girl was sorting pages of typescript. Cleeve's

26

own room was next door; large and L-shaped, a combination of office and library with creature comforts catered for, but it was in total contrast with what he had seen of the rest of the house: Edwardian; thick red Wilton on the floor, heavy mahogany bookcases, straight-backed leather armchairs and a huge desk with an inset leather top.

'Sit you down. You'll find my chairs comfortable. If a soldier marches on his stomach a writer writes on his backside, so I've made a study of chairs. You can lounge in one of these or you can sit at a desk – both in comfort; and you can push it around on its castors. I abominate those articulated swivel things which remind me of the dentist's. Darwin wrote his *Origin* sitting in one like this so that gives me a chance.'

He opened a drinks cupboard. 'What will you have? Whisky is my tipple.'

'A small one then – no water.'

Cleeve brought over the drinks; half a tumbler for Wycliffe.

They prepared to engage. Wycliffe said, 'This is good whisky.'

'Whiskey with an "e" – it's Irish. My publisher has a house in Kerry. I've no idea where he got this but, knowing him, I wouldn't be surprised if it was moonshine out of a Kerry bog.' Cleeve was watching Wycliffe, trying to gauge his responses, but Wycliffe was at his most bland, wearing what Helen called his 'well-meaning-vicar look'.

'Have you read any of my books?' The question came with a disarming grin.

'All of them, I think.'

'And?'

A thoughtful pause. 'I think they are extremely well written and compelling. Does that sound patronizing?'

'If it does, I asked for it. So you don't like my books, but do you take them seriously?'

Wycliffe drank some more whiskey with an "e": it

27

really was very good – smoother than the scotch to which he was accustomed. 'I take them very seriously.'

'But in official jargon you probably feel they tend to corrupt and deprave; is that it?'

'No, it isn't!' Wycliffe was short. 'Your books depress me because you write about a world without hope. God is dead; heaven is empty. I'm simple enough to hope and believe that there must be some chink of light in the darkness somewhere.'

Cleeve laughed. 'I've said already, this is my lucky day. Drink up! The prophet of doom and gloom! One critic called me Bunyan without a pilgrim.' He became serious again and looked at Wycliffe quizzically. 'A non-conformist background? Liberal-cum-Fabian Socialist? Don't be offended; it's no good if we waste time being polite. Have I got it right?'

'Just about.'

A satisfied smile. 'I'm out of the same stable. Totally backslid, I tell myself, but it sticks like shit to the proverbial blanket. It left Arnold Bennett too inhibited to indulge the one vice he really fancied – screwing nubile girls under pink lampshades. I must say it's never got me that way – stopped me, I mean.'

Wycliffe pursued his theme in self-defence. 'Even your "good" characters seem doomed through circumstance to add to the evil in the world—'

Cleeve cut in sharply. 'And that worries you? Don't you think it worries me? But I write about the world as it is – at least as I see it; a world with no sense of guilt because it has lost its sense of sin. After thirty years in the police you must surely go some of the way with that.'

Wycliffe smiled. 'I will admit I sometimes wonder if our generation was the last to be burdened with a sense of guilt. I don't think it follows that people no longer distinguish right from wrong or that the future is wholly black.' He emptied his glass. 'Anyway, now that the courtesies have been exchanged and the ice broken, perhaps you will tell me why I am here.'

Cleeve's face was like water which takes on the changing moods of the sky; the blue eyes and the fresh, open countenance could darken in an instant. They did so now.

'I do want something from you; something I'd be very unlikely to get from the nearest cop-shop – advice without strings. Your profession is one of those where it's very difficult to bypass the GP and get to the consultant direct.'

'Except by kidnapping the consultant.'

A brief smile. 'The fact is, my life is threatened. I know that sounds dramatic but I'm satisfied that it is the case.'

Wycliffe waited.

'The threats have come through the post – four so far, extending over a period of about nine months.' Cleeve's nervousness showed; he fingered his rather ragged moustache and looked at Wycliffe with obvious anxiety.

'Have you any idea who is threatening you?'

A momentary hesitation. 'None.'

'Is it David Cleeve or Peter Stride who is threatened?'

A quick, appreciative glance. 'Oh, Cleeve. Because of the kind of books I write all sorts of cranks send abusive and threatening letters addressed to Stride. I take no notice of them.'

The casement window was open and voices came from the garden below. Patricia Cleeve's, rather high-pitched but musical; Helen's softer, her words inaudible. Wycliffe felt irritated; they were on holiday and they had come, casually, to look at an archaeological dig, now they seemed trapped in other people's lives. He made an effort.

'So the threats are personal and you take them seriously. In that case I think you must have some idea why you are threatened.'

Cleeve picked up the whisky bottle. 'Let me top you

up!' Wycliffe refused and Cleeve replenished his own glass. 'I've told you I don't know who is threatening me.'

'May I see these threats – I suppose they take the form of letters or cards?'

'I destroyed them.'

Wycliffe was patient. 'You say you received the first one about nine months ago; when did you get the last?'

A frown. 'About a month ago. It indicated that time was running out.' He grinned self-consciously. 'Sounds like something out of Agatha Christie, doesn't it? "The end is near." '

'Is that what it said?'

'Of course not, but that is what it amounted to.'

It was obvious he was lying; at least suppressing most of the truth.

'Did these communications have postmarks?'

'Oh yes – all over the place – one was from London, another from Durham and the last was posted in Exeter. I think the third one came from Bristol – something like that anyway.'

Wycliffe took refuge in the official manner and sounded pompous. 'Mr Cleeve, if you want help from the police you will have to be more open with me. Originally you said that you wanted my advice – it's this: whatever the circumstances, if you think you are in danger, you must be completely frank. Without more to go on it isn't possible for me to tie up for your protection men needed elsewhere.'

Cleeve said quietly, 'I am not asking for protection; I don't want it.'

'What, then?'

He leaned forward across the desk and spoke with great seriousness. 'I want to be sure that if anything happens to me – if these threats are carried out – my family will not be plagued by the police. You understand?'

'I'm not sure that I do.'

Cleeve sighed. 'It's not easy to explain; that is why I'm talking to you instead of some cloth-eared detective sergeant in the nearest nick. If a man in my position is murdered the police will dig into his private life and find God knows what reasons for suspecting his relatives and close associates – money, jealousy, sex . . . I don't have to tell you what the family of a murdered man has to go through if there is any mystery about the crime.' A twisted little smile. 'I don't have to tell you either what may come out when the lid is lifted off that Pandora's box which we call family life.'

'You are saying that if you are murdered the police should look for suspects outside the circle of your family and friends.'

'Exactly! I would rather they didn't look at all, it wouldn't do me any good, but that would be too much to hope for. I've thought of putting this in writing and attaching it to my will or something of the sort, but when you turned up out of the blue it seemed too good a chance to miss.'

He was smiling, a nervous, tentative smile. 'I'm trouble enough to my family alive; I don't want to haunt them when I'm dead.'

Wycliffe was brusque. 'There is very little I can say to you, Mr Cleeve. Your obvious course is to allow the police to investigate the threats to your life and prevent them being carried out. If you decide to do this or if you have any more to tell me, you can get in touch at any time. I advise you to think it over.'

Cleeve nodded. 'The official line; I couldn't expect anything else but I've said my say and you will remember it if anything happens.' He got up from his chair. 'Now, let's see how the women are getting on.'

Wycliffe felt uneasy; even guilty, but what more could he do? His irritation increased. Why couldn't he and Helen have a holiday like anybody else?

They ate coq au vin with a green salad and drank a bottle of over-age Beaujolais in a restaurant close to the harbour. The other diners were mostly unisex boating

31

buffs in blue jerseys and carefully bleached jeans with expensive labels on their bottoms. They wore canvas shoes and talked a cryptic jargon incomprehensible to the uninitiated. The meal was second-rate, but for the buffs it was the chance to talk that mattered. Wycliffe seemed preoccupied.

Over coffee Helen said, 'What exactly did David Cleeve say to you? You've been broody ever since we left them.'

Wycliffe looked around at the other diners, babbling away for dear life and none of them listening. It depressed him. A character in one of Cleeve's books had been made to say: 'Once people were individuals; they struggled; at least with the illusion that they might change things; now, unresisting, resigned, they're swept along by a great wave which must soon break.'

For Wycliffe, that was the real trouble with Cleeve's books, they focused the mind with the unrelenting intensity of a burning glass.

He muttered, 'I'll tell you later.'

When they left the restaurant the sunset was glowing red over the castle, and overhead the sky was pale blue-green. The air was silky and people were sitting out at tables in front of the pubs, feeling just a little awed by the vast stillness of it all. The trippers had gone home, there was no traffic, and the waters of the harbour mirrored the moored craft. Herring gulls, nicely spaced on the sea wall, meditated on eternity.

'Well?'

'He thinks his life is in danger.'

'You mean someone wants to kill him?'

'That's what he says. Someone is threatening him; he doesn't know who or why. Of course he's lying.'

'You mean he isn't being threatened?'

'I mean that if he is, he knows where the threats are coming from and why.'

'What are you going to do?'

He snapped, 'What can I do?' Then quietly, 'Sorry!

But unless he is prepared to give me the facts I can't spend police time on him; he doesn't even want it. Did you get any impression of the family from his wife?'

Helen considered; always careful about making judgements of other people, she made a dull gossip. 'She seems a very pleasant woman, fond of her children and interested in what they do.'

'And her husband?'

Longer consideration. 'I had the impression that she looks upon him not so much as a man and a husband, rather as a kind of monument or institution to be preserved.'

'Not much affection between them?'

'I don't know. People can become very attached to monuments and institutions even when they are something of a liability.'

Back at the cottage he lit his pipe and stood in the doorway, watching the dusk take possession of the creek, the hill opposite, the pine trees and the bay. Finally he turned away. 'I'll sleep on it.'

CHAPTER TWO

Sunday July 17th

They agreed to split up for the morning. Helen would walk along the coast path to St Just then on to Philleigh in time for a snack lunch at the pub and Wycliffe would join her there with the car.

'I want to find out what the local sergeant knows about the Cleeves.'

Sunday, a day like any other; there would be the same tourists, and even more trippers, the same parade along the waterfront, the same sailing and wind-surfing (given some wind) but it would all take a little longer to get started. Sunday is a sluggish day, as though God, unable to preserve His day of rest, has nevertheless applied the brakes.

As Wycliffe climbed Zion Steps to the house which was home and office for the police sergeant, the single bell of the village church called to worshippers with a blatant and monotonous insistence. In the chapel they were already singing. 'There is a land of pure delight . . .' Let's hope so.

Sergeant Pearce answered the door in his shirt sleeves, a grey-headed old warrior with his years of service recorded on his countenance like notches on the stock of a gun.

'Just a courtesy call,' Wycliffe said.

'I heard on the grape-vine that you were with us, sir.'

Wycliffe took him out for a drink and Pearce introduced him to a bar at the back of The Buckingham Arms.

34

'Non-emmet,' Pearce said. (The word emmet derives from the Old English for ant and is the Cornish vernacular for a summer visitor.)

The Buckingham presents a brash face to the waterfront but keeps a little bar at the back for locals.

Pearce explained: 'The emmet who strays in here soon begins to feel like a pork butcher in a synagogue – unless, of course, he's somebody's guest.'

They drank lukewarm beer, sitting on hard seats, but without space invaders, fruit machines or juke boxes, and with plenty of privacy. The bar had just opened and they were the only customers.

'They'll get busy later.'

Wycliffe mentioned the Cleeves.

'We hardly ever see Cleeve himself but his wife and daughter do a bit of sailing and they're members of the club. Mrs Cleeve seems a nice woman. Then there's a son – the children are twins – he's about quite a lot in the vacations. He's got a rebuilt MG which is the envy of all the young blood in the village.'

Pearce got out his tobacco pouch. 'I hear you're a pipe smoker – try some of this, sir. I grow it and cure it myself but it's not at all bad.'

They filled their pipes and smoked peaceably. Wycliffe found the tobacco pleasant; mild and sweetish to the tongue. Rum and molasses.

'Going back to Mrs Cleeve, she's got a brother in the village, a chap called Tull – Geoffrey Tull – he runs a herbalist's shop further down the Steps; you may have noticed it. He calls himself a naturopath, whatever that is. He seems to have a good business but I fancy he spends faster than he gets and I've heard that his sister has had to bail him out of trouble more than once.'

Wycliffe diverted the flow. 'I gather Cleeve isn't too popular with some people over these excavations.'

Pearce chuckled. 'The Roseland Celtic Society. Chairperson, Mrs Laura Wynn – she's got a shop on the

Steps too – jewellery, near the top. She's a strange one. If she was ever married I don't know what happened to her husband but it wouldn't surprise me if she'd eaten him.'

'Is the feeling over the dig very strong?'

Pearce scratched his cheek with the stem of his pipe. 'I doubt if the real Roselanders care a cuss either way, but some of the newcomers want a bit of colour in their lives and they've decided to revive what they call the Celtic tradition.'

'What do they do?'

Pearce was intrigued by Wycliffe's interest but he asked no questions. He took a swallow of beer and wiped his lips. 'Until this excavation lark started, not much that I could see. They have a bonfire on the Stone Field twice a year – Mayday eve and Hallowe'en, and I believe they go up there sometimes at sunrise to dance round in their nightshirts in a yoghurt-induced frenzy, pretending to be druids or something.' Pearce spoke with a vast tolerance of human vagaries bred of a lifetime in the force. 'I got to admit I was never up there to see.'

'And since the excavations started?'

'Ah! Officially I don't know anything about that as nobody made any complaint, but I understand they went up there two or three times in the early stages and pulled up all their markers – that sort of thing. It seems they've stopped that caper now and decided to play it legal; they're getting up a petition and talking about an injunction, though I can't think who'd put up the money for any court case.'

'I don't suppose it bothers Cleeve too much.'

'You wouldn't think so, but about the same time as they began talking about the dig in Henry's Field, Cleeve employed a firm of private inquiry agents to investigate Laura Wynn.'

'How do you know that?'

'A complaint from the lady herself about a strange

36

man asking her questions and talking about her to her neighbours. I made a few enquiries, asked around a bit, and it turned out to be Charlie Cox who used to be a DC at sub-division and now works for Sowest Security Services. Over a jar Charlie told me his agency had been briefed by Cleeve.'

'To do what?'

'To find out who the woman was and where she came from – that was all.'

Wycliffe looked at the empty glasses. 'Shall we have another?'

'No, sir; thank you. Not for me; I've had my ration for a morning session.'

'Me too; I'd like to get back to your office and use the telephone.'

In a neat little office, looking out over Zion Steps, where even the rubber stamp knew its place, Wycliffe telephoned his headquarters.

'Who's on duty in CID?'

'DS Watson, sir, but Chief Inspector Scales is in his office as it happens.'

'Good! Put me through, please.'

He talked to his deputy, John Scales. The usual smokescreen of words which takes the place of the sniffing ritual in lower animals, then: 'I want you to set going a few enquiries, John. Have you heard of Peter Stride?'

'Who hasn't? But he's not a favourite of mine at the moment. Jane has an American girl over here doing a PhD thesis on *The Man and his Work*. (Jane Scales was a lecturer at the university.) She can't get near him. Just a note from his secretary: "Mr Stride thanks you for your interest but he does not give interviews, neither does he furnish details of his private life. He prefers to be judged on his published work alone." '

'He may have a good reason for that! Anyway, I want you to find out what you can about him through the usual channels. You probably know already that his real name is Cleeve – David Cleeve; he's a little older than me, married to Patricia née Tull – an Oxfordshire family. She's several years younger. They have twin children, boy and girl, aged about nineteen . . . They've lived here for several years . . . No, I don't mind if he gets wind of our interest . . . As far as I know he hasn't done anything except tell me a half-baked yarn about his life being threatened . . . No, I'm quite prepared to believe he's being threatened but he won't give us enough detail to help him . . . Yes, it's pretty obvious he's afraid of incriminating himself in some way . . .'

That and a word to sub-division arranging for the Panda patrols to keep an eye on Roscrowgy, made him feel better. Not that it would do Cleeve any good if someone had decided to stem the flow of contentious masterpieces with a bullet or a loaded sock, but it was all he could do.

He joined Helen at the Philleigh pub for lunch and afterwards they crossed by the chain-ferry to Trelissick and spent the afternoon walking in the gardens and woods. Wycliffe grew nostalgic about life in the great days of houses like Trelissick, until he remembered that he would have been among the forelock-touching minions on the wrong side of the green-baize door.

A pleasant tea in a former barn with the chaffinches more than ready to go shares.

Monday July 18th
Cleeve was following his morning ritual, counting the pine trees. The sun was shining directly into his room and it was already hot. He opened the window and let in the fresh air along with the sounds from outside, the gulls screeching, the shouts of children playing in a garden further down the hill, a helicopter pulsing distantly, somewhere over the bay. For most people it was another summer's day; for him it was Monday July 18th and he was waiting for Milli to bring in the mail.

She came at last, wearing a sleeveless frock with shoulder straps and a plunging neckline, more provocative than if she had been nude. But today he hardly noticed.

The routine 'Good morning!'

Milli said, 'There are a couple of queries from Lester about a TV serialization of *Medicus* you'll have to look at. Apart from that. . .'

'Leave it on the desk with the others.'

On the way out she stopped. 'Are you all right?'

'Why shouldn't I be?'

A shrug of the bare shoulders.

After an all but sleepless night he had been up since first light and from eight o'clock he had felt like a man living on borrowed time, as though the minutes, the seconds, were being doled out to him with miserly reluctance. Once more he seemed to bestride two worlds.

He crossed to his desk; the Cleeve mail was there, five or six envelopes . . . the third was white, addressed in block capitals, postmark Truro. He opened it, the card was there but it was in two pieces; a Jack of Diamonds roughly torn across. In the margin of each half, the date: Monday July 18th and the number 5.

After a while he returned the torn card to its envelope, unlocked the bottom left-hand drawer of his desk and added the envelope to the four others contained in the cigarette box. Automatically he checked the other contents of the drawer: his pistol, three clips of ammunition, the current volume of his journal, and a slim file of documents.

He closed the drawer and locked it. For a while he stared out of the window, watching a squadron of herring-gulls perform breathtaking aerobatics as they mobbed one of their number who carried a coveted morsel of food in its beak. He reached a decision and went out into the corridor, calling to Milli.

'I'm going out.'

'Out? What if Lester phones?'

'Tell him.'

'Tell him what?'

'You'll think of something.'

He collected his stick and let himself out of the house by a little-used side-door, crossed the garden, and passed through the rhododendron tunnel and the wicket gate to Henry's Field. There he followed a path diagonally across the field to the wooden shed. He raised his stick in salute to the students at work on the dig, and came to the shed and the narrow, rutted lane which led in from the road. He continued down the lane and reached an area of woodland, part of what was once a much larger area preserved for shooting. As he entered the trees he felt calmer; there was an atmosphere of claustrophobic seclusion and remoteness which brought to mind the sombre fairy-tale forests of childhood and, paradoxically, made him feel safe.

He came to a house in a clearing, pushed open the slatted gate and walked up the garden path. The garden had run wild, a paradise for butterflies and bees. An old wicker chair with sun-bleached cushions stood by the front door; the door was open and Cleeve could see into the dimly lit interior of the cottage. A table covered with a green chenille cloth, shared between an ancient Remington portable, a pile of books, and a sleeping tabby cat. Peace descended upon him like the holy dove.

'Anybody home?' He tapped on the door with his stick.

A moment, and Kitson's lean figure emerged from the kitchen at the back, stooping to clear the low lintel. In an old cotton shirt and trousers which were too short he looked like a broomstick man.

'Ah! The squire on a tour of inspection of his property.' The voice was soft and the words were accompanied by a smile which, because of his disfigurement, involved only half his face.

40

Years of mortifying self-consciousness had established a conditioned reflex so that he usually contrived to present his uninjured profile.

'Aren't you going to ask me in?'

Kitson turned back into the house and Cleeve followed him into the front room which was a combination of living- and work-room. Sparsely furnished, with just the table and three or four chairs, the room overflowed with books; there were shelves everywhere. Two small, square windows looked out on the garden wilderness and in each was a jam-jar of wild flowers – foxgloves with flowering shoots of meadowsweet.

Cleeve was tentative. 'I know you don't like day-time visits . . .'

Kitson said, 'You're here now. What about a drink? Elderberry, dandelion or blackberry . . .'

'Christ! I should have brought a bottle.'

'Yes. The squire should never visit empty-handed.' The gentle and whimsical manner seemed to belie his words.

Kitson went into the kitchen and came back with a bottle and glasses. They sat on the hard wood chairs – Windsor strutbacks, and Kitson poured two glasses of slightly viscous purplish wine.

'Elderberry; said to ease the bowels.'

Cleeve said, 'My bowels won't need easing today.'

Kitson sipped from his glass. 'My calendar says Monday July 18th. I can guess why you're here.'

Cleeve nodded. 'You guessed right.'

But he felt relaxed here as nowhere else. There was an atmosphere of timeless serenity and for a little while it was possible to believe in Shangri-La and Santa Claus.

Kitson earned a meagre living, translating Russian texts for publishers and others.

Cleeve, self-absorbed, said, 'It's an uncomfortable feeling, Roger – unnerving. I would never have believed it could have affected me so.'

41

Kitson smiled. 'You're a fraud, Davy! You write as though it needed more courage to live than to die but, come the crunch, and you tremble before the Old Reaper like the rest of us. "Be absolute for death", Davy, then "either death or life shall thereby be the sweeter".'

Cleeve laughed despite himself. 'You always were a Job's comforter, you old devil!'

On that same Monday the Wycliffes crossed to St Anthony and visited Place House, site of an ancient Celtic religious foundation, made holy in the first place, according to local tradition, by earlier visitors of greater distinction, none other than the boy Jesus and his uncle, Joseph of Arimathaea. Later visitors are supposed to have included Henry VIII and his new bride, Ann Boleyn, completing a honeymoon begun at Hampton Court. Now it can look with condescension on other houses whose only boast is "Queen Elizabeth slept here."

Tuesday July 19th
A hot, sticky night; the Wycliffes had tossed and turned in bed, disturbing each other, then at first light they had fallen into a dead sleep and awakened unrefreshed.

They planned to drive to Pendower, to walk the coast-path to Portloe, and return to the car by way of Veryan.

'Have we got the map?'

'It's in the car.'

'The binoculars?'

'They're on the window-seat.'

'We're ready then. . .'

The telephone rang and Wycliffe answered it. Sergeant Pearce.

'Divisional Inspector Knowles's compliments, sir. He'll be over as soon as possible. He's notified headquarters, but as you're here he thought you should be told. . .'

'Told what?'

'There's been a death by violence, sir – here in the village; suspected murder.'

Wycliffe thought of Cleeve and his heart missed a beat. 'Who?'

'A young woman found dead on her bed.'

'How did she die?'

Pearce was cagey. 'There's some doubt about that, sir – not straightforward at all. Dr Hodge spoke of poison which, he said, was not self-administered.'

Wycliffe looked out of the little latticed window. The sun was still shining on the water and on the fields beyond; there were still dinghies whistling for a wind, and people continued to pass to and fro along the waterfront, but he was no longer part of it.

'Where is she?'

'Mount Zion Steps; two doors down from my place. The house is in two flats and hers is the lower one.'

'Who found her?'

'The milkman, and he came to my place to telephone for a doctor. It wasn't until Dr Hodge had seen her that there was any thought of foul play.'

'All right; I'll meet you at the house shortly.'

He looked across at Helen; she was standing by the window with her back to him but when she turned round she was already resigned. 'A murder case?'

'It looks like it; too early to say for certain. What will you do?'

'Don't worry. I may drive into Truro if you don't want the car, or I could take the ferry to Falmouth.'

He telephoned John Scales.

'Ah! I'm glad they got hold of you, sir. . .'

It was all arranged. Initially, Scales was sending Detective Sergeants Smith and Lane with three constables. 'I'll get two more DCs off to you later in the day, sir.'

Detective Sergeant Lane – Lucy Lane, a recent recruit to his squad. Wycliffe professed freedom from

43

sex prejudice but he recalled Dr Johnson on the subject of women preachers – 'like a dog walking on his hinder legs. It is not done well; but you are surprised to find it done at all' – and reserved judgement.

Time would tell.

'What about Franks?' Franks was the pathologist.

'I caught him at the hospital; he's hoping to be with you about midday.'

Wycliffe turned once more to Helen: 'I'll be off then.'

Helen said, 'A floral shirt and light-fawn slacks might raise a few eyebrows, don't you think?'

He had to change.

The little house was half-way up Zion Steps, almost opposite the jewellery shop where Helen had bought her brooch. It was like being suddenly transported backstage from a seat in the stalls.

The sombre granite frontage had been tarted up with bright-blue paint on the woodwork of windows and door. Pearce was waiting for him outside.

'Better go round the back, sir.'

A little way down, there was a passage giving access to a narrow lane running along the backs of all the houses in the block, and the house of the dead girl had a yard from which blue-painted steps gave separate access to the upper flat.

Pearce pointed to a ground-floor sash window, open several inches at the bottom; the curtains were drawn but didn't quite meet. 'She's in there, sir; that's her bedroom.'

'Who is she?'

'Celia Dawe – a girl in her early twenties; a real eye-catcher, the sort men turn to look at in the street – women too, for a different reason.'

'Local?'

'Yes. She was an orphan, brought up by her uncle and two maiden aunts – the Borlases, who keep the photographer's shop further up the steps. She's been away for a few years but she turned up again last season. Jack Polmear, the landlord of The Buckingham Arms, gave her a job and let her have this flat which used to be his mother's until she died a year or two back. There's an old lady in the top flat still – Maggie Treloar – she worked for the Polmears for donkey's years.'

'The girl didn't go back to her relatives?'

Pearce scratched his long nose. 'I don't think it would have worked; she probably left in the first place because she couldn't get on with her uncle and aunts – they're an odd family, great chapel people and probably very strict.'

'Have they been told?'

'Dr Hodge went over there. I thought I'd better not leave here more than I had to.'

'This chap Polmear seems to have put himself out for the girl.'

A sly grin. 'Jack's wife divorced him a year or two back but as long as I've known him he's had a succession of girl friends; this one is just the latest in line.'

'Was she a tart?'

Pouted lips. 'I wouldn't say that; I think she looked on a man as security. Incidentally, she's been seen about a lot with young Cleeve since he came home on vacation a few weeks ago.'

'I gather the milkman found her?'

'Yes, it seems they had an arrangement; if she wasn't up and about when he came he was to bang on her bedroom window. He did this morning but got no reply, then he saw her through the gap in the curtains. He realized something was wrong when she didn't wake and tried the back door; it wasn't locked and he went in. . .'

'Have you got his statement?'

'No, when the doctor came he went on with his round but we can pick him up.'

'Is there access to this yard other than through the alley from the Steps?'

45

'Yes, the back lane continues up into Chapel Street.'

Wycliffe found it hard to realize that he was starting on a murder inquiry. So far these people were not real to him; he still felt detached, as though he were reading about them in a newspaper; he was still on holiday.

'Let's go inside.'

Through a small kitchen which was modern, though none too clean; the remnants of a fish-and-chip take-away on the table; dirty dishes in the sink.

Pearce said, 'Apart from this and the bathroom she only had the two rooms – a little parlour facing out on the Steps and her bedroom overlooking the yard.'

In the passage Pearce pushed open a door and they stood just inside the girl's bedroom. There was a carpet on the floor; a double bed and a dressing table took up most of the space. A television set on a stand was placed at the foot of the bed; the clothes she had been wearing were in a little heap on a tub chair, and there was a floor-to-ceiling cupboard, presumably her wardrobe. White curtains were drawn across the sash-window but they did not meet and the window itself was open a little at the bottom so that the curtains were stirred by a draught. Despite the fresh air, there was a stale smell blended of cosmetics and woman.

Celia Dawe, completely naked, lay on her right side; a grubby sheet and a duvet trailed over the foot of the bed; her shoulder-length blonde hair spread over the pillow. There were no obvious signs of injury or violence but her features were contorted as though in a spasm of pain.

'She was lying on her back,' Pearce said, 'but Dr Hodge shifted her. You see he's marked a small punc-ture wound in her left buttock.'

A reddish ring, apparently drawn with the girl's own lipstick, surrounded a tiny puncture high up on the left buttock where the hips began to narrow to the waist.

The puncture itself was at the centre of a brown spot like a mole.

They were standing by the dressing table which was littered with cosmetic bottles and jars. Pearce pointed to a glass specimen tube lying in the lid of a jar of face cream. In the tube was a little dart-like object which seemed to consist of a fine needle in a brass holder. The needle was stained brown as though by rust.

'Dr Hodge found the dart on the floor by the bed; he reckoned it must've dropped out of the wound and rolled there.'

Wycliffe examined the tube, removed the stopper and sniffed. 'Nicotine!'

'That's what the doctor said, sir.'

There was nothing they could do until the technical people had done their work so they went out into the yard.

'You haven't had a word with the old lady upstairs?'

'No, sir, I haven't had a chance but I'll do it now.'

Wycliffe said, 'Leave it. There's something else I want you to do. We shall need an incident room; I'd prefer a large room or a small hall — somewhere with a bit of space. I hate those caravan things where you're afraid to breath for fear of upsetting somebody else's cocoa. Any ideas?'

Pearce nodded. 'I'll see what I can do, sir.'

The divisional inspector had left again with his DC, relieved to be let off so lightly. Wycliffe had said, 'It's too early; I'll let you know if I need more local assistance, it depends on the amount of leg-work. At the moment I want Pearce freed of normal duty and assigned to me. In addition, you can leave me your uniformed man to defend us from snoopers.'

The truth was that he preferred to work with a small team of his own men.

Now he was going up Zion Steps to the photographer's shop. Tourists were plodding up and ambling down in a thin stream, women with sun-reddened skins, paunchy men and bored children. Nobody showed the slightest interest in what might be happening in the little house with the blue paintwork, but that could change once word got round.

A tall, bald-headed figure threaded his way among the tourists; an animated scarecrow, his head and face were terribly scarred on one side; Kitson, carrying a plastic bag, doing his shopping. Mutual recognition and acknowledgement.

It was hot, Wycliffe could feel the damp patches under his arms and he promised himself a cold beer at lunchtime.

W. Borlase and Son, Photographers: faded gilt lettering on a brown fascia; a double-fronted shop with one window devoted to wedding photographs and child studies while the other was filled with historical photographs recording the life of Roseland through more than a century.

Joseph Borlase stood in his shop, a little back from the door, watching the approach of his visitor. He was a soft, fleshy man of about fifty with the unformed features of a plump baby; he wore a fawn linen jacket, a white shirt with a bow tie, and dark trousers. He saw Wycliffe pause for a moment outside, sizing the place up, then the door opened and a bell sounded discreetly. Everything in the shop was both dusty and discreet, the potted palms, the framed photographs on the walls and displayed on easels, the ornately carved screen with velvet curtains which separated the shop from the studio; the place could scarcely have changed in 50 years.

Wycliffe introduced himself. 'I think Dr Hodge broke the news of your niece's death . . . I'm very sorry . . . I understand that you and your sisters are her next-of-kin – is that correct?'

Borlase was sweating though it was cool in the shop; there were beads of sweat under his eyes and he wiped them away with a silk handkerchief from his breast pocket as though they were tears.

'Celia's parents were killed in an accident when she was three . . .' His voice was soft as melting butter. 'My sisters and I brought her up . . . My sisters are a good deal older than I . . . it wasn't easy.'

Wycliffe said, 'I don't know what Dr Hodge told you but we suspect that your niece was murdered.'

'Murdered!' A murmured exclamation of horror.

'Did you think she had died a natural death?'

'What?' The blue eyes were troubled. 'Dr Hodge mentioned poison . . . I thought it must have been an accident. Perhaps that she had taken her own life – not murder . . .' His words seemed to hang in the air, breathy and moist.

'Your niece left home several years ago, I believe. Where did she go?'

Joseph rolled his handkerchief into a ball and was kneading it with both hands. 'I don't know, super-intendent . . . After breakfast one morning she went out and never came back . . . We found that her clothes were missing . . . She was eighteen. Three days later we had a card with a London postmark. It said that she was well and that she wouldn't be coming home . . . We heard nothing more until at the beginning of last summer she arrived back in the village.'

'Didn't she offer any explanation of where she had been or why she had come back?'

'She never came near us – we heard she was back from neighbours and then she came to live just a few doors away. She never came to see us.'

'Did you or your sisters go to see her?'

He looked mildly shocked. 'It wasn't our place . . . After all we'd done for her, to be treated like that!' He wiped his face once more; his pores seemed to ooze moisture.

'So you have had no contact with her since she came back?'

49

'None.'

'For practical purposes, Mr Borlase, I have to ask whether you are willing to act as next-of-kin – there will be formalities, the body will have to be identified, there will be an inquest and arrangements to be made for the funeral.'

A sigh. 'I quite understand. I hope I know my duty.'

Wycliffe looked round the shop with its air of dusty, fossilized gentility. Celia Dawe had lived in the place with this man for fifteen years of her life. 'Is there anything you would like to ask me, Mr Borlase?'

'Ask you? No . . . I don't think so . . . There is, perhaps, one thing . . . I mean her belongings.'

'What about her belongings, Mr Borlase?'

'I wondered . . .' He hesitated. 'Shall I be able to claim them? I'm sure that my sisters will feel . . . I mean things of family interest . . .'

'If she has left no will I imagine all her property, whatever it is, will come to you and your sisters eventually.'

It was evidently not what he had hoped to hear. The handkerchief was kneaded more vigorously. 'Perhaps I could come over and go through her things . . . I mean, we ought to know exactly what her circumstances were . . .'

Wycliffe was puzzled. He said firmly. 'I'm afraid there can be no question of that until our investigation has gone a good deal further than at present. Of course, there is nothing to stop you getting in touch with your solicitor regarding your rights.'

He shook his head with unaccustomed vigour. 'No! No, we wouldn't want to do that . . . I merely thought . . . The whole business is so very painful.'

Wycliffe decided to leave it there. Borlase came and stood on the step, watching him as he crossed over.

Cleeve was at his desk; he had the typescript of *Setebos* in front of him but it was no more than an excuse, he had scarcely turned a page for the morning. He was not drinking either, he was waiting. Since half-past nine when Milli brought the mail he had seen no one and no one had telephoned. Unless he gave specific instructions it was rare for him to be undisturbed for so long.

The windows were open and from time to time he went over to stand, looking out. Not a cloud in the sky, the sun blazing down, the air shimmering in the heat, and everywhere, silence. A strange silence it seemed to him, even a conspiracy of silence. He dismissed the fanciful notion but without conviction. He looked at the long-case clock which he wound religiously every Saturday morning – ten minutes to eleven. In ten minutes Milli would bring him his coffee. Perhaps then . . . Milli had her own way of gathering news; he suspected her of operating her own KGB in the village.

The night of Monday July 18th . . . last night. An incredible coincidence and an incredible stupidity on his part; he could almost believe that the events of the night had been a dream.

The old clock cleared its throat, as it always did a couple of minutes before striking, and just then there was a tap on the door. Milli came in with the coffee on a little tray.

'Do you really want this? Or is it too hot for coffee?'
'Don't I always have coffee?'
She shrugged. 'As you like. Do you mind if I have a shower? It's sticky in that room.' She squirmed inside her frock and her hard little nipples protruded through the thin material like beansprouts.

She was signalling; he could have her if he wanted, as he had done before, still wet from the shower. He was tempted, but this was not the time.

He said with contrived casualness, 'By all means have a shower if you want one. No calls?'
'No, it's quiet this morning.' She paused, looking at

him. 'All right, I won't be long. I'll switch the phone through.'

He could imagine what she would do in the shower. 'Little whore!'

He laced his coffee with whisky. Two or three minutes went by and there was another tap at the door; he thought it was Milli, back on some pretext, but to his astonishment it was Patricia. He couldn't remember the time when she had come to him in this part of the house.

As always, Patricia looked relaxed and cool. 'I hope I'm not disturbing you?' Her calm gaze took in the whole room and he was sure she had not missed the lingering fragrance of whisky.

'Of course you're not disturbing me! Sit down. Will you have something? Coffee? A drink?'

It was absurd, he was treating her like a visitor.

She remained standing, aloof. 'I was in the village this morning and I met Nancy Hodge – the doctor's wife.' Patricia was never sure how much he knew of the village. 'Hodge was called out this morning to that little house on Zion Steps which Polmear turned into flats . . .' Her eyes were on him, unwavering. He sat at his desk, gently stroking the ragged ends of his moustache.

'Celia Dawe – Borlase's niece – has been living in the bottom flat and working at The Buckingham . . . The milkman found her this morning, dead on her bed.'

'Dead? What did she die of?' His voice sounded unreal.

'That's the point. Hodge called in the police and now your friend Wycliffe is down there. Nancy hinted that they think the girl was murdered.'

'Murdered? That is ridiculous!'

'Why is it ridiculous?'

He realized that he had been too emphatic. 'Well, who would want to murder the girl?' Feeble.

Patricia did not relax her gaze. 'I'm worried, David.'

'Worried?'

A flicker of annoyance. 'Please don't fence with me! You think if you close your eyes you can't be seen.'

Cleeve spread his large freckled hands on the desk and seemed to study them.

Patricia went on: 'There is Andrew to consider.'

'Andrew?'

'You must know that he has been seeing a lot of that girl since he came home this time. That at least will be common talk in the village.'

Cleeve said nothing. Patricia remained standing; she had gone as far as she was prepared to go.

'You remember that we shall have guests this evening?'

'I hadn't forgotten.'

The headquarters party arrived; they trooped into the back yard of Celia Dawe's flat led by Detective Sergeant Smith – the squad's photographer, fingerprint man and resident Jeremiah. He was trailed by Detective Constable Shaw – the administrative assistant, and two DCs carrying gear – like porters in darkest Africa. Smith would take charge at the scene-of-crime; Shaw would look after communications and records.

'We had to park a quarter of a mile away.' Smith, the eternal victim.

Wycliffe said, 'Is DS Lane not with you?'

'She's coming in her own car.' This, too, seemed a matter of grievance.

Franks, the pathologist, was not long after the police party. By contrast, Wycliffe had never known the plump little doctor anything but cheerful. He was ruled by two passions, women and fast cars, and age had not withered nor the years contemned.

'Seventy minutes from the hospital, Charles! Not bad over these roads.'

Wycliffe, whose speedometer rarely touched 60, was unimpressed. 'One of these days a bright lad in traffic

53

will stay awake long enough to book you. I only hope it happens before you kill somebody.'

Franks grinned. 'Still the same old Charles! Where is she? It is a she, isn't it?'

Wycliffe led the way into the house. Smith had already taken a number of shots of the room and the body; now he would record each change of position during the pathologist's examination.

Franks looked down at the dead girl. 'She was beautiful, Charles! "The nakedness of woman is the work of God . . . The lust of the goat is the bounty of God." You wouldn't approve, you old Puritan! But Blake said that – it's poetry . . . What's the hieroglyph on her bottom in aid of?'

Wycliffe pointed to the specimen tube containing the dart. Franks picked it up and examined it through the glass, then took out the cork and sniffed.

'Nicotine, my God! Fancy stuff, Charles. It's a long time since we've had a decent poisoning – gone out of fashion. Too much bother; needs a bit of nous – planning. Easier to clump somebody over the head.' He held up the little tube. 'Who has a go at this? Me or Forensic?'

As always, Wycliffe reacted to Franks with gloomy disapproval. 'You know better than that. You do your Stas-Otto on the tissues and leave the clever stuff to the whiz-kids at Forensic.' After a moment, he added, 'I suppose there's no harm in you taking a look before passing it on.'

Franks said, 'You'll want to know whether she had a man.'

Wycliffe waited in the yard. The professional callousness of pathologists made him uncomfortable. But things were beginning to move. After a while, Pearce came back wagging his tail like an old spaniel with his master's slippers. He had found a little building once used by the village school, now in planning limbo.

'Where is it?'

'In Chapel Street at the top of the Steps. It belongs to the chapel and they're always glad to make a few pounds by letting it.'

'Good! Put DC Shaw in the picture and let him get on with it. I want you here.'

Shaw would arrange for a pantechnicon to bring furniture, office equipment and a communications unit from central stores.

Detective Sergeant Lucy Lane put in her appearance; this would be the first time she had worked directly under Wycliffe. She had applied for a vacancy in Serious Crime Squad from a divisional CID and, with an ear for his conscience and an eye on the discrimination acts, Wycliffe had agreed to the appointment. Her qualifications were impeccable, beginning with an honours degree in English Literature. She had the vital statistics of a Miss World and at first had been a major distraction in the duty room, with cases of the wandering hand as well as the wandering eye. In the end she had put a stop to it in a single memorable sentence; she said simply, to all within earshot: 'If you want sex in your work you can play with each other or with yourselves, not with me.'

Wycliffe gave her her instructions: 'I want you to brief yourself with the local man, Sergeant Pearce; let him put you in the picture about the place and the case. Then you can start on house-to-house with DC Curnow to assist. There's an old lady who lives alone in the flat above this; she might have something to tell us. Obviously we want to know whether anybody saw or heard anything last night – they probably didn't; but we also want gossip. Don't turn your nose up at gossip. More than half the leads in a case like this stem from it.'

The dark eyes were innocent.

'Yes, sir. I remember you making that point in a lecture you gave when I was in training school, way back in '78.'

55

First blood to the lady.

Franks's preliminary examination did not take long and he rejoined Wycliffe in the yard.

'You can have her shifted, Charles. In my opinion she's been dead between fifteen and twenty hours, which puts it between nine and two last night. The only sign of injury is the puncture wound and what I've seen is consistent with her having died of a quick-action poison injected into her system. Nicotine would fill the bill very well and that dart stinks of the stuff. Of course I'll be able to tell you more when I've done the PM and the tests.'

He wiped his bald head with a silk handkerchief. 'God, it's hot! Nicotine – where would he get it? It used to be used by horticulturalists as a pesticide but I don't know if it still is – you and Helen are the gardeners. Vets use it as a vermifuge . . .'

'Surely penetration of the skin by a needle simply dipped in nicotine wouldn't be fatal?'

'No; there must be more to that dart. You're after a man of ideas, Charles, and God knows, there aren't many of them left. Murders these days are merely brutal. The Borgias invited their victims to dine; this chap coaxed his into bed – I like that.'

'She definitely had a man with her?'

'Definitely! I might be able to tell you his blood group from the semen, though much good that will do you at this stage.'

The mortuary van came to the top of the Steps and the girl's body had to be carried up on a stretcher, providing a brief diversion for the sightseers. End of Celia Dawe who left home at eighteen for the big city but came back to her village five years later to work as a barmaid and sleep with her boss. Wycliffe muttered irritably, 'Stupid youngsters! Chasing rainbows!'

But now they could get on.

Wycliffe went back to the flat. Smith and his assistant

were creating havoc in the bedroom, looking for uncon-
sidered trifles. Smith was good at his particular job
because he could be single-minded about little things;
no detail would escape him, his problem was to see the
broader picture.

Wycliffe poked about in the kitchen. Celia had not
been a housekeeping girl. The cupboards were empty
except for a few basics – tea, coffee, sugar, a packet
or two of breakfast cereal and a few tins. She had
probably eaten most of her meals out. In the bathroom,
the bath and basin had a soapy rim and the loo cried
out for that wonder liquid which kills 'all known germs
DEAD!'. Knickers and bras were draped on a string
stretched over the bath.

He went into the front room – the parlour; a dreary
little room with a window looking out over the Steps.
No sun and little enough light. It was furnished with
a dusty three-piece suite, a sideboard, a table . . . There
was a carpet on the floor and framed prints of soulful
maidens looked down from the walls. Even on this hot
July day it smelled of damp and disuse; it was almost
certainly as Polmear's mother had left it. The girl had
used the flat only as a place to sleep.

Wycliffe let himself out by the front door and stood
for a moment looking up and down the narrow street,
taking it all in afresh. Subconsciously he was beginning
to see the place through the eyes of a local. Opposite
was the shop where Helen had bought her brooch,
and he was aware of being watched by the lady with
the long blonde hair. She must be wondering what
he had to do with the happenings across the road.
Next door to the jeweller's was the photographer's
and it was in those rooms with the bay windows
over the shop that Celia Dawe had spent most of her
childhood.

Feeling more at home he strolled down the Steps to
the waterfront and the lounge bar of The Buckingham.
The pub did a good trade in light lunches; most of the

tables in the bar and in the walled courtyard were occupied by people eating crab or prawn salad, cold meats, or grilled fish. He chose the prawns and found a table in a corner by the bar. He wondered where Helen was lunching and felt hard done by at missing his holiday in such ideal weather.

Waitresses in blue nylon overalls flitted between the tables with trays held high. He felt conspicuous in a suit. Behind the bar a middle-aged man, running to fat, kept an eye on it all. He wore a white shirt, a bow tie and black trousers: Polmear, the landlord. His fair hair was thinning but carefully combed to disguise the fact. His eyes rested momentarily on Wycliffe, registered his presence and moved on.

Wycliffe took his time over the meal; drank two glasses of chilled lager and followed this with coffee. By that time customers were dwindling, a bell sounded. 'Last orders for drinks, please.'

The waitresses were beginning to clear the tables; Wycliffe went over to the bar where Polmear was lighting a cigarette.

'Mr Polmear?'

Recognition, not of the man but of his mission. 'You are . . .?'

Wycliffe told him: 'I think you know why I'm here.'

'Yes, it was a shock.'

'I would like to talk to you in private for a few minutes.'

Polmear called through a hatch to another bar. 'Chris! Take over here for a bit. . . This way.'

Wycliffe followed him into a little office where there was just room for a desk and two chairs; no natural light. 'Will you have something?'

'Not now, thanks.'

Polmear tapped ash from his cigarette into an ashtray advertising lager.

'You've known her a long time?'

'Since she was a kid – three or four years old. Her

58

parents were killed in an accident somewhere up north and she came to live with her aunts and uncle – the Borlases – they're a brother and two sisters.'

'You've taken an interest in her since she came back?'

A shrewd look. 'I gave her a job and found her somewhere to live.'

'Altruism?'

Polmear trickled smoke through his thick lips and watched it rise. 'Not altogether; I did feel sorry for her – she was down on her luck but I also thought she'd make a good barmaid, and she did; she had looks, a pleasant manner, an eye for the till and, when necessary, she knew how to cool it.'

'Couldn't she have gone back to the Borlases?'

A broad grin. 'You must be joking! I mean, she stuck it as long as she could the first time round. The Borlases have to be seen to be believed and he's as kinky as they come, in spite of his chapel-going.'

'So Celia Dawe was simply an employee of yours whom you helped in various ways?' Wycliffe at his most bland.

Polmear grinned. 'You know damn well she was more than that; the whole village knows I spent most nights up there. It suited us both, I'm divorced and Celia had got into the habit of having a man in her bed.'

'Were you there last night?'

He looked shocked. 'My God, I wasn't! I haven't been up there for more than two months.'

'Why not?'

'Because she found somebody else. That was fair enough. She was looking for security and she knew she couldn't expect it from me. She told me she'd taken on somebody else and that was the end of it as far as I was concerned. No hard feelings; I've never gone short.'

'Who was this other man?'

'I don't know – none of my business.'

'But I expect you could make an informed guess.'

He shook his head. 'Straight up, I couldn't. They must have kept it pretty quiet because I never heard a whisper. Now, I suppose, he's done for her. She was an unlucky kid – never got it right.' His manner was relaxed and natural, concerned but not nervous. He was playing with a ball-point, flicking it in and out. 'She liked to play it rough: some women do; I suppose he went too far and strangled her.'

'She wasn't strangled.'

'No?'

'She was poisoned.'

'*Poisoned!*' Polmear was incredulous. 'Then I'm a long way out . . . If that's the case it sounds like a woman. . . . Are you sure it wasn't an accident?'

'Could her new bedfellow have been young Cleeve?'

Polmear shrugged. 'It started before he came home on vacation. It's true she's been running round with the boy but I guess that was fun, not business.'

'When did you last see her?'

'Last night when we closed.'

'Was she her usual self?'

'She seemed so to me; she was in the other bar and I didn't see a lot of her.'

'One last question. Have you any idea where and how she spent the years she was away?'

Polmear lit another cigarette. 'I know she was in London and that she had several jobs; she had a spell in a strip club then, through her boy friend, she got bit parts in the theatre. By the time she decided to chuck it and come home she was sharing a flat in Bayswater with a girl friend and working in a café in Queensway . . . Come to think of it, she used to hear from that girl so you may find letters.'

Wycliffe left the pub and joined the crowds on the waterfront. The holiday circus was in full swing, the car park was full, boats peeled off from the quay, laden with their quota of emmets, to 'cruise round the creek and view the lighthouse' or 'tour the harbour and docks at Falmouth'. Laughs, cries, shouts and occasional shrieks came from the shingle beach, now at its greatest low-tide extent. Village, creek, castle and pine trees shimmered in the afternoon heat.

He was beginning to get some sort of picture of the dead girl – of whom he had never heard until that morning. Like thousands of others she had set out with little more than an undiscriminating greed for life. Such a girl might, conceivably, end up being strangled by a lover; it was a credible climax. But this girl had been poisoned – poisoned by someone who had carefully and deliberately planned to murder; someone with a knowledge of poisons and access to one of the most lethal; someone with the ingenuity and skill to prepare a dart which must have functioned as a miniature hypodermic.

Not a crime of passion but of cold, festering hatred.

The man who had slept with her on the night of her death was the most obvious suspect but, in Wycliffe's view, not the only possibility.

He saw the bedroom in the eye of his mind; the bed across the window, with only a couple of feet of space between; the window open at the bottom to the yard, the flimsy curtains scarcely stirring; the night sultry and still. The girl on the bed quite naked.

He sensed that this would be a plodder's case, nothing to be gained by running round in ever diminishing circles to meet the fate of a certain legendary bird, but step by step; stone on stone.

Back to the present. He had been leaning on the sea wall staring at nothing. In his sombre suit he must have looked like an undertaker at a party. A few feet away a woman painter in water colours had set up her easel; her colours were spread out on a little tray and a water-pot dangled from a hook. It needed courage, so nakedly to expose one's talents.

61

Wycliffe made for Zion Steps. As he passed the herbalist's he was recalling his encounter with Cleeve. Within three days of his arrival in the village on holiday he had been consulted about threats to a man's life and confronted with the murder of a girl. Coincidence? Reason said 'Yes', but instinct, cautiously, 'Perhaps not'. Was young Cleeve's association with the dead girl a significant link? Cleeve had made a deep impression on Wycliffe and though his first reaction was antagonistic he sensed the man's profound disquiet, his self-disgust, and wondered what the cause might be.

At the girl's flat Smith was still in the bedroom, his assistant, DC Edwards, had been assigned to the other rooms. The bedroom looked as though the removal men were expected at any moment. The dressing table had been cleared of cosmetics and toiletries and in their place was an array of labelled polythene envelopes, large and small. Smith, wearing his rimless half-glasses, sat on the stripped bed writing in his notebook – always an exercise in copy-book script which magistrates and even judges had commended.

'Anything to tell me?' One had to be careful with Smith, a too-precise question might elicit a long exposition of some side-issue while more vital information waited in the queue.

Smith got up from the bed, removed his glasses, and pointed to his envelopes. 'There's a lot of stuff to go through when I get back.'

'Anything of immediate interest?'

Smith smoothed his lantern jaw. 'She was saving money.' He picked up one of the envelopes. 'Building Society pass-book. In the past year she's paid in four thousand pounds, a hundred or two at a time, and she didn't do that on a barmaid's wages, even allowing for tips.'

'Anything else?'

Smith looked over his collection in the manner of a connoisseur selecting his best pieces. 'A few letters –

not many – but one recent, from a girl she seems to have been with in London. That might mean something.' He searched through another envelope and came up with a two-page letter written in large, round hand and almost devoid of punctuation. 'I've marked the bits which might be interesting.'

Wycliffe skimmed the lines. 'It looks as though you was right to go back you seem to have struck it lucky for once. I never heard of him but I wouldn't would I. The boy seems nice even if he is a bit wet but I think you could make trouble that way . . . What about your uncle. Have you seen him again . . . Yes I would like to come down for a week in September if I can get time off then . . .'

The letter was signed 'Liz' and there was no address.

I never heard of him but I wouldn't would I. The boy seems nice even if he is a bit wet but I think you could make trouble that way . . . The boy was obviously young Cleeve. Could the other, of whom Liz had never heard, be his father? *You could make trouble that way.* By running father and son in tandem?

Wycliffe shrugged. Perhaps he had Cleeve on the brain.

Polmear had said that Celia had worked at a café in Queensway; if necessary the Met would find the café and from there it should be possible to find Liz.

Smith was scratching his grey cheek with an earpiece of his glasses – one of many idiosyncracies which would have endeared him to a cartoonist. He said, 'I had a visitor this afternoon, sir – the girl's uncle who keeps the photographer's shop. He wanted to help in sorting through her stuff. I told him we could manage. He seemed upset.'

Wycliffe went through to the back yard; he wanted to satisfy himself that it would have been practicable for the killer to enter the yard and approach the open window of the girl's bedroom without any great risk of being seen.

The yard was too small to swing the proverbial cat but it was private, only overlooked by windows belonging to the two flats and, standing close to the bedroom window, one was shielded from view in the upper flat by the projecting landing at the top of the stairs. Wycliffe stood there without being noticed by Smith who was sitting on the bed with his back to the window.

A blue-painted door in a stone wall opened into the back lane. Wycliffe let himself out and walked up the narrow, grass-grown track which had a step or two at intervals, until he joined Chapel Street. He was satisfied that at any time after dark the killer would have been very unlucky to be spotted if he approached the house that way.

CHAPTER THREE

In the chapel schoolroom Shaw had worked a trans-
formation; it had already acquired the atmosphere of a
duty room in a rather sleazy nick with the traditional
amenities: battered furniture, ancient typewriters,
buckled filing cabinets, and tin-lids for ashtrays. On
the whole it was a convenient arrangement, certainly
preferable to those mobile rabbit hutches where it is
scarcely safe to sit down without warning. There was
even a little cubby hole with a window which would
serve as an interview-room. There had been three or
four calls from press and radio, routed through sub-
division. Shaw had handed out Wycliffe's prepared
statement to the effect that a young woman had been
found dead in bed in suspicious circumstances, and
that the police were investigating the possibility of
foul play.

Wycliffe was facing the prospect of coming to terms
with the Lane girl and regretting the loss of his old
sergeant – now inspector – Kersey. ('You lose your
best men in the promotion stakes.')

There she was, sitting at one of the typewriters,
looking cool and competent in a butcher-blue frock
which seemed right for her colouring. He had to
admit that she dressed sensibly; that she had a professional look, crisp and clean as a new banknote, which
was more than could be said for some of her male
colleagues.

Shaw was duty officer and Sergeant Pearce was
helping DC Edwards with his share of the scene-of-

crime report. Two old-timers got together! Add Pearce's service to Edwards's and you had a lifetime.

Shaw said, 'Cuppa, sir? Tea or Instant?'

The chipped mugs were lined up, plastic spoons at the ready; home from home.

Shaw went on: 'Dr Franks would like you to ring him at this number, sir, and Mr Scales rang to say that Potter and Dixon will be here sometime this evening.'

Wycliffe was put through to Franks.

'How's this for service, Charles?' Franks full of himself as usual. 'Your girl died of nicotine poisoning – no doubt about that. No doubt either that it was injected by that dart which was really a miniature hypodermic, crude but ingenious: a bit of brass tube, sealed at one end and fitted with a hardwood plunger, well greased and pierced with a sawn-off length of hypodermic needle. The nicotine was contained in the tube behind the plunger and as the needle entered the skin it was forced through into the tissues. Not exactly a precision job, but effective. I estimate that it delivered the equivalent of sixty milligrams plus of the pure alkaloid. I expect the boffins at Forensic will set up all sorts of elaborate gadgets to demonstrate how it worked, but you can take it from me the girl died because that thing was jabbed into her backside.

'What puzzles me is why he didn't use an ordinary hypodermic; they're easy enough to come by. I suppose it would be a bit awkward, going to bed with one and biding your time . . . but the more you think of it the more extraordinary it seems that a man should choose that way of murdering his mistress.'

Wycliffe said, 'We are assuming that she was killed by the man who slept with her.'

'Surely that's the most likely?'

'I don't know. What is the external diameter of the brass tube?'

'External? I can't say offhand, but I made a detailed

66

sketch of the thing before passing it on. I'll check.' He was soon back: 'Almost exactly five millimetres – why do you want to know?'

'Just curiosity.'

Franks sighed. 'Well, if it wasn't the guy who was screwing her then your case really is wide open. I wish you joy, Charles.'

As Wycliffe put the phone back on its cradle he muttered to himself, 'Not that wide.' The killer must have had access to nicotine and the knowledge and manual dexterity to contrive a suitable dart for its injection. Added to that, he had, presumably, sufficient acquaintance with Celia Dawe to generate a motive for murder. Really a fairly neat set of crossbearings.

He! Always he! But might not the killer have been a woman? It is a cliché to say that poison is a woman's weapon, but statistically true. And there was something about the sustained rancour suggested by the careful and lengthy preparation which pointed, perhaps, to a feminine cast of mind.

He had been standing in the middle of the room, hands in pockets, brooding; now he turned to Lucy Lane and tried out his thoughts after bringing her up to date.

She met him half-way.

'I agree, it's hardly the way a man would murder his mistress.' She had a way of wrinkling her forehead as she spoke which gave her words an added seriousness. 'All the same, the man who was with her must have been there up to a short time before, if not actually when she died, and you would expect him to come forward.' She hesitated, then went on, 'As to the feminine cast of mind when it comes to nursing a grievance, my brother teaches in a school where three male members of staff haven't addressed a single word to each other in fifteen years.' She grinned. 'But I suppose you would call them "old women" anyway.'

Wycliffe laughed. 'Speaking of old women, have you seen Borlase yet?'

'Borlase and his two sisters. I saw them in the house-to-house routine and I'm just writing up my report. They're a weird trio and I feel sorry for any girl brought up by that lot. Incidentally, the old lady who lives above Celia Dawe's flat says Borlase has been to see his niece several times since she came to live there and that more than once she's heard voices raised as though they were quarrelling.'

No surprise there. He had suspected as much. 'She may have been trying to blackmail her uncle – perhaps succeeding. He was desperately anxious to take possession of what he called "her things" and when I turned him down he had a go at Smith, offering to help with the sorting out. He's obviously scared of what we might find, but in point of fact Smith has almost finished there and we've found nothing that need worry him.'

Wycliffe had perched himself on the edge of her table, now he got out his pipe and started to fill it; a sure sign that he was relaxing his guard. 'Did you get anything from the old lady in the top flat about the girl's night visitor?'

'Nothing. She either couldn't or wouldn't help. She said she went to bed to go to sleep and that was that.'

'Anything else?'

She shuffled through her papers. 'Nothing much. I talked to Laura Wynn, the woman who runs the jewellery shop.'

'Boadicea.'

A polite smile. 'She's certainly a dragon; I didn't get beyond the shop and I had very little to show for a ten minute fencing match. Her attitude was: "Surely, with girls like that, murder is an occupational hazard." She says she saw nothing and knows nothing.'

'What do the neighbours say about Mrs Wynn?'

'What don't they say! They call her "the duchess".

68

It seems she has a habit of casually referring to "my family" as though she belonged to the landed aristocracy. Among her other accomplishments she tells fortunes – not for money, of course! "Just leave a little something for charity." But according to her neighbours, her charity begins at home and stays there.'

Wycliffe said, 'You know she was investigated by a private detective working for Cleeve?'

'Sergeant Pearce told me. I think there might be more to be got out of Mrs Wynn.'

'Then perhaps you should try again.'

A small smile. 'With respect, sir, I think you would inspire greater confidence in the lady.'

A working relationship? Something like it, anyway. A start. He had to admit that he wouldn't have got a more concise or shrewder summing up from any of his men. And she had tolerance, a quality he looked for in all of his staff.

He gave her her instructions: 'I want you to tackle the nicotine angle – people who would have access to nicotine through their work – horticultural, veterinary or agricultural . . . The county advisory services would probably help in identifying trades in which the stuff is used. Then there are others likely to have the knowledge and resources necessary to extract nicotine from tobacco leaves as grown, or as sold for smoking. I don't think it's all that difficult. . .

'Anyway, you've got enough to be going on with. I think we'll let Borlase simmer for a while and I'll talk to Madam Laura later.'

He left the Incident Room and walked down Zion Steps. It had occurred to him that few people could be in a better position to extract vegetable poisons from their source than a practising herbalist. Of course, it was too obvious; no man in his senses would risk drawing attention to himself so blatantly . . . and yet, enterprising criminals, especially the clever ones, often have a blind spot. In any case,

Wycliffe was too old a copper to ignore the obvious.

For the first time he looked at Geoffrey Tull's shop with more than casual attention. A colourful sign showed a bouquet of herbs, apparently well painted, but he was too ignorant to identify them. The bow-fronted window exhibited only a printed card with an ornamental border of which the text read: 'Infusions, decoctions, extracts, tinctures and tablets, prepared on the premises from finest ingredients. Consultations by appointment. Geoffrey Tull MB, BCh.'

Beyond a low screen at the back of the window he could see into the shop. A large number of little varnished wooden drawers with white-enamelled labels and, above them, shelves with rows of glass bottles carrying gilt labels. It was reminiscent of a shop in a city museum: 'Pharmacy – circa 1910.' The era of Seidlitz powders, castor oil and ipecacuanha wine.

Although it was half-past six the notice on the door read 'Open'. He entered and a bell buzzed somewhere as he stood on the mat, but there was no response. The shop was elegantly neat, the glass jars gleamed in the dim light and there was an attractive smell of aromatic herbs. The labels on the drawers and bottles read like an index to one of the herbals; a cornucopia of healing.

'Can I help you?'

A voice almost at his elbow. Geoffrey Tull was tall, somewhat overweight, with a carefully trimmed mous-tache. He had his sister's colouring though his features were plump and soft, the face of a spoilt child.

'My name is Wycliffe – Detective Chief Super-intendent Wycliffe.'

'Oh, yes?'

'I am investigating the murder of Celia Dawe.'

'Your sergeant has already spoken to me. I knew the girl, of course, but I can tell you nothing which isn't common knowledge.'

70

'You have heard how she died?'

'I have heard rumours – no more.'

There was something familiar about Tull; not that Wycliffe had ever seen him before, but he belonged to a type, a type once familiar in seaside hotels in the company of widowed or divorced ladies. Not a crude con-man, rather a professional companion for well-to-do lonely women.

'She died of nicotine poisoning; the nicotine was injected into her body by means of a hypodermic device.'

'I see.'

Getting nowhere, Wycliffe tried another approach. 'You are a registered medical practitioner?'

'I am medically qualified but I practise only as a naturopath. I am not in medical practice.'

An evasion; he had probably been struck off.

'You prepare your own medicines?'

'I prepare most of my herbal prescriptions.'

'So you have a laboratory or dispensary – something of the sort?'

'Something of the sort.'

'Have you any objection to showing me where you work?'

Tull did not reply but he moved aside to allow Wycliffe to pass between two counters to a door at the back of the shop.

'Through here.'

The room, looking out on the back yard, was more like a kitchen than a laboratory.

Tull said, 'Most of my preparation work is in the nature of cookery. As you see, I use slicers, shredders and mincers to deal with leaves, roots and stems. The heating is done on an electric hotplate . . . I suppose one of the main differences is that I use glass utensils exclusively, though most of these are bought at kitchen shops.'

'What about distillation?'

71

A faint smile. 'Few of my preparations involve distillation but I am equipped.' He opened a cupboard door. 'See for yourself. For distillation I use ordinary chemical glassware – flasks and condensers. I also have apparatus for boiling under reflux in certain extraction processes.'

His manner was casual, teasing. He closed the cupboard door. 'You see, Mr Wycliffe, I have quite enough equipment to extract nicotine from tobacco but I have never had occasion to use it for that purpose.'

Patronizing bastard! Wycliffe was becoming irritated but Tull was no fool, he hadn't put a foot wrong.

'You live alone?'

He received a long cool look before an answer. 'I do.' A brief pause, then: 'I think I've answered all your questions frankly, Mr Wycliffe, so if you will excuse me, I am expecting a patient.'

'Do you have an assistant?'

'I do. She looks after the shop while I am dealing with patients who come for consultations, but she finishes work at five-thirty.'

'Does she have anything to do with the preparation of medicines?'

'Nothing whatever.'

'You receive your patients here?'

'Certainly not! I have a consulting room upstairs.'

'Perhaps you will give me the name and address of your assistant.'

He would have liked to refuse but realized there was no point. 'Sonia Penrose, 4 Veryan Close. I hope . . .'

'Yes?'

Tull shook his head. 'Nothing.'

The shop doorbell sounded and a moment later a woman stood in the doorway of the dispensary.

Tull said, 'Oh there you are, Mrs Wynn! Do come in, Mr Wycliffe is just leaving.'

The statuesque proprietor of the jewellery shop.

Outside, Wycliffe wondered how much his suspicion of Tull was due to dislike.

The Cleeves and their guests were taking coffee in the paved courtyard by the ornamental pool: Cleeve and Patricia, her brother Geoffrey, the archaeologist Gervaise Prout, and Roger Kitson. Andrew had not put in an appearance at dinner and Christie had excused herself immediately afterwards.

Patricia explained: 'She is very upset about the dead girl.'

Otherwise there had been no mention of Celia Dawe.

Carrie Byrne was in the house supervising two daily women from the village who stayed on to help whenever the Cleeves were entertaining.

The air was warm and sensuously soft; heavy with the scent of dracaena palms in flower. Colours were muted by the dusk, and water trickled musically from an incontinent Cupid into the pool.

Cleeve had been drinking before, during and since the meal; now he was flushed and his eyes were heavy. He had himself in hand but he was edgy and from time to time his temper showed in barbed sallies. Patricia, by adroitly changing the subject or deliberately misunderstanding her husband's words, had so far avoided unpleasantness.

Prout sat erect in his cane chair, his suit almost white – like tropical 'drill', a pukka sahib. Through dinner they had talked largely of the dig and he had bemoaned his lot as a 'prehistoric' archaeologist with no written records to help in interpreting his finds. 'Think of some of those classical chaps with a library of contemporary literature at their backs!'

Later, by some quirk or, perhaps, by intent, the conversation had turned to herbal medicine and Cleeve had made a couple of snide jokes about his brother-in-law, referring to him as 'our resident shaman'. Now Kitson, in a threadbare suit, his long body half coiled in his chair, his injured profile turned from his audience, was holding forth on remedies to be found in the great herbals of the Chinese Sung. Kitson was an encyclopaedia of unlikely information and he had that rare gift which can make a railway timetable interesting.

Cleeve said, 'When I was getting together background for *Medicus* I remember being impressed by the number of really virulent poisons which could be extracted from quite common plants.'

Prout, apparently anxious to make himself agreeable, said, 'Yes, it really is remarkable. I've often wondered why we bother so much with legislation about the sales of poisons when anybody with a bit of nous can prepare extremely toxic alkaloids from plants which grow freely in hedgerows and gardens. Isn't that so, Mr Tull?'

Tull had seemed to be absorbed in contemplation of the carp in the pool and he looked up, startled, at being addressed directly. There was an awkward silence while he studied Prout as though trying to decide whether some innuendo had been intended, then he said, 'I am not interested in toxicology.'

Kitson gave a shrill little laugh. 'I think you two are at cross-purposes. Gervaise is amazingly well informed about the migration of Celtic tribes over the face of Europe two thousand years ago but not so well briefed on today's or yesterday's news. I doubt if he has heard that the Dawe girl was poisoned by one of his toxic alkaloids.'

Prout flushed with annoyance but it was Cleeve who demanded in a harsh voice, 'Where in hell did you get that tale, Roger?'

Patricia's voice warned: 'David!'

But Kitson was unperturbed. 'I never reveal my sources.'

Tull said, 'I told him.'

Cleeve turned on Tull. 'You? Is it true?'

74

Tull, clearly annoyed by Cleeve's manner, contrived to keep his dignity. 'Of course it's true! The superintendent told me that the girl died of nicotine poisoning.'

'And did the superintendent say that she had been murdered?'

'He did.'

Cleeve was frowning and intent. 'Did he say how the stuff was administered?'

'By some hypodermic device.'

'Why should he tell you all this?'

Cleeve's manner was offensive but Tull's calm replies were an effective rebuke. 'I assume it was because he thought I would have the knowledge and resources to extract nicotine from tobacco and might therefore rank as a suspect.'

Cleeve looked like a man who had received a considerable shock but he laughed self-consciously, beginning to feel foolish. 'A suspect. I see! Well, well!' His eyes travelled round the little group. 'Who's going to help me out with this brandy?'

When Wycliffe got back to the cottage, Helen was in the kitchen, wearing an apron, ready to get to work.

'Ah, you've come! I was afraid you would be late. How do you feel about having a meal here instead of going out?'

'I doubt if I could keep awake in a restaurant.'

'A rough day?'

He yawned. 'It didn't feel much like a holiday. What have you been doing?'

'I went across to Falmouth on the ferry and I've been extravagant. We're having fresh salmon steaks, cooked in white wine. There are a couple bottles of Muscadet in the fridge. If you feel like sampling it you can pour me some; I shall only need a little for the salmon.'

Just like home; drinking in the kitchen while the food was being prepared.

They had their meal in the front room with its latticed windows open to the waterfront so that voices of passers-by sounded as though they were in the room. They ate their salmon with small boiled potatoes garnished with parsley and they finished the Muscadet.

Wycliffe began to feel human. 'And for dessert?'

'Peaches. There's clotted cream if you've given up worrying about your cholesterol.'

Coffee, and then a walk. A circuit of the village, returning down the hill by the castle in time to see the estuary and the whole western sky glowing red.

Red sky at night; shepherds' delight. Emmets' too.

Early to bed.

Wednesday July 20th

Wycliffe was a small boy again, back on his parents' farm; the little square window overlooked the farmyard and he could hear the cows' hooves pattering on the cobbles. His mother's voice came from downstairs: 'Charles! Charles! You'll be late for school again!' His mother had been the only member of the family who, like Helen, refused to call him Charlie.

It was Helen calling up the stairs. 'It's half-seven, Charles!'

A fine day as promised but, according to the radio, a temporary change on the way, with drizzle and coastal fog in the outlook period.

'I'll make the most of today,' Helen said. 'There's a trip across the bay to Helford.'

It was almost nine before he arrived at the Incident Room in Chapel Street. Two more DCs, assigned from headquarters, had arrived – Dixon and Potter, known to intimates as Pole and Pot in reference to Dixon's height and Potter's paunch. Potter was duty officer, and alone. He did not hear Wycliffe come in; only a close encounter detached his feet from the table and his attention from the sports pages of *The Sun*.

'Sorry, sir!' He reached for the log. '08.33 hours: message from Mr David Cleeve of Roscrowgy. He would like to see you as soon as possible; he will call here at your convenience or be available at Roscrowgy at any time to suit you.'

'Very accommodating of him. Where is DS Lane?'

'Due on at 10.00 hours, sir, with Edwards, Curnow and Shaw. DC Dixon has gone round the back to the loo.'

'A veritable hive of activity.'

'Yes, sir.' After a moment, Potter added brightly, 'Coffee, sir?'

'No.' He sat at his table, sucking the end of his ball-point and brooding over Celia Dawe. The girl had been mercenary; she had slept with men as an investment in security and hoarded her gains. Her upbringing probably accounted for that. Otherwise there was nothing special about her but her looks. Only by being murdered did she stand out from the crowd in false perspective. Who would have cause to hate or fear such a girl enough to plan and contrive her death with such patience and care?

Lucy Lane arrived, wearing green, and cheerful with it. 'Good morning, sir! Another lovely day.'

He preferred the morose taciturnity he was accustomed to from his male colleagues. He answered glumly.

She went to her table, opened her shoulder bag and took out a bulky envelope. 'I think this is what has been worrying the Borlases.'

She emptied the contents of her envelope on to her table. Wycliffe went over. About 20 full-plate photographs; all of girls of different ages either nude or scantily clad; a voyeur's collection. Then he realized that they were photographs of one girl – of Celia Dawe, a record of her growing up from the age of three or four to early maturity. The quality was high and though the studies were intimate they were neither vulgar nor obscene. All the same, they made Wycliffe feel uncomfortable, as though he had stumbled into the very private world of a young girl. He had to admit that in all his years in the police he had never seen anything quite like them.

'How did you get them?'

'Luck, sir. I thought it might be useful to talk to the other girls who worked at The Buckingham, so I looked in there yesterday evening. Well, they couldn't or wouldn't tell me much about her. It was obvious they didn't like her, probably because she slept with the boss. Anyway, as I was leaving, one of the girls asked me what was to happen to Celia's belongings because they needed her locker. In the season they have a staff of five women and three men and each of them has a locker for personal things. Of course I didn't have her keys but Polmear found a duplicate. Her locker contained an overall, a raincoat, an umbrella, a pair of shoes, and these.'

'Good for you! What do you make of them?'

She turned the prints over, puckered brow. 'At least they explain what Borlase was so agitated about. He couldn't afford to have these passed round among his chapel friends.'

'Do you think his sisters know about them?'

It was a silly question and she looked surprised. 'They must have done; this was going on for thirteen or fourteen years. I imagine they were glad to keep his rather mild sexual vagaries in the family. I don't suppose they did anybody any harm.'

'Not the girl?'

'I shouldn't think so. I doubt if he touched her; he's a brooder, not a doer. It would be enough to have her to gloat over; and for her it would be routine. On Thursday night you wash your hair; Friday is bath night; and on Saturday afternoon or whenever, you strip and pose for uncle. She might have thought it a bit odd as she got older but she would be used to it.

I doubt if these were among her reasons for leaving home.'

Wycliffe told himself that women in general and this one in particular were full of surprises. He said, 'All the same, it seems likely that she was getting money out of him on the strength of the pictures. In other words, he had a motive.'

The brown eyes looked incredulous. 'For murder? I can't honestly see Borlase as a killer unless one imagines a homicidal rabbit.'

Wycliffe laughed; their relationship was beginning to gel. 'Do you want to follow this through?'

He thought of Borlase's torturing embarrassment at being questioned about his photographs by a girl, and decided he deserved it.

But Sergeant Lane had other ideas. 'In the long run I think there's more to be got out of his sisters and they're more likely to talk to you than me, sir.'

'I'll think about it. Meanwhile Cleeve wants to see me.'

'About the case?'

'What else? I suppose you know he's Peter Stride, the author?'

'I had heard.' Drily.

'You know his work?'

'I'm an addict; I took him for my special paper in finals.'

'Good! You may have a chance to get to know him better.'

Wycliffe was regretting that he would have to talk to Cleeve before he had news from John Scales of the man's background but, on cue, the telephone rang.

'Mr Scales for you, sir.'

'Well, John?'

'I've got something on Cleeve at last; it doesn't amount to much – nothing you'd think he'd want to conceal unless he really is a very shy bird. No biographical titbits in any of the tomes which list the works and whims of the literary. I got on to him finally by chance, through a chap who works on the *News*. A couple of years back he thought of doing a piece on the man but he came up against the same brick wall as Jane's student. It made him inquisitive and he did some poking around but the game wasn't worth the candle and he packed it in. Anyway, he gave us a start and we were able to carry on where he left off. David Paul Cleeve was born in Bristol, September 5th 1931, son of David Gordon Cleeve, solicitor's clerk and Elizabeth née Cotterell. Nothing so far on his childhood or education but in either '47 or '48 he joined the staff of the local paper as a trainee journalist. National Service was still in force then but he was exempted on medical grounds – he was an epileptic. He's still remembered on the paper as the reporter who had fits – he had one in a council meeting.

'In 1953 he moved out into our territory at Exeter, and set up as a freelance, contributing to newspapers and writing articles for magazines. But by the time he published his first book – *Xanadu* in October 1955 – he was living in London. *Medicus* followed in '57, *Magistra* in '59 et cetera.

'In April 1962 he married Patricia Elizabeth Tull at a register office in Oxford, a successful author, already very well-heeled. They lived in Surrey, then in Dorset, and moved to Cornwall in '74 or '75. Of course by then they'd had their twin children who were at boarding school.'

'Is that the lot?'

'I'm afraid so up to now.'

'A blameless career in fact.'

'It looks that way. Do you want the enquiry kept open, sir?'

Wycliffe hesitated. 'I'm seeing Cleeve later this morning so carry on unless you hear differently.'

They talked for a while about other cases then Scales, with good-humoured cynicism, wished him a happy holiday.

Wycliffe said to Potter: 'Ring Roscrowgy and tell them I'm on my way.'

He decided to walk to give himself time to think.

He left the Incident Room and turned up the hill by the chapel, leaving the tourists' village behind. Larger houses modestly concealed their virtue behind high dry-stone walls topped with escallonia in crimson flower. Only the bees disturbed the stillness and in the dry, fragrant heat it would have been easy to believe that he had the Mediterranean at his back instead of the English Channel. But his mind was on other things.

David Cleeve, Peter Stride . . . Why was he bothering his head about this man? Did he believe that Cleeve had killed the girl? He had no reason to think so, and yet . . . '*I never heard of him but I wouldn't would I. The boy sounds nice even if he is a bit wet but I think you could make trouble that way . . .*' The gospel according to Celia Dawe's friend, Liz. He had asked the Met to contact the girl. But even if Cleeve was sleeping with Celia Dawe was there any reason to link her death with Cleeve's past and the nebulous threats he had been so coy about?

He left the villas behind and came out on the *ros*, or heath, which gives Roseland its name. He walked on past the gates of Roscrowgy until he could see what was happening in Henry's Field. They were there, working like beavers preparing for a flood. Nothing had changed except that there were posters on boards set up in the hedge: 'Stop this desecration of land sacred to the Celtic People!' Followed by small print explaining how to set about doing it; all nice and legal.

Wycliffe retraced his steps and went through the white gates and up the long drive to the house. It brought him to a different entrance from the one Cleeve had taken him to – how long ago? Just four days! He was about to ring the bell when the door was opened by Cleeve himself.

'I happened to see you from the window . . . good of you to come.' Bland good manners which failed to conceal an underlying anxiety.

Wycliffe followed him along a short passage which joined the main corridor, then up the stairs to the study. The little dark girl looked up and saw them as they passed the open door of her office.

'Sit you down . . . whisky?'

'Not just now, thanks.'

A wry smile. 'I suppose not. You won't mind if I do? I shall probably need it.'

Nothing had changed; the sunlit creek, the estuary, the white-sailed yachts weaving their slow patterns on a smooth sea. In the study the smell of polished wood, of leather, of books and whisky . . .

'You wanted to see me?'

'I had to. Of course, it's about this girl – Celia Dawe. All this talk of her being murdered – poisoned.'

'You knew her?'

Cleeve made an impatient movement. 'Let's not beat about the bush! If you haven't heard already you soon will; I've been sleeping with her.'

'You visited her at her flat?'

'A couple of times a week over the past two months.'

'At more or less regular intervals?'

'Usually Monday and Thursday of each week.'

'You are being very frank.'

'I need to be. I was beginning to wonder when I was going to be haled off to the nearest cop-shop – "a man is helping the police with their enquiries". All this nonsense about murder . . .'

'Were you with her on the night of Monday/Tuesday – the night she died?'

Cleeve fingered his moustache, belatedly hesitant at the final fence. 'Yes, I was.'

'Then I should warn you –'

'To hell with that! I want to tell you what happened, then you can tell me what it's all about.' He paused, fiddling with his whisky glass, twisting the crystal tumbler between finger and thumb. 'I was with her when she died and I can see no way in which she could have been murdered.' He broke off and looked at Wycliffe. 'They're talking about nicotine poisoning – injected. Surely that would be quick acting?'

'Very.'

'Then there is no way she could have been murdered! I can't understand how all this started . . . I'm putting myself in your hands, I've got to rely on you to believe what I tell you.'

Wycliffe said nothing and Cleeve paused to collect his thoughts. When he spoke again it was in a different vein, he even summoned up a grin.

'I wonder how much you know about women. I suppose most men imagine themselves to be experts but I don't mind admitting they defeat me . . . You know those boxes of assorted chocolates with a little chart to tell you what's inside the different shapes? I need something like that in dealing with women; it's too late when you've bitten through the chocolate coating . . . Looking at that girl you'd have thought all that was needed was a match to the blue touch paper but, in fact, she was frigid. She put on a damned good act, but an act it was, and in a dozen subtle ways she let you know it . . . I always thought she was laughing at me; she was clever, I think she got a kick out of it, but it was tantalizing – humiliating, I suppose . . . A man likes to think . . .'

He looked at his glass which was empty. 'Are you quite sure you won't?' Wycliffe shook his head and Cleeve pushed his glass aside. 'I suppose I'd better not either. I've had enough already.'

He shifted heavily in his chair. 'I was going to say that on Monday night it seemed different.' He looked boyishly embarrassed. 'I thought I'd made it – you understand? I mean, all the signs, the sort of thing they can't fake – that shuddering spasm . . . Then she went limp and I must admit, my only thought was, "Got you this time, my girl!" '

Wycliffe found it hard to remember that he was listening to the creator of *Medicus*, and not to any man only haltingly articulate on the subject of his sexual experience. An author without his typewriter is a soldier without his gun.

'She was dead.'

The words hung uncomfortably in the air.

It was hot and getting hotter. Cleeve was red-faced and sweating; he got up and opened a window, letting in the sounds from outside with a breath of air and the smell of freshly cut grass. Someone was mowing the lawns.

He returned to his chair. 'It took me minutes to realize what had happened, and when I did I thought she must have died of heart failure or a blood clot or something of the sort. . . I did all I could—'

'Except call a doctor.'

He nodded. 'I was a fool, but I couldn't face it, and once I was certain nothing could be done . . .' He hesitated. 'I was right, wasn't I? Nothing could have been done?'

'As it happens, you were right.'

'Then I don't understand all of this talk of murder – of poison. She died in my arms – literally, and I was with her for about two hours before that. You see, it's not possible.'

'The girl was killed by a dart made from part of an ordinary hypodermic needle set in a brass tube which held the nicotine. It functioned like a miniature hypodermic syringe. The needle entered the girl's left buttock and the poison was injected into her system. Subsequently – perhaps when you moved away from her, the dart fell out and rolled onto the floor where Dr Hodge found it.'

Cleeve was looking at him in ludicrous astonishment. 'I suppose you know what you are talking about, but I was there—'

84

Wycliffe cut him short. 'The sash window of the bedroom was open a little at the bottom?'

'Yes, it was; I remember the curtains moving slightly but I don't see — '

'She could have been killed by someone in the yard; someone standing by the window.'

'You mean that someone reached in and plunged that thing into her when we were . . .'

'I think it's more likely that the dart was fired from some sort of air weapon or spring gun.'

Cleeve had lost his high colour and for a moment Wycliffe wondered if he would faint. It was some time before he could speak then he said in a low voice: 'So she really was murdered! Murdered while . . .' It was obvious that he was deeply affected, unable to come to terms with what he had been told. All his 'man-to-man-let's-settle-this-together' attitude had deserted him. He got up from his chair and made a slow circuit of the room, pausing now and then to stare at books on the shelves then, abruptly, he turned to Wycliffe. 'Have you any idea who did it?'

'None.'

'Or why?'

Wycliffe shook his head. 'I can think of no reason why anyone would want to murder Celia Dawe, can you?'

He looked startled. 'Me? Of course not! I've told you, I couldn't understand this talk of murder.'

Wycliffe was impressed by the change in the man. Celia Dawe had died in his arms yet he had been sufficiently detached to gossip, even make little jokes, but now that he understood how she had died he was overcome. Wycliffe thought that he knew the reason for that.

'What time did it happen?'

A moment to consider. 'Between half-past one and two; I can't put it closer than that.' He came back to stand by his chair, looking down at Wycliffe. 'So you believe me – my version of what happened?'

Wycliffe made a small movement with his hands. 'It's too early to say; I can say that, in the light of what I already know, what you have told me is believable.'

Cleeve nodded. 'That's all I can expect. Thanks. What happens now?'

'You will be invited to make a statement. I suggest you come to the Incident Room in Chapel Street this afternoon. One of my officers will be expecting you and you will be asked about the events of Monday night and invited to make a statement in writing. Shall we say at four o'clock?'

'I'll be there.' He seemed to answer mechanically, preoccupied with his thoughts.

Wycliffe went on: 'At the same time I want you to allow your finger-prints to be taken.'

Cleeve looked surprised. 'Finger-prints? I've admitted being in the room with the girl; my prints are probably all over the place.'

'All the same we shall need your prints for comparison purposes.'

A shrug. 'As you wish.'

Wycliffe allowed a silence to drift on. Cleeve resumed his seat and the two men were once more facing each other across his desk. When Wycliffe spoke again his manner was less formal.

'Have you thought any more about our conversation on Saturday?'

'What? Oh, yes, I'm getting a security man to patrol the grounds at night.'

'Have there been any more threats?'

'No – none.'

'Do you feel at greater risk because of what happened to Celia Dawe?'

Cleeve reacted sharply. 'Why do you ask me that? Why should I?'

Wycliffe was matter-of-fact. 'Because since I told you that Celia Dawe had been murdered and explained how it was done, you have been wondering whether the dart that killed her found its intended target. That is reasonable. After all, it would be a very odd coincidence if, while your life was being threatened, the girl who shared your bed was murdered in an unrelated incident.'

Cleeve's powerful hands were lightly clasped, resting on the desk. A craftsman's hands, stout fingers, square ends. He seemed to be studying his hands and did not raise his eyes. 'Of course the idea occurred to me.'

'And?'

He shook his head. 'I don't know.'

Wycliffe got to his feet. 'You must think about it; but whatever you decide, now that I know you were with the girl, I have to look at the case from a new angle. Unless there is fresh evidence soon, which makes sense of the girl's murder, we shall assume that you were the intended victim; then your reticence about these threats will have greater importance.'

'Is that a warning?'

'Not a warning. I'm pointing out the direction our enquiries will take, and giving you the chance to make your voluntary statement as complete as possible.'

'I see.'

'Once we know the nature of the threats you received and once you have told us something of the reasons behind them, we can provide you with whatever protection is needed.'

Cleeve, too, got to his feet. 'I shall be at the Incident Room at four o'clock. I'll see you out.'

They walked down the long, inhospitable corridor and Cleeve saw him off at the front door. Wycliffe felt depressed. Sometimes it seemed to him that his was a degrading occupation, exposing the nakedness of men, the deceits and evasions of the weak and the pathetic deviance of the wicked; pinning out their sins, like insects in a box, and saying, 'This is what you are!' Not that he would condone crime, but sometimes he yearned for a more inspiring concept of justice, perhaps like the classical Chinese – the restoration of the pattern.

Back to earth: he was convinced now that his hunch had been correct, that the little dart had been carefully and cunningly contrived to be fired from an airgun or something of the kind. Franks had said that the external diameter of the brass tube was close to five millimetres and that meant it could be fired from a variety of air and spring weapons. Further than that, he was convinced that it had been aimed at Cleeve, not at the girl.

It was twelve-thirty – time for lunch and, on the spur of the moment, he decided to try The Vegetarian.

It was comfortably full and he was asked to share a table with a man of about his own age, a lean man of saturnine countenance. He looked at the menu; the waitress said: 'The sweet-corn-and-cheese-bake is our special today.'

'All right. Are you licensed?'

'No, but you can have fruit-juice, tea or coffee, or various herbal drinks.'

Depressing. 'I'll have coffee later.'

The saturnine man said, 'I've never understood why vegetarianism and total abstinence seem to go together.'

'I'll start with the soup.'

'Are you ready for your main course, Dr Hodge?'

Dr Hodge. The eyes of the two men met and Dr Hodge smiled. 'I think it's Chief Superintendent Wycliffe . . .'

They talked about the village.

Hodge said, 'I've been here for twenty years. It's not a village, it's a suburb without any urb to be sub to; a cosmopolitan collection of people with nothing in common but the conviction that they've escaped from something – from what, they're not quite sure. Interesting though. You'll need a side-salad with that bake thing when it comes. There aren't many of the original inhabitants left and those that are don't count any more; no more than mice in the woodwork.'

Wycliffe lowered his voice though there was no need; people were chattering nineteen to the dozen. 'You found the dart.'

The waitress came with the doctor's main course – a three-egg omelette with a brown-bread roll and butter. High cholesterol. 'My wife won't let me have eggs at home; says they're bad for me. Yes, cunning little thing, wasn't it? Somebody spent the whole winter concocting that, brooding on it. They're great brooders hereabouts – nothing else to do in the winter. But why the girl? That's what puzzles me. She was a good-looker but apart from that she was ordinary enough. The trouble was she had old-fashioned ideas – she thought somebody would be fool enough to set her up and keep her for what they could get in bed. It's funny; some of these girls don't seem to realize that sex is off ration now so there's no longer a black market. Leathery!' The doctor was prodding his omelette. 'Cooked too slowly; they're usually better at it here.'

'Do you mind if I ask you a professional question?'

'Why not? Everybody else does.'

'Would you say that epilepsy – *grand mal* epilepsy, where the patient is subject to recurring seizures – is curable?'

Hodge shrugged. 'It depends; every case is different, but for a young person who submits to treatment and behaves sensibly, the prognosis is good.'

'Is there a chance that he might be able to come off drugs and lead a normal life?'

'In many cases – yes.'

'Alcohol?'

A quizzical look. 'Oh, no, I'd strongly advise anybody with a history of epilepsy to lay off the booze.'

'For good?'

'Certainly, he'd be tempting providence otherwise.'

'Thanks.'

They finished their meal.

'If you and your wife are still here on Saturday afternoon, you might care to come sailing . . .'

Back in the Incident Room he briefed DC Edwards to take Cleeve's statement. Edwards was slow but nothing got past him and he had the integrity of an elephant. 'Also, get hold of Sergeant Smith and ask him to be here to take Cleeve's prints – I want them checked with CRO immediately.'

At a quarter to four Wycliffe pushed open the door of the photographer's shop, the bell buzzed, but no one came. He went through to the studio at the back, pushing aside the velvet curtains: a camera on a stand, various lamps and screens and an assortment of studio props dating from the 'twenties. Carpeted stairs to the floor above.

He could hear the photographer's voice, softly insistent. He stood at the bottom of the stairs and called: 'Is anyone at home?'

An interval, and Borlase came to the top of the stairs, wiping his mouth with a table napkin. Afternoon tea: the photographer's too-solid flesh needed frequent nourishment. He was anxious, startled.

'Mr Wycliffe!'

'Don't bother to come down; I'll come up.'

Before Borlase could stop him he was at the top of the stairs, on a landing with several doors. Two of the doors at the back were open, one to a gloomy kitchen and the other to a dining-room, furnished in oak which would have been thought handsome 60 years before. Smells of cooking, stale clothes, dust, and dog blended uneasily.

Borlase's sisters had come on to the landing to see what was happening.

'This is my sister, Helena, Mr Wycliffe.' Tall, gaunt and grey, supporting herself. 'And this is Posy.' Younger and stouter than Helena, having split a packet of genes with her brother.

'This is Mr Wycliffe, the gentleman from the police.'

Helena rounded on her brother. 'I know who he is; the question is, what does he want?' Her voice was harsh and masculine.

The photographer, embarrassed, said, 'Perhaps you will come into the dining-room, Mr Wycliffe . . .? Will you join us in a cup of tea . . .? Are you sure?'

On the table was a plate of sandwiches, another of sausage rolls and a third of dough buns.

A yellowish dog of dubious provenance, an obscene-looking creature, patchily bald, roused itself from sleep on the hearth-rug and lumbered across to Wycliffe, wagging a truncated tail. Wycliffe took a large envelope from his bag with a police inventory tag stuck to the outside. The photographer brushed crumbs from his shirt front, his gaze riveted on the envelope.

'I think these are what you are looking for, Mr Borlase.' Wycliffe slid the photographs on to the table top.

Borlase was speechless; he squeezed his napkin into a ball and began to knead furiously.

Helena glared at the photographs, then at Wycliffe, finally at her brother.

'How did he get hold of these?' The voice was menacing.

Wycliffe said, 'You told us lies, Mr Borlase. You said you hadn't been in touch with your niece since her return; in fact, you've been to visit her several times and, on more than one occasion, you quarrelled.'

Borlase shook his head helplessly and little beads of sweat appeared on his forehead and lips. 'It was the photographs, Mr Wycliffe . . . I had to get them back. She took them when she went away and she was threatening me. When a painter paints a nude, it's art, but when a man like me, a photographer . . .' He picked up one of the prints. 'This is work of very high quality, Mr Wycliffe – any authority would tell you . . . You have to believe me; there was nothing . . . it was entirely 'innocent, I assure you . . .' The weak, rather sensuous mouth was trembling.

'Then why did you allow your niece to blackmail you?'

He shuddered. 'Blackmail! Dear God, I assure you—'

Wycliffe's expression was blank. 'An unpleasant word, but still not so unpleasant as murder.'

'Murder!' A whisper; his voice all but let him down completely. 'You can't think that I . . .'

Helena hammered on the floor with her stick and shouted. 'Will you tell me how *he* got them? You said you'd made her give them back!'

It was Posy's turn. With a grim I-told-you-so smile, she said, 'You should never have gone to see her in the first place, Joe! You wouldn't have gone if it had been left to me, but other people knew better.'

Helena snapped: 'If people listened to you they would never do anything, not even keep themselves clean.'

They were laying the foundations for a future quarrel in which Joseph's role would be no more than that of a carcass squabbled over by jackals. But there was no time now. Helena concentrated on her brother; her wrinkled lips quivering with frustrated rage:

'Five hundred pounds you said you gave her! What happened to the five hundred pounds?'

'She took the money but she wouldn't give me . . .' Words failed him.

Helena shouted and banged her stick on the floor. 'Fool! Fool! Liar!'

And Posy said, 'They really will come to lock you up one of these days if you go on like that, Lena.'

Lena and Posy. A long time ago they must have been young girls, a few years' difference in their ages; Lena, slim and dark; Posy, fair, plump and rosy-cheeked. In fact, there was a hand-coloured enlargement of two such girls over the mantelpiece.

But it was not his sisters who were worrying Borlase

at that moment, but the seemingly impassive policeman. He turned to Wycliffe.

'Celia said they were photographs of her, so they were hers, and if I wanted them back I would have to pay for them. Then, when I gave her the money she asked for . . .'

'But why did you want them so badly? Surely you had negatives?'

The photographer raised his hands in helplessness. 'You don't understand, Mr Wycliffe! She threatened to show them round the village! In a place like this I would never live it down; they would say that I . . . that I . . .' His voice broke in a sob and he covered his face with the wretchedly crumpled napkin.

His sisters watched him and Helena said, 'Murder? You can see for yourself. He couldn't step on a cockroach!'

Wycliffe was feeling grim. He gathered up the photographs and replaced them in the envelope. 'These will be retained until the case is over; then you will have them returned to you. It would have saved a lot of trouble, Mr Borlase, if you had told us the truth in the first place.'

Early in his career he had discovered that if one has greater sensitivity than a punch-bag, humiliation recoils. Ashamed of this scene he turned to the window and stood looking out, giving them a chance to recover some semblance of dignity.

From the window he could see down into the yard next door. Laura Wynn was in her workshop, bending over a sink, her golden hair like a crown. The houses on this side of the street had long narrow gardens. The Borlases' was a wilderness but Laura Wynn had put hers in grass and not far from the house there was a little gazebo.

'Keeping an eye on her?' Lena's harsh voice at his elbow. Incredibly, after all that had gone before, her manner was relaxed and conversational. 'You should!

She and her cats! She's been there two years and still nobody knows who she is or where she came from. You should ask her what she was doing the night Celia was murdered – prowling round till all hours.'

'You said nothing about that to Sergeant Lane.'

She sniffed. 'Perhaps I forgot.'

'Well, you've remembered now; what did you see, and when?'

'I've told you. It was Monday night. I'm an old woman and I can't sleep. My bedroom is in the front and sometimes I get out of bed and sit in a chair by the window for a bit. I saw her in the street, wearing some dark-coloured dressing-gown sort of thing.'

'What was she doing?'

'She was crossing the street when I saw her.'

The photographer had recovered sufficiently to intervene. 'I think Lena should tell you that Mrs Wynn is often out at night, looking for her cats. She's got four Siamese and they wander away.'

To Wycliffe's surprise Helena did not seem to resent the interruption. She said, 'That's as maybe, but it's funny why she had to go down the alley that leads round to the backs of the houses.'

'You saw her go down the alley?'

'It looked that way to me.'

'You either saw her or you didn't.'

She shrugged. 'It was dark on that side of the street.'

Wycliffe said, 'I shall have to ask you to make a statement about this. It's obviously important to get it right. Are you sure—'

She interrupted. 'I don't trust her. She calls herself Mrs but there's never been any sign of a husband nor talk of one and she came here in the first place because of that man, Cleeve.'

'Because of Cleeve? What makes you say that?'

She looked smug. 'It was obvious. She hadn't been in the place five minutes before he way paying her visits and staying half the night. I thought he'd set her up here.'

'And you no longer think so?'

'If he did, it didn't last long – not more than four or five months; then he stopped going there. It wasn't long after that they started on about digging up Henry's Field and she was all against it – spite!'

She was a thoroughly unpleasant old woman but what she said made some sort of sense.

'I'll send someone to take your statement, Miss Borlase.'

'Suit yourself!'

Borlase came with him to the shop door. 'I hope . . .'

'Yes, Mr Borlase?'

'Nothing, I'm sorry.'

Wycliffe found himself out on the Steps with a sense of relief, wondering why people, families in particular, contrive their own peculiar hells.

He arrived back at the Incident Room as Cleeve was signing his statement. Cleeve in checked shirt and khaki slacks, looking like the lord of the manor who has called on his steward to sign a few boring documents before proceeding to more interesting concerns. Edwards, sitting opposite him across the table, was respectful but firm.

'The declaration at the start, then each page separately, sir, then the declaration at the end.'

Cleeve signed with a flourish and a gold pen, disregarding the miserable little ball-point he had been offered. When the last signature had been given he looked up and saw Wycliffe.

'Oh, it's you, Mr Wycliffe.'

'Good afternoon, Mr Cleeve.'

Very formal, Wycliffe took the statement and turned over the pages, unhurried. When he had finished he said, 'I see you have included nothing fresh in your statement.'

'No, it covers the same ground we discussed this morning – everything relevant as far as I can recollect it.'

Wycliffe nodded. 'There will be two men on duty round the clock – in the grounds close to your house, if you will allow it, otherwise outside.'

'Am I under observation, house-arrest, or what?'

'You are being given police protection.'

'Am I free to come and go as I please?'

'Of course! But I shall be grateful if you will keep my men informed of your movements, for your own safety.'

'I see.'

When Cleeve had gone, Wycliffe talked at length to Lucy Lane.

'Cleeve must know as well as I do that Celia Dawe was killed in an attempt on his life. He must know too that the attempt could only have been made by someone with an intimate knowledge of his movements.'

Lucy Lane thought he seemed preoccupied, unsure of himself. He stood by one of the windows, watching the unexciting life of Chapel Street. Another meal time loomed and the emmets had drained away from the streets as though someone had pulled the plug on them. A grey-haired woman stood in her open doorway, staring at nothing; a dog sniffed along the pavement; a man in a blue jersey went by, carrying three or four mackerel strung together by their gills.

'The attempt on Cleeve's life must have been made by someone intimately acquainted with him and his routine.' Wycliffe repeated the words to himself as though to lend them emphasis. Yet Cleeve's whole point at that first, fortuitous meeting had been that he was being threatened by someone outside the circle of his family and friends . . .

In any case, there could hardly be many who could claim close acquaintance with the man. Who were the initiates? Patricia and the twins, the brother-in-law Geoffrey Tull, the housekeeper Carrie Byrne, and, according to Helena Borlase, Laura Wynn. Were there others? What were Cleeve's relations with Gervaise Prout? With the mutilated Kitson?

Whether or not the attempt on his life had arisen from something in his past, whoever made it must belong to the here and now.

Wycliffe sighed. He had committed men to Cleeve's protection; he had little choice once it became obvious that the man's life really was under immediate threat. With or without Cleeve's co-operation the obligation remained, but whether the protection could be effective was another matter.

CHAPTER FOUR

Thursday July 21st

Wycliffe was standing on the edge of a trench; it could have been part of the dig in Henry's Field or it could have been a grave. Lying in the trench was a man, fully dressed. It was Cleeve and he was looking up at Wycliffe with an enigmatic smile. Wycliffe felt giddy and was afraid of falling into the trench; at the same time there was a ringing in his ears. Helen's voice came, peremptory but irrelevant:

'It's the telephone, Charles!'

Consciousness returned. The telephone. It was ringing downstairs; no bedroom extension in the cottage.

'Damn!'

He went down the narrow, break-neck stairs, mumbling to himself. It wasn't completely dark, just light enough to see the time by the wall-clock with the brass pendulum: four forty-five.

It was Pearce. 'I'm ringing from Roscrowgy, sir.' He spoke in a low voice as though concerned not to be overheard. 'There's been a fire on the Henry's Field site, the wooden shed they use as an office and museum has been burned down. The brigade was on the spot before me, and Bert Chinn, the fire officer, says it was burning so fiercely when he arrived that he suspects arson.'

Wycliffe was not pleased to be woken at dawn to be told that the Celtic Society might have had an unscheduled bonfire. He muttered something under his breath.

'Sir?'

'Never mind. What do you want me to do? Arrest the Wynn woman?' Heavily humorous.

But Pearce had saved his real news. 'I knew you wouldn't want to be got out of bed just because Laura Wynn might have got the bit between her teeth, but there may be more to it than that, sir. It looks as though Cleeve is missing.'

'Missing?'

'It seems that way.'

'Either he is or he isn't. What about our chaps who are supposed to be patrolling the place?'

'It was one of them who spotted the fire and phoned the brigade, but it looks as though Cleeve must have given them the slip. When the son went to tell his father about the fire, father was nowhere to be found. Mrs Cleeve is obviously worried but I can't get her to admit that she hasn't a clue where her husband is. I think she's afraid of starting something then having him turn up saying, "What the hell?" '

'All right. You were quite right to phone; I'll be along.'

He went back upstairs and groped for his pants.

'You've got to go out?'

'They think I'm the fire-brigade.'

The weather had changed – only temporarily, according to the forecast – the creek was obliterated by heavy mist, and moisture condensed out of the chill morning air. He seemed to be the only human being out of bed. His car was parked behind the cottage on a little rectangle of beaten earth advertised as 'space for car' – barely space enough to manoeuvre into the narrow lane, so testing his modest driving skills to near their limit. He cursed silently, and the engine was dubious about this early start on a damp morning. Further up the hill the mist became a fine drizzle.

Henry's Field was a dreary prospect; the large wooden shed had collapsed in on itself and was no more than a tangled heap of carbonized timbers, still smoking and steaming. The firemen had decided that the fire was out but they were in the cab of their tender, maintaining a watching brief. No sign of the archaeologists; the flaps of the bell-tents were down and the curtains of the caravan were drawn. Henry's Field was a depressing sight and Wycliffe decided it could hardly have been a health resort for its Iron-Age occupants.

Pearce was waiting. He nodded towards the tents. 'They've gone back to their sleeping bags.'

'What did Gervaise Prout make of it all?'

'Prout isn't here; he went off early yesterday and he isn't expected back until lunchtime today – some university meeting. It seems he took the site records with him to show his mates. Just as well, otherwise they would have gone up in smoke too.'

'So who's in charge?'

'Young fellow called Wrighton; Prout's assistant; all hair and glasses, looks at you like an owl.'

'What does he have to say?'

'That the fire must have been started deliberately; that there's no way the place could have caught fire otherwise. The lighting is electric, powered by a pocket-sized Jap generator in that dog-kennel over there and it's switched off at night.'

'Anything inflammable stored in the hut – petrol? Paraffin?'

'According to Wrighton there was a five-gallon drum containing about two gallons of paraffin. They use it for the generator.'

'And one of our chaps raised the alarm – at what time?'

'He logged it at 02.07.'

Wycliffe shivered; the chill dampness seemed to be seeping into him. Hard to believe that only the day before the site had been sweltering under the sun. He looked at his watch. 'Half-past five. Have the

Roscrowgy contingent gone back to bed too?'

'I very much doubt it, sir.'

'Then I'll try talking to them. I want you to find out from the fire officer when this debris can be handled without people getting choked or burned. If necessary, get them to damp it down some more. I would like somebody down from Forensic this afternoon – somebody with experience of arson.'

Pearce seemed surprised. 'You're taking this very seriously, sir.'

'Yes.'

He left Pearce and crossed the field to the wicket gate, he passed through the rhododendron tunnel where water dripped from the foliage and as he emerged from the tunnel one of the uniformed men on duty came towards him.

'PC Julian, sir.'

Wycliffe, becoming an expert on the brogues of the two counties, placed him as a Camborne man.

'I spotted the fire, sir. I was doing my rounds behind the house when I saw a glare in the sky somewhere over Henry's Field. It was clear then, the mist came in just before dawn. I reported in on my pocket-set and Control alerted the brigade. I heard them arrive ten or fifteen minutes later.'

'You didn't go over to the site?'

'No, sir. I talked to my mate and we decided our brief was here. I hope we did right?'

'In the circumstances – yes. Did you wake the people in the house?'

'We thought about it, sir, then decided not; but at about half-two or a bit later, young Cleeve turned up; he'd been to some party in Truro and he'd seen the fire on his way home. He was a bit shirty because we hadn't told his father and went off to do it.'

'And?'

Julian shifted uneasily. 'Well, his father wasn't there, sir.'

'When did you last see Mr Cleeve?'

'Neither of us have seen him since we came on at ten, sir. With respect, it's very nearly impossible to keep this place boxed up between the two of us. Altogether, there are five doors—'

Wycliffe said, 'I know; I'm not blaming anyone.'

He walked on towards the house. There were lights in several of the windows, competing with the grey morning. He rang the bell and the door was answered by a youth immediately identifiable as Andrew Cleeve because of his likeness to his sister.

'Mr Cleeve?'

The boy was pale, and hollow-eyed with tiredness. 'You are Mr Wycliffe – I think my mother will be relieved to see you.'

He took Wycliffe's raincoat and led him through a large drawing-room to a small boudoir which opened off it; an hexagonal room, plainly furnished: a dove-grey carpet, a business-like desk and a couple of spoon-back chairs; the whole redeemed and relieved by an Ivor Hitchens flower study over the fireplace and a bowl of pink roses on the window-sill; the office of an up-market headmistress. Patricia Cleeve was fully dressed, pale, but apparently composed.

'Mr Wycliffe, I'm so glad you've come; I scarcely know what to do.' She said this in the manner of a lady putting at ease a guest who feels that he has arrived at an awkward moment. 'May I offer you something?' She made sure that he was comfortably seated. 'Thank you, Andrew.'

Wycliffe refused refreshment though he would have given a great deal for a cup of black coffee. 'I expect you are very concerned for your husband.'

She arranged her dress to cover her knees. 'I must admit that I am, and very puzzled.'

'You would have expected him to tell you if he intended to stay out?'

'Of course! We don't share a bedroom because we

have different sleeping habits but he usually tells me if he intends to spend the night or any part of it away from home.'

Different sleeping habits . . . the night or any part of it – no beating about the bush; these are the facts; why pretend otherwise?

'You have no idea where he might have gone?'

'No.' She considered carefully before enlarging. 'In the circumstances, I was very surprised to hear that he had gone out.'

She did not say, 'with that girl lying dead', but her meaning was clear.

'Sometimes in the past he would take a stroll round the grounds before settling down for the night but not, I think, recently.'

'Can you tell me when you last saw your husband?'

'At our evening meal which we have at seven-thirty. Afterwards he went back to work as usual.'

'You have been to his room?'

'His bed has not been slept in.'

With caution, Wycliffe said, 'When you were speaking to Sergeant Pearce earlier he had the impression that you were reluctant to admit that you had no idea where your husband was.'

A little smile. 'Was it so obvious? I'm sure you will see that my husband would not have welcomed a hue and cry about nothing.'

'Since then, something has occurred to change your attitude?'

She played with her thin gold wedding-ring, twisting it round and round on her finger. 'Only that some hours have gone by and he still hasn't come home.'

She was superficially calm but underlying nervousness showed in her restless hands. She went on: 'When you were here on Saturday you had a private conversation with David and I'm sure he must have confided in you to some extent.' She added with a shrewd smile, 'Otherwise I hardly think you would be interested in

103

a man who has been missing from his home for only a few hours.'

Wycliffe nodded. 'And by the same token, if he hadn't taken you into his confidence, you would probably be less anxious now.'

She swept back her blonde hair with an impatient movement. 'I assure you, Mr Wycliffe, that David doesn't share his troubles with me; he seems to think that it is his duty to shield me from worry, which of course means that I worry all the more.' Her voice became brittle. 'You are probably in a better position to form an opinion about what danger he may be in than I am.'

'Is he on friendly terms with anyone in the neighbourhood whom he might conceivably have visited last night?'

She considered her reply. 'Leaving aside his affairs with women, about which there can hardly be any secret, there is only one person he is in the habit of visiting, that is Roger Kitson. I think you met Roger, he was with David when you were at the dig on Saturday. Roger has a little cottage in the plantation and David often goes there; they seem to have a lot in common. But he wasn't there last night; Christie and Andrew went over to enquire. We tried to telephone but Roger's phone is out of order. Since then they've been searching the whole area in case there's been an accident of some kind. I gather that Roger has been out too.'

Wycliffe was thinking that the mating game brings together strange partners. This woman, perceptive, forceful, but restrained; probably tantalized by sex though prudish by nature . . . she must have had a hard time with her brilliant, often sombre, always wayward and egocentric husband.

Wycliffe said, 'Forgive me, but I suppose there is no possibility that he was visiting another woman?'

A faint smile. 'I think not.' She added after a moment, 'He would allow a decent interval.'

'Could he have left the area for any reason? Simply cleared out?'

She looked surprised. 'Walking? The cars are in the garage, and as far as I can tell he had only the clothes he stood up in.'

Difficulties easily solved with money but he did not press the point.

He allowed a minute or two to pass before putting his next question and she waited, quite still now.

'Do you think there may be a connection between your husband's absence and the burned-out hut?'

'If there is I can't imagine what it could be.'

Wycliffe thought: That makes two of us. He said: 'Yesterday afternoon he came to the Incident Room and made a statement in connection with Celia Dawe's death. The statement did not incriminate him but it makes him a key witness so he is certain to be called to give evidence at the inquest and at any trial there may be.'

She looked at him, her blue eyes non-committal. 'So?'

'Do you think he would have been very upset at such a prospect?'

'I'm sure that he would. David has an intense dislike of publicity which amounts to a phobia; he even tries to prevent it being generally known that Peter Stride and David Cleeve are one and the same.' She smiled, as at the whims of a child. 'He never gives interviews, never fills up biographical questionnaires, and his photograph doesn't appear on the dust cover of his books.'

Wycliffe thought: Let it go at that for the moment. He dispensed balm with professional skill and it was received by one adept in the art of acknowledging courtesy with grace . . . 'I know that you will do all that is possible, Mr Wycliffe.'

Wycliffe got to his feet; then, as though the thought had just occurred to him, he said, 'Do you know if your husband, as a young man, was subject to epileptic seizures, Mrs Cleeve?'

She too was standing, and she looked at him in astonishment. 'David? What makes you ask that?'

'Was he?'

'If he was, he told me nothing of it and there has never been the slightest suggestion of anything of the kind since our marriage. I would like to know—'

Wycliffe cut her short, gently but firmly. 'We have to think of every possibility.'

Andrew Cleeve was waiting for him in the big drawing-room. 'I'll see Mr Wycliffe out, mother.' The boy clearly doted on his mother and wanted to save her from distress as far as he could.

In the hall he helped Wycliffe on with his raincoat. Wycliffe said, 'Walk back with me to the site.'

It was obvious that Andrew was waiting for a chance to talk.

'Take a coat or something, it's quite wet out.'

Andrew went to a hall cupboard and came back, struggling into an anorak that was already wet.

Outside, it was the boy who spoke first. 'Do you think that something has happened to father?'

'I don't know what to think; what is your opinion?'

The question took him by surprise. 'I don't know . . . he's been very odd lately. Since I've been home this vacation he's hardly been outside the grounds except . . . It's true he never went out much. Then he's been talking of employing a security johnny to patrol the grounds at night; he says it's because there have been one or two burglaries in the neighbourhood but I can't help feeling he's scared of something . . .'

'Do you get on well with your father?'

He thought about the question or, perhaps, about the answer he would give, then he said, 'No – not really.'

'Rows?'

'Not rows; we just keep out of each other's way.'

106

'Is this strain something new? Is it connected with Celia Dawe?'

In a dead-pan voice the boy said, 'So you know about that; I suppose you are bound to.'

'I know about your father and Celia and about you and Celia.'

'Yes, and that's what caused the trouble. I don't want to say much now but it's disgusting! He's more than old enough to be her father and, in any case, it's so humiliating for mother.'

'You weren't madly keen on the girl?'

They passed through the wicket gate and were able to walk side by side over the wet grass.

'I liked her; she was good fun but it wasn't serious for either of us. She was a really nice girl who'd had a very rough time and I felt sorry for her. But first Polmear, then my father, treated her like a tart.'

'How did you find out about her and your father?'

'She told me. She was very straight about it; she wouldn't let me take her out until I knew the situation. I thought that was very honest.'

Wycliffe thought that there might be other words to describe it but he said nothing.

'So your father sometimes went out at night if he didn't by day.'

'Yes! Sneaking out of his own house like a delinquent schoolboy!' He was silent for a while and they came to a halt in order not to reach the fire-tender before they had finished their conversation. 'Of course, the rules that apply to ordinary people are not for The Great Writer. I know that sounds harsh, but all that crap makes me sick!'

'There are many people, all over the world, who think your father is a great writer.'

'So what? My tutor at university is internationally known as a geologist but he's an ordinary, pleasant chap; he takes his wife and kids on holiday, he watches telly, and when he gets drunk he does it in company because he's enjoying himself – not alone in his room as an outlet for creative frustration.'

'But don't you think that the emotional demands on a first-rate writer or painter or musician are probably greater than those on your geologist?'

The boy shrugged. 'Possibly; I don't know, and I don't want to know. I prefer to be stupid and live like other people.'

Wycliffe changed his ground. 'Do I need to tell you that your father didn't kill Celia Dawe?'

The young man seemed to consider this for a while though he made no comment but after a little more time the question came, hesitant and a little fearful, 'Was he with her that night?'

'I'm not going to answer that; I've said more than I should already. Now, you must tell me something. Did Celia say anything to you which might have implied that she was frightened of someone or threatened by them?'

'Never!'

'Did she talk about her uncle?'

'Only about the way she was treated by him and her aunts.'

'Ill-treated?'

'Not exactly that; they were incredibly old-fashioned and she was made to dress and behave as if she was living when they were young. Even after she was sixteen, there was a row if she didn't go to chapel every Sunday, and she had to tell them exactly where she was going before she was allowed to go out of an evening. It was Victorian!'

'I understand you spotted the fire on your way back from Truro at about half-past two this morning.'

'Yes. I'd been to a sort of farewell party to a chap I was at school with; he's off to work in Tunisia . . . I know it sounds a bit heartless with Celia and all that . . .'

'It's natural enough; I shouldn't let that worry you.

108

You didn't see anything unusual along the road – apart from the fire, that is?'

'No, nothing. In fact I don't think I saw a soul – not a thing on the road – from Tregony home.'

Wycliffe thanked the boy and they parted. Andrew turned back towards the house and Wycliffe continued across the field. There was more activity on the site: unisex students in all manner of dress, looking damp and dismal, drifted to and fro between the tents and the screened-off wash-ups and loos. Near the burned-out hut Sergeant Pearce was in conversation with a sturdy, bearded young man with a mass of curly black hair and king-sized spectacles; presumably Prout's assistant.

Pearce turned to Wycliffe. 'Mr Wrighton tells me he knew nothing of the fire until a student came banging on the door of the caravan where he was sleeping. By that time the fire-tender was already entering the field.'

Wrighton looked at Wycliffe, solemn and anxious. 'I must admit to being a very sound sleeper.' He confessed it as a fault.

Wycliffe said, 'I suppose this is a major set-back for your work?'

The young man removed his glasses to wipe them and blinked myopically. 'I shouldn't think so. Ours won't have been the first hut to be burned down on this site; it must have been a fairly common occurrence when the original inhabitants were in possession.'

'But they weren't archaeologists working to a budget.'

A quick smile. 'They weren't insured either. No, most of our artefacts are pretty durable; they wouldn't be here otherwise after so many centuries. I expect most of our finds will turn up again in the debris. Luckily all our instruments are kept in the caravan.'

'And your records?'

The glasses were replaced. 'Ah, there we really had some luck. Dr Prout had the bulk of our records with

109

him and I was working on the current stuff in the caravan last night.'

'I understand that you and Dr Prout live in the caravan, but that he is away.'

'Dr Prout is away and he'll be returning some time this afternoon, but I only sleep in the van when he's away. At other times I'm in the tents with the others.'

'Is he here most nights?'

'Oh, yes, he's never away more than one or two nights a week. Although he only lives at St Germans and could, I suppose, go home every night, he prefers to stay on the site.'

'Tell me how you spent yesterday evening.'

'I was in the caravan writing up our log. I worked until about ten-thirty, then I made myself a hot drink and went to bed and to sleep.'

'Did you see Mr Cleeve at all?'

'No, I didn't; he hardly ever comes here in the evenings.'

'When you went to bed, had the students settled down for the night?'

A tolerant smile. 'No, they certainly had not. On Wednesday evenings there is a disco in the village and they went off in a body. I understand they came back at about half-past eleven but I'm afraid I didn't hear them.'

'How many students do you have on the site?'

He considered. 'Let me think . . . yes, twelve – ten of them, six girls and four boys, are living in the tents; the other two are local and one of them is Christie Cleeve.'

Wycliffe thanked him.

'If there is anything more I can do . . . I'm sure that Dr Prout would want me . . .'

'We may ask you for a written statement later.'

Pearce's owl seemed to Wycliffe more like an earnest, myopic teddy-bear.

Back in his car, Wycliffe put through an RT call to

division, asking for additional men. No point in ringing Forensic until the witching hour of nine a.m.

It was still a little short of eight o'clock when he let himself into the cottage. The mist showed no sign of clearing and a very fine rain had spread down from the hill. No sailing today; no trippers; no cruises round the docks or to the lighthouse.

Helen was in the kitchen, in her dressing-gown. 'Coffee?'

Her auburn hair was set off by the blue of her dressing-gown and he thought how young she looked to be the mother of grown-up children. He kissed her on the nape of her neck.

'What was that for?'

They sat on stools in the kitchen, eating toast and drinking coffee.

'What happened? You said something about a fire.'

'The archaeologists' hut has been burned down – almost certainly with malice aforethought. More important, it looks as though Cleeve is missing.'

Helen paused with a piece of toast half-way to her mouth. 'Missing?'

'It seems he went out late last night and he hasn't come back.'

'You've talked to his wife?'

'Yes. She didn't miss him until they were all woken up about the fire. They don't sleep in the same room.'

Helen nodded. 'I thought there was something. Poor woman! With all her breeding she couldn't hide the fact that she had her troubles. It can't be easy living with a man like Cleeve. Since we were there I've thought about them a lot; it's one thing to read the work of a man who is obsessed by the evil in the world but it's quite another to have to live with him.' She grinned. 'I suppose there are worse things than being married to a policeman.'

After a pause she said, 'Do you think there's a

111

connection between the fire and Cleeve's disappearance?'

Wycliffe sighed. 'I wish I knew.'

'Surely in a village of this size, a murder, arson, and a missing man, all in the space of three days, are more likely to be linked than not?'

He nodded. 'You'd certainly think so, but piecing them together is another matter. It reminds me of homework we used to get at school: "Put the following incidents into a story of three hundred words—".'

'Taxis and hire-cars in Roseland itself and the district up to and including Truro and St Austell; you'll need a description of Cleeve and of the clothes he was wearing when he went out. If we haven't found him by late afternoon I shall issue a press release then we can ask for public co-operation – anyone driving along the A3078 after 20.30 hours last night blah blah . . .'

Lucy Lane was making notes. 'You really think he's cleared out of his own accord?'

'Or he's under the debris of the burnt-out hut, or he's lying injured or dead somewhere in the neighbourhood, or he's been kidnapped by the little green man with an Irish accent.'

'Sorry, sir.'

'No, it's me.' Wycliffe sighed. 'After talking to him yesterday I feel I should have kept closer tabs on him. Then there are the watermen.'

'Watermen?'

'Down at the harbour. It's not impossible that he took a boat, his own or somebody else's. We also want to know where everybody was yesterday evening and night. I've asked Division for more men.'

'Anything else?'

'Yes. Laura Wynn's Celtic circus. It seems that somebody set fire to the hut and arson is arson whether or not it is connected with Cleeve's disappearance. So: anybody seen loitering in the neighbourhood with a dangerous box of matches . . .'

112

'But seriously—'

'Seriously, you get from Pearce a list of Laura's dyed-in-the-wool activists and make 'em account for themselves. It will be a waste of time but "no stone unturned" and it might teach 'em a lesson.'

Six constables, including three dog-handlers with their dogs, arrived from Division and were allocated to Sergeant Pearce to work over the fields and lanes, the cliffs and shore lines to the north of Roscrowgy – the area within which Cleeve might conceivably have walked and met with some mishap without being found. Before turning them loose, Wycliffe telephoned Patricia to make sure there had been no news. In telling him there had not she effectively hid whatever feelings she may have had under the veneer of her impeccable manners.

Dr Bell, an old friend at Forensic, telephoned to say that Horton, the fire expert, would be on the scene by three o'clock. He also confirmed that the dart had probably been projected from some sort of air or spring gun: they had found traces of oil on the brass tube probably from the barrel of the weapon and, more significantly, tiny fragments of hard wax adhered to the blank end of the tube, almost certainly a substitute for the flaring of the pellets normally fired from airguns, which stops them sliding down the barrel.

The killer had thought of everything.

Tests were being carried out to determine the effectiveness of the dart when fired from different types of air weapon.

Wycliffe said, 'The killer couldn't have counted on an open window and a naked target. He might have had to wait for his victim to leave, fully dressed. What about the effectiveness of the dart then?'

Bell was definite. 'I think it would have penetrated all but the thickest clothing and remained effective when fired with a modern airgun or pistol.'

113

For an hour Wycliffe created an atmosphere of unease in the Incident Room, standing about, brooding, drinking cups of Potter's coffee and smoking. He spoke with two reporters who were quite content to be briefed with the details of Celia Dawe's murder; they showed no interest in the fire, and had not yet heard that the country's most controversial and best-selling author was missing from home.

Cleeve missing. Since yesterday's encounter Wycliffe had been convinced that Celia Dawe was the accidental victim of a dart intended for Cleeve. The middle of the night, the lighting poor, the killer nervous, and the two bodies on the bed anything but still; a sudden convulsive movement on their part had probably reprieved the man and condemned the girl. Polmear, landlord of The Buckingham, had said it: 'She was an unlucky kid – never got it right.' Wycliffe hadn't been a policeman for nearly 30 years without knowing that there were such people – Fate's preferred targets.

But it was Cleeve, missing or not, on whom the investigation must concentrate now.

He said to Potter: 'I'm going to talk to Laura Wynn.'

The mist had thickened; on the Steps visibility was less than 20 yards; a sea mist with the tang of salt. Invisible, a jet-fighter ripped through the air above the mist – in yesterday's weather. In this steep narrow lane between granite cottages it was easy to imagine that the figures looming out of the fog were fishermen returning from sea; in fact they were disgruntled emmets in plastic macs, wondering what there was to do but eat. Now and then the fog-horn on the lighthouse boomed out like some monstrous animal in its last sad hours.

Wycliffe pushed open the door of the jewellery shop and stepped down into the well-like area in front of the counter. A moment or two went by before Laura Wynn appeared; Laura in working rig – blue nylon

114

overall, her hair caught back in a youthful ponytail, no torque, no bangles. Probably she did not expect customers in such weather and she looked at him without enthusiasm.

'Mr Wycliffe, isn't it?'

'I would like to talk to you, Mrs Wynn, in connection with the murder of Celia Dawe.'

She indicated by the slightest movement that there was nothing stopping him.

'It would be more convenient if we could sit down.'

She seemed on the point of refusing but changed her mind. She went to the door, lowered the catch and changed the sign to closed. 'This way, then.'

Through the door at the back of the shop, along a narrow passage to a room which looked out on the back garden. A pleasant room, white walls, chintz upholstery, shelves on either side of the chimney-breast filled with zany books. The pictures were framed reproductions of mediaeval illustrations of the Arthurian legend. She indicated a chair on one side of the empty fireplace and sat herself opposite him.

'I've already told your detective that I know nothing of the dead girl or of the people she associated with.'

A woman striving to achieve a serenity which did not come naturally to her; one could imagine her attending yoga classes, and dutifully consuming her fruit and fibre with live yogurt. At least she had achieved a clear eye and an intimidating gaze. Not a woman who had spent much of her life with men.

'You are acquainted with David Cleeve?'

It was obvious that the question came as a surprise. 'Why should—'

Wycliffe was firm. 'Perhaps you will allow me to ask the questions. Of course you don't have to answer them but I hope you will. This is a murder inquiry and I assume you wish to help.'

'All right. As we live in the same village it would be surprising if we were not acquainted.'

'Do you know that he was on intimate terms with the dead girl?'

A hardening of the facial muscles. 'It doesn't surprise me.'

'But did you know?'

A momentary hesitation. 'No, I did not know.'

'You were out on the Steps very late on the night of Monday/Tuesday.'

'So?'

'What were you doing?'

'I was looking for Tripitaka. Although he has been neutered he is very wayward at night.'

'Did you go down the alley which leads to the backs of the houses opposite?'

'A short distance – yes. I called Tripitaka and suddenly he was there at my feet. I picked him up and came back here.' Her manner was detached, objective.

'What time was this?'

'About half-past twelve.'

'Did you meet or see anyone while you were out?'

'No one.'

She was a good-looking woman – splendid was the word; too statuesque for Wycliffe's taste, but she might well have been a challenge to Cleeve. A modern Hera. Wasn't it Hera who annually renewed her virginity at the Argos spring? Women like Laura never really lost theirs and he suspected that this was true of Patricia too. Psychological virgins.

'David Cleeve is missing.'

'*Missing?*'

'He went out last night and he hasn't come back.'

She looked incredulous. 'You think something has happened to him?'

'That's what I'm trying to find out.'

'But why come to me?'

'The big wooden hut on Henry's Field was burned down during the night. Arson, by the look of it.'

A worried frown. 'You don't think that any of our people would do such a thing?'

'No? It seems they've been pretty active on the site before now.'

'But nothing wilfully destructive!' Anxious, shocked.

He moved in. 'I suspect that you knew Cleeve before you came to live here.'

Hesitation. She was saved from immediate reply by the arrival of one of her tribe of cats, a wicked-looking seal-point. The creature leapt on to her lap, flexed its claws in a way which must have been painful, and settled down, sleek and graceful as a snake.

Laura made up her mind to be co-operative, though her manner was more aggressive. 'I suppose I shall be badgered until I tell you, and I've nothing to hide. When I was at school I lived with my mother in a flat in Exeter. We had been deserted by my father who went off with another woman. David Cleeve and a friend moved into a flat on the same landing.'

'What year was this?'

She reflected. 'It must have been early in the summer of 1953, I remember the city was decorated for the coronation. They were still there when we left in September '54.'

John Scales had established that Cleeve moved from Bristol to Exeter in 1953 and set up as a freelance journalist. Now, here he was pin-pointed in an Exeter flat with a friend. Nice when the wires crossed on target.

'Where was this flat?'

'In Mellor Road – number fourteen. The houses in Mellor Road were four-storey Victorian town houses and most of them had been converted into flats. They're all gone now – replaced by modern flats, half the size and ten times the price.'

'Cleeve would have been about twenty-two at that time?'

'I suppose so, about that.'

117

'This friend he lived with . . .'

'A young man of about the same age. He was called John – John Larkin. They were journalists of some sort and they were both writing books.' She seemed slightly embarrassed. 'At that time I had visions of becoming a writer and I was impressed.'

'Did you know them well?'

She shook her head. 'No, we just met occasionally on the stairs. I was never in their flat or they in ours. I was only a schoolgirl and my mother didn't like me talking to them; she thought they were a bit odd.'

'I suppose they chatted you up?'

She frowned. 'No, it wasn't like that. We talked about books and they used to tease me about being serious. Anyway, when I was seventeen we moved to London and a bit later I went to the School of Art and Design.' She smiled, a rueful little smile. 'No more writing.'

'Did you see either of them again?'

'No, it wasn't until just after I came to live here – David came into the shop to buy a present for his wife and I recognized him.'

'After nearly thirty years?'

'Why not? People don't change all that much.' She smiled, softened by recollections of youth. 'I got mixed up, though, and called him John.'

'These two, when you knew them in Exeter, how were they living? Lots of friends – parties – girls?'

'No, nothing like that; they lived very quietly. Of course they were out a lot because of their work. They seemed quite well off; one of them had a car and not so many people did then.'

'I suppose your mother remembers them?'

'Mother died before I came to live here.'

'Perhaps you will tell me your maiden name?'

She hesitated, then made up her mind. 'I've never been married. I adopted the "Mrs" to avoid unwelcome attentions.'

118

'That's understandable. Did Cleeve seem pleased to see you again?'

'He didn't remember me at first.'

'And afterwards?'

She actually coloured. 'I saw him from time to time.'

'Do you know what happened to his friend – John Larkin?'

'No; I asked him, but it seems they lost touch. Not long after we left Exeter David moved to London himself and published his first book – *Xanadu*, the one that made his name. It was strange, I suppose, I actually read all the Peter Stride books without having the least idea that they had been written by him.'

'Can you give me the names of other people who were living in the Mellor Road flats who might remember the two young men?'

He got three names. Progress of a sort; at least a Knight's move.

As he was leaving he asked to see her workshop. She looked doubtful, but led him to a room which had been built onto the kitchen. Not very big but meticulously arranged to make use of every inch. Two benches, one for the metalwork, the other for enamelling. Tiny tools – snips, pliers, various little hammers, some of metal others of hard wood, tweezers and tongs; doll-size anvils and vices; a kiln and another little furnace; bottles labelled with cabalistic signs containing the enamelling colours . . . No doubt at all that Laura would have found the making of the dart well within her capability.

'Very interesting – thank you.'

Lunch, he thought, at The Buckingham.

The Buckingham was full of people and talk; waitresses dodged between the tables while people queued at the bar for drinks. Wycliffe hovered at the entrance to the lounge bar and was instantly spotted by the all-seeing Polmear. A signal to one of the waitresses and

119

he was piloted to an alcove where there was a table laid for one – presumably for Polmear, when he found time to eat.

'The plaice is very good, sir. Fresh-caught this morning . . . With a side-salad . . . dressing? . . . And a lager?'

Near the end of the meal Polmear came and sat opposite him, nursing a bottle of brandy. 'To sweeten the coffee.'

Wycliffe said, 'Weather not so good today.'

'I'm not complaining, a couple of days a week like this and the money just rolls in – they've nothing to do but eat and drink; but if the weather stays bad longer than that they think about going home.'

The ethology of the emmet.

'Progress?'

Wycliffe shrugged.

Polmear said, 'I hear they had a fire up at the dig last night.'

'I heard that too.'

Polmear poured brandy into balloon glasses. 'Since you told me about Celia, I've been thinking: it could have been a jealous wife. There are women who can't take that sort of thing . . .'

Whatever Polmear had or hadn't known before, he knew something now.

'Thanks for the brandy.'

Wycliffe strolled along the waterfront; he found the tangy mist invigorating. One of the ferry boats was berthing with hardly anyone aboard. He turned up Zion Steps, loath to get back to the grind. The herbalist had a 'Closed' notice in his glass door; the vegetarians were champing away; the jewellery shop and the photographer's had a sealed look. In the Incident Room Dixon had taken over from Potter.

'Coffee, sir?'

'I'm awash already.'

He stood by one of the tall, narrow Gothic windows

of the little building, looking out into the grey gloom with a morose unseeing gaze.

In a murder case the rules are clear; you look to the oracles, the Three Wise Monkeys of criminal investigation: Motive, Means and Opportunity, and the greatest of these is Motive. He had asked: Who had a motive for murdering Celia Dawe? And the oracle had remained dumb. Now it seemed the question should have been: Who had a motive for killing Cleeve? But the oracle was no more communicative.

Cleeve had been threatened and there had been an attempt on his life; now he was missing.

Wycliffe brooded on Cleeve. The reporter on the local paper who had 'fits'; the freelance in Exeter, sharing a flat with another journalist, John Larkin; the schoolgirl Laura Wynn, living in the same building. Then, London, *Xanadu, Medicus, Magistra* . . . fame, marriage, the twins, Roseland . . . no more fits.

Patricia had said, 'If he was (an epileptic) he told me nothing about it and there has never been the slightest suggestion of it since our marriage.'

There was another remark playing hide-and-seek on the fringes of his consciousness, a remark someone had made recently. He made an effort of memory – almost always fatal to the trapping of such will-o'-the-wisps – and failed. He thought it might have been something from Laura Wynn but could get no further.

Perhaps it would come back if he stopped trying.

He turned to Potter. 'See if you can get Mr Scales on the telephone.'

Scales would be in his – Wycliffe's – office, sitting in his – Wycliffe's – chair. It was an odd feeling; somehow the job seemed more important when someone else was doing it. When he sat in that chair he felt at everybody's beck and call; when someone else sat there they seemed to acquire a certain eminence. Absurd!

'I've got the address of the Exeter flat, John, but it's been pulled down.'

Scales already had men working on the Exeter angle, so far without success, but with the address and the names of occupants contemporary with the two young men they might do better.

'Has Horton arrived yet, sir?'

'I'm expecting him at any moment.'

'No news of Cleeve?'

'No, the search party is out and as soon as Horton arrives we shall start turning over the debris of the fire. Keep watching this space, John!'

A man had come into the room and was talking to Potter. Wycliffe reconized Horton, a dark, undistinguished little man with whom he had worked before and admired for his self-effacing manner as well as for his professional skill. He did not look like a veteran of the courtroom but he had a reputation among criminal lawyers for never getting ruffled and for never being jockeyed into saying more or less than he intended.

They shook hands. 'Are you coming with me to wherever it is?'

'I'll run you up to the site.'

Henry's Field was a bleak prospect. The drizzle had stopped but the landscape was obliterated by mist, and the fog-horn on the lighthouse punctuated the silence with its eerie blast. They were working on the dig and figures were dimly visible through the mist. It was arranged that the earnest Wrighton would work through the debris of the hut with the police to rescue the second-hand artefacts.

Horton cast a professional eye over the tangled mass of carbonized and charred timbers and seemed mildly surprised.

'This is important?'

'If there is a man underneath.'

'A funeral pyre?'

'Could be.'

Horton turned to the two men who would do the heavy work. 'All right, you can get started. As you work, try to cause a minimum of disturbance and lay the timbers out in order as you remove them.'

Wycliffe walked over to the dig. Christie Cleeve was the first to see him. 'Is there any news?'

'I'm afraid not.'

She looked grey-faced and heavy-eyed. 'Mother says it's better for me to carry on here.'

'I think she's right and I'll make sure you know the moment we hear anything.'

Gervaise Prout's slim figure emerged from the mist, his white hair glistening with moisture. 'Mr Wycliffe! I'm so glad to see you.' He turned to Christie: 'Jane has found something at number five and she's not sure what it is, see if you can help her.'

The girl went off.

Prout said, 'I feel so annoyed with myself for not having been here, but I really had no option. There was a symposium in Exeter at which I had to read a paper.'

'I don't see what you could have done if you were here.'

Prout made a gesture of impatience. 'It's such a blow to our work when it was going so well.'

'Are you thinking of the loss of your hut or the disappearance of your patron?'

He received a quick appraising glance as though Prout suspected him of sarcasm but Wycliffe's bland features gave nothing away.

'I was referring to the loss of the hut.'

'I understood from your assistant that it would be no great set-back because you had the bulk of your records with you and the rest were in the caravan.'

A frown. 'Wrighton is an enthusiastic youngster, a good field-worker in the making, but he has no idea of administration and its problems.' Prout rubbed

123

his bony chin until it shone like a little red apple. 'I was deeply shocked to hear about Cleeve. What does it mean?'

'That he went out last night and didn't come back.'

'You know no more than that?'

'At present, no. We are searching the neighbourhood, so far without result.'

'Do you suspect foul play?'

Wycliffe shrugged. 'Do you? You probably know the man and his circumstances better than I.'

Prout seemed to resent having his question turned back on him. 'I'm naturally very concerned. David is not only our patron here but I may say that he has become a friend. Have you spoken to Kitson?'

'Not yet. You think he might be able to help?' Naïve.

'I don't know . . .' After a pause he went on, 'I certainly have the impression that David and Kitson are very close.'

Wycliffe was casual. 'I suppose that is natural; two very intelligent men, living as neighbours . . .'

Prout would have liked to let it go at that but he was urged on by the desire to seem well informed. 'You may be right but I feel there is more to it than that . . . Whenever David visits the dig, Kitson is rarely far away and one frequently comes upon the two of them in seemingly intimate conversation. What really strikes me as odd is that David seems to defer to him in a way that he would do to nobody else.'

Wycliffe recalled the curious moment of strain when, on his first dig, returning to the hut with Prout, they came upon Cleeve and Kitson in earnest discussion.

Prout had talked himself into yielding confidences. 'You may think it petty, but raising funds even for a small project like this is difficult – one has to nurse one's patron, to catch and hold his interest . . . It is true that we have sufficient money for the present dig but I had interested Cleeve in a more ambitious scheme . . .'

'And Kitson talked him out of it?'

'I'm sure that he did.' Prout had his eyes on the wall of mist which all but hemmed them in. 'Altogether, I felt that Kitson must be a . . . must have very considerable influence on David.'

'Are you suggesting that there might be something sinister in their relationship?'

Prout shied away from that like a frightened colt. 'Not sinister! Of course not! I'm merely saying that for Kitson to have so much influence over David he must know him better than anyone else. I suspect that they have known each other a long time – certainly before Kitson came here to live.'

Wycliffe said, 'Do you know anything of Kitson's background?'

Prout prodded a clump of heather with the toe of his bespoke fell-walkers. 'I met him for the first time when I came here to talk to David about the dig eighteen months ago.'

'But you've been making a few enquiries among your academic friends – quite natural in the circumstances.'

Prout let this pass though he looked uncomfortable. 'I really know very little about him. He doesn't seem to have a formal academic background. I gather that he translates Russian and other Slav languages for anybody who will pay him and he's made something of a reputation as a linguist. I've heard that he undertakes hack-work for scholars in the field of Slavonic studies – manuscript reading, indexing, proof checking – that sort of thing.'

Wycliffe guessed that he had got all that he was likely to get from Prout and he was anxious to move on. 'Thank you for being so helpful. I shall treat what you have told me in confidence.'

The Land Rover which had brought the searchers from Division, parked on the skyline at the highest point in the field, looked grotesquely enlarged by the mist. Sergeant Pearce was in the cab, a map spread in front of him, a flask of coffee on the seat beside him; he was monitoring the search through the personal radios of his men.

'This has worked well, sir. Very few radio blind spots and no blisters on my feet. Unfortunately, no luck either. They've covered the ground we mapped out for them and, in any case, I shall have to call them off for refreshment shortly.'

'Don't send them back until you hear from me.'

'You don't think he can be out there, sir?'

Wycliffe growled something unintelligible. Why did they all ask questions as though he had a crystal ball?

He plodded through the heather and joined Horton by the burned-out ruin. Already a large quantity of charred timber had been laid out on the ground and the site was looking less like a Guy Fawkes bonfire which had been caught in a deluge.

Horton said, 'I think we've found what you are looking for.'

CHAPTER FIVE

Thursday July 21st

It was a moment before Wycliffe, peering down through the still considerable tangle of carbonized wood, saw a human foot; a foot burned through to the bones of the toes but, for the rest, still enclosed in the ghostly remnants of a shoe. The leg, dealt with in the same freakish manner by the fire, was visible to the knee, but what-ever remained of the body was hidden under more charred timbers.

'Is that what you expected?'

Wycliffe was subdued. 'I think this is the man we are looking for.' He glanced across at the industrious Wrighton, squatting on his haunches, sorting through ashes and rubble with no eyes for anything else. 'Does he know?'

'No.'

'Then find some pretext to send him away. I don't want the news to get around until we are sure. Another thing: it's possible that he died in the same way as the girl – injected with nicotine by a hypodermic dart. Obviously it's vital to find the dart if there is one.'

He went over to the Land Rover and made a number of calls on the RT; to the coroner; to Franks, the pathologist; to the local GP; to his headquarters and to the Incident Room.

Another half-hour and the body was completely uncovered. It was Cleeve; no doubt about that. In the whimsical way of fires, objects near the ground had suffered less actual burning than others higher up, probably due to the reduced oxygen supply. Horton said, 'A body takes a lot of burning.'

All the same, Cleeve was no sight for the public gaze and Wycliffe posted Pearce and his men to keep people away until the screens were delivered.

Dr Hodge, the local GP, came in his battered Metro, bouncing over the rough ground. He got out, slammed the door, and came to stand, looking down at the remains of the dead man. He muttered: 'Is it Cleeve?' Then he turned to Wycliffe, 'If at first you don't succeed, try, try again – is that it?'

'We don't know how he died yet.' Wycliffe was terse.

'No, but we can make a good guess.' Hodge rubbed his dark chin, always a little in need of a shave. 'Well, it makes more sense; I couldn't believe that anybody would take that trouble over a silly girl. Poor little so-and-so! Ah, well!' The doctor sighed. 'I suppose you've notified the coroner?'

Wycliffe made his way across to the dig. He spotted the auburn head in one of the trenches and was immediately seen himself. Christie was like a young doe, alert to the slightest signal. She came to him, frowning, anxious, 'You've heard something?'

'I'm afraid it's bad news.'

'Tell me.'

He told her. The news of her father's death did not come as a great shock, rather a confirmation of something feared; it was the circumstances of his death which distressed her.

She murmured: 'He died in the fire . . . in the fire . . .'

Wycliffe said: 'I'm sure we shall find out that your father was already dead when the fire started.' He added after a moment: 'I mean that. Now you must go to your mother.'

She seemed to hesitate and he said: 'Would you like me to break the news first?'

She shook her head. 'No, but I must find Andrew.'

Wycliffe was reminded of his own twin son and

daughter, several years older, but still in moments of crisis reaching out to each other. He watched her set out across the field to the wicket gate, deeply puzzled and distressed. In his turn he was being watched curiously by the students working on the dig; they must have realized that there had been some development.

Cleeve was dead and Wycliffe was in no doubt that he had been murdered, though he would have to wait for Franks to provide official confirmation.

Why had he gone out late at night knowing that his life was threatened? Wrighton, who had spent the evening working in the caravan, had not seen him, though his body had been found in the shed.

Lucy Lane arrived and he put her in the picture. 'I want you to be with me when I talk to Mrs Cleeve.'

Just short of the wicket gate they were waylaid by Dr Prout, very subdued. 'I've just this moment heard . . .' And then, 'I suppose it's too early to call on Patricia?'

Wycliffe agreed that it was.

Through the wicket gate and the rhododendron tunnel. The mist was lifting at last and, as is often the case on this coast, there was a prospect of a fine evening after a dismal day. He led the way round to the front door and rang the bell.

The door was opened by a woman Wycliffe had never seen before, a little brown mouse of a woman, probably still on the right side of forty but she would look very different at sixty. Her features looked pinched and he had the impression that a single harsh word would send her scurrying for cover, or that she might burst into tears.

Wycliffe introduced himself and Lucy Lane. She said, 'I am Mrs Cleeve's cousin; my name is Byrne – Miss Byrne.'

'I suppose you have heard?'

She nodded without speaking, eyes cast down like a nun.

'This is a distressing time for you all . . . I am anxious to find out exactly what happened last night and I hope you will answer a few questions . . .'

Another nod.

'Did you see Mr Cleeve at all?'

'We all had dinner together, as usual.'

'At what time?'

'At seven-thirty.'

She seemed so distressed that he felt heartless in questioning her. 'Can you tell me what happened after dinner?'

She made an obvious effort. 'The same as usual. David had a strict routine which he followed unless we had guests. He worked in the morning, then he was free until dinner. After dinner he would go back to work until midnight or even one in the morning.'

He saw with surprise that her eyes were glistening with tears.

'You were fond of him.'

She flushed. 'He was his own worst enemy. He was a hard-working man and except at odd times when he'd had too much to drink, a kind man – too kind, sometimes.' She turned her head away.

'Were you surprised to hear that he went out last night?'

She nodded. He was afraid that if he questioned her further she would break down. He said something soothing and asked her to find out if Mrs Cleeve would see them.

'She's expecting you.'

They were taken to the big drawing-room. 'I'll tell her you're here.'

A clock in the passage chimed and struck five. Several minutes went by before Patricia Cleeve came into the room. After being introduced to Lucy Lane she apologized for keeping them waiting, sat herself in one of the armchairs and smoothed her skirt.

'Christie and Andrew have each other; I've left them

together.' She was completely controlled but there was tension in every little line of her body.

Wycliffe repeated the usual phrases with obvious sincerity and she accepted his sympathy with dignity. Wycliffe thought: These are the forms, and she is the kind of woman to be strengthened and supported by their observance. No hiding away; no hole-in-corner grief, self-indulgent and destructive; there is a ritual for bereavement as for everything else.

'There are questions I shall have to ask you, some of them very personal, but if you would prefer to put it off until tomorrow . . .'

In a deliberate, emphatic tone she said, 'I would prefer, Mr Wycliffe, that you do whatever you think necessary to find out what is behind all this; how David came to die. It is certainly not pleasant to be interrogated but it is much worse to be kept in the dark . . . in the dark about almost everything.'

Wycliffe nodded. 'I understand.'

The windows of the drawing-room looked out on a terraced lawn, falling away to a fringe of trees and, beyond the trees, to the creek, the headland and the pines. The mist had vanished magically, like the lifting of a veil, and already a watery sunshine was restoring colour to the scene.

'As you know, your husband's body was found in the ruins of the archaeologists' hut – can you think of any reason why he would have gone there late at night?'

A slight shrug. 'No, I certainly cannot. It's true that he was more interested in the dig than he was willing to admit and I think Gervaise Prout sometimes worked very late but I understand he was away.'

Wycliffe cleared the decks. 'So far, of course, we have no evidence that his death was other than accidental but—'

She cut across his words. 'Please don't feel that you have to spare me, Mr Wycliffe. David was murdered.

131

You know that as well as I do. The horror of publicity he has had ever since I've known him arose from some sort of fear and in recent months that fear has been catching up with him. Although he would never discuss or even admit the existence of anything of the kind, I've no doubt in my mind that he believed his life to be threatened. When I saw how anxious he was to talk to you on Saturday, I hoped that he was going to tell you about it.'

Few women in his experience could have disciplined themselves to speak so objectively of a husband, recently dead.

'Up to a point your husband did confide in me; he told me that he was being threatened but he claimed to have no knowledge of the source of the threats or of any possible reason for them. He was extremely vague as to their nature though he did say that they had arrived through the post – four of them spread over the past nine months. When I asked to see these communications, whatever they were, he said that he had destroyed them.'

Lucy Lane had been sitting bolt upright in her chair, her bag on her lap, here eyes moving from one to the other, taking in every nuance of the exchanges; now she said, 'When someone makes that kind of complaint to the police, Mrs Cleeve, it usually means that he or she is well aware of who is threatening them and why, but without embarrassment or some incriminating admission they can't or won't speak out. With no facts it is impossible for the police to act.'

'Yes, I see that.'

Wycliffe said, 'And the situation hasn't changed so far as those threats are concerned; we still need to know more about them, which means that we must know more about your husband's past.'

She made a gesture of helplessness. 'But I know so little – virtually nothing about his life before our marriage.'

132

'And you feel that whatever made him so . . . so wary of publicity of any kind, must have occurred before you met him?'

She was emphatic. 'I do! Very early in our marriage I questioned him about it.' A wry smile. 'Needless to say, I learned nothing except not to ask such questions in the future.'

'Did you ever meet any of his relatives?'

'No, his father and mother were already dead; he was an only child and, though he admitted to cousins, I don't think he was ever in touch with them.'

'When did you first meet?'

'It was one Christmas, in London – Christmas 1961 it must have been. We were married the following April.' She smiled. 'It was hero-worship on my part. I had read his books and I was an eager disciple. I saw him as a genius.' She glanced across at Lucy Lane as she said this.

'Where was he living at that time?'

'When we met? In a bachelor flat off Gower Street. As far as I could tell he had few, if any, friends – a loose acquaintance with a couple of fellows in a neighbouring flat – they, in fact, came to our wedding, the only ones from his side.'

'Not his publisher or his agent?'

She spoke with deliberation. 'You may find this incredible but at the time of our marriage, David had never met either his publisher or his agent. All the business was conducted by correspondence.'

Wycliffe kept the questioning in a low key, allowing intervals of silence when the three of them sat, each apparently absorbed in private thoughts.

'This man, Roger Kitson – is he a recent acquaintance?'

Another frown. 'I think David has known Roger for some years. Very occasionally David had to go to London to deal with the business side of his work and when he came back from one of those trips he said that

133

he had offered the cottage to someone. That was nearly two years ago, and a month or so later Roger turned up and took possession.'

For a while she sat, looking down at her hands, clasped in her lap, then she raised her eyes and looked straight at Wycliffe. 'You must think it very strange that after twenty years of marriage I know so little about my husband but ours was not a conventional marriage. I've already said that I regarded David as a genius; certainly he was no ordinary man and he did not behave like one. He lived much of his life in a sort of limbo between imagination and reality and, as you will know from his books, the world of his imagination could be strange and terrifying.'

Her gaze shifted from Wycliffe to Lucy Lane as though the girl fitted more easily into the pattern of her thoughts. 'Even as a young wife I realized that I could not expect to monopolize any part of such a man – that it would have been inviting disaster to try.

'When we had the children I asked only that he would not allow the assertion of his own personality to blight or smother theirs and, in the main, he kept that bargain.' She made a small gesture with her slim hands. 'Of course, he had many women; there were occasional bouts of drunkenness, he was sometimes thoughtlessly cruel, and obsessively secretive . . . But I knew that he couldn't be otherwise; he was the man I married.'

She was looking down at her hands once more. 'I flatter myself that I understood his needs and that I made life easier for him. I saw that as my role. But you will see that I am not in a position to tell you much about him.'

Wycliffe was beginning to feel stifled in this atmosphere of reasonableness and studied calm which seemed to create its own peculiar tension. He admired the woman's self-control but it was unnatural. Oddly, he felt sympathy for Cleeve; such repression would probably have provoked him to either violence or obscenity and either response would have been incomprehensible to Patricia.

'What an extraordinary woman! I never really thought of him as having a wife, but a woman like that . . .' Lucy Lane in admiration.

They walked along the broad corridor with its disturbing pictures and erratic changes of level and climbed the stairs; Lucy all eyes. As they reached the secretary's office the girl came to the door and Wycliffe introduced himself and Lucy Lane.

Milli looked them over in cool appraisal. 'I know who you are.'

It was the first time Wycliffe had seen the girl at close quarters. 'I suppose you know that Mr Cleeve's body has been found?'

'Mrs Cleeve told me.'

'Did he seem much as usual yesterday? Or was he nervous, edgy – you know the sort of thing?'

She shrugged her thin shoulders. One had the impression that her body was infinitely pliable rather than jointed and, though she was perfectly proportioned, she was very small. She said, 'You were here yesterday, you saw as much of him as I did.'

'But you knew him, you could compare his behaviour with some sort of norm.'

'There was no norm; he was never the same two days together, it depended on how the work was going, whether he had slept the night before – even on the weather.' She added grudgingly, 'But he was upset yesterday. I noticed it when I arrived in the morning, then you came, and he was out most of the afternoon so I didn't see much of him.'

'Do you live in the house?'

'I do not! I live in the village but I have my lunch here.'

'With the family?'

'Of course.'

'How long have you worked here?'

'Nearly five years.'

'We shall be in the library for a while but I would like to see you again afterwards.'

She glanced at her watch. 'I finish work at half-past five and it's already quarter to six.'

'I won't keep you longer than necessary.'

For the third time in six days Wycliffe found himself in Cleeve's library, so much in contrast to the rest of the house.

Lucy Lane exclaimed in astonishment: 'It's Edwardian! I'd always imagined him against a background of white walls, steel-framed abstracts, and Giacometti figures on the bookcases.'

'That sounds more like his wife.'

Looking round the big room he experienced a mild elation and immediately felt guilty. The truth was that he always had a pleasurable sense of anticipation when he was able to look behind the scenes of another man's life. Asexual voyeurism, he called it – the vice which sells autobiographies, published journals and diaries. Wycliffe was one of that army of unassuming people who feel the need to match themselves against the grain of other people's lives; perhaps that was why he had found his vocation in the police.

Cleeve's desk was orderly: a thick wad of typescript in a limp cover, labelled *Setebos*, presumably the next novel in final draft, waiting for the author's finishing touches and seal of approval. But even without them, good or bad, *Setebos* would be 'Peter Stride's last and greatest masterpiece, published posthumously'. And if publication could coincide with a well publicized trial of his killer then the sky would be the limit.

Wycliffe said, 'Why Setebos, I wonder?'

'Setebos was Caliban's creator-god, and in Browning's

136

poem Caliban thought Setebos had created the world for his own amusement.' Lucy Lane, BA Hons (Eng Lit). Very prim.

'Ah!'

On the desk there was a crystal pen-tray with coloured ball-points and pencils; a paper-knife with an ivory handle in the form of a lion couchant, a memo pad, and two telephones . . . On the memo pad were three lines of notes: 'Lester . . . RC WE 9/8 . . . Saunders for Medicus???' The notes had been written in green and below them there was an odd little doodle of a man upside down.

'Ask Miss Who-is-it to come in.'

Lucy was looking at the bookshelves; she fetched the girl from the office. Milli came in and looked disapproving when she saw Wycliffe sitting in Cleeve's chair.

'I wonder if you can explain these notes?'

She glanced at the pad. 'I think so. Colin Lester is Mr Cleeve's agent and this is a memo to ring him; RC is Russel Cowdray, his English publisher. Mr Cleeve was arranging for Cowdray to spend the weekend beginning Friday August 9th here. Saunders for *Medicus* – that refers to dramatizing *Medicus* – one of Mr Cleeve's books – for TV. The company want to use Neville Saunders but Mr Cleeve wasn't sure they'd chosen the right man for the job.'

'And these notes were made yesterday?'

'Oh, yes.'

'Thank you; that is very helpful. But what about the little upside-down man?'

A ghost of a smile. 'That's typical of Mr Cleeve – a doodle.' She looked more carefully at the little drawing. 'I think it's a version of the hanged man in the Tarot pack. He thinks – thought in symbols, he really did. Even people who read his books (the inference being that Wycliffe was unlikely to have done so) don't realize the amount of symbolism there is in his writing.' She waved a hand vaguely. 'You'll find a whole section of the library devoted to books on the subject.' She paused. 'Is that all?'

'For the moment, thank you, but don't go home yet.'

So Milli was something more than an animated doll.

The room would have to be meticulously searched and this was a job for Smith but he wanted to get the feel of it, to glimpse the private world of David Cleeve. It wasn't possible to step into the dead man's shoes but from the things he kept close to him one could, perhaps, guess at the vision he had of himself.

The room was L-shaped and he had never seen the other leg of the L. Here there was a second window, looking out from the back of the house to a wooded area of the estate. As in the rest of the room the walls were lined with mahogany bookcases which reached to within a couple of feet of the high ceiling. There were eighteenth-century library steps with hand rails, and a long, polished table with several of the favoured straight-backed armchairs so that wherever one happened to be there was a convenient place to sit and look up a reference or make a note; there was even another telephone. One whole section of the bookcases was devoted to Cleeve's own works in a babel of languages and a rainbow pattern of jackets. An impressive card index stood next to a sinister electronic device with a blank screen, no doubt scheming a take-over.

There was a door in the end wall of the L. Wycliffe opened it and found himself in a bedroom, very simply furnished; aseptic like a private room in a hospital, but with a double bed. A wall-cupboard turned out to be a well-stocked wardrobe. There was a bathroom and a loo, accessible from the corridor as well as from the bedroom.

Wycliffe, hands in pockets, returned to the library and mooned about, feeling none the wiser. He was thinking of the young man who had started it all, the

138

acquaintance Laura Wynn had made in a block of Exeter flats. He had moved to London and, through his talent as a writer, he had become rich and famous, but after 28 years it seemed that he had still felt menaced because of something which had occurred in those early days.

He rejoined Lucy Lane. 'We must let Smith loose in here, and make a note to get Inspector Royal down. Somebody will have to look into Cleeve's affairs and cope with his lawyers.' Royal was the department's legal and financial expert.

They moved to Milli's office which she shared with two kinds of copier, a word-processor, a duplicator which looked like a space machine and, surprise, surprise, a finger-powered typewriter – no doubt in reserve like an oil-stove against a power cut.

'Is there a safe where Mr Cleeve kept valuables?'

She was filing correspondence and she did not stop in her work. 'If there is I don't know of it; he kept important documents and all his manuscript material at the bank.'

'What other rooms are there on this level?'

'Apart from the library and this office there is a stationery store, a bathroom, loo and bedroom.'

'Do the rest of the family come up here?'

She slammed shut the drawer of the filing cabinet. 'I've never seen Mrs Cleeve on this floor – that's not to say she doesn't come here. The twins used to come up here when they were younger – not now.'

'Does Mr Cleeve sleep up here?'

'I suppose so. I'm not here at night to see.'

'What is your impression of the household; do the Cleeves get on well together?'

She shrugged. 'So-so, like most families, I suppose.'

'You know that Mr Cleeve had other women?'

'It doesn't come as a surprise.'

'You?'

'On occasion.'

'Did Mrs Cleeve resent these relationships?'

'I don't know; I've never asked her.' She glanced at her watch. 'Now, if there's nothing more . . .'

The burned-out hut was now screened from the public gaze and two uniformed policemen, bored to their boots, stood guard. Franks's automobile, looking as though it had escaped from a James Bond film, stood at a sprawling angle to a line of other parked vehicles which included the mortuary van. Wycliffe recognized Smith's Land Rover among them.

The constables, galvanized into efficiency, saluted. Wycliffe passed behind the screens into more or less ordered chaos. Franks saw him and came over.

'Ah, there you are, Charles! I must say you go in for variety; a pretty tart on Tuesday and on Thursday, Britain's up-market answer to the horror comic. He'll be missed, Charles, and not least by those sharks at the Inland Revenue.'

Wycliffe said, 'You haven't shifted him yet.'

'No, there's a little problem of keeping him more or less in one piece. They're getting a plastic sheet under the body now.'

'I hope they're keeping their eyes open.'

'Horton is, and he won't miss much.'

The debris had been almost cleared away and four men in green overalls were bending over what remained of David Cleeve, manipulating the edges of a plastic sheet while Horton crouched, watching every move. Sergeant Smith was packing photographic gear into two custom-made holdalls of his own design.

The plastic sheeting was patiently edged under the body and folded over to make a secure envelope which was finally lifted clear and carried to the mortuary van. Inspector Knowles had arrived from sub-division and he would accompany the body and attend the post-mortem to maintain continuity of evidence.

End of an author. The rag-bag of contending emotions

and creative energy that was Cleeve had been obliterated, and in its place were the charred remnants of a body in a plastic envelope. Wycliffe, despite his years of experience, was always deeply shocked and angered by murder; he found it difficult to conceive of the arrogance which allowed one man to take all from another, leaving no possibility of restitution. And in this case his emotions were more than ever involved because he had known the dead man; just five days earlier he had been drinking his whisky.

Horton was beginning the detailed examination of the ground where the body had lain and, later, the rest of the debris would be removed and the whole area subjected to a minute scrutiny, as thorough as anything undertaken by the archaeologists.

Back in the Incident Room Wycliffe dictated a press release: 'The body of Mr David Cleeve of Roscrowgy in Roseland has been found in the ruins of a burned-out shed used as an office and site-museum by a group of archaeologists excavating in a field near his home. Mr Cleeve went out on Wednesday evening and did not return. During the night, the fire brigade was called out to a fire which completely destroyed the wooden shed and Mr Cleeve's body was discovered late on Thursday afternoon when the debris was being removed under the supervision of a forensic expert. The police are investigating the possibility of foul play.'

Wycliffe sighed. 'Once the press realize that David Cleeve is Peter Stride we shall have a hornet's nest about our ears.'

The routine of the case seemed to acquire a life of its own; nourished by large quantities of paper and by an increasing number of people. Every table in the Incident Room was occupied; reports were being typed, duplicated and filed; index cards, recording every item of information collected during the investigation, were lodged in the carousel; lists were prepared and compared . . .

141

DC Curnow was checking a list of people who, for one reason or another, used or had access to nicotine. As far as he could see, none of them had the remotest connection with the dead girl or with Cleeve. Another list recorded those who might have sufficient skill and apparatus to extract nicotine from tobacco leaves or from tobacco on sale in the shops; these included two teachers of chemistry and a former professor of pharmacology, but here again, there seemed to be no link with the girl or with Cleeve; the single exception was the herbalist, Geoffrey Tull.

Quite a number of people appeared on a third sheet – those likely to have the skill and tools necessary to contrive the dart, but few of these cross-checked with either of the other schedules and, of them all, only Laura Wynn was known to have been aquainted with Cleeve and Celia Dawe.

Wycliffe digested it all and was depressed. Sufficient unto the day – and it had been a long one. 'I'm going home.'

Helen was concerned for him. 'I had no idea when you were coming so I couldn't get anything ready but it won't take long, then early to bed!'

'Can't we go out?'

'Of course, if you really want to.'

Helen had heard good reports of a restaurant at Veryan and, encouraged by the dramatic improvement in the weather, they decided to eat there.

Veryan is a neat little village which somehow manages to escape the worst symptoms of the emmet plague. They had their evening meal in a small restaurant which offered a simple menu, the food well-cooked and presented, the wine sensible, and value for money. A vegetable soup, chicken-in-cider, followed by a delicious apple crumble and the cheese board. Half a bottle of German hock.

Helen said, 'This is definitely holiday eating; we mustn't make a habit of it.'

Wycliffe had been unusually silent; now he said, 'Cleeve is dead. They found him in the ruins of the hut.'

Helen was shocked but she said little, there was no point.

They were silent for a while then Wycliffe said, 'In the mirror – that couple who have just come in . . .'

Laura Wynn with her golden hair. (How long would she contrive to keep it like that?) Another green frock – she must think that green was her colour and certainly she drew attention from all over the room. The hair and the frock were discreetly garnished with jewellery from stock. Her companion was the herbalist, Geoffrey Tull, in a suit of fine grey cord. They were obviously known to the proprietor.

Wycliffe muttered, 'Those two together . . .'

'What about them?'

He made an impatient movement which meant that he didn't want to commit himself to words. 'Shall we have our coffee?'

When they were leaving they had to pass close to the other couple's table. Tull looked sheepish but Laura greeted them with the aplomb of a real duchess.

It was half-past ten when they got back to the cottage and quite dark. He had been up since before five that morning but he was disinclined for bed.

He said: 'I'll be up later.'

He opened the front door, crossed the road, and smoked his pipe leaning on the sea wall. The sea was quiet, just the ripple and swish of wavelets advancing and retreating over the shingle. Navigation lights and street lamps cut paths across the dark water and at 20-second intervals the lighthouse flashed. He counted the seconds through three or four cycles and got it wrong every time. It was then, by one of those subterranean tricks of the mind, that he remembered what it was that Laura Wynn had said, the remark he had tried so hard to recall.

It came as an anticlimax. She had been telling of her first meeting with Cleeve after more than 28 years, when he came into her shop and she had recognized him.

Wycliffe had said, 'After nearly thirty years?'

'Why not? People don't change all that much . . . *I got mixed up though, and called him John.*'

A natural enough mistake; on her own admission she hadn't known the two young men at all well . . . All the same, taken with the epilepsy . . .

He went back indoors to the telephone and dialled John Scales's home number.

'I hope you are not in bed, John.'

'I should be so lucky! Jane is entertaining some of her departmental colleagues. Did you know that academic shop is even more boring than police shop? That academics have more expensive taste in booze and that they get tipsy quicker?' John sounded a bit tipsy himself.

'It's a very long shot, John, but there could be something in it. I want you to get somebody to check registrations of death in the Exeter area between September '54 and, say, June '55. The chap could have died in hospital and that might be a different registration district from his home address.'

'Does this chap we are talking about have a name, sir?'

'Yes: David Paul Cleeve, born September 5th 1931 at Bristol – will that do?'

Scales was impressed. 'So that's the way the cookie crumbles! I'll get somebody on it as soon as the office opens. Anything else?'

'Yes. I don't want Jane to break any professional confidences but I suppose she must know Gervaise Prout. If she does, I'd appreciate her off-the-record summing up.'

Scales chuckled. 'We've been talking about him recently, since he cropped up in this case. Jane knows him, though he isn't employed by the university. He's a freelance with private means. He's a bachelor, with a house near St Germans. It seems he's well thought of academically and he's got a knack for raising funds for his digs. He does some extra-mural work for the university and he's a visiting lecturer at several places. The funny thing is he's a bit of a joke, but nobody knows quite why.'

'Thanks, John. Enjoy the party!'

Wycliffe climbed up the narrow, twisted stairs to bed. Helen was propped up, reading a dog-eared copy of *Magistra*.

CHAPTER SIX

Friday July 22nd

A fine sunny day but with a light breeze; enough for the sailing fraternity and for the wind-surfers, not too much for the beach loungers. The emmets, convalescing after yesterday's gloom, agreed with each other: 'We were right not to go to Spain this year after all.'

Helen had decided on a rather special trip – up the coast to Portscatho then on to the Gull Rock and the Nare.

'It will be choppy.'

'You know I enjoy it.'

Wycliffe didn't, he was prone to sea-sickness.

At half-past eight he was walking up the Steps to the Incident Room. Hardly anyone about; cats sprawled elegantly on the sunny side, performing their morning toilet; the postman was on his round; Borlase, with bucket and mop, was washing down his shop-front.

A nervous 'Good morning' from the photographer.

Already the press-release had brought reporters with photographers in tow and there was a group outside the Incident Room.

'Is it murder? . . . Any connection with the girl? . . . Is it true that he was scared of something? . . . Is that why he was press-shy?'

Wycliffe made his way through. 'I can't tell you anything because I don't know anything. As soon as I have the result of the post-mortem I'll talk to you.'

In the Incident Room there was a feeling of being under siege and it must have been the same at Roscrowgy

146

for there had already been a report from the man on duty about fending them off.

His table was dotted with little piles of paper neatly arranged. Horton had left a memo, preliminary to his full report. Wycliffe glanced through the clipped sentences:

'. . . fire almost certainly started in the area where the body was found. The initial intensity of the blaze suggests paraffin or similar . . . A 20-litre drum, screw-top missing, was identified by Prout and his assistant as the drum in which they stored fuel for the generator . . . it was said to have contained less than half that amount . . . Possibly that paraffin was poured over the body, then set alight . . .'

Nothing really new, he was waiting for Franks to pronounce.

Potter said, 'The chief for you, sir.'

Mr Oldroyd, the big-chief in person. 'You've run into a hornet's nest there, Charles! Sorry about the holiday. . . . The case is bound to draw a lot of attention and there will be plenty of sniping . . . Have you got all the assistance you need? I know you like to work with a small team. I'll do my best to keep the press off your back. Pity about Cleeve. I can't say I *enjoyed* his books but they were compulsive reading. They seemed to catch the spirit of our time, like Terry Wogan and sliced bread.'

The chief, dispensing moral support.

Another memo on his table informed him that CRO had no record of Cleeve's prints so he had never been convicted of any crime. A criminal record might have explained his fear of publicity and, perhaps, his fate.

Detective Sergeants Smith and Lane were at Roscrowgy with a DC to assist. Smith and the DC would make a systematic search of Cleeve's suite of rooms while Lucy Lane smoothed their path with the family.

Franks came through at last, and after the usual preliminaries, salted with Franksian cynicism, he said,

'I have had a hell of a job with this chap, Charles, but there's no real doubt; he was killed in the same way as the girl.'

'Have you found the dart?'

'Yes, among the odds and ends that were gathered up with the remains, but God knows where it got him.'

'Have you been able to do any tissue analysis?'

Franks laughed. 'Don't rush me, Charles! I'm fragile this morning. I've done preliminary tests on liver tissue and on muscle preparations taken from the rump – both show unmistakably the presence of nicotine. I've got other samples and later I may be able to give you some idea of probable concentration but I think you can take it that they poisoned Cleeve before they cooked him.'

That was what he wanted to hear, if not in those words. It would give the press something and be of some consolation to the family. He translated the pathologist's words for the benefit of the waiting reporters:

'The preliminary indications are that Mr Cleeve was poisoned and that he died before the fire.'

'Poisoned in the same way as the girl?'

'It seems so.'

'Are you saying that he was murdered?'

'This is now a murder inquiry.'

'That makes two.'

'Yes, I had worked that out.'

'Is it true that Stride made a statement to the police in connection with the murder of Celia Dawe?'

(Of course it would be 'Stride'; the public for whom these boys were working had never heard of Cleeve.)

'Yes, he did.'

'Was he wanted by the police in connection with that case?'

'No; his statement, along with facts already known to us, made it possible to eliminate him as a suspect.'

'Stride has always avoided publicity like the plague;

148

is it possible that something in his past caught up with him?'

A leak, or a shrewd deduction? Wycliffe said, 'I don't know the answer to that. There must be many reasons why a man would want to avoid publicity; I can think of several at this moment.'

They let him go, more or less good-humouredly, but a crowd was gathering and that would take up the time of another uniformed man who could be better employed.

Wycliffe drank Potter coffee and moped about the Incident Room trying to clarify his ideas. The case seemed to split into two – the Exeter end, where Sergeant Mitchell was digging into Cleeve's past and trying to establish a motive; and the Roseland end, where the murders had been committed and the job of the police was to identify the killer. Laura Wynn linked the two locations but was she the only one?

He let himself out into the sunshine; the reporters had gone but they would be back; the emmets had resumed their wanderings in search of God knows what – the Golden Fleece or the Second Coming. He turned up the hill towards Roscrowgy.

What if, after all, it turned out to be a purely local crime – even a family affair? Then what of the threats Cleeve had talked about? Were they real or had he invented them to draw attention to a danger which he saw but dared not name? With Cleeve out of the way Patricia would surely be a wealthy woman in her own right . . . Was it possible that someone – Tull, for instance . . . ?

He was wool-gathering. Cleeve's whole point had been that, whatever happened, it would have nothing to do with the family. But Celia Dawe and David Cleeve were dead and they hadn't been killed by remote control.

At the top of the hill he turned in through the white gates where there was a policeman on duty;

he walked through the garden and into Henry's Field.

Henry's Field was like a painter's palette, with splashes of yellow gorse, a whole spectrum of greens, and some synthetic purples from the heathers. Nature advertising her wares, blatant and shameless. The bees were busy, the students too; plump girls in tight bras and shorts in uneasy alliance with awkward angular youths.

They watched him pass and answered his wave with suspicious reserve. He wondered how Prout was managing without his hut.

He was taking the short-cut to Kitson's cottage; the path led past the ruined hut and joined the lane just beyond it. He continued along the lane and entered the trees – trees that were wind-blasted at first but rose later to the dignity of a high canopy. It was utterly silent. Abruptly he came upon the clearing with the cottage set in a neglected garden surrounded by a decaying fence. Wycliffe thought it might be a good place to live for anyone not bitten by the improvement bug.

Kitson was sitting in an old wicker chair by the front door, reading.

He looked up as Wycliffe pushed open the creaking gate. 'Ah! I expected you yesterday.'

They went into the living-room where a pleasant smell of stew came from the kitchen and one could hear a lid trembling on a saucepan that was simmering too vigorously.

'Excuse me, I must see to my lunch.'

When Kitson returned he sat at the table, one elbow resting on it, the injured side of his face cupped in his hand.

'You know, of course, that Cleeve's body has been found?'

Kitson said, 'I was over there last evening. My telephone has been out of order and it was only repaired this morning.'

150

'Was it out of order on Wednesday night when Cleeve went missing?'

'I don't know; I only found it out when Christie and Andrew came over in the morning to ask me if I had seen their father.'

'So you didn't telephone him on Wednesday night?'

Kitson's manner became more reserved, cautious. 'No, I did not.'

'Someone or something induced him to go out late at night and to cross Henry's Field in the dark.'

Kitson said nothing and Wycliffe went on: 'What was wrong with your phone?'

'The engineer said the line had broken opposite the hut where the fire was; he seemed to think it might have been something to do with that. The telephone to the hut came off the same pole.'

'When did you last see Cleeve?'

'On Tuesday evening. Periodically Patricia takes pity on her bachelor acquaintances and then she lays on a decent meal for them. She did on Tuesday.'

'Who were the bachelors?'

'Her brother – Geoffrey Tull – Gervaise Prout and myself. Prout, of course, is a bird of passage.'

Kitson had very dark brown eyes of bovine serenity, in sharp contrast both with his pallid skin and his almost bird-like awareness. He avoided looking at a companion directly and spoke, as it were, in profile so that he seemed to be talking to someone else.

'Have you known the Cleeves long?'

A quick glance from the dark-brown eyes before answering. 'I met David in London in '61, I think it was. That was before he married Patricia. He had a flat off Gower Street and he was spending his days at the British Museum reading room, getting together material for *Caliban* – his best book, in my opinion, but the one we hear least about. As it happened I was working in the museum too, but we actually met in a pub. We found that we had interests in common,

151

and we've kept loosely in touch ever since.'

He spoke slowly with pauses between each sentence in the manner of a man who is much alone.

The room was long and narrow with low ceiling beams – two of the cottage rooms knocked into one. A paraffin lamp hung from gimbals over the table. The walls were lined with improvised shelving, loaded down with books, and there were books on the table along with a sheaf of manuscript notes and an ancient portable typewriter. Most of the books were in Russian or in some other language which used the Cyrillic alphabet. Furniture was minimal and basic. A tabby cat slept on one of the two window-sills, next to a jam-jar of wild flowers.

'So you've known Cleeve for more than twenty years; when did you come down here to live?'

'I moved in here nearly two years ago. I was fed up with London and I asked David if he knew of some little property I could buy or rent. He offered me this, so I cast off the ball and chain and here I am.'

'Did you see a lot of Cleeve?'

Kitson produced a little machine for rolling cigarettes and charged it with tobacco. He worked mainly with his right hand for his left shared in the injuries to the left side of his body and the fingers seemed to be stiff and poorly co-ordinated.

'He would drop in here three or four times a week, usually in the early afternoon.'

'And the last time?'

'The last time he was here on Monday morning, but that was unusual.'

'He had a particular reason for coming?'

Kitson extracted a passable cigarette from his machine, tapped it down, and lit it. 'Yes, he had a particular reason; he wanted somebody to talk to.'

'Something was worrying him?'

Wycliffe received a sidelong glance. 'I think you

152

know – at least the kind of thing I'm talking about. He told me he had spoken to you.'

'He told me a story about warnings or threats he had received through the post but he refused to give me enough detail to take any action.'

An emphatic nod. 'Exactly! According to him he had been receiving these things for months but he never discussed their nature or the reason for them. All I can say is that he got very agitated when one was due.'

'You mean that he knew when to expect them?'

Another quick glance. 'Didn't he tell you that? Oh, yes, he knew when one would come. Sometimes I wondered if it wasn't all in his imagination or even whether he was sending them himself, but he seemed genuinely scared and now he's dead.'

'He had one of these things on Monday?'

'Yes.' A pause while Kitson re-lit his cigarette which did not seem to draw very well, then he went on: 'Like a lot of highly creative people David lived in a world largely of his own imagining and, to some extent, signals from outside had to be tailored to fit.'

Wycliffe was looking out of the window through tiny panes which gave a chequered view of the sunny wilderness. Everything was still and the silence was so profound that one felt subdued by it – muted. He shifted irritably on his chair. 'But he *is* dead so it seems the threats must have been real enough and if you or I had persuaded him to talk he might still be alive.'

Kitson shook his head. 'I don't deal in "ifs". As I see it, we are born and we die, we have little say in either event so what gives us the idea that we can influence the bit in between, I don't know.'

'Did Cleeve ever speak to you of his life before you met?'

'We never discussed the past; I assumed that like me he preferred to forget what had gone by.'

153

'When you first knew him was there any question of him being or having been an epileptic?'

Kitson's astonishment showed in his face. 'Epileptic? I've never heard anything of the sort. Whatever gave you that idea?'

'Apart from these threats which he discussed with you, did he ask your advice on other aspects of his affairs?'

Pursed lips and a longish pause. 'David needed some-one to talk to about himself and about his nightmare view of the world which, I believe, was genuine – and damned uncomfortable to live with. Sometimes it seemed to me that he felt guilty for being human; he would quote papa Nietzsche – "this disease called man" and all that . . . Once he said – no doubt he thought it up in advance – "We are God's sick joke; automata with a sense of sin." ' Kitson stubbed out his ailing cigarette. 'He was a man possessed by a tormenting spirit and his books were intended to be an exorcism, but they didn't work.'

'Do you think he talked to his wife?'

Hesitation. 'That's what he should have done. Patricia would have been a source of strength, but she was a woman and that would have injured Davy's self-esteem. In any case, he was afraid of her.' A short laugh. 'I suppose he needed an ego-boost from an neutral corner and he sometimes came here to get it.'

'Did you influence him in his dealings with Prout?'

A slow smile. 'Poor old Prout is an academic wheeler-dealer like so many of his colleagues these days, scrambling for grants and subsidies; he might as well be selling motor cars or replacement windows but it happens to be archaeology. David had little sales resistance.'

'One more question Mr Kitson, were you here the whole of Wednesday evening and night?'

'I didn't leave the cottage.'

Kitson came with him to the gate; so did the tabby

cat, stretching its legs and arching its back after a long sleep.

Wycliffe returned to Henry's Field and by the burned-out hut he stopped to look at the dumpy telephone pole perched on the hedge. A new length of wire marked the repair, while the line which had served the wooden hut was coiled and secured to the pole. He continued on, through the wicket gate and into the grounds of Roscrowgy. He rang the door bell and once again he was admitted by the cousin-housekeeper, more mouse-like than ever. She looked at him as though fearful that he might be the bearer of still more bad news.

'I've come to see my people who are working in the library; I know my way.'

She let him pass without a word and closed the door behind him. He walked along the now familiar corridor and up the stairs.

Milli's door was open and she saw him pass, glancing up from her work. Strange girl! Wycliffe wondered what would happen to her now. Probably Cleeve's literary executors would be glad to use her, in which case her future would be secure for a long time.

The library looked much the same except that Smith and Curnow were standing by the big table examining a heterogeneous collection of objects: their haul so far.

Smith complained, 'There's not much here to tell us about his present, let alone his past. According to the little vixen next door, he kept all his papers, including his manuscripts, in a safe deposit.' Smith had met his match in Milli.

Wycliffe pointed to two chargers for an automatic pistol which were among the collection. 'No gun?'

'We haven't found one and he's not a registered holder.' Smith picked up one of the chargers. 'These are Mauser 7.63 mm – what we used to call .30 in the days before we went continental. There are quite a few pistols which might fire them.'

Of course, it was quite likely that Cleeve had provided himself with a gun and that he had taken it with him on his late-night excursion, but no gun had been found.

'You might take a look at these, sir.' Smith handed him a cardboard box which had once held cigarettes. 'That was in the same drawer as the ammo, the only locked drawer in the desk. Take a look inside . . .'

Wycliffe lifted the lid and found several ordinary white envelopes addressed to Cleeve in block capitals. He glanced at the postmarks – Durham, Bristol, Exeter, London and Truro.

Smith said: 'Look in the envelopes, sir. Don't bother about dabs, I've been over them.'

Wycliffe slid out the contents of the envelopes on to the table – five Jacks of Diamonds. Each card was numbered and dated in one of the margins. One of the cards had been torn in two and was numbered and dated on both halves. All were from mint decks and were identical with each other except that the backs of two were pink while the others were blue.

'What do you make of them, sir?' Smith's questions were usually in the nature of a challenge.

'Not much.'

Wycliffe spread the cards out and arranged them in numerical order – one to five; the dates then read; Saturday September 4th; Tuesday March 8th; Friday May 13th; Thursday June 16th and, finally, Monday July 18th – the card which had been torn in two.

Smith said: 'Celia Dawe was murdered on the night of July 18th.'

'So?'

'I don't know.'

'Neither do I but it's worth remembering.'

Wycliffe stared at the five cards: five Jacks of Diamonds which had seemingly arrived through the post at irregular intervals over the past ten months and been interpreted by Cleeve as threats. There was something melodramatic, something juvenile about it all – the Black Spot updated, yet Cleeve was dead and Celia Dawe had died apparently in a first abortive attempt to kill him.

Smith said: 'What about the intervals between the dates?'

'Work them out and see if they mean anything to us.'

Smith set to work, his glasses on the end of his nose. 'The interval between the first and second dates is one hundred and eighty-five days – near enough for six months; between the second and third, it is sixty-six days – just over nine weeks; between the third and fourth, thirty-four days – five weeks; and between the fourth and fifth, thirty-two days, or just over a month. Means nothing to me, sir.'

'Nor to me.' Wycliffe grinned. 'In *Alice* the jurymen added up the dates given in evidence and reduced their answers to pounds, shillings and pence.'

Smith did not smile. 'That would be before we went metric, I take it, sir.'

Wycliffe wondered, as often before, what went on behind that grey and gloomy facade.

They brooded over the cards then Wycliffe said: 'As it happens, the day of the week and the day of the month in the card dates correspond with the present year, but it surely meant more to Cleeve than simply the day on which they were sent. The intervals must have meant something too.'

Smith was staring at the cards over the tops of his glasses. 'You think these dates refer to events in the past?'

'I think they must do; otherwise what significance could they have? We might make a guess at the year.'

DC Curnow, a studious young man with old-fashioned ideas of self-improvement, was browsing through the books on the shelves. Wycliffe called to him: 'There's a whole shelf of *Whitaker's* just on your left, bring over a recent one.'

Wycliffe leafed through the almanack to find the perpetual calendar. 'If his wife is right, Cleeve's fears date from before their marriage in 1962.' His finger moved over the tables. 'Here we are, 1955 is the first year before that in which the days fit the dates; the one before that again in 1949. But in 1949 Cleeve was only seventeen – a bit young to start a feud which lasted through the rest of his life. My bet is that the card dates refer to 1955.'

Smith took off his glasses and polished them with a lens tissue. 'You are saying that the dates on the cards refer to events between September 1954 and July 1955 – is that right, sir?'

'I think it's a strong possibility.'

With magnanimity Smith said: 'You may be right at that.' He went on: 'There's something else in the same line.' He handed over a lapel badge in the form of a playing card club. 'This was also in the locked drawer.'

A pretty thing; the trefoil shape was done in black enamel and set in plaited gold wire. In the centre of the badge a gilt 'J' was embedded. A Jack of Clubs?

Wycliffe turned the thing over in his fingers. The whole business was acquiring an Alice-in-Wonderland zaniness. 'I'll give you a receipt for this and the cards.'

He was driven back to the Incident Room. No news from John Scales but Inspector Royal had arrived and Wycliffe put him in touch with Cleeve's solicitors.

Afterwards he walked down the Steps; the parade had thinned because it was lunchtime. The photographer and his sisters would be tucking in to something substantial – something with suet in it; Boadicea would probably be toying with a little steamed fish washed down with fruit juice. And Geoffrey Tull? What was the diet of naturopaths in captivity? To judge from Geoffrey's smooth, slightly oily skin, something rich. Perhaps in terms of food he and Laura Wynn would not see eye to eye, but in the matter of preparing a hypodermic dart

158

charged with nicotine they could be an unbeatable combination.

It occurred to him that Cleeve had moved to the Exeter flat in '53 and that he was still there when the Wynns left in September '54 – the most probable date for the event recorded by the first card.

Having made himself diet-conscious by his speculations about food he settled for The Vegetarian and ordered an omelette with salad. Afterwards he walked down to the waterfront and went into a pub he had not visited before. He drank a pint of lager, standing at the bar, while a step away from him a group of reporters were having a liquid lunch, but they were far too busy talking shop to notice him.

Jack of Diamonds . . . Jack of Clubs . . . the sort of aliases young crooks might have fancied; tearaways with romantic notions of crime. A gang? The 'fifties were, after all, the era of the Teddy-boy, boot-lace ties and winkle-picker shoes.

By two o'clock he was back in the Incident Room and at a quarter-past John Scales telephoned.

'You've found the man who died twice, sir.' John in buoyant mood. 'David Paul Cleeve, born September 5th 1931 at Bristol, son of David Gordon Cleeve, solicitor's clerk, died October 12th 1954 in Exeter General Hospital of multiple injuries sustained in a road traffic accident earlier in the day.'

Wycliffe sighed with relief. 'Any details?'

'Some, but this goes back to the days of the old city force. Records stirred themselves and blew the dust off a couple of files. It seems that Cleeve had an epileptic fit in Queen Street during the morning rush-hour. The RTA report says he was struck by a bus as he fell, sustaining injuries from which he subsequently died without recovering consciousness. The body was identified by his flat-mate, John Larkin, and the next-of-kin was given as Elizabeth Cleeve, mother.'

'No question of foul play?'

'No hint of it. I've seen the inquest report. Cleeve's doctor testified that he was subject to epileptic seizures and that he was unreliable in taking his medications so that the seizures were not kept in check as they might have been.'

So John Larkin had become David Cleeve and David Cleeve had become the celebrated Peter Stride, one of the western world's best-selling and most controversial novelists. But why had he taken another man's name?

Scales said, 'This will be a meal ticket for the media when they get hold of it.'

But Wycliffe was not thinking of the media. 'You realize, John, that the stuff we scraped together on Cleeve's background no longer applies. The man who was killed on Wednesday night, who married Patricia Tull, and was responsible for the Stride canon, was John Larkin, and we knew virtually nothing about him except that he didn't have a criminal record. We start from there. I imagine Larkin had other than aesthetic reasons for changing his identity and we've got to know what they were. We've only got the Exeter flat as a starting point; I know it's nearly thirty years ago, but there must be people in Exeter who still remember him. Get some men on it, John, and see what you can do.'

The widow took the news with no outward sign of shock or distress and she made no attempt to contest it. She was silent for a while then in a resigned voice, she said, 'If what you say is true, and I have no reason to doubt it, who was the man I married?'

'At the time of Cleeve's death your future husband was calling himself John Larkin and I have no reason to think that was not his real name. The two men, Cleeve and Larkin, were journalists and they shared a flat in Exeter. Laura Wynn, the woman who makes jewellery, lived with her mother in another flat on the same floor.'

A tremor of distaste. 'That is unfortunate! Did this woman know that my husband was . . . that he was impersonating someone else?'

'No, she thought that her memories of the two men had become confused; she had not known them very well.'

'But she recognized him?'

'As one of the two – yes. At the time Cleeve was killed, she and her mother had already left Exeter.'

Another prolonged silence. One of the large casement windows was open and a cool breeze stirred the curtains. Patricia sat very still; obviously she was trying to grasp the implications of what she had heard.

'Was my husband a criminal?'

'He was never convicted of any crime but he must have had some compelling reason for taking on another man's identity.'

'To escape being caught?' Wycliffe did not answer, and after a pause she said, 'Will all this have to come out in the press?'

Cleeve's words came back to him: 'I don't have to tell you what the family of a murdered man has to go through if there is any mystery about the crime.' He felt sorry for the woman but there was no reassurance he could give. 'It must come out; the reason for your husband's change of identity is almost certainly connected with how he came to die.'

'Yes, I'm sorry.'

He changed the subject. 'Do you know if he had a gun?'

'A gun?'

'An automatic pistol; we found ammunition for an automatic in a locked drawer of his desk, but no pistol.'

She shook her head. 'If he had a gun, I knew nothing of it, but there was so much I didn't know.'

'In the same drawer – the only locked drawer – we also found these.' He drew out of his pocket the envelope containing the playing cards and laid the

161

cards out in order on a small table close to her chair. Finally he added the little lapel badge.

'May I?' She picked up one of the cards, then another; when she had examined all five, she put them back on the table and picked up the lapel badge. 'I don't understand – what are these things?'

Wycliffe said, 'Each of the cards, as you see, is dated, and the dates run from September 4th to July 18th. Without going into detail, we think those dates refer to the years '54 and '55. There can be no doubt that these were the warnings which he spoke to me about.'

She looked from the cards to Wycliffe. 'They mean nothing whatever to me. It seems all the more strange because he hated card games and I doubt if there is a pack of cards in the house.'

Wycliffe said, 'We shall have to find out what they meant to your husband.'

She nodded. 'I suppose so, but I shall be sorry if what you discover about his past casts a shadow over his memory and over our children.'

He had no more questions and he stood up. She was apologetic. 'I really am sorry not to be more helpful but I know so little . . .'

'If anything occurs to you, however trivial it may seem . . .'

'I will let you know, of course.'

She came with him to the door. He had left his car down the drive by the white gates but instead of making in that direction he walked round the house to the rhododendron tunnel and on through the wicket gate to Henry's Field.

He felt vaguely depressed, for despite the news about Cleeve's true identity he could see no way ahead. He reminded himself that Celia Dawe's body had been found on Tuesday morning, Cleeve had gone missing on the night of Wednesday and it was now Friday afternoon. Not long for the investigation of a double

162

murder, but his case was by no means wide open. It was not what he called a computer exercise. A girl is found raped and strangled in a ditch by the motorway; a householder is stabbed to death in his burgled house – these are computer exercises – crimes without an obvious context. Thousands of scraps of information have to be matched against each other and correlated – or not. Finally, something like an answer may pop up on the screen if you are lucky enough to have fed in the vital facts and clever enough to have pressed the right keys. But this was definitely not such an exercise; there were clearly defined links between the murdered man and a small number of people.

He muttered to himself a list of names: Patricia, Geoffrey Tull, Laura Wynn, Roger Kitson, Gervaise Prout. . . . He might have added Borlase, the photographer, but he had ceased to take him seriously. Then there was a possible unknown who might have sent the card messages through the post but would need to have been on the spot on Monday night when Celia Dawe was murdered and again on Wednesday night when Cleeve died.

As he emerged from the garden on to the heath he was astonished to see men erecting a small marquee close to the dig; two of the girls were conducting parties round the site – probably made up of people more interested in homicide than archaeology; Gervaise Prout was supervising other students who were taking out a fresh trench near one of the excavated huts. Only a large, roped-off area round the site of the fire, and the presence of a bored policeman, remained as evidence of the tragedy. For the archaeologists it was business as usual. The press had been and gone.

Wycliffe followed a newly made path through the heather and was greeted by a lugubrious Prout.

'I suppose we are right to carry on, Mr Wycliffe. Patricia says that we should, though I have little heart for it at the moment.' After a pause he went on: 'We have come across a length of walling linking this hut with another, not yet excavated, and the interesting thing is that the wall seems to have been built from stones brought up from the seashore . . .'

Wycliffe said, 'I see you have a marquee going up.'

Prout sighed. 'Yes, we had to have something if we were to carry on and that will serve as long as we don't have any unseasonable gales.'

They stood for a while, watching the students clearing soil from either side of the newly excavated wall.

Prout said, 'I suppose you have just come from Patricia? I met her briefly yesterday evening in the lane on the way to the cottage. She is a remarkable woman.'

'The cottage?' Wycliffe playing dumb.

'Kitson's place.' Prout stooped to examine the loosened soil by the wall. 'You have something there, Donald . . . Let me see . . .' He came up with a piece of pottery which he rubbed free of soil with his thin fingers. It was part of a largish pot and it included a segment of the rim with an area decorated with a spiral motif. 'Glastonbury ware – rather later than most of our finds, perhaps first century . . . Go carefully, Donald, there is probably more.' He turned back to Wycliffe. 'What was I saying? Oh, yes – Patricia, a dear lady, so kind and generous. I dare say Kitson arouses her compassion.'

The reporters were back outside the Incident Room, though not in strength. Perhaps his proper course would have been to prepare a statement on the Cleeve/Larkin change of identity and issue it then and there but he decided not to be precipitate.

'No developments I'm afraid. Believe me, we're working on it.'

'The widow won't talk to us.'

'Can you blame her?'

'Is it true that Cleeve's life was threatened?'

'I've told you – no developments. I'll give you a statement when I've got something to say.'

Sunlight streamed in through the tall narrow windows of the old schoolroom and there were splashes of coloured light on his table, due to a bit of stained glass in one of them. He was in a strange mood, suddenly everything had become unreal: the bare schoolroom with its peeling green walls, the battered tables, the scratched filing cabinets, his colleagues bending over their reports . . . He had known such experiences since childhood when, quite suddenly, everything seemed remarkable, nothing was ordinary any more. His mother would say: 'Why aren't you playing with your toys, Charles?' Later, at school, it was 'Day-dreaming again, Wycliffe!' Now DS Lane was watching him and probably thinking, 'Why does he just *sit* there?'

He forced his thoughts back to the case, to his brief catalogue of names: Patricia, Geoffrey Tull, Laura Wynn, Roger Kitson, Gervaise Prout – one of them? Or two of them in collusion? Of the five, three were newcomers: Laura Wynn had lived in the village for just over two years, Kitson for less, and it was only eighteen months since Prout's first visit to talk about the dig. Cleeve's playing cards had started to arrive ten months ago. Laura Wynn and Kitson admitted to an acquaintance with Cleeve going back more than 20 years. Those were the facts.

And those cards; the five Jacks of Diamonds, their dates as enigmatic as the strangely stylized features of the two-headed knaves. Taken along with Cleeve's secrecy about them and the Larkin/Cleeve identity switch, they must surely mean that Larkin had been involved with others in some criminal act. Yet Records had no trace of him, so he had escaped the law. Had his accomplices been so lucky? If not, the threats and his reaction to them might be explained.

But after 28 years?

He brooded while the little splashes of coloured

165

light on his table crept nearer the edge.

Cleeve had employed a firm of Exeter inquiry agents to investigate Laura Wynn; had he thought it worth doing the same for others? Such firms were notoriously cagey but with a little pressure they could usually be induced to co-operate and it was a line worth following. It occurred to him too that whatever had prompted Larkin to adopt his flat-mate's identity must have happened while he was in Exeter. DS Mitchell was looking after enquiries at that end but a visit would do no harm and it would be a chance to look in at headquarters . . . He was talking himself into it. The truth was that he felt the need to look at the case from a different perspective.

He turned abruptly to Lucy Lane: 'I'm going home this evening; I shall be in Exeter tomorrow and I expect to be back either tomorrow evening or early on Sunday morning. I'll keep in touch.'

'Any special instructions, sir?'

'Yes, I want a round-the-clock watch on Kitson. Unobtrusive, so try not to use the foot-putters. I simply want to know his habits, his comings and goings and any visitors he may have.'

'Is he to be followed if he goes out?'

'No, that won't be necessary.'

At a little before five o'clock Wycliffe was on the quay, waiting for Helen to return from her trip.

'There she is now, Mister. That's Billy's boat jest rounding the point. I told 'ee Billy wouldn't be late tonight, 'ee got a fishing trip laid on for six an' no gear aboard yet.'

The tubby little man in a squashed sailor-cap was pointing to a beamy craft, low in the water, making her way up the creek.

'What's it been like today outside – rough?'

'No; sou' east by east, a bit o' breeze. They'd run into some chop going but they've 'ad wind an' tide be'ind 'em coming back. I reckon they'll be coming ashore direc'ly thinking they'm bloody Nelsons.'

'Wasn't he sick at the start of every voyage?'

A fat chuckle. 'So'll some o' they 've bin I reckon.'

Helen came ashore, flushed by sun and wind but there were a few pale faces.

'Had a good day?'

'Marvellous! I wish you could have come.'

'I thought of going home tonight; I want to look in at the office and there are one or two enquiries in Exeter ... I shall be back Sunday morning if not before. Do you want to come?'

She hesitated. 'No, I don't think so, we might as well get what we can from the cottage, it seems silly to go home. You'll sleep at the house?'

'Where else?'

'Then I'll ring Nora and ask her to air the bed.'

Nora was a daily woman who had agreed to sleep at the house and look after the cat while they were away.

CHAPTER SEVEN

Friday evening

Wycliffe arrived home in the late evening. The Watch House, an old coastguard station, stood overlooking another estuary, another river. A mile upstream was the little village of St Juliot, and beyond that the naval base and the city sprawled over its creeks and hills like a grey lichen encrusting the landscape. But of this, nothing could be seen from the Watch House, here there was only the channel and the slopes and fields opposite. Now they were visible through a golden haze, the last rays of the setting sun.

'Why do we go away?'

Nora, a pragmatist, said, 'I suppose because you want to. I'll get you something to eat.'

He poured himself a drink and took it out into the garden. A tour of the demesne, taking stock, his every movement monitored by Macavity, green-eyed and standoffish after days of having only Nora for company. Grass to be cut, weeding and dead-heading to be done, hedges to be trimmed, but no damage – no damage because no gales.

A makeshift supper, then bed.

Saturday

By eight o'clock next morning he was in his office but his personal assistant was already waiting for him. Diane, alias the Snow Queen, alias the Ice Maiden.

'Mr Scales intended to be here but there's been a big

robbery somewhere near Buckfast – silver and glass, a connoisseur's job, he said.'

She was blonde and exquisite, made up with resolute restraint, a hint of eye shadow, a touch of lipstick, a whiff of perfume – no more. She could have been of any age between twenty-two and thirty; the record said twenty-eight but she would hardly change for many years to come. 'Beauty in cold storage,' Scales said. With it all she was inexorably efficient.

'Your appointment with Sowest Security is for twelve o'clock, with a Mr Jim Harris. It will take you an hour to drive to Exeter (she always allowed for his sedate driving) which means you must leave by ten forty-five.

'Mr Scales asked me to remind you that DS Mitchell is in charge of the enquiries in Exeter and you can contact him at the Central nick there.'

He was fiddling with the things on his desk, the telephones, the clock calendar, the desk diary – putting them back where they *belonged*.

Diane said, 'I was sorry about your holiday; I hope Mrs Wycliffe wasn't too disappointed.'

He spent an hour dealing with the paper work she presented to him and left for Exeter on schedule.

He liked Exeter, it was his idea of the right size for a city and it was still a cathedral and market town not dominated by industry. Despite Hitler, post-war architects and developers, enough of the old town survived to preserve a sense of history. He parked off Fore Street and walked to Langdon Row where Sowest Security had their offices over a building society. He presented himself at the reception desk on the second floor at one minute to twelve. Diane had done it again! A pert brunette with a high and prominent bosom admitted that he had an appointment and he was shown into a rather seedy office where a little man with dark curly hair was feeding papers into a pocket file labelled with the name of a famous firm. Mr Harris had rehearsed the occasion.

'Ah, Mr Wycliffe! I'll be with you in one minute . . . Do sit down.'

Harris put the file in a drawer and extended a soft hand. 'Always a pleasure to assist the official arm – provided there is no betrayal of a client's confidence, eh?'

'This client is dead.'

Mr Harris had broad, squat features and his wide mouth had been extended in a toothy smile, now it contracted promptly. 'Dear me —'

'Murdered. David Paul Cleeve of Roscrowgy-in-Roseland. He employed you just under a year ago to investigate a lady called Laura Wynn and, more recently, you may have been asked to supply a security guard for his property.'

'Indeed?' Harris spread his hands. 'At any one time, Mr Wycliffe, we have on our books —'

'I'm quite sure, Mr Harris, that you don't run your business by not remembering clients as celebrated as David Cleeve, or by not knowing that the report of his murder was spread over yesterday's papers.'

Harris was unperturbed. 'I don't concern myself with the day-to-day work of my operatives, but I do know that Cleeve was a client, as you say. I also saw the report of his tragic death in the paper yesterday. What, exactly, did you want to know?' The smile was back but less expansive.

'Whether Cleeve employed you to investigate other subjects and, if so, who they were and what you found out.'

A hoarse chuckle. 'It's a good job we don't stand on ceremony round here, Mr Wycliffe. Some of my acquaintances in the business would want an application in triplicate pinned to a court order before they would part with that much.'

'Does that mean that you did have other commissions from Cleeve?'

'One other.' A sly smile. 'But I really shall have to

170

refer to our records if you want details.' He shouted: 'Bring in the Cleeve file, Sue!'

A minute or two passed then the girl with the high-rise breasts teetered in and dropped a pocket file on her boss's desk; she went out again without a word spoken.

Harris riffled through the contents of the file and came up with a few pages of typescript clipped together. 'Here we are! The subject was male, Caucasian; name of Shirley – Jack Philip Shirley. Our client said the man had been released from Parkhurst in October 1960 after serving five-and-a-half years of an eight-year sentence for burglary. At that time Shirley was twenty-nine years old . . . six-foot-one in height, and weighed approximately two hundred pounds. We received our instructions last March . . .'

'What were you expected to do?'

'To find out what had happened to him in the last twenty-odd years.'

'And what did you find?'

Harris showed his yellowing teeth. 'I hope you'll remember this when the occasion arises, Mr Wycliffe . . . We had no trouble in picking him up after Parkhurst. He was an electrician by trade and he got a job with a firm near Southampton docks. Eighteen months later he was still there but then he was caught flogging material from the firm's store and sacked. They didn't prosecute and Shirley just faded out. We didn't pick up any trace of him again until a fortnight ago. I'd even asked Mr Cleeve if he wanted us to go on with it because these enquiries cost money –'

'What happened a fortnight ago?'

Harris turned the pages of the report. 'You can see for yourself. We had a report – largely by chance – that Shirley was dead. Not long after he left Southampton he was working for a fly-by-night firm in Brixton and it seems he contracted pneumonia and was taken to hospital where he died within forty-eight hours – a weak ticker. Here's a copy of the death certificate, dated August 15th 1962.'

'You reported this to Cleeve?'

'On the 15th of this month I sent him a copy of this.'

'Have you any idea why Cleeve was interested in this man?'

A grimace. 'We don't investigate our clients, Mr Wycliffe; we shouldn't keep 'em long if we did.'

'I would like a copy of that report; the department will pay reasonable clerical charges.'

'Really?' Harris was ironical. 'But I wouldn't like to milk the Law. I'll get Sue to run off a copy, it will stop her brooding on her boobs for ten minutes. As you go out, tell her where to send it.'

Wycliffe was beginning to like Harris and they parted with mutual regard.

He joined the Saturday-morning shoppers. One could still catch the atmosphere of a country market-town with the farmers and their wives coming in from the villages for a morning's shopping and a meal out. He promised himself a decent lunch later.

In March, probably at the time he received his second playing card warning, Cleeve had instructed this security firm to investigate Jack Philip Shirley, released in October 1960 after serving five-and-a-half years. That meant that Shirley had been tried and sentenced early in 1955 – the key year as Wycliffe saw it.

He made for the Central nick and received VIP treatment. He drafted a telex to CRO – 'Urgent and Immediate. Details of offence for which Jack Philip Shirley received eight years in 1955.' He directed that the reply should be sent to his headquarters. Criminal Records would have to dig in their card indexes for Shirley's offence ante-dated Big Brother's computer.

DS Mitchell arrived; he was responsible for trying to fill in the detail of Larkin/Cleeve's stay in Exeter. Mitchell was young, hard, and ambitious; a career cop with a very clear idea of where he thought he was

172

going. Mr Polly would have recognized him instantly as a fully paid-up member of the Shoveacious Cult. At the moment he was bright-eyed and bushy-tailed.

'I've got something on the Mellor Street flats, sir.'

Perhaps Wycliffe looked vague, for Mitchell went on: 'Where Larkin shared a flat with the real Cleeve on the same floor as the Wynn woman when she lived there as a girl . . .'

Wycliffe re-orientated. 'Well?'

'There's an old man, living in a home out at Heavitree, who occupied the flat below the two men.'

'Good! You've talked to him?'

'This morning, sir. He's quite with it – I mean he's mentally alert.'

Wycliffe had a feeling that Mitchell might have been reluctant to say the same of him.

'He remembers Larkin and Cleeve and he says Larkin gave up the flat immediately after Cleeve's death which wasn't long after the Wynns went. As he put it, "It was all-change on that floor." '

'Anything else?'

'Yes. He says that about six months after Larkin went, the police came enquiring about him; they questioned everybody in the building, but he had no idea what it was all about.'

'You'd better see if you can find anything in our records.'

'I'll get right on to it, sir.'

When Mitchell had gone Wycliffe leafed through the telephone directory in search of Prouts. There were more of the clan than he had supposed, but only one Gervaise C. and his address was given as Bankside, St Germans. He wanted to see where Prout called home and it turned out to be not a great way from the Watch House; both were on the Cornish side of the river. He could drive over that evening or leave it until he was on his way back to Roseland in the morning.

Before leaving Exeter he ate fillet of sole with cream and onion sauce and drank a single glass of lager, sharing a table with an aged clergyman who must have slipped from between the pages of Trollope. He lectured Wycliffe on the relative merits of Bath, Portland and Caen stone for building churches. All this within sight of the great west front of the cathedral.

Afterwards, feeling philosophical, he walked to the car park, collected his car, and drove back to headquarters.

Saturday afternoon: the big, ugly building, a honeycomb of glass and concrete, was almost deserted and his footsteps echoed in the empty corridors. His own department was reduced to one detective sergeant and two constables.

He spoke to Mr Oldroyd, his chief, on the telephone, then drafted a statement for the press. Saturday afternoon was a good time to issue a press release as nobody would expect him to lay on a briefing until Monday morning. The statement confirmed that the murdered man had been threatened for some months before he was killed. It went on to say that the man known to the public as Peter Stride, and in private, as David Cleeve, was in fact, John Larkin. All this was as neatly wrapped up as a potato in its jacket and Wycliffe hoped that it would take the media a while to work out the implications.

There was a reply to his telex, succinct, but heartwarming in its promise: 'Jack Philip Shirley sentenced eight years Bristol assize 13th May 1955 for his part in burglary of Shotton House, Yeovil, Somerset 4th September 1954. Indicate further details.'

Wycliffe was pleased, and it was the dates which pleased him; they checked with those on the first and third of the playing cards sent to Cleeve; which must mean something. But Shirley was dead and had been for 20 years when the cards were sent. He certainly needed details but he preferred to get them from a less impersonal source than Criminal Records.

He telephoned Jim Clarke, his opposite number in the

Somerset police and a companion of various jaunts and jamborees.

'Yes, I know about the case, Charles, but it was before my time here. The papers called it The Shotton House Shooting —'

'Shooting?'

'Yes, a police constable was shot and killed by a man resisting arrest after a burglary. As far as I remember there were four men involved but only two were caught – one of them got the chop.'

Murder! And murder of a police officer, a crime which at that time was almost certain to incur a death sentence.

Clarke was saying: 'Officially I suppose the case is still open. What's this all about, Charles?'

Wycliffe explained and Clarke offered to turn up the files.

'I'd rather talk to someone who worked on the case; is there anyone still around?'

Clarke laughed. 'I'll say! Joe Enderby; it was Joe's hour of glory as a chief DI. He's retired now, of course – living with his daughter near Chard.'

'Do you think he would talk to one of my chaps or to me?'

'Joe would talk to a brass monkey about that case if he thought the creature was listening. I'll give you his number . . .'

But ex-Chief Detective Inspector Joe Enderby was at a cricket match and Wycliffe arranged to ring him later in the evening.

Scales arrived and for a couple of hours they discussed administrative matters and cases on hand, while in the real world outside the flow of traffic into the city, with people returning from the countryside and beaches, reached its peak. It was seven o'clock when he and Scales parted company in an almost empty car park. He could have driven straight back to Roseland but he had told Nora he would be home for a meal. He decided to take a look at Prout's house, then go home as arranged.

Bankside was not the name of Prout's house, as he had thought, but of a road, lined with detached houses on one site; houses in the upper bracket, worth £80,000 to £100,000 out of anybody's piggy bank. They overlooked the river but the tide was out, leaving an expanse of mud which gave off a rank smell of decay. Trees were obviously encouraged, gardens were immaculate, and those houses which had names avoided the worst excesses – no Dunroamins or Beuna Vistas, and certainly no Teddimars or Patruths. The cars in the driveways were Rovers, BMWs, Audis and Jaguars. In one of the gardens a military-looking gentleman was shaving his hedge with an electric clipper.

'Gervaise Prout? Let me see . . .' He squinted into the evening sun. 'Two, three – four houses along, the one with an *Amanagowa* cherry sticking up like a blasted maypole in the middle of his lawn – quite absurd!'

No car in the drive and the grass around the *Amanagowa* in need of a trim; Wycliffe rang the doorbell. A short delay, then the door was opened by a plump little woman in a floral dress reminiscent of a seed packet. She looked very slightly dishevelled, as though disturbed during a nap.

He introduced himself. 'Is Dr Prout at home?'

A rich brogue and an obvious desire to please. 'I'm afraid not, sir. He's away at present, but I'm his housekeeper. Do come inside, sir, perhaps I can help . . .'

With plausible mendacity Wycliffe said, 'I thought I might catch him at home; I know he's working on a dig down west but it seemed likely that he might come home at the weekend.'

He was shown into a large room, nominally a drawing-room, with lounge chairs; actually a library where bookshelves were interspersed with display cases containing reconstituted pots, querns, spindle whorls, and tools and ornaments of bone, ceramic and metal

176

. . . Above the cases and shelves the walls were hung with framed photographs of archaeological occasions.

'Like a museum, isn't it? That's what I say to him; more like a museum than a sitting-room.' The housekeeper had obvious pride in her charge. Wycliffe looked in vain for a desk or table. 'Is this where he works?'

'Oh, no! His study is next door – here, I'll show you.'

She opened a communicating door into an adjoining room which looked out on a patio and the back garden. A large, square table, more shelves but this time they were loaded down with proceedings and transactions of learned societies. Above the mantelpiece there was a portrait in oils of a young girl, a compelling portrait conveying an impression of fragility, so vulnerable that one could scarcely imagine the subject cooking a meal, catching a bus, playing a game, or doing anything other than being her lovely self. But her eyes were strange – oddly blank.

'Isn't she beautiful?' The housekeeper, aware of his interest. 'She must have been his sweetheart when he was young – I suppose she could have been his wife. He never mentions her but there's a photograph of her on his dressing table.' She added, speaking in a lower voice: 'Some tragedy, I reckon. You've only got to look at her to see she wasn't the sort to make old bones.'

Wycliffe changed the subject. 'I should have thought Dr Prout would have been home fairly often, seeing his dig isn't all that far away.'

She shook her head. 'He came up last Wednesday for a meeting at the university, and he spent the night here on the way back – the first time I'd seen him for nearly a fortnight and then it wasn't for long. He was late home from the meeting and not in the best of tempers because he had trouble with his car. He'd left it in the garage down the road and he was afraid it might not be ready for him in the morning.'

'And was it?'

'Oh, yes. I told him it would be; Mr Trewin looks after his regulars.'

As she spoke she was constantly tidying this or straightening that, her hands were never still. 'I suppose you wanted to talk to him about those terrible murders?'

'Yes, I did, but I shall be down there tomorrow, so it's of no importance. I'll talk to him then.'

'He'll be so upset. If I got it right, this Mr Cleeve, apart from being a friend, was paying for the work down there.' She turned to him, shrewdly confiding: 'There's no money in archaeology, you know, sir. If the doctor wasn't well off he couldn't carry on. He's a director of a company – Fecundex – you've probably seen their adverts on the television.'

She came with him to the gate, after failing to persuade him to stay for a cup of tea.

At the corner, there was a garage on what was virtually an island site. 'Bankside Garage: Petrol and Repairs.' Wycliffe slowed down, hesitated, then pulled in on to the forecourt. Thirty years of experience had made him cautious. A dark, youngish man came out of the cave-like interior of the repair shop, wiping his hands on a rag.

'Mr Trewin?'

'He's not here. Can I help?'

Wycliffe produced his warrant card. 'A routine enquiry to eliminate one of your customers from a hit-and-run case.' A euphemism rather than a lie.

'Fire away.'

'Dr Gervaise Prout – his car is a dark-green Granada saloon?'

'You must know that it is.'

'Were you here on Wednesday evening?'

'I've been on every evening this week.'

'On Wednesday evening did Dr Prout bring his car in for attention and leave it with you?'

'He did; the engine was missing – a bit of trouble with the electrics. I told him I'd see to it right away. He said he wanted to drive down west in the early

178

morning and would I leave the car ready on the fore-court where he could pick it up before we opened.'

'You did that?'

'Yes, but Bert – that's Mr Trewin, told me he didn't pick her up until well on in the morning, then he was in a tearing hurry.'

'Thanks, that's all I wanted to know. It eliminates Dr Prout from our enquiry.'

So much for that.

He drove through a tortuous maze of lanes to the Watch House. Nora had a cold meal ready for him – sliced ham with potato salad.

'If you wanted something hot you should've said when you was coming.'

'This is fine.'

'There's beer and a bottle of white wine in the fridge if you want it.'

After the meal he put through a call to ex-Detective Inspector Enderby. A woman answered the telephone. 'I'll get father, it will take a minute or two because he's not as spry as he used to be – arthritis, you know.'

'I'm sorry.'

A few words of introduction and explanation then Enderby was launched.

'Yes, there were four of 'em involved – Jonathan Welsh, Jack Shirley, John Larkin, and Roger John Cross – all in their early twenties . . . At that time Shotton House was in the hands of the Wallis family and the old man collected boxes.'

'Boxes?'

'Snuff boxes, bonbonnières, patch boxes, rouge boxes – you name it, little things in silver and gold and porcelain; easy to carry, easy to fence – made for it. Lovely! Worth a bit, too.

'We'd had three or four of these robberies with the same MO in less than six months and nobody to put 'em down to. You couldn't use the motorway alibi in those days because there was no motorway.'

'How did the shooting come about?'

'It was as the four were leaving the house; one of our patrol cars came up the drive and they were spotted —'

'There was nobody in the house?'

'The family was on holiday abroad and the married couple who had charge of the place were in Wellington overnight for their son's wedding. Somebody who knew the house should have been empty, saw a light in one of the rooms and phoned the nick.'

'Go on.'

'Well, the plan was for the four of them to split up as soon as they left the house and, according to Shirley, that's what they did. Welsh had a different tale; he said that when they saw the patrol car, Shirley and Cross bolted, but he and Larkin stayed together. They hared off through the shrubbery in the direction of the boundary fence and the road. It was then that they ran into our young copper using his initiative.'

Enderby was shaken by a spasm of coughing. 'Sorry about that! It's these damned cigarettes – they'll be the death of me yet. Anyway, Welsh admitted threatening the PC with a pistol but he said he had no intention to shoot.'

'Did he admit that it was his pistol which killed the man?'

'He didn't have any choice because we were able to show that the bullets taken from the body had been fired from a gun of the same calibre and type as one purchased illegally by Welsh a fortnight earlier.'

'Wasn't the gun ever found?'

'Never.'

'Go on.'

'Welsh claimed that he merely threatened the PC to frighten him off but that Larkin grabbed the gun from his hand, slipped the safety catch, and fired three times at point-blank range. He said Larkin had panicked and would have gone on firing if the gun hadn't jammed.'

'It doesn't sound very likely.'

180

'No, and it didn't impress the judge or the jury. In his summing up the judge said, "You may think, members of the jury, that a man who carries a loaded weapon while perpetrating a crime, intends to use that weapon if the occasion arises." Anyway, Welsh got what was coming to him. Killing a copper in those days was a sure way to the big drop.'

'Did the others know that Welsh was armed?'

'Shirley swore that he didn't and he didn't think the others did either. I was inclined to believe him – Welsh was a wild man – a vicious streak there.

'As you know, it was six months later when we got two of them and, to be honest, we wouldn't have got them if Shirley hadn't tried to flog a couple of snuff boxes. He fingered Welsh but he'd lost touch with the others and didn't know where they were. We eventually traced Larkin to Exeter but the bird had flown long before . . . That was it – until now.'

'Presumably Welsh had a family?'

'Oh, yes. Very respectable people; his father owned a business in Newton – fertilizers and horticultural supplies – that kind of thing. Of course it was a great tragedy for them. There was a sister too; it seems she doted on her brother and I remember reading a long time after that she had committed suicide.'

'What was Shirley like?'

'Not very bright – that was my impression anyway, though he was supposed to have been a wizard with alarm systems. He learnt his trade as an electrician in a factory that made the things so I suppose he knew something about them. I don't know what happened to him when he came out of jail but it wouldn't surprise me if he got back in soon after.'

'I suppose there was a hue and cry after the other pair – Larkin and Cross?'

'You're telling me! More hours and overtime than I care to remember, and all for nothing. There was a rumour that Cross had tried his luck abroad and ended

181

up as a mercenary in darkest Africa but I've no idea if it was true.'

'Presumably you had some background?'

'Yes, but they were both loners to some extent. Larkin had been brought up as an only child by his mother; they lived in Crewkerne and she made a small income painting and selling pictures. When Larkin left school he got a job on the local paper; mother died, the boy had to do his National Service and that's where he met the others . . .'

'And Cross?'

'Something of the same story except that mother was a former member of the *Ballets Russes* – Ukrainian by birth, and married to a British businessman who died young and left her fairly comfortably off. The boy went to Oxford and read languages, then he had to do his National Service and, like I said, that was where the four of them got together.'

Wycliffe's thanks were sincere; the kind of information Enderby had given him wasn't the sort one finds in the files.

'When I'm your way we'll have a jar together.'

Enderby said, 'No bother! It's nice to be taken down and dusted now and then.'

Early to bed.

On most fine Sunday mornings at some time between eight and nine he would be walking along the foreshore to St Juliot, the village nearest the Watch House, to collect his newspapers. But this Sunday, by half-past seven, he was already well on the way back to Roseland. The roads were quiet, hardly any traffic down the county and only a sprinkling of cars and caravans the other way. The bulk of the weekly emmet migration and counter-migration takes place on Saturdays, much of it under cover of darkness.

Wycliffe took stock. On the whole he was pleased with his weekend's work. He had identified the criminal act, 28 years ago, which seemed to be the source of Cleeve's fears and the motive for his murder. Four men: Jonathan Welsh, Jack Shirley, Roger John Cross and John Larkin – the Four Jacks? Was that too fanciful? Whether it was or not, three of them were dead. Welsh had been executed, Shirley had died a natural death, and Larkin/Cleeve had been murdered. That left Cross. . . . It occurred to Wycliffe that Cleeve had not, apparently, made any enquiry about Cross. Did this mean that he knew where Cross was or what had happened to him?

Progress. But was he any nearer finding out who had first threatened, then murdered Cleeve? Both he and Cross had escaped the law; they had that much in common . . . His thoughts chased each other in circles but he was beginning to feel optimistic. He even sang in a cracked voice:

'There'll be blue birds over the white cliffs of Dover...' and on a few open stretches of road his speedometer clocked an almost unprecedented 70.

'I'm high,' he told himself, 'it must be Nora's egg and bacon.'

He turned off the spine road which links the granite moors through the county and travelled south-westwards into china-clay country. A glimpse of sunlit sea as he approached St Austell entranced him and even the grim moonscape of the china-clay workings failed to depress. By half-past eight he was back in Roseland and entering the village, past the villas which bordered the creek. The pines and palms and a limpid quality of the light created a Mediterranean air, then he rounded a bend and the whole waterfront of the village was before him. It really was a toy-town village, the little houses painted in pastel colours, self-consciously neat, most of them with their tubs of flowers outside. There were few people about, only the boatmen getting their craft ready for the day, carrying cans of fuel and waterproof cushions across the quay and down iron ladders to their moored boats.

Wycliffe parked his car and let himself into the cottage. Helen had just got up and was making coffee.

A welcoming kiss and, 'Shall I get you some breakfast?'

'I've had the full treatment from Nora – bacon, egg and tomato – "A man needs a good breakfast inside him," Nora said.'

'I'll bear it in mind but what about a cup of coffee for now?'

He telephoned the Incident Room to say that he was back; and Division with instructions to send another telex to CRO – the full treatment on Welsh and Shirley.

Helen said, 'Any chance of meeting for lunch?'

He was tempted but decided against. 'No, I can't promise anything.'

A few minutes later he was turning off the waterfront up Zion Steps. The shops were closed. He wondered how Geoffrey Tull would be spending his Sunday. With his brother-in-law's money on the family horizon the future must look brighter. And Laura Wynn?

In The Vegetarian benches were stacked on the tables and a woman was on her knees washing the floor. As he approached the photographer's Borlase came out of his shop followed by the hideous yellow dog on a lead. The photographer was in his Sunday suit of mottled grey. He saw Wycliffe, pretended not to have done, and turned up the Steps, then he changed his mind and faced about with a nervous smile.

'Ah, Mr Wycliffe! I wasn't expecting to see you, they told me you were away.'

'Did you want to see me?'

Borlase looked paler, more pasty than ever; his eyes were bloodshot and his manner was timid. 'Only to tell you about the arrangements for Celia's funeral. I've got the coroner's certificate and I – we have arranged the funeral for two o'clock tomorrow. Celia is being taken into our chapel in the morning and we shall gather there for a short service at two o'clock before proceeding to the cemetery.'

184

'I shall try to be there.'

He walked along Chapel Street to the Incident Room and felt that he had been a long time away. DC Shaw was duty officer and DS Lane was sitting at her table; both were reading Sunday newspapers so crime did not press on the Lord's day.

'I thought you might want a word, sir.'

'I do.' He gave her an account of his progress. 'What news of Kitson?'

'He hasn't done anything exciting; he seems to have a regular routine –'

'Does he know that he's being watched?'

'It seems not. Weekes and Trembath have divided the daylight hours between them and they say he's never given the slightest sign. If he does know he must be playing some sort of game.'

'That wouldn't surprise me.'

Lucy referred to her reports. 'On Saturday morning he was up at half-past seven when he let the cat out, then there was music, apparently from a record player. Trembath, who has an ear, says it was Schumann. At a little before nine Kitson came out of the cottage leaving the door wide open and went off carrying a shopping bag. An hour and a half later he was back with a load of groceries and whatever.'

'And after lunch?'

'After lunch he was typing for a while then he had a visit from Mrs Cleeve who went in without knocking. She had her dog with her and the dog settled by the front door, very much at home. Mrs Cleeve stayed until four and after she'd gone, more typing, then music for the rest of the evening and bed at about half-past ten.'

'No other visitors?'

'No, sir.'

Wycliffe was restless, unsure of his next move. He ambled about the drab hall, stooping now and then to retrieve screwed-up bits of paper which had missed the waste bins, fiddling with the carousel, staring out of

185

the window at the drama of life in Chapel Street. From time to time he checked the wall clock against his watch. Finally, at twenty minutes to eleven, he came to a stop by Lucy Lane's table.

'I'm going to talk to Kitson; he's on the telephone so you can reach me there if you want me.'

'Good luck!'

For some reason he felt cheered.

CHAPTER EIGHT

Sunday July 24th
The single bell was clanging out its summons to
loyal members of the establishment, while dark-suited
men waited at the chapel door to welcome the non-
conforming elect. Exactly one week earlier Wycliffe had
been calling on Sergeant Pearce and was taken to The
Buckingham Arms for a drink. At that time Celia Dawe
would have been in one of the other bars and David
Cleeve was probably pottering about in his library-study
afflicted by that Sunday-morning lassitude which is the
fate of unbelievers. Now they were both dead, but
nothing seemed to have changed, the village went about
its business and its pleasures and the sun still shone.
Wycliffe recalled that someone had said, 'Living is like
making a hole in water.'

He was walking up the now familiar hill; the prolonged drought was taking its toll, the hedges were
dustier, the grass browner and the last of the foxgloves
had lost their petals. He passed the gates to Roscrowgy.
Somewhere across the river they were harvesting –
unthinkable on the Sabbath when he was a boy. At first
sight Henry's field seemed deserted but as he turned
off the road he saw a couple of the students, towels over
their shoulders, strolling from tents to wash-ups. He
crossed the field, passed the caravan, and glimpsed
Prout's white head bent over some task with the spec-
tacled Wrighton at his side. Neither of them looked up.
He reached the burned-out hut, turned down the
lane through the wood, and approached the clearing.

187

DC Trembath emerged from the trees like Uncas, the last of the Mohicans.

'He's working, sir; every now and then the typewriter clatters away for a bit, then it's quiet again.'

Trembath had been seconded from Division; a mountain of a man but light on his feet, and with the gentle features and manner which often go with great bulk.

'Have you seen him today?'

'Only when he put the cat out just after seven.'

Wycliffe said, 'I want you to come in with me.'

He opened the creaky gate and together they walked up the path to the front door. Kitson was at the table with the typewriter in front of him. In the middle of the table the cat was fast asleep.

Kitson looked up in mild surprise to see Trembath blocking the doorway. 'Ah! The spy has come in from the cold.'

Wycliffe said, 'Detective Constable Trembath.'

'Won't you both sit down? Bring up a chair from the corner there . . . Mr Trembath, make yourself comfortable if you can.'

Wycliffe said, 'One or two points . . .'

'I thought you people kept that for when you've been interrogating some poor devil for days on end – "One or two points . . ." '

Kitson's manner was light, bantering, but Wycliffe sensed that he was keyed-up, braced for a climax, and this would be the more understandable if he knew that he had been under observation for 36 hours.

In a conversational tone Wycliffe said, 'Jonathan Welsh, Jack Shirley, John Larkin, Roger John Cross.' A lengthy pause, then: 'All four were involved in a burglary at Shotton House near Yeovil on September 4th 1954.'

Wycliffe had settled as comfortably as he could on his hard chair and was filling his pipe. 'Do you mind?'

'No! Smoke by all means – you too, Mr Trembath.

I've noticed that during your vigil you favoured cigarettes; so do I, though Cleeve used to call them coffin nails.'

Poor Trembath looked like a naughty boy.

Wycliffe went on, 'In trying to avoid arrest, Jonathan Welsh shot and killed a policeman. Six months later he and Shirley were arrested. Welsh was hanged for murder and Shirley was sentenced to eight years for burglary . . .' Wycliffe's speech and actions were deliberate and slow, as though he was setting the tempo for a protracted session. He added, 'But I think you know all this.'

Kitson turned briefly to face Wycliffe. 'Why should I know anything of these people?'

Wycliffe said: 'Cleeve must have known them; he employed a private inquiry agent to find out all there was to be known about Shirley, and you were very well acquainted with Larkin.'

'Indeed?'

'Of course, you prefer to speak of him as Cleeve and I find it difficult not to but, as we both know, Cleeve was the name he adopted when he was wanted by the police after the Shotton House killing.'

Kitson tapped ash from his home-made cigarette. Trembath stared at a threadbare rug on which there was no trace of pattern remaining. A little clock wedged between books on a shelf became obtrusively audible in the silence.

Kitson said, 'Is this going on for much longer? If so I would like to do something about my lunch.'

Wycliffe shook his head. 'I shouldn't worry, Mr Kitson; if the only inconvenience one suffers from all this is a late lunch then it will be nothing to complain of.

'Returning to these four young men; they must have had romantic notions of crime. The Four Jacks – I wonder why they picked on jacks? The knaves in the pack, I suppose?'

189

The sun was shining through the little square panes of glass, directly on to the faded spines of rows of books. Another very hot day but small windows and thick walls kept the room pleasantly cool.

'I wonder which of the four was the Jack of Diamonds? The five playing cards sent to Cleeve were Jacks of Diamonds.' Wycliffe was speaking very quietly as though half to himself. 'Roger John Cross is the only one of the four not accounted for; the other three are dead.'

Trembath shifted his position and the strut-back Windsor creaked in protest.

With a sudden briskness of manner Wycliffe said: 'Do you have a birth certificate, Mr Kitson?'

'Not in my possession.'

'But you could get one?'

'I suppose so, if necessary.'

Wycliffe reverted to his former casual, rather sleepy manner. 'I wonder what it would tell us? That your name isn't Kitson but Cross? Of course, birth certificates are not to be relied upon; look at your friend Cleeve; I've no doubt he had a birth certificate – don't you have to in order to get married?'

Kitson was silent for a long time then he said, very quietly: 'All right, having got so far you are sure to find proof if you look for it.'

'You are Roger John Cross?'

'Yes.' He said it with a sigh which might have been of relief.

A plane flew low over the cottage, shattering the silence; the cat leapt off the table and padded about the floor bemused. Kitson lifted the creature on to his lap and made soothing sounds. Then, without any prompting, he began to talk:

'It was bound to come to this when David was murdered and perhaps I wouldn't have wanted it otherwise. . . . We met, the four of us, by chance or fate or whatever you like to call it – four beds in a row in a barrack

190

room when we were National Service rookies. For some reason we formed a natural group – at least it seemed natural in the circumstances. Shirley could scrounge anything anywhere; Welsh could talk his way round the recording angel, while Larkin and I were as green as grass and scared of the whole business – the cretinous NCOs, the military bull, and the stark reality of dossing down with twenty others in the same room. We were more than glad to latch on to a couple who seemed to know their way about. I'm not sure what we contributed but there were no complaints.' One side of Kitson's face twitched in a smile.

Aware of legal thin ice, Wycliffe warned him that he was under no obligation either to answer questions or talk about events which might incriminate him.

He responded with a laugh. 'What have I got to lose?'

Outside the long grass, the nettles, the docks and the brambles got on with the business of take-over in silence.

'The Korean war was going strong and, after training, we were drafted with the British contingent and largely owing to Welsh's wire-pulling we kept together.'

Kitson paused and began the lengthy process of rolling one of his cigarettes. He spoke, concentrating on the manipulations involved. 'Fifteen months out there strengthened the bonds between us, whatever they were. We became known as The Four Jacks – inseparable and slightly crazy.'

'Was that when you adopted the playing cards as symbols?'

'No, not then, it was just that we happened to have – all four of us – names that might be reasonably shortened to Jack.'

Wycliffe reminded himself that he was engaged in a police investigation; the atmosphere was more conducive to quiet nostalgic recollection.

'When we finally got back to this country, Welsh said

191

that we mustn't just separate and lose sight of each other so, at his suggestion, we agreed to meet every three months. As I said, Welsh was a persuasive talker, but I don't suppose any of us thought it would last long. Our first get-together was on a Saturday early in September '52, and it came as a surprise to three of us. We met at a pub we had frequented during training but after a drink or two we went to an hotel where Welsh had laid on a little dinner – very civilized. There were place cards, each one a jack from a deck of playing cards with our names on them – that was how the playing card business started. Typical Welsh, by the way, he had a strong element of fantasy in his make-up.'

'Who was which of the four jacks?'

'Shirley was the spade, Larkin the club, Welsh the diamond, and I was the heart.' A twisted grin. 'Don't ask me on what grounds the allocation was made. Anyway, in addition we were each given a little lapel badge in the shape of our suit with a 'J' in the middle.'

'These quarterly meetings continued?'

'They became a ritual.'

'Did you communicate with each other in between?'

'No, at each meeting we fixed up the next. It was Welsh's idea that they should be our only contact and as we settled back into civilian life and moved around we didn't even know each other's addresses.'

'What sort of man was Welsh?'

Kitson took time to consider his answer. 'Blond, with almost feminine good looks; slight of build but hard as they come.'

'I was thinking of his character.'

'I know, but that's more difficult. Have you read *Medicus*?'

'Yes.'

Kitson re-lit his cigarette. 'I've always thought that Aldo in *Medicus* was based on Welsh.'

'Wasn't he the chap who in some way or other mutilated every girl he slept with?'

'Yes, but at other times he was a pleasant, entertaining fellow, generous, affectionate, even sentimental. That was Welsh; I'm not saying that he mutilated girls but he certainly had a cruel streak which didn't show most of the time.'

It was odd, this concentration on Welsh, the man of the four who had been dead for 28 years; yet Wycliffe felt convinced that he was the key. Even the warning cards sent to Cleeve had been Jacks of Diamonds.

'Did you know anything of his family?'

'Only that they were in some sort of business. They must have been well off because Welsh was always in funds and he was sometimes absurdly generous – embarrassingly so. As to the family, I remember some mention of a sister – Barbara, I think she was called.'

'What about the burglaries?'

Kitson continued stroking the cat for a while without speaking then he said: 'If you mean how did they start, it was a casual conversation at one of our get-togethers – at least I thought it was casual at the time. When we met again we seemed to go on talking from where we'd left off; there was a lot of nonsense about a modern Raffles but I didn't think anyone took it seriously. By the second or third meeting after it was first mentioned, we were actually planning a robbery – just for an experiment. That was the way things went when you were with Welsh – he was a remarkable chap. He would float an idea, let it hang around for a bit, start a discussion leading to argument, then say, "Why not put it to the test? Just for the hell of it . . ."

'The idea was to pick a smallish country house where the owners were away or just out for the evening, take only small, easily portable objects of moderate value, then separate – no get-away car or any of that nonsense; each to find his own way home with his share of the loot, to meet later at an agreed rendezvous. Welsh knew something that I didn't at the time – Shirley had worked in a factory where they made alarm systems.

'Well, it worked and, inevitably, we had to repeat the experiment. Welsh did all the planning; he selected the houses, decided on the timing and the kind of thing we should take. He seemed to know these houses from the inside and I suspect they were the houses of friends of his family.'

'What happened on the night of the killing? Did you know that Welsh was carrying a gun?'

Kitson paused long enough to collect his thoughts. 'No, I didn't know. As to what happened, we came out of the house and immediately saw a police car in the drive with two uniformed men getting out. We scattered and I saw no one after that but I did hear three shots which seemed to come from the other side of the drive.'

'Do you think it likely that Welsh and Larkin kept together?'

'According to what Larkin – strange to call him that now – told me, they did not, and I believed him.'

'When did you first meet Larkin again after the Shotton House affair?'

'It happened just as I told you, when we were both working in the museum. By that time, of course, he was calling himself Cleeve and I was Kitson. We stuck to our new names quite firmly, even when we were alone together.'

'What happened to you in the meantime?'

The cat was clawing at the tablecloth and Kitson lifted her down to the floor and straightened the cloth. 'A great deal, but nothing relevant to your case.'

'Your injuries?'

'Yes, but don't get any wrong ideas about them.' A grim smile. 'I spent some time abroad and this was the work of an unfriendly gentleman I met.'

'Did you kill Cleeve?'

Wycliffe's manner was relaxed, conversational, as though they were having an academic discussion rather than pursuing a police inquiry. 'There is the point that if you didn't kill him, who else could have had sufficient knowledge to do it in the way it was done – cards and all?'

Kitson turned to face him and his manner was grave. 'I did not kill him – why in God's name should I? As to who might have done it, don't you think I've racked my brains over that?'

'With any result?'

'None. When David received those cards I thought it was leading up to a blackmail attempt, and I said so. I could just about see Shirley in that role, but we know now that Shirley was dead and, in any case, the cards led not to blackmail but to murder.'

'What did Cleeve himself think?'

Kitson made a helpless gesture. 'I really never knew what he was thinking about anything, I sometimes wonder if he knew himself. He lived so much in that strange fantasy world of his books that he half believed in the reality of situations he had created. He pretended to believe that he was a guilty man – deserving of punishment – that was the image he presented.'

'And it was false?'

A frown. 'I'm not saying that it was false, but it was exaggerated.'

Wycliffe stood up. 'I shall leave DC Trembath to keep you under surveillance until the Somerset police take over responsibility.'

'What happens then?'

'I don't know; you may have to face a charge of burglary.'

'And?'

Wycliffe turned away and when it seemed that he

would not answer, he said: 'After twenty-eight years?'

As a small boy Wycliffe had played Snakes and Ladders with his sister. On their board an awesome snake writhed across from within a few squares of Home to somewhere quite near Start. He could still recall what it felt like to land on that repulsive head and have to slither down all the way under his sister's watchful eye. He felt much the same now, oppressed by a sense of anticlimax. The playing card nonsense had been unscrambled and that should have been the end of the case. But why would Cross want to kill Larkin or Kitson kill Cleeve? For his wife? Wycliffe had already decided that that kite wouldn't fly. He doubted if they were having a real affair and to imagine Kitson setting up that elaborate charade with the cards – for what? It would only point back to him in any case.

Lunchtime. Nora's breakfast at six-thirty was only a memory. He hesitated between a pub meal and The Vegetarian, but pub food on a Sunday was often below its best and he wanted something light. He was glad to find The Vegetarian still with several empty tables, then he saw Dr Hodge, but not before Dr Hodge had seen him.

'Come and join me!' Hodge was having soup with a crusty roll. 'My wife has gone to St Ives to see her mother; I'm on call. This soup is good if you like celery. What's the matter with you? You're taking all this too seriously – you look wisht about the gills, as the Cornish say . . . So our late lamented genius was hiding under yet another name – hiding from something pretty nasty I should say, reading between the lines.'

'Is there something in the papers?'

'Radio – I haven't seen a paper today, too busy. I heard it on the car radio.'

The waitress came.

'I'll have the same as Dr Hodge.' He was in a strange mood, weak and suggestible.

Hodge said, 'Now there's a rumour going round that Mrs C wasn't Caesar's wife after all. It's a wicked world, but surely a woman like her wouldn't fancy poor old Kitson?'

There were a few enterprising reporters outside the Incident Room but he got away after promising a Monday-morning briefing. Inside, most of the tables were occupied, the ponderous routine of the case churned on – most of it precautionary, in case things turned sour, then everybody could say: 'No avenue unexplored! No stone unturned!' Nobody with egg on his face. Well, he didn't make the rules of the game, thank God.

He sat at his desk and looked across at Lucy Lane feeling mildly guilty. The girl seemed to be there whether she was officially 'on' or 'off' and he wasn't bringing her into the conduct of the case as he would have done with her predecessors. He called her over and they talked for half an hour.

'So where do we go from here?'

She didn't answer at once, then she said, 'Do you think we know all we should about the Welsh family? I mean, if they really believed in the young man's innocence and in Cleeve's or Larkin's guilt, then there would be a powerful motive, even after this lapse of time.'

He was impressed because it was the conclusion he had reached himself. 'But it's not only a question of motive; there must be someone here and now —'

'There's a Miss Byrne wants to speak to you, sir; she won't say what it's about.' Dixon, the duty officer, in a low voice.

Wycliffe glanced across the room to the duty desk. Carrie Byrne, the housekeeper-cousin from Roscrowgy, looking anything but dowdy in a plain emerald-green frock. 'I'll talk to her.'

It was only as he got close to her that he saw her face was blotchy and the skin round her eyes was creased with tiredness. The woman was on the point of breakdown.

'You want to speak to me, Miss Byrne?'

'In private.' The words seemed to be jerked out of her and she looked round the room with apprehension.

'Of course!' He led the way between the tables to a little room at the back which was probably a store-cupboard when the place was a school. Now it had a little table and two bentwood chairs. Light came from a small window high up; like a cell.

She sat, holding her handbag with both hands. 'I haven't been able to sleep since that night . . . I feel so ashamed . . .'

Wycliffe, sitting opposite her, said nothing, but tried to look kindly and attentive.

'Patricia has always been good to me – more like a sister than a cousin, and I've everything to thank her for.'

'What do you want to tell me?'

'It's about the night David . . .'

'Wednesday night.'

'Yes, he had a telephone call saying something had happened to Roger.'

'Roger Kitson?'

'Yes. That was why he went out and if he hadn't gone he wouldn't have been killed.' She suppressed a sob which became a snort; she took out a handkerchief and held it to her nose and mouth.

Light dawned on Wycliffe.

'You were with Mr Cleeve at the time?'

She nodded, helplessly, like a child.

'You were upstairs in his part of the house?'

'We were in bed.' Words came in a rush now. 'I wasn't really being disloyal to Patricia; I mean, if it hadn't been me it would have been one of the others and he had to go out for them. David couldn't do without women . . .'

'Is there a telephone in his bedroom?'

'No, it rang in the library but the door was open.'

'You could hear what he said?'

She nodded again.

'Tell me.'

She wiped her nose and her eyes. 'He sounded irritable; he said: "Oh? What do you want at this time of night? . . . Of course I'm alone!" Then his voice changed and he was obviously worried. I can't remember his exact words but they were something like: "Is he hurt . . . Don't be a fool, you must know . . . No, don't do that, I'll be right over . . . tell him I'm on my way." I heard him drop the phone then he must have picked it up again because I could hear him dialling, but he couldn't have got through because he didn't speak to anybody. He came back into the bedroom and dressed very quickly.'

'Did he say anything?'

She hesitated. 'He just said, "It's about Roger. You'd better get back to your room." He went into the library again, I suppose to fetch something, then he was gone.'

It left a pathetic picture; Carrie gathering together her clothes with the shreds of her modesty and stealing back to her room.

'Did you get the impression that he was speaking to Kitson?'

'No, I didn't; I thought he was speaking about Roger to someone else.' Her lower lip trembled. 'I should have told you this before but I couldn't bear . . .'

'Never mind, you've told us now. I'm going to hand you over to Miss Lane and she will write out what you have said and ask you to sign it. We shan't use it unless it is absolutely necessary.'

He left the two women together in the glorified cupboard which had to serve as an interview room. The unassuming, unaspiring Carrie Byrne had solved one problem which had troubled him – how Cleeve had been lured out of his house late at night and induced to cross Henry's Field in the darkness. Now he knew how, but by whom?

199

He went back to his table. It was very hot and the atmosphere was somnolent. He was thinking about Welsh, the young man with whom it had all started. Jonathan Welsh, Jack of Diamonds; blond with almost feminine good looks, slight of build, but hard, a great talker, affectionate, sentimental, but with a cruel streak; sometimes absurdly generous, a strong element of fantasy – Kitson's assessment. Enderby had said ' . . . a real wild man – a vicious streak'.

Contradictory, mutually incompatible elements provide the mix for every one of us but this recipe must have added up to more than ordinary instability and on a July morning 28 years ago that young man had been led out from his cell to the scaffold.

'Welsh is dead!' Wycliffe muttered to himself.

Dixon came over from the duty desk. 'Somerset police are sending a detective sergeant and a constable to interview Kitson, sir.'

'Do they want to take him back with them?'

'No, sir. Their instructions are to take his statement, then all the papers will be sent to the DPP for an opinion.'

Which probably meant that Kitson and the police would be let off the hook.

He had thought about Welsh, now he was thinking about the crime, the crime of the Four Jacks. Four young men had set out to commit a particular type of crime – robbing country houses. It was a good recipe; there was something in it for everybody – profit, risk and for the squeamish it was all down to insurance. Shirley was dim and probably went along with the others because one way of avoiding slog was as good as another. Larkin and Cross probably needed the element of adventure, even of romance. If it wasn't robbing the rich to pay the poor it was the next best thing. And the playing-card Jacks were a symbol of their camaraderie; they even had badges.

All this planned and organized by Welsh who had thought up the scheme and skilfully sold it to the other three . . . And Welsh was the wild man.

Did it really add up? Wycliffe wasn't sure.

It was Sunday and he had been on the go since six-thirty. Suddenly he was very tired. 'I'm going home.'

The trippers were returning after a day in the sun. On the waterfront there was a general movement towards the car park; at the quay one ferry was loading and another waited for the berth. He had no idea how Helen had spent the day and he felt guilty.

She was waiting for him. 'I've had a lazy day. This morning I went to church at St Just; I had lunch in the wine bar and this afternoon I took a book and lay on the grass below the castle. I think I slept most of the time.'

'Do you want to go out for a meal?'

'If you like, but I've got a couple of veal cutlets in the fridge . . .'

'Suits me.'

They drank sherry in the kitchen while the meal was prepared. Afterwards they sat in the living-room with the window open to the waterfront. Helen was browsing through the Sunday supplements, Wycliffe was drifting between sleeping and waking, slumped in his chair. 'Do you think we know enough about the Welsh family?' Lucy Lane's question; the answer was an emphatic 'No!' It occurred to him that the Welshes had run their business in Newton and it was there that his former sergeant – Kersey – had been transferred as CID inspector. He got up from his chair.

'What are you going to do?'

'I'm going to ring Kersey.'

It took a little while speaking of this and that then they got to business. 'Do you know anything of a family called Welsh who run some sort of horticultural business in Newton?'

'Afraid not, sir. There's no horticultural firm trading under that name.'

Wycliffe explained what he was after. 'The son was executed in '55; I think there was a daughter who later committed suicide. I want to know what happened to the family after '55 and to their firm . . . Phone me at the Incident Room sometime tomorrow afternoon, you should have something by then.'

When he replaced the phone Helen said, 'Are they all right?'

'What?'

'The Kerseys – how are they getting on?'

'Oh, fine . . . fine!'

'Is Joan still having trouble with her back?'

'I forgot to ask.'

'Oh, Charles!'

CHAPTER NINE

The promised press briefing was held at sub-division, partly because there were better facilities, partly to keep the reporters out of the village. He had to drive to King Harry, cross the river by the chain-ferry, then drive up the hill past Trelissick to the Truro road. As a way to work there was much to recommend it, especially on a morning when the air was fresh and sweet as on the first day of creation. Georgian Lemon Street was a pleasant sight too, but the nick, though newish, was much like any other when one was inside.

He gave a succinct account (he hoped) of the case so far; a digression on the Four Jacks, and a brief résumé of the Shotton House affair. Hard luck on the Cleeve family but there was no way around that. A young man was involved in several burglaries, in the last one a policeman was shot and killed; one of the young man's accomplices was hung for murder, but he adopted a false identity and wrote himself into fame and fortune. Then, nearly 30 years later, after a series of melodramatic warnings, he was killed by a poisoned dart and his body cremated . . . Plenty of column-inches there; not only for the proverbial nine days but for a re-hash at each stage of the legal grind if it ever came to that.

A little monkey-face reporter whom Wycliffe knew of old, said, 'It's like The Ten Little Nigger Boys, Mr Wycliffe, except that there are only four. One was executed, one died a natural death, one was murdered and then there was one – what happened to him?'

'The police are in touch with the fourth man.'

'Is he in custody?'

'No, we have no case against him and the Shotton House burglary is the concern of another force.'

'May we know the fourth man's name?'

'The Jack of Hearts.'

Guffaws. They were in a good humour, with more than enough to be going on with.

When they had gone the DI was waiting for him. 'There's a package from CRO and another from the Somerset Police – I was going to send them on by messenger but –'

In the DI's office he unpacked his parcels and laid out their contents. He spent an hour working through the material and ended up with three mug-shots of Welsh, a copy of his official record, and a series of notes taken from statements made at the time. He had also constructed a little table which pleased him:

Dates on the playing cards	Events which they recorded
Saturday September 4th	The Shotton House killing
Tuesday March 8th	Arrest of Welsh and Shirley
Friday May 13th	Trial verdicts
Thursday June 16th	Rejection of Welsh's appeal
Monday July 18th	Welsh executed
(The card symbolically torn across)	–

A riddle finally solved.

A uniformed copper brought coffee on a tray, a whole pot with a cup and saucer instead of a mug; rich tea biscuits – luxury.

Wycliffe studied the photographs while he nibbled his biscuits. Despite the white-sheet background and the front lighting the man came through. There was certainly something immature as well as feminine about the features, and his mouth had that curious delicacy which one associates with cruelty. But it was the eyes which compelled Wycliffe's attention; they were empty

204

of expression, looking out with a disturbing blankness at the camera and the world. Wycliffe was reminded of young, blond, brainwashed Nazis in their field-grey uniforms with swastikas on their arms. Perhaps that was why this man's face seemed familiar . . .

Then he remembered the girl in the painting.

It was not an experience comparable with Saul's on the Damascus road, not even with that of Archimedes in his bath, but from that moment Wycliffe knew that he was at last pointed in the right direction.

Enderby had said that the Welsh family ran some sort of horticultural business in Newton, way back in 1955; Prout's housekeeper had told him with pride that her employer was a director of Fecundex – a firm in the same line of business. Coincidence? Perhaps, but add to that the fact that Welsh had a sister and that his mugshots, despite the unsubtle techniques of HM prison photographer, vividly recalled the painting of the girl which hung in Prout's study . . .

He picked up the telephone and spoke to the switchboard operator: 'I want to know if Fecundex Limited are listed in the Exeter district directory – I'll hold on . . .'

It took only a moment. 'They're listed as Fecundex Horticultural Products —'

'And the address?'

'Tanner's Lane, Newton, sir.'

That seemed to clinch it, but there would be news from Kersey later.

Another telephone call, this time to the Incident Room; he spoke to Lucy Lane: 'I want a couple of DCs to keep an eye on Prout – as discreetly as possible but he mustn't be allowed to give us the slip.'

As he approached the village on his way back he turned off the road and up the drive to Roscrowgy. He parked in front of the house and caught sight of Patricia deadheading a rhododendron bush not far off. He was mildly shocked. Would Helen go on with her gardening routine if he were lying dead? Why not? He had to admit that she probably would; the sensible thing to do . . . He walked over.

'I wonder if you will spare me a few minutes?'

She dropped a couple of browning heads into a plastic sack. Her features were drawn and she looked tired, but she seemed pleased rather than otherwise to see him.

'I was just thinking that I'd earned a cold drink and I'm sure you could do with one. Let me take you to the courtyard then I'll see about something long and iced.'

They sat on the white metal chairs in the shade of an umbrella maple. The drinks turned out to be lager in tall glasses, misted over. Very refreshing.

He said: 'You may have heard from Kitson how the case has developed?'

'Yes; Roger telephoned.' She was silent for a while, sipping her drink, then she said: 'It is an humiliating experience to discover that for twenty years one has been . . .' She hesitated for a word then went on: 'one has been totally ineffective.'

'Ineffective?'

Her face was turned away from him but her voice betrayed her emotion. 'When I married David I saw it as my job to make it easier for him to do the work I so much admired. Yet in twenty years I never succeeded in winning his confidence sufficiently to help him in the one way which might have meant something.'

Wycliffe said, 'I think you are very hard on yourself.'

'That is kind.' She turned to him, suddenly brisk. 'Forgive me! I am being morbid. What did you want to ask me?'

'About the dig in Henry's Field: I wonder if you know how it came about that Gervaise Prout undertook the work?'

She was clearly surprised and diverted by the question. 'You mean how it all started?'

'Did the initiative come from your husband?'

206

'No, David was interested in the remains and he spoke of the possibility of a dig and Christie was keen, but it was a letter from Gervaise which set it going.'

'They knew each other?'

'No, the letter came out of the blue. It simply said that the sight was an interesting one and might be important for Iron-Age studies in the south-west. He wondered if David would consider the possibility of a dig if funds could be raised.'

'What happened?'

She placed her empty glass with Wycliffe's on a tray. 'I think David made some enquiries about Prout's academic standing then he invited him down. He was impressed by Prout's enthusiasm and not only agreed to the dig but offered to finance it.' She smiled. 'Something must have impressed him.'

'Didn't it strike you odd that, avoiding all forms of publicity as he did, he should invite a stranger down and be willing to co-operate in a venture like that?'

She nodded. 'I suppose I did, but I was very pleased; it came at a time when he was beginning to . . . to loosen up, to go out more and to be more responsive to contacts. I see now that he was beginning to feel more secure.'

It was an idyllic spot; the sunshine and shade, the patterns of shadows, the fragrance of flowers and the sound of water trickling into the pool . . . Wycliffe thought that it might be hard not to feel secure in these surroundings.

'What was your husband's opinion of Dr Prout?'

Such a direct question jarred on her sense of propriety but she responded. 'I think he was amused by him – by his single-mindedness, but also a little irritated. He said once that Gervaise was like an iceberg, only one-seventh above water. Although David was so secretive himself he couldn't stand that characteristic in others.'

'And you – what do you think of Dr Prout?'

A frown and a moment to consider. 'He is an agreeable man with enthusiasm for his subject which he can communicate to others.'

'But?'

She laughed despite herself. 'There are no buts – or only a little one. I have to confess that at first I was irritated by his curiosity. I was a victim, so was Christie.'

'About what was he curious?'

'About us as a family. At one point I wondered if he was trying to steal a march on David's would-be biographers. When he found that we had nothing to tell he stopped asking questions.' She smiled. 'It was only a small thing, mildly irritating.'

Wycliffe got up. 'Thank you for the drink and for being patient with my questions. Do you mind if I go through the tunnel to the dig and leave my car where it is?'

'Please do whatever is convenient.'

She walked with him back to the spot where she had broken off her work and he continued through the tunnel and through the wicket gate into Henry's Field. As he crossed the field he saw that Prout's caravan had been shifted to a position near the marquee and the site of the wooden hut. Nearby a man was working on the telephone pole which carried the wires to Kitson's cottage. Wycliffe went over and found Prout, standing in the shade of his van, watching the man at work.

'I'm having our communications restored, Mr Wycliffe.' Prout being rather self-consciously jovial. 'The phone was previously in the wooden hut and as they are not willing to connect it to a marquee I'm having it in the van.'

'I suppose you need the telephone?'

A quick glance. 'Without it one feels cut off on these digs, and the students like to be able to ring home. I had to go into the village this morning to phone my housekeeper; one doesn't like to disturb Patricia at this time.'

'I expect your housekeeper told you that I called on her on Saturday?'

A frown. 'Yes, she did. I suppose one must get used to having one's every statement checked in these circumstances.'

'I'm afraid so.'

Wycliffe was no longer watching the telephone engineer, but Prout. 'Odd that Kitson's line should have been cut on the night of the fire, don't you think? His wire came nowhere near the hut.'

'These things happen.' Prout met his gaze, blue eyes unflinching.

With a casual parting word Wycliffe made his way across the site. After a month of almost unbroken sunshine the students were as brown as Indians. Christie, wearing shorts and a bra, her auburn hair caught in a pony-tail, was trowelling away soil from a trench, occasionally dropping sherds of pottery into a plastic bowl. She looked up as Wycliffe's shadow fell across the trench.

He said something fatuous: 'Everything under control?'

She smiled. 'Yes, I think so, thanks.'

He returned to his car and drove back to Chapel Street and the Incident Room. A few minutes with Lucy Lane, then it was lunchtime. He went down the Steps. How long was it since he first set eyes on Zion Steps? Nine days; yet the Steps had taken their place in his daily routine. Now the episode was almost over; in a day or two all that had happened in those nine days would be condensed into just another case-file and the people he had met would either be forgotten or they would be remembered as witnesses who would wait their turn to enter the box at any trial there might be . . .

At any trial there might be . . . a trial in which the innocent would suffer more than the guilty.

Borlase was in his favourite position, just behind the glass door of his shop, looking out. Laura Wynn had customers, he could see her standing behind the counter, serenely detached, while they examined her wares. Farther down, Geoffrey Tull was on his doorstep, talking to a pin-stripe suit with a brief-case. In The Vegetarian all the tables seemed to be occupied.

Wycliffe would have found it hard to say what was in his mind. Was he conning the field? Hardly, because he was no longer in doubt of the outcome. Scarcely aware of any intention he ended up at The Buckingham Arms. Business was good but he was immediately signalled from behind the bar. Polmear's heavy features were flushed and covered with little beads of sweat.

'If this weather goes on I shall just melt away and trickle down the nearest drain.'

'Leaving a fortune behind.'

Polmear grinned. 'You should be here for the other nine months of the year.' He called a waitress. 'Here, Judy, lay-up for Mr Wycliffe in the cubby.'

'Are you going to the funeral this afternoon?'

'Of course! She worked here, didn't she? And she was damned good at her job. I miss her. Life isn't all about bed, Mr Wycliffe – only mostly.'

Wycliffe meditated on this observation while he ate a very tasty quiche with a green salad and drank a carafe of Liebfraumilch.

The graveyard was on the slope above the village; the air was filled with the resinous scent of pines. The mourners gathered at the graveside and they could look down on the houses, descending in steps to the creek. Wycliffe was surprised by their number, most of whom were unknown to him. Borlase was much in evidence in a black suit which must have survived many funerals and now was turning green with age. His sisters had not come. Polmear had squeezed him-self into a grey suit which was too small for him and sported a black tie. Wycliffe spotted Dr Hodge and, next to him, Andrew Cleeve, wrapped about with a dark raincoat several inches too short, probably a relic of his schooldays and looking ludicrous in the sunshine.

The words of the burial service, rendered with all the elocutory skill of an auctioneer in a cattle market, still came through as solemn and moving. Celia Dawe's coffin was lowered into the grave and the party was over. People moved away, murmuring platitudes. Wycliffe lingered and so did Andrew Cleeve. The boy looked across at him, tentative, anxious.

Wycliffe walked over to join him. 'A lot of people.'

'Yes, but not many bothered with her when she was alive.'

They walked down the steep slope together. Andrew slipped off his coat and rolled it under his arm. As they reached the gate he said: 'There's something I have to tell you . . . Mother agrees that I should.'

Wycliffe waited.

'We were talking about what you said to mother this morning when Christie mentioned something I hadn't heard before – that Gervaise Prout was in Exeter on Wednesday and that he didn't come back until Thursday lunchtime.'

'He went to the University for a symposium. Didn't you know?'

'No, I didn't, but his car was in its usual place on Wednesday night. He keeps it in the lane to Roger Kitson's cottage, just off the road. When I was coming back from Truro and saw the fire I got out of the car and ran down the lane far enough to see where it was before haring off home to raise the alarm. Prout's car was there then but I thought nothing of it. Of course when I got home I found that one of your chaps had already called the brigade.'

Wycliffe walked back to the Incident Room, feeling lucky; he had not dared to hope for such direct evidence. Andrew's evidence would clinch a possibility which had been in his mind since he had seen the relatively isolated garage where Prout's car was supposed to have spent the night on the forecourt. An hour's trip either way, the job done, and back before anyone was about. Very cool.

Prout had called Cleeve on the telephone from the wooden hut and Wycliffe thought he could make a good guess at providing the other half of the conversation overheard by Carrie Byrne:

'This is Gervaise.'

'Oh? What do you want at this time of night?' Irritated.

'Are you alone?'

'Of course I'm alone.'

'I'm speaking from the wooden hut; Kitson is here, there's something very wrong with him —'

'Is he hurt?' Anxious.

'I don't know, he —'

'Don't be a fool, man, you *must* know —'

'No, I don't; he was talking wildly and he kept asking for someone called Larkin. Now he's gone quiet and I can't rouse him. Do you think I should call a doctor?'

'No, don't do that, I'll be right over . . . Tell him I'm on my way.'

That or something like it would have lured Cleeve out of his house into the open. Even so he had tried to check. Carrie Byrne had heard him dial a number to which there was no reply – no reply because Kitson's telephone had been cut beforehand. And Cleeve had gone back into the library – to fetch his pistol?

In the Incident Room Potter was duty officer.

'Anything from Mr Kersey?'

'No, sir.'

But Kersey came through a few minutes later.

Wycliffe said, 'I think I know something of what you've got for me – that the Welsh family business is now Fecundex Horticultural Products.'

'That's right. They changed their name way back in

'56 after all the notoriety over the murder case. I've just been talking to the managing director – a chap called Bannister. I know him slightly, we use the same local, and he's been with the firm since the flood.'

'Is the family still involved?'

'There's none of 'em left. They had only the one son, and a daughter, the daughter was a couple of years older and she married – guess who?'

'Gervaise Prout?'

'Ah, you knew. Anyway, he was a research student without twopence to his name but it seems to have been a real love match and Papa Welsh approved. He even persuaded Prout to come into the firm.'

'Did it work?'

'Very well, apparently. Prout was soon in charge of sales and he also showed a flair for gadgetry. He patented several bits and pieces for crop spraying, for greenhouse control systems and that sort of thing. His patents made a nice fat profit for the firm.

'The Shotton House affair came three years after Prout had married into the family and it was the beginning of the end of the Welshes. The parents were devastated, and the sister devoted herself first to proving her brother's innocence then, when that failed, she went all out for a reprieve. It seems she spent her time chasing lawyers, gathering what she imagined to be fresh evidence, and God knows what else. She took a room near the prison and visited her brother as often as the authorities allowed – right up to the last.

'Of course, she didn't stand a chance, it was an open and shut case, and it broke her. Eighteen months after the execution she was put in a mental home and spent a year there, then she was sent home, supposed to be cured. Within a fortnight of coming home she went out into the garden, soaked her clothes in paraffin and set herself alight . . . Poor old Prout found her while there was still life in her body.'

213

Wycliffe said: 'And afterwards?'

'Prout stayed with the firm and in 1962 Papa Welsh died; his wife had died three years before. In his will the old man left all his personal estate and a two-thirds' interest in the firm to Prout – the other third went to Bannister.'

'Was that when Prout felt the call back to archaeology?'

'No, it seems he kept up his interest all through but it wasn't until the 'seventies that he began to spend most of his time away from the factory; now he's only there two or three days a month.'

'Did Bannister query your interest in all this?'

'No, he'd read about Cleeve's involvement in the Shotton House business and he seemed to think it natural that we should come asking questions about the Welshes – God knows why.'

'Do you think he'll pass on news of your visit to Prout?'

'I shall be surprised if he doesn't. Is that bad?'

'It doesn't matter at all. In fact, there's something else I want you to see him about, and you can make this official. We need to know whether his firm manufactures or stocks any compounds containing nicotine. If so, we want to know the nature of the preparation, its nicotine content and its availability to anyone with access to the factory. We shall also want a sample for analysis.'

Wycliffe remembered Joan Kersey's back just in time.

'Oh, she's found an osteopath who seems to have a winning way with backs – at least I hope that's what it is.'

Wycliffe's feelings were oddly ambivalent. The three Wise Monkeys must be satisfied at last: Motive, Means and Opportunity, but if it hadn't been for the luckless Celia Dawe . . .

One more gap: he spoke to John Scales on the telephone. 'I want you to send someone to Prout's house at St Germans with a warrant. There's a housekeeper. We want to know whether Prout has a work-shop – any sort of DIY set-up: once upon a time he patented gadgets for horticultural equipment . . . If there is such a place, put seals on it until we can arrange a proper examination by Forensic.'

Four o'clock and the weather seemed even hotter. Wycliffe's shirt stuck to his back and he was con-scious of damp patches under his arms; he was tempted to go back to the cottage for a shower and a change of clothes but decided against; he was inventing ways of putting off the inevitable. Perambulating around the room he came to a stop by Lucy Lane's table. 'I'm going up to the site and I want you to come with me.'

She brought his car to the door; they drove up the hill past the entrance to Roscrowgy, and turned down the lane to the dig. They parked behind Prout's Granada, left the car, and walked down the dry rutted track as far as the burned-out hut.

Henry's Field seemed deserted, the caravan, the tents and the marquee were still there but there were no students to be seen, only the hairy, bespectacled Wrighton, a pathetic figure trailing a plastic sack and stooping now and then to pick up a sweet paper or cigarette packet left by litter-bugs. DC Curnow emerged from behind the marquee. 'He's in the caravan, sir; been there since just after one.'

Wycliffe approached Wrighton: 'All on your own?'

The young man looked at Wycliffe through his big round lenses. 'It was too hot to work out of doors so Dr Prout gave them the afternoon off and they've all gone swimming. Dr Prout is in his caravan and doesn't want to be disturbed.' Wrighton seemed to feel excluded from both camps.

Wycliffe knocked on the door of the caravan; no response, so he knocked again. Wrighton had stopped work to watch. Still no answer.

'You wait outside for the moment.' To Lucy Lane.

He turned the handle, opened the door, and found himself in the kitchen section. To his left he was vaguely aware of the sleeping compartment but to his right there was a more roomy area resembling the saloon of a yacht: a table, bench seats, shelves and cupboards, all built in. Prout was sitting at the table and open in front of him was a bulky ring-file of the kind used by students.

He raised his eyes from the file in the manner of one who suffers an unwelcome though anticipated intrusion. 'Ah, you've come.'

Prout had changed, he looked older, but more than that it was as though a mask had been discarded and it seemed to Wycliffe that he was seeing the real man for the first time. Gone the defensive bonhomie; gone, too, the high-pitched voice which had seemed always to tremble on the edge of a nervous little laugh. The face of the man at the table was grave, introspective, and closed.

Speaking very slowly, Prout said: 'There is no point in prolonging this; I am very tired. Of course I realized from the start how it might end and I have no doubt that your case against me is a strong one. I shall make no attempt to defend myself in law.' He paused, resting a slender hand on the open pages of his file. 'For the rest, my justification is here. Nothing of this is mine, it is my wife's work, a record of her fight to establish her brother's innocence and of her efforts to secure a reprieve.'

The door of the caravan had remained open and Wycliffe could see Lucy Lane waiting only a few feet away. He should have yielded to protocol and called her in but he wanted to gauge the temper of the situation first.

Prout had gone back to his file; he was turning the pages with deliberation, almost with reverence, as a monk might turn the pages of a holy book. Wycliffe waited. Only when he reached the end of the file did Prout look up:

'See what she wrote on the last page.'

The page was blank except for three words, written in a schoolgirlish hand: 'I failed him.' Melodramatic but, in the context, moving.

Prout's voice became harsh. 'It destroyed our life together and in the end it destroyed her. She spent a year in a nursing-home under treatment . . . They said she was cured but within weeks of her coming back to me . . .'

A long pause, then he went on, 'I made him suffer – though not as much as I would have wished.' He closed the file. 'I've no regrets.'

'And the girl? What about Celia Dawe?'

Prout passed a hand across his face. 'That girl . . .' He shook his head. 'Isn't it always the innocent who suffer most?'

'You believe in your brother-in-law's innocence?'

For the first time Prout showed signs of anger, his pale features flushed. 'Would I have done what I have done otherwise?'

'You could have been wrong, you may still be wrong.'

A faint smile. 'Oh, no! I can't deny moments of weakness – of doubt, but now, thank God, I'm sure.' He turned in his seat to open a little cupboard. 'This is my proof.' He laid an automatic pistol on the table. 'Your experts will tell you that this is the pistol which killed that young policeman at Shotton House, twenty-eight years ago – the crime for which my wife's brother was hanged. It is of the same calibre and make. I took it from Larkin's body on Wednesday night and you will find his prints on it as well as my own.'

Wycliffe reached across for the gun and Prout made no attempt to stop him, then Wycliffe signalled to Lucy Lane to join him. Prout glanced up as she entered but made no comment.

'Gervaise Adam Prout, I am taking you into custody

in connection with the murder of John Larkin, alias
David Cleeve. You are not obliged to say anything but
anything you do say may be taken down in writing and
used in evidence.'

Tuesday July 26th

In the Incident Room Wycliffe was turning the pages
of the ring-file. On the first page was a single word:
'Jonathan'. The file was a detailed record of everything Welsh's sister had done, over a period of four
months, to save her brother. It included correspondence with lawyers, Welsh's own letters from prison,
correspondence with Members of Parliament, with
the Home Office, and even a petition to the Queen.
There were detailed accounts of visits and interviews;
of rebuffs and, more rarely, of encouragements.
There was nothing of sentiment or bitterness in this
stark record which spoke for itself, and Wycliffe was
moved. Only in two places did emotion break through:
a photograph of four young men in battledress was
labelled with their names: John Cross, Jack Shirley,
John Larkin and Jonathan Welsh. The figure of Larkin
was ringed about in pencil so heavily that the point
of the pencil had cut into the print; the other instance
came at the end where the girl had written, 'I failed
him.'

On an adjoining table the contents of Prout's
pockets were laid out: a ring of keys, a few coins, a
handkerchief, a notebook and pencil, and a wallet of
tooled leather. The wallet contained a few pounds
in notes, a couple of credit cards, and four photographs – one protected by a polythene envelope. This
was the girl in the painting, his wife. The other
three had been 'taken off' and enlarged from a group
– Shirley, Cross and Larkin; the prints were faded
and creased.

Had Prout arrived at Roscrowgy in all innocence
and found his quarry by chance? Or had he tracked

the man down and made a plausible approach? That was what the photographs seemed to suggest. At any rate, within eight months of his first visit, on the precise anniversary of the Shotton House killing, Cleeve had received the first of the five playing cards.

The atmosphere in the Incident Room was lethargic, deflated; the process of winding down had started. In a day or two they would be moving out and their precious files would be transferred to headquarters, there to provide the ingredients on which lawyers would go to work. The mass of paper would continue to grow and the personalities and events of the case concerned would be slowly digested into a legal soup.

Wycliffe, brooding, shifted irritably in his chair and muttered: 'Adolescent games!'

'Sir?' Lucy Lane at the next table, preoccupied with filing reports.

'Adolescent games and attitudes. That's what this case has been about – people who have never grown up.'

'I'm sorry; I don't understand.'

'I'm not surprised. But didn't all this start with four young men in the throes of a retarded adolescence? They dressed up their crimes in romantic trappings – all the nonsense of reunions, and badges, and calling themselves by the names of cards – like kids playing cops and robbers, or star wars . . . Then we have the ineffable Prout, married to and deeply in love with a beautiful though fundamentally unbalanced young woman. When she was overwhelmed by the terrible consequences of her brother's wildness and killed herself, he turned real tragedy into melodrama with his absurd vendetta; working out his fantasy at the cost of two more lives – one of them certainly innocent.' He spread his hands in a gesture of helplessness. 'Don't you agree that such people corrupt themselves through a sort of juvenile naïvety?' Then he broke off, slightly embarrassed. 'End of sermon!'

'You believe that the Welsh boy was guilty?'

'He was convicted and sentenced after what seemed to be a fair trial.'

She persisted with diffidence. 'But?'

A vague gesture. 'I've talked to Cleeve and read his books; you've made a study of his work: what impressed you most about the man who wrote them?'

She smiled. 'Write your answer using one side of the paper only; do not write in margins . . . I suppose it was his obsession with evil and with our apparent helplessness to control or contain it.'

Wycliffe nodded. 'Perhaps he was one of the Four Jacks who finally grew up and realized his responsibilities.'

'For responsibilities, read guilt.'

'Perhaps.'

The mills continued to grind. Kersey reported that Fecundex held a small stock of an outmoded pesticide containing 40 per cent nicotine; a sample had been sent for analysis. Scales telephoned to say that a garden shed in Prout's back yard was fitted up with the usual home-handyman's equipment and it had been sealed pending the arrival of the man from Forensic.

The message from Ballistics did not arrive until late afternoon. Wycliffe spoke briefly on the telephone then turned to Lucy Lane. 'It seems the gun Prout handed to us is the one purchased illegally by Welsh a fortnight before the Shotton House killing. They are carrying out further tests but they've no real doubt that it fired the bullets which killed the policeman.'

It was the last day of his official holiday and the Wycliffes decided they would have one more excursion to look back on. They would drive to Pendower, walk along the coast to Portloe, and return to the car by way of Veryan.

'Have we got the map?'

'It's in the car.'

'The binoculars?'

'They're on the window seat.'

'We're ready then . . .'

Instinctively they both turned to look at the telephone, but it did not ring.

THE END

available from
THE ORION PUBLISHING GROUP
Other books by W.J. Burley

WYCLIFFE AND THE SCHOOL BULLIES

Two very different young women have been murdered within the same week. One was a singer in a nightclub, the other was a nurse, but both were strangled in their own homes in strangely efficient attacks that appear to be remarkably similar. The press are quick to assume there is a psychopath on the loose but Detective Chief Superintendent Wycliffe suspects the truth may be somewhat more complex than that...

When another attack is aborted halfway through for no apparent reason Wycliffe becomes certain that this is no random spate of murders. But with his superiors and the media uninterested in his theories Wycliffe knows he will have to work alone to find the killer. As he searches for a link between the victims his investigations take him back in time ? to a school trip, and isolated hostel and a cruel joke on a lonely student.

WYCLIFFE AND THE SCAPEGOAT

Each year, at Hallowe'en, high on the Cornish cliffs, a life-size effigy of a man is strapped to a blazing wheel and run into the sea ? a re-enactment of a hideous, ancient legend where the figure had been a living sacrifice.

So, when Jonathan Riddle, a well-known and respected local builder and undertaker, disappears it seems all too likely that his corpse has gone the way of the historic 'scapegoat'.

As Chief Superintendent Wycliffe begins to investigate the family life of Riddle, more and more unpleasant facts begin to emerge until eventually he is left with an incredible, and seemingly impossible, solution...

WYCLIFFE'S WILD GOOSE CHASE

Wycliffe's home overlooks a peaceful, West Country estuary ? but even here he can't get away from crime.

One Sunday morning he is walking along the shore when he comes across a service revolver with one chamber recently fired. In recent years Wycliffe has often regretted the fact that his rank cuts him off from the early stages of an investigation, but here he is, in at the very start.

The case takes Wycliffe into the world of art robberies and crooked dealers, to a suicide which may be a murder, and a hunt for a missing yacht. As the investigation escalates, Wycliffe begins to wonder exactly where the clues are leading.

WYCLIFFE AND DEATH IN STANLEY STREET

In a sprawling West Country port lies the insalubrious Stanley Street, a dubious cul-de-sac off the busy main road. And when a prostitute is found naked and strangled in her bed there, Chief Superintendent Wycliffe is called in to investigate.

But things aren't quite as straightforward as they seem. The victim, Lily Painter, is the kind of girl who likes Beethoven and has plenty of qualifications to her name ? not the usual sort of prostitute at all.

The more Wycliffe investigates, the more surprises he uncovers. But it takes a dangerous arson attack and a second murder before the solution to this complex and fast-moving puzzle can be found.

WYCLIFFE AND THE REDHEAD

When the body of an attractive young woman is discovered in a flooded quarry, suspicion naturally falls on her employer, Simon ? a lonely, middle-aged man who lives above his antiquarian bookshop. Rumours had already been spreading about his relationship with Morwenna and people are quick to jump to conclusions.

Detective Superintendent Wycliffe finds it hard to tally his impression of the shy bookseller with the violent crime he's investigating. Everything he discovers suggest Morwenna was manipulating her boss. But why? The people of Truro are not as cautious, however, and Simon is soon the target of some disturbing vigilante attacks. When Wycliffe discovers that the victim had reason to bear a grudge against Simon the case is turned on its head. But Morwenna was hiding more than one secret…

WYCLIFFE IN PAUL'S COURT

Paul's Court is a quiet corner in the heart of the city: an oasis of peace and safety ? until the night when there are two violent deaths. Willy Goppel, an émigré from Germany, is found hanging from a beam in his home; and fifteen year old Yvette Cole, who may or may not have lived up to her wildest reputation, is strangled and thrown half naked over the churchyard hedge.

Chief Superintendent Wycliffe has the aid of a shrewd local sergeant, Kersey, but they still find this is a difficult case to crack. Did Willy assault the girl and then hang himself? Or was his death not suicide at all?

As Wycliffe and Kersey dig deeper, they gradually untangle a complex network of secrets in the quiet of St. Paul's Court…

WYCLIFFE AND THE DUNES MYSTERY

Cochran Wilder disappeared fifteen years ago while on a walking holiday in Cornwall. Recently released from a psychiatric hospital after being convicted of indecent assault, he had been a serious embarrassment to his father, a prominent MP. Now his body has been found, buried in the dunes. It is clear that he was murdered.

Wycliffe suspects the involvement of six people, now well-established figures in the community, who at the time has been spending an illicit weekend at a chalet near where Wilder's body was found. All are disturbed by Wycliffe's interest and by a series of threatening anonymous communications. But then a second murder is committed and the investigation takes on a new urgency…

WYCLIFFE AND THE PEA-GREEN BOAT

When Cedric Tremain is charged with murdering his father by booby-trapping his fishing boat, all the locals are agreed that he is an unlikely murderer. But the case against him is strong: he has the motive, the opportunity and the know-how; not to mention the fact that there is some hard circumstantial evidence against him. So Cedric is arrested.

But Chief Superintendent Wycliffe has a strong sense that something about the case just doesn't fit. As he quietly continues his investigations a confusing picture emerges. Twenty years ago Cedric's cousin was convicted of strangling his girlfriend and served fourteen years of a commuted death sentence.

As the wheels of justice begin to grind, Wycliffe searches for a link between past and present…

WYCLIFFE AND THE WINSOR BLUE

Gifford Tate, a well-known Falmouth painter, and Edwin Garland, a local businessman, had been inseparable companions until Tate's death several years ago. Now his paintings are much sought after and each year a work not previously shown is sold at a London gallery.

When Garland dies of a heart attack no one is suspicious ? until the eveing of the funeral, when his son is shot dead and Chief Superintendent Wycliffe is faced with a seemingly motiveless killing.

Then another relative disappears and the most promising clue Wycliffe has is an artist's pigment called Winsor Blue. He finally identifies the motive behind the crimes ? but is it too late to prevent another death?

WYCLIFFE AND THE HOUSE OF FEAR

Detective Superintendent Wycliffe is holidaying in Cornwall when he meets the intriguing Kemp family. The Kemps have lived in Kellycoryk, their decaying family seat, for almost 500 years and have a tragic history. Roger Kemp's first wife disappeared mysteriously in what was presumed to be a boating accident and now the Kemps are struggling to maintain their family home. When Roger's wealthy second wife, Bridget, also disappears Wycliffe is inevitably drawn into the case,

Wycliffe is troubled by the dysfunctional family he is investigating. Can the loss of their mother account for the Kemp children's strange behaviour or is there a more sinister explanation? And why is his main suspect doing so little to save himself?

WYCLIFFE AND THE CYCLE OF DEATH

When Matthew Glynn, a respectable bookseller, is found bludgeoned and strangled, Chief superintendent Wycliffe is mystified. Why would anyone want to kill him, and in such a brutal manner?

But a look at Glynn's background reveals tension within the family. Alfred Glynn, an eccentric recluse, has held a grudge against his brother for years and the older brother, Maurice, argued bitterly with Matthew over the sale of the family land. Add to this a discontented son, valuable documents in the bookseller's safe, and the mysterious, still unexplained disappearance of Matthew's wife years earlier, and Wycliffe is facing one of his most impenetrable cases.

Then another Glynn dies and the murderer's identity seems obvious. But Wycliffe is not convinced ? and soon uncovers some very murky secrets, and the possibility of another murder…

WYCLIFFE AND THE TANGLED WEB

A beautiful schoolgirl goes missing from a Cornish village on the day she has told her boyfriend and sister she is pregnant. The possibility that she has been raped or murdered ? or both ?grows with every passing hour, and Chief Superintendent Wycliffe is brought in on the case.

The investigation reveals a complex network of family relationships and rivalries centred on the girl; and then Wycliffe finds a body ? but not one he expects. Have there been two murders? And if so, are they connected?

Wycliffe digs deeper, and soon realises that just beneath the normal, day-today surface of the community lies a web of hatred and resentment ? a web he will have to untangle if he is to find the key to the mystery…

All Orion/Phoenix titles are available at your local bookshop or from the following address:

Mail Order Department
Littlehampton Book Services
FREEPOST BR535
Worthing, West Sussex, BN13 3BR
telephone 01903 828503, *facsimile* 01903 828802
e-mail MailOrders@lbsltd.co.uk
(Please ensure that you include full postal address details)

Payment can be made either by credit/debit card (Visa, Mastercard, Access and Switch accepted) or by sending a £ Sterling cheque or postal order made payable to *Littlehampton Book Services*.
DO NOT SEND CASH OR CURRENCY.

Please add the following to cover postage and packing

UK and BFPO:
£1.50 for the first book, and 50p for each additional book to a maximum of £3.50

Overseas and Eire:
£2.50 for the first book plus £1.00 for the second book and 50p for each additional book ordered

---

BLOCK CAPITALS PLEASE

name of cardholder ....

delivery address
(if different from cardholder)

address of cardholder ....

....

postcode ....

postcode ....

☐ I enclose my remittance for £ ....

☐ please debit my Mastercard/Visa/Access/Switch (delete as appropriate)

card number ☐☐☐☐☐☐☐☐☐☐☐☐☐☐☐☐

expiry date ☐☐☐☐   Switch issue no. ☐☐

signature ....

prices and availability are subject to change without notice